STAGE WHISPERS

Kealan Patrick Burke

Copyright © 2013 by Kealan Patrick Burke

Cover Design Copyright © 2013 Elder Lemon Design

All rights reserved. No part of this publication may be reproduced, distributed, or transmitted in any form or by any means, including photocopying, recording, or other electronic or mechanical methods, without the prior written permission of the publisher, except in the case of brief quotations embodied in critical reviews and certain other noncommercial uses permitted by copyright law.

ISBN: 1482333929
ISBN-13: 978-1482333923

For the readers who've come this far along the ghost road
My thanks

BOOKS by KEALAN PATRICK BURKE

THE TIMMY QUINN SERIES

The Turtle Boy
The Hides
Vessels
Peregrine's Tale
Stage Whispers
Nemesis

NOVELS

Kin
Master of the Moors
Currency of Souls

NOVELLAS

Thirty Miles South of Dry County
You In?
Midlisters
Seldom Seen in August
Saturday Night at Eddie's
Underneath

COLLECTIONS

Ravenous Ghosts
The Number 121 to Pennsylvania & Others
Theater Macabre
Dead Leaves: 8 Tales of the Witching Season
Dead of Winter
Digital Hell

"Introduction: A Kind of Haunting" originally appeared in a slightly different form in the Thunderstorm Books edition of *Stage Whispers*, 2012.

The Turtle Boy was originally published by Necessary Evil Press, 2004

The Hides was originally published by Cemetery Dance Publications, 2005

Vessels was originally published by Bloodletting Press, 2006

Peregrine's Tale and "Genesis" were originally published by Cemetery Dance Publications, 2010

TABLE OF CONTENTS

Introduction: A Kind of Haunting
7

Prologue: Genesis
11

Book One: The Turtle Boy
25

Book Two: The Hides
79

Book Three: Vessels
194

Book Four: Peregrine's Tale
286

INTRODUCTION
A Kind of Haunting

It's been almost ten years now since I wrote *The Turtle Boy*, almost a decade since I looked out my office window one day in July and saw my stepson and his best friend navigating the cornfield behind our house, headed back to the small manmade pond our neighbor claimed was full of turtles the size of Buicks. I had no idea at the time that the book would prove to be as popular as it has been. I just wanted to preserve in amber a moment of childhood innocence that even in those days, with technology doing its best to steal our children, was a rare thing. In so doing, I found myself telling the tale of good kids on the threshold of adolescence who find out that the adults they trusted unconditionally, as most kids do, harbor dark secrets. It's a story about the moment in which you realize the world has as much darkness as it does sunlight, that your dreams may never be realized, and that there are things out there that can and will hurt you. It's a story about the end of magic.

After the publication of *The Turtle Boy*, I was pleasantly surprised to see just how much the story resonated with people, and I think it does so because we all keep those memories of our childhood summers locked away in a special place in our hearts. Even now, as I write this, it's early May and the weather has finally gotten good after weeks of storms and cold. The air smells of cut grass, and it's still light out at nine p.m. And just the sound of the streetlights humming to life brings me back to evenings spent with my bike propped up against one of them while I sat around with my friends discussing superheroes.

Summer casts the brightest light through the window of memory.

Remember waking up and looking forward to no school because it meant you got to run free all day? Nobody told you where you could and couldn't go, nothing was off limits (even if your parents said it was; that only increased the appeal), your bike was a rollercoaster that could take you to the ends of the world if you let it; every neighborhood had at least one creepy old house you were just *sure* was haunted; girls were an object of fascination and fear; twilight meant you started watching the clock to see how long before you heard your parents yelling for you, a cry you could somehow hear no matter how far away you were. Remember tire swings and swimming holes? Rain, nor snow, nor hail stopped you from your adventures, only changed the color of them. You lived to get dirty, to rip your good clothes on thorns and branches. Trees were skyscrapers, hills were army bunkers, holes were tunnels to China, rocks came from the moon, and sticks were guns. Remember flying through town on your bike, weaving in and out of cars, pulling up to the bookstore and feeling the thump of excitement in your chest that the new book by that author you liked was out? Remember how the air seemed to smell cleaner and even when it didn't, it smelled *right?* Perfection was rain on the skylight of your library while you lost yourself in the rows and tried to drum up the nerve to inveigle your way into the adult section. At home, your parents shook their heads and said "he always has his face in a book" but you could see the pride in their eyes.

The stars looked brighter, the moon looked closer, and there was nothing we believed we couldn't do.

We are walking time capsules and summer makes it hard to avoid looking inward.

And I think it's this nostalgia that defines the Timmy Quinn series, something I might not have realized had I not come across a particularly insightful review of *The Hides* and *Vessels* a few years back. In it, the reviewer shared his belief that the series had more to do with familial relationships than ghosts, and in particular, the relationship between Timmy and his father. I found this startling, and upon revisiting the books, more than a little true. My relationship with my own father has been rocky at best over the years, but I honestly don't recall ever setting out to resolve anything by engaging in fictional therapy. Perhaps it's a form of catharsis. Perhaps I'm reading too much into it all. Or perhaps I've just been writing what I know.

When I wrote *The Hides*, what I really wanted to do was revisit my hometown, both because I missed it and didn't know when I was going to get the chance to go back, and because it's an ideal location for a ghost story: ancient and seething with a troubled history. And yet it's also where I grew up and lived until I was seventeen, and the scene of lots of adolescent strife.

With *Vessels*, I wanted to put Tim somewhere that reflected his own isolation and the erosion of his mind and body after years of enduring the attention of the dead. Blackrock Island *is* Tim—weathered, alone, still there despite the best efforts of the elements to erase it from existence. On that lonesome island, he finds more secrets, of course. He also finds his father. So perhaps there is indeed something to the reviewer's claim. Am I simply writing ghost stories or using them as a canvas for my own psychological bugbears? I guess we'll never know.

If *The Turtle Boy* is a summer story then *The Hides* and *Vessels* are bleak, unforgiving tales of winter. *Peregrine's Tale* is autumnal and redolent of change, and *Nemesis*, the final volume, is spring, wherein death feeds new life.

These are my seasons and whether populated solely by ghosts of the fictional dead or troubled revenants from my own psyche, or an amalgam of both, with them we come full circle, and everything ends. It's been close to a decade coming, but I think Tim Quinn, like his creator, has to say goodbye to the harsh weather and find his place in the sun. And that's why *Nemesis*, like *Vessels*, is dedicated to my father. We have come full circle, old wounds have healed, and it's time to move on. It's the closing of a door that has long been held open. It's the end of one story, and time for another.

I want to very much thank you, the reader, for coming along on this journey with me. It represents the summer in which everything began for me and all the seasons in between. Some of them have been rougher than others, but I'm still here and so are you, hale and hearty (I hope), and ready for whatever comes next.

Here's hoping this finds you warmed by the sun in the summer of your days with the coldest winters behind you.

One final note: I would like to thank you for continuing to support the independent press by purchasing this book and others like it. It's people like you that keep the magic (and the careers of writers) alive, for as much as I embrace (out of necessity) the advent of digital publishing, my heart belongs to real books such as this one. Nothing invokes more nostalgia in me than glancing at the stacks of books to my left. I refuse to part with them and continue to add to their ranks, because that's what I've always done. And while in the end it is the words themselves that matter more than the medium in which they reach us, you just can't beat the feel and physical presence of a book.

So again, thank you, and I hope 100,000+ words collected here prove sufficient reward for your investment. If you like it, I hope you'll check out the concluding volume, the full-length novel *Nemesis*, now available in print as a hardcover limited edition from Thunderstorm Press, and also in digital format from all the usual vendors, with a paperback release scheduled over the coming months.

Now, enough banter. Let's walk that shadowy road.

Our ghosts await.

— Kealan Patrick Burke
Columbus, Ohio
May 2012

PROLOGUE:
Genesis

1895

Matheson awoke with a woman's name on his lips and a bullet hole in his chest. When he rolled off the couch, the first came slithering painfully from between his clenched teeth, the second sucking the breath in through a fiery vortex somewhere east of his heart. He dropped to the floor, nausea clutching at his throat, making him gasp for air that seemed in desperately short supply. Eyes watery with tears, he was nevertheless able to make out the deep burgundy carpet spread out around his hand like blood. *The drawing room*, he realized as yet another breath caught somewhere it shouldn't have, making him want to retch and gasp at the same time. Pain tickled his throat and painted his tongue with the taste of copper. On all fours, he raised one quivering hand and brought it to the wound. His white shirt was sodden red, his black dinner jacket still slung over the arm of the couch where he remembered Professor Canavan had tossed it shortly after Matheson arrived. The ragged hole seeped blood, but the oozing was slow and not at all critical, it seemed. He was no doctor, however, so finding someone who knew more about the ramifications of such a wound seemed the most logical step. But that would require rising, and the thought of it made him sick to his stomach.

Memory distracted him.

Canavan's face swum into his addled brain, a mirror image dusted with pain. The professor was beaming, his eyes more alive than Matheson could ever recall seeing them before. *You won't believe it, old friend*, he'd said, his excitement almost palpable. *You won't believe it when you see what I've done.* And while Matheson had the good manners to smile and nod and allow the old man to take his coat before leading him into the entryway, he was a little disturbed by the professor's zeal. Given Canavan's field of research and expertise, this was hardly surprising. There was more than one person on the staff at Hartford University who thought that the old man's obsession had long ago sent him waltzing into the ugly dark, from which there was no hope of return.

But Matheson had accepted his old friend's invitation, ostensibly to hear Canavan's news, but also because he knew the professor's daughter Cynthia would be in attendance. He had been willing to endure hours of her father's pontifications if she were in the room with him, and though twelve years his junior, he had sensed on previous visits an admiration in her for the breadth of his botanical knowledge and the gentleness with which he shared it, a sharp contrast to her father's melodramatic and vociferous outbursts of fancy. Such admiration could hardly be taken as significant interest, but it was a foundation on which he hoped to build a romance. He had no doubt that her father would object, simply because it was expected of him, and because it might lose him the only member of his immediate family still too young to have flown the roost. But in time he would realize that such protestations would result in nothing but time away from the experiments and equations that had consumed him for so very long. He would return to them with a disgusted flap of his hand, and Cynthia would be his.

But this night in Canavan House had been anything but romantic, and upon waking from his slumber, the fragmented recollection of it felt more to Matheson like a nightmare.

He managed to rise, one bloody hand splayed on the arm of the couch for support, his head filled with tumbling rocks that set off sparks behind his eyes and threatened to pull him back to the floor. For a brief moment his thoughts swept away from him and he panicked, shook his head to clear it, and took a very tentative step forward.

Canavan went mad, he thought, and the lucidity of it reassured him. He was not going to faint, not going to give in to the seductive pull of unconsciousness. *Stark, raving mad.*

The agony increased the further he went. He squinted against it, one hand hovering over the wound, afraid to touch it. He looked up and saw the door to the hall was ajar. Little light waited beyond it.

He went mad, and he shot me. The memory gave him pause, but as soon as gravity began to coax him again, tugging on invisible threads that had spun from the bullet hole, he moved on. Gilt-framed portraits of distinguished gentlemen—Canavan's idols and forebears—viewed him with disinterest as he staggered forth, breathless and shaking.

It was not the memory that had halted him, but concern, for only now had it reminded him of the other guests—the curious assemblage gathered here at Canavan's request—who had greeted him in this very room.

He stopped again, frowned and glanced to his left where there stood a large oval mahogany table, draped in a skin of lace and studded with lighted candles. A gentle breeze from somewhere shouldered the flames.

There were seven of them, he remembered, seven women varying in age from prepubescent to elderly, all of them gathered at that table with their curios and symbols—he spotted colored stones, parchment pages, an ankh, a crucifix, a battered old doll missing an eye, even a Ouija Board—and all of them wearing beatific smiles as if they had come prepared to raise Jesus Christ himself, and not just the common dead.

"Psychics?" Matheson had asked, careful to keep the skepticism from his tone.

Canavan had clucked his tongue in annoyance. "Not *psychics*, man. *Receivers.*"

Matheson had no idea what the difference was, and cared even less to find out, so he'd nodded politely to the women as they were introduced, then excused himself to the bathroom. When he'd returned, they were gone, only his dearest Cynthia waiting for him.

He could no longer remember their names, but the memory of the Receivers' faces, so eager and full of excitement, now filled him with dread. He'd guessed that what Canavan was planning would be something dramatic—it was the nature of both the man and his obsession—but the sight of those women, despite his conviction that their abilities were completely fraudulent, troubled him deeply.

At last he reached the door, though the journey had seemed as long and arduous as a trek across the Sahara. He stopped for breath, one hand already gripping the doorknob as if fearing it might disappear if he dallied too long.

The candles fluttered. A soft breeze swept through the drawing room. It was night beyond the tall mullioned windows, but Matheson had no idea how late it might be. The house was quiet, though that was hardly comforting. He imagined the sextet of charlatans whimpering under the black hole threat of Canavan's gun in one of the other rooms. Would Cynthia be among them? Of course she would. Despite the professor's abrupt descent into madness, he'd never have hurt his own daughter.

Unless he thought she betrayed him too.

It was an awful thought and he willed it away. It made his head ache and he winced. His chest felt as if acid had been poured into the hole and was even now finding its way through his veins.

She'll be all right. I know she will.

Resolute, he composed himself as much as the injury and fear would allow, eased open the drawing room door, and stepped into the dark hallway.

* * *

The lights in the hall were out, the only illumination provided by the carriage lamps outside the front door, their feeble amber glow through the door's glass panels casting a confusion of jaundiced shadows across the walls and floor. Matheson's shoes dragged across the tile. He was fading, but hoped his sudden lethargy had only come about at the thought of another long walk rather than because of blood loss, or worse.

It bothered him, now that he thought about it. There should have been more blood. Even though his shirt was soaked with the stuff, the hole itself had stopped bleeding. He wanted to believe it was because the injury was superficial, that maybe he'd survived because Canavan knew about as much about guns and ammunition as Matheson did about flesh wounds and coagulation, but still it puzzled him. He couldn't probe the wound, or test the depth of it—

he knew he'd vomit, or worse, lose consciousness—but it *felt* deep, and the pain was excruciating, almost as if his chest was caught in a slowly tightening vice while an invisible torturer thrust a red-hot poker into his breast. Perhaps it had been cauterized.

He struggled on, leaning against the wall for support. Once, he tried to cry out, but stopped himself in time. He had no idea where Canavan was, no idea where *anyone* was, and alerting them to his presence might end in disaster. At least if the professor thought him dead, he had the element of surprise on his side.

Do you believe in Purgatory, Jim?

Canavan's question, posed some weeks before in the professor's office at the University, had not come as a surprise, particularly given the title of the book he'd had spread open in front of him when he'd asked it. It was a battered red leather-bound volume of *The Apocrypha Obscura*.

"Do you believe our loved ones go on to a better place despite their sins? Or do you think the slightest of missteps is enough to guarantee them, and us, a place in Hell? And would you, if you knew how, attempt to save them, to bring them back and spare their suffering?"

"I don't know," Matheson had answered truthfully. It was a question he'd assumed hypothetical, as any rational man would, but it quickly became clear that Canavan saw it as much more than that.

"If your wife or lover leaves you and you think of precisely the right thing to say to keep them with you for another while, would you not try to reach them at the train station, on the platform, in those last few moments before they board that train and begin the journey to their final destination? Would you not try to save them if you knew nothing but pain and suffering awaited them at the other end?"

"I suppose so, yes. But I don't understand what—"

"That, my good friend, is what I hope to achieve. Salvation for the suffering, the opening of a door that will enable us to give peace to the tormented."

After that, he'd said no more, for which Matheson had been deeply grateful. The more he listened to his friend and colleague, the more he became convinced Canavan's work had consumed him and affected his brain. He supposed the death of the professor's wife had been the catalyst, turning dutiful study to frantic research, and in the weeks that followed, Canavan confirmed it.

"Are you free next Friday night?"

"I'm not entirely sure. I'll have to check my engagements. Why do you ask?"

"I'm holding something of a get-together at my house. A few friends, a few toasts, to celebrate."

"To celebrate what?"

"Ah, but it wouldn't be half the fun if I told you now. Can I assume any previous engagements can be rescheduled in favor of my little soirée? I promise you won't regret it."

Though reluctant to accept an invitation from a friend who seemed to be quickly coming apart at the seams, the idea of seeing Cynthia again forced him to acquiesce.

* * *

Up ahead there was a narrow band of hazy light beneath the library door. Matheson focused on it as he shuffled his way forward, almost knocking over a planter he hadn't seen in the gloom.

The pain was unbearable now, every step punctuated by a ragged hiss, a poor substitute for a scream he couldn't allow himself for fear of detection. The advantage he'd been counting on seemed ridiculous now. He was losing strength at a rapid rate. In his present condition if he 'surprised' Canavan, the professor would have ample time and opportunity to reload his gun and finish the job he'd started. But the alternative option—that of turning around and heading out and away from the house—was quickly dismissed. There were still people here, and though weak, he was no coward. He could not, in good conscience, flee this place knowing there were many others who might still be in grave danger.

Golden specks lit his vision and he paused again, his breath sounding like a pneumatic pump as it escaped him. In the instant he closed his eyes, he relived the memory of Canavan storming into the drawing room, face a portrait of rage. At Matheson's side, Cynthia stood, her own ire a softer but no less potent reflection of her father's.

"Is this what you came for?" Canavan shouted, one hand behind his back, the other clenched by his side. "My daughter? Are you so vacuous that you'd abandon the most spectacular scientific pursuits of our time to fondle my youngest child? Get out of my house."

"He's not going anywhere," Cynthia said, raising her chin in defiance and slipping her hand into Matheson's. He remembered wishing she hadn't done it, for it was clear it was an act of rebellion meant to provoke her father further, and not a gesture borne of affection. "I wish him to stay."

"What you wish doesn't matter to me." The look of contempt that crossed Canavan's face was so powerful it elicited a gasp from his daughter. "Now step away from him."

Matheson had not yet begun to panic, though he could feel it gathering its troops in the hills behind his courage. "We were just talking, Canavan, nothing more. Please, you're overreacting."

"Am I?" the professor said, and brought his other hand out from behind his back. In it, he held a pistol, which he leveled at Matheson. "I've seen you watching her, seen the lechery in your eyes. You haven't an ounce of interest in my studies. None! So enshrouded have I been in them that I've failed to recognize your true intent." He nodded. "But I see it now."

"Canavan, this is madness," Matheson said, his hands floating out to placate the man. "You're mistaken."

Matheson opened his eyes, sparing himself the memory of the roar, the smoke, Cynthia's scream, the feeling of being punched in the chest by a massive fist, and, just before the trigger was pulled, Canavan's gleeful reply, *As are you, my friend.*

* * *

He reached the library and collapsed against the door, entrusting his weight to the heavy polished oak. The air seemed thicker now, and darker, as if the dust had swollen. It made it hard to breathe. His nose tickled and he rubbed it until it was sore.

He shot me. A single pulse of anger flashed through him at the thought that his old friend had tried to kill him, and for nothing. He hadn't even touched Cynthia, no matter how much he'd wanted to. Sitting next to her had been enough, basking in the intoxicating smell of her, being close enough to study her soft pink lips, the slender slope of her cheek, the ginger-colored fall of her hair. The promise that maybe in the weeks to come she would accept his kiss, accept his advances without hesitation, sated him.

With considerable effort, he turned the knob on the library door. It resisted, then gave, and swung creakingly open.

Please let her be alive.

As the room came into view he saw it shimmer and wobble, as if he were gazing into a poorly lit aquarium. He brought a hand to his eyes, shielding them from the disorientation he hoped was the fault of the room and its feeble light and not a product of his waning consciousness. But when he looked again, the air was still thick and shifting, a carnival mirror with amber glass.

And through the oddly rolling waves of dust, he saw that all of them were there. All of them, watching him with fear etched on their honey colored faces.

The charlatans sat in a ragged semicircle around another oval table, almost an exact duplicate of the one he'd seen in the drawing room, right down to the lace cloth and drooling candles, which burned slowly with sepia fire. It might, Matheson supposed, be the expectancy thickening the air, for he could feel it radiating from the assembly. Their eyes were wide and frightened, their mouths agape, each of the Receivers clutching the tools of their trade tightly to quivering breasts. Cynthia sat among them, her pallid face wet with tears, draining away some of her beauty, but despite his sluggishness, Matheson felt elation coarse through him.

She's alive. Somehow he'd known she would be; the certainty felt like the line that had drawn him to this room.

He smiled. "He didn't hurt you."

Everyone in the room jolted upright at the sound of his voice, startling him in turn. And from the stacks of books that lined the walls, a shadow detached itself, crossed the room and stopped in front of him.

Even through the strange amber filter the air had become, Canavan looked euphoric, none of the madness Matheson had seen in his face in evidence now.

"You made it," he said, studying Matheson as an archeologist might a rare find. "I knew you would."

Matheson frowned and tried to take a breath considerable enough to allow him to sound threatening. He couldn't, and the effort drained him further. His legs began to feel numb and now he clutched the doorjamb for support. "I need help. I'm hurt," he whispered and again watched his words make ripples in the faces of the gathering. *They're looking at me as if* I'm *the madman*, he thought, his gaze coming to rest on Cynthia's horrified expression as she wept anew.

"You look wonderful, old friend," Canavan said, unable to disguise the awe in his voice.

Matheson tried to take a step forward but his foot refused to move. "Wonder...ful? I need a doctor. You shot me. I'm dying," he said, and knew all of it to be true. "*Please*." He suddenly, desperately, wanted nothing more than to sleep, just for a little while. Anything to force back the raging tide of agony lapping at his insides.

Canavan shook his head and smiled. His voice sounded very far away. "My friend, you are a hero," he said. "And soon pain will not be something you'll need to worry about. You're already dead, you see, and in coming back, you've not only validated my theories and made my experiment a success, but you've also given me the opportunity to help you."

Matheson snorted laughter and it hurt his head. He closed his eyes, praying for an end to the insanity, whatever the source. "I need a doctor," he repeated. "And the police."

Cynthia sobbed aloud, momentarily drawing the attention of everyone in the room. She raised a crumpled linen handkerchief over her eyes.

Why won't she look at me? Matheson thought, alarmed. *What's going on?* Then a terrible possibility dawned on him. Was it conceivable that she he had worked in collusion with her deranged father? Had her interest been merely a lure, meant to lead him away from the group so he could be murdered in private? But surely Canavan would have feared being heard? After all, his chosen method of execution had hardly been subtle.

Unless...

The next thought almost robbed him of consciousness then and there, so terrible were the implications of it.

Unless they're all *in on it.*

He moaned, and noticed a moment later that the blood had begun to run again. It was warm against his otherwise cold flesh, but the pain was no more, no less than it had been before.

"Splendid, isn't it?" Canavan addressed the crowd of fearful watchers like a ringmaster at a circus. "We've done it, ladies. We've discovered the Door to Purgatory!"

"You're insane," Matheson said. "This is the bloody...door to your hall. I'm not dead, despite your efforts, and when I recover, my first order of...business will be to see you hanged."

Canavan turned back to him. "What is it like?"

Matheson said nothing. It was getting harder to breathe and the sight of all their faces being pulled in different direction by the watery air made him nauseous.

"What does it feel like where you are now?" The professor didn't wait for an answer. He was alight with excitement, barely content to await the response his professional curiosity demanded. "How do you feel?"

How do you feel?
What is wrong with the air?
What is wrong with the women?
What is wrong with me?

Too many questions. He wanted to wake up and find himself home in bed, safe and sound beneath the covers and safe from this outrageous fantasy. He was not dead, of course he wasn't—the notion was beyond preposterous—but there was something afoot here, something critical he was too feeble and tired to grasp.

He opened his mouth to speak, but it was Cynthia's voice he heard.

"Make him go away, Father. I beg you, let him go."

It's all right, Matheson wanted to assure her but the words wouldn't come, so he had to hope she'd read them in his eyes, though it was getting hard to keep them from closing. *I won't leave without you. He can't make me leave you in this madhouse.*

"Father, please. Look at him! He's suffered enough."

Canavan sighed. "My dear, I thought you understood. He's here because I, we, summoned him. We're not going to add to his suffering. We're going to take it away from him, so he can go on to wherever he's bound without pain."

"This is blasphemy," Cynthia said. "You're meddling with things you have no business meddling with. You cannot influence ghosts!"

I'm not a ghost. Matheson's head began to sink. *I'm alive.*

"He's not a ghost," Canavan told her, as if Matheson had transmitted the thought to him. "He's significantly more than that. We've made history tonight, ladies. We'll all forever be remembered as mortals who unlocked Purgatory. And he's going to be our subject."

Kill him.

Matheson's raised his head, his eyes drifting dreamily from one face to the next.

After a muddled moment, he found that there was someone in the room he hadn't noticed before, a shadow, darker than any of the others, standing behind the ladies at the oval table. Its head was misshapen, the body too lithe to be natural.

Kill him, it said. Now that he had recognized it, Matheson was sure he'd found the source of the voice, despite it seeming to come from inside himself. *He's a murderer, a fool, and he's set us free. Control does not—cannot—belong to him. Now kill him.*

"How?" Matheson mumbled aloud.

Canavan, mistakenly assuming the question was directed his way, grinned. "We're going to study you, unlock the secrets of your new domain, discover how much you take with you to that awful prison. You'll achieve an importance in death you could never have dared dream of in life. You, my old friend, are the key to everything."

"I'm not dead."

Yes you are.

Matheson looked at the shadow looming over the women at the table. "Who are you?"

Canavan frowned. "Oh come now, you know who—"

I'm you, and everything you've become. Now have your revenge on this imbecilic old fool.

"I don't know how."

"Who is he talking to?" one of the women at the table said, as symbols were raised and orbs consulted. The youngest of the group, a blind girl with hair the air turned amber, said tonelessly, "There's someone else here with him."

Cynthia rose and crossed the room. "For God's sake, Father, this has gone far enough!" Matheson followed her terrified gaze to an apparatus he had failed to notice before. It stood beside the door, large as a bureau, a contraption made of dark oak, with all manner of coils and devices hissing and spitting sparks and tongues of electricity, while dials peaked and hummed beneath a protective bell-shaped glass case.

Cynthia headed for it, pretty face set in grim determination, but her father moved with a speed that belied his years. "Don't," he warned, one finger thrust in her face. "I'm telling you—don't."

"Father, get out of my way. You have to stop this."

"The most miraculous and important discovery of our time...and you wish to *stop* it?" He shook his head in amazement and turned to point at Matheson. "You want to stop a machine that can do *this*? Are you *mad*?"

"No," she said, averting her gaze. "But I fear you are." Defeated, she marched back to her seat and sat, not looking at Matheson, who felt an ache inside for her. It was lost in the torrent of pain and he winced, felt something abruptly surge up and out of him. He sagged against the frame, then just as quickly felt his spine contort, forcing him to stand. Something cracked and new pain blossomed in his neck, twisting his head back and forth.

"What's happening to him?"

"Canavan, it may have gone far enough. I'm sensing a peculiar amount of negative energy now."

"Is he dying?"

"You... For Heaven's sake, he's *dead!* Why can't anyone understand that! I killed the bastard and yet here he stands on a threshold that no longer leads only into my darkened hallway, but into another plane, into the fields from which God and Satan pluck their fruit! Here before us is the proof man has sought for an eternity. Here, is nothing less than—"

KILL HIM.

There was a buzzing in Matheson's head. He raised his hands as if to contain it and black fire burst from his mouth, eyes, and ears. He screamed in utter terror, pain...and finally rage, as he thrashed at imaginary bonds and shoved himself away from the wall. A thousand voices filled his head, goading him, mocking him, driving him to do what it was now clear he had to do if he hoped to survive. He had to kill the source of all this wickedness and hate. He had to kill Canavan.

The old man whirled as the air around him became a vortex. Shadows crept like lizards from the doorway and clambered up the walls, stealing the light and scaling their way up and across the ceiling. The room was alive with them. The ladies began to scream. Cynthia ran, though there was nowhere to go. She hid, with the youngest of the Receivers, under the oval table. Canavan barked commands, but there was fear in his voice now.

"Canavan," Matheson said as the shadows slipped inside him, changing him, painting his eyes with darkness, giving him the sight and the strength he would need to escape this hellish place to which the professor had condemned him.

Canavan backed further into the room. The women's screams continued unabated, increasing in pitch as the shadows flattened themselves and began to ooze down the walls. On all four, thick glutinous streams ran down over the baseboards, and crept across the floor like tar, toward where the women were huddled and desperately trying to escape.

"This is not how it's supposed to be," Canavan said angrily. "We were so careful!"

The pain was still tearing at his insides. Matheson could feel it, but it no longer presided over him. Now rage and an overwhelming bloodlust had taken hold of him, and he welcomed the distraction.

"I followed the passages precisely, don't you understand? I brought only the best Receivers in to draw you. Their energy, the spells, and the machine...it was all perfect. I checked it myself...a thousand times before I dared open the door! This cannot be. I won't allow it!"

Cynthia screamed, and Matheson glanced over to where she was lying, something resembling a shivering, tar-covered dog standing over her, its jaws worrying at her throat.

He felt nothing.

Canavan followed Matheson's gaze, and his daughter's screams, and started to go to her. Matheson's hand on his shoulder stopped him cold.

"I'm not your experiment," Matheson told him, some distant part of him jarred by the sound of his voice, for it was not one he recognized. "And you'll be the one remembered, but not for your accomplishments." His grip on the old man's shoulder tightened, almost of its own volition, and Canavan began to lean into it, a moan escaping him. Bones popped and cracked. Matheson clenched his teeth together so hard they began to splinter. Fury made him shudder. He watched as his other hand reached out, the fingers pale, marked only by the jet-black veins he could see beneath the skin, and reached around to grab Canavan's jaw.

The shadows crowded the room, the screaming all but finished but for the few still audible beneath undulating skins of tar, then that too came to an end.

"Please, this is not how it's supposed to be," Canavan protested, his voice growing strained as Matheson, one hand still holding him in place, began to slowly, carefully, turn the old man's head around to face him.

BOOK ONE
The Turtle Boy

CHAPTER ONE

"All the world's a stage, Timmy Quinn, but it's not the only one…"

DELAWARE, OHIO
FRIDAY, JUNE 9th 1979

"Timmy, Pete's here!" his mother called and Timmy scattered a wave of comics to the floor with his legs as he prepared himself for another day of summer. The bedsprings emitted a half-hearted squeak of protest as he sidestepped the comics with their colorful covers.

School had ended three days ago, the gates closing with a thunderous finality the children knew was the lowest form of deception. Even as they cast one last glance over their shoulders at the low, hulking building – the antithesis of summer's glow – the school had seemed smug and patient, knowing the children's leashes were not as long as they thought. But for now, there were endless months of mischief to be perpetrated, made all the more appealing by the lack of premeditation, the absence of design. The world was there to be investigated, shadowy corners and all.

Timmy hopped down the stairs, whistling a tune of his own making and beamed at his mother as she stepped aside, allowing the morning sunshine to barge into the hallway and set fire to the rusted head of his best friend.

"Hey Pete," he said as a matter of supervised ritual. Had his mother not been present, he would more likely have greeted his friend with a punch on the shoulder.

"Hey," the other boy replied, looking as if he had made a breakthrough in his struggle to fold in on himself. Pete Marshall was painfully thin and stark white with a spattering of freckles – the result of an unusual cocktail his parents had stirred of Maine and German blood – and terribly shy around anyone but Timmy. Though he'd always been an introverted kid, he became even more so when his mother passed away two summers ago. Now when Timmy spoke to him, he sometimes had to repeat himself until Pete realized he could not get away without answering. The boy was all angles, his head larger than any other part of his body, his elbows and knees like pegs you could hang your coat from.

In contrast to Pete's shock of unruly red hair, Timmy was blond and tanned, even in winter when the bronze faded to a shadow of itself. The two of them were polar opposites but the best of friends, united by their unflagging interest in the unknown and the undiscovered.

According to Timmy's mother, it was going to get into the high nineties today but the boys shrugged off her attempt to sell the idea of sun block and insect repellent. She clucked her tongue and closed the door on the sun, leaving them to wander across the yard toward the bleached white strip of gravel-studded road and the fields of ocean green beyond.

"So what do you want to do today?" Timmy asked, kicking a stone he knew was big enough to hurt his toes if he got it at the wrong angle.

Pete shrugged and studied a curl of dried skin on his forefinger.

Timmy persisted. "Maybe we can finish digging that hole we started?"

Convinced there was a mass of undiscovered treasure lying somewhere beneath Mr. Patterson's old overgrown green bean field, the two boys had borrowed some shovels from Pete's garage and dug a hole until the earth changed color from dark brown to a Martian red. Then a storm had come and filled the hole with brackish water, quashing any notions they had about trying to find the rest of what had undoubtedly been the remnants of a meteor.

"Nah," Peter said quietly. "It was a stupid hole anyway."

"Why was it stupid?" The last word felt odd as it slipped from Timmy's mouth. In his house, "stupid" ranked right up there with "ass" as words guaranteed to get you in trouble if uttered aloud.

"It just was."

"I thought it was pretty neat. Especially the chunks of meteor. I bet there was a whole lotta space rock under that field. Probably the bones of old aliens too."

"My dad said it was just clay."

Timmy looked at him, his enthusiasm readying itself atop the downward slope to disappointment. "What was clay?"

Pete shrugged again, as if all this was something Timmy should have known. "The red stuff. It was just old dirt. My dad said it gets like that when it's far enough down."

"Oh. Well it *could* have been space rock."

A mild breeze swirled the dust around their feet as they left the cool grass and stepped on to the gravel. Although this path had been there for as long as they could remember, it had only recently become a conveyor belt for the trucks and bulldozers which had set up shop off beyond the tree line where new houses were swallowing up the old corn field. It saddened Timmy to see it. Though young, he could still remember his father carrying him on his shoulders through endless fields of gold, now replaced by the skeletons of houses awaiting skin.

"How 'bout we go watch the trains then?"

Pete looked at him, irritated. "You know I'm not allowed."

"I don't mean on the tracks. Just near them, where we can see the trains."

"No, if my dad found out, he'd kill me."

"How would he know?"

"He just would. He always knows."

Timmy sighed and kicked the rock back into the grass, where it vanished. He immediately began searching for another one. As they passed beneath the shade of a mulberry tree, purple stains in the dirt all that remained of the first fallen fruit, he shook his head, face grim.

"I wish that kid hadn't been killed up there."

Pete's eyes widened and he looked from Timmy to where the dirt road curved away from them along Myers Pond until it changed into the overgrown path to the tracks.

The summer before, thirteen-year-old Lena Richards and her

younger brother Daniel had been riding their dirt bikes in the cornfield on the other side of the rails. When a freight train came rumbling through, Danny had thought it a great idea to ride along beside it in the high grass next to the tracks and despite Lena's protests, had done that very thing. Lena, thinking her brother would be safer if she followed, raced up behind him. Blasted by the displaced air of the train, Danny lost control of his bike and fell. Lena, following too close behind and going much faster than she realized to keep the pace, couldn't brake in time. The vacuum wrenched them off their bikes. Danny was sucked under the roaring train. Lena survived, but without her legs.

Or so the story went, but they believed it. The older kids said it was true.

As a result, Timmy and Pete and all the neighborhood kids were now forbidden to venture anywhere near the tracks. Even if they decided to ignore their parents, a funny looking car with no tires rode the rails these days, yellow beacon flashing in silent warning to the adventurous.

"They were stupid to ride that close to the train anyway," Pete said glumly, obviously still pining for their days of rail walking.

"Naw. It sounds cool to do something like that. Apart from, you know...the *dying* part an' all."

"Yeah well, we can't get close enough to watch the trains, so forget it."

"Well then you come up with something to do, Einstein."

Pete slumped, the burden of choice settling heavily on his shoulders. Beads of sweat glistened on his pale forehead as he squinted up at the sun. To their left, blank-faced white houses stood facing each other, their windows glaring eyes issuing silent challenges they would never have the animation to pursue. To the right, hedges reared high, the tangles of weeds and switch grass occasionally gathering at the base of gnarled trees upon whose palsied arms leaves hung as an apparent afterthought. In the field beyond, high grass flowed beneath the gentle caress of the slightest of breezes. The land was framed by dying walnut trees, rotten arms severed by lightning long gone, poking up into the sky as if vying for the attention of a deity who could save them. A killdeer fluttered its wings in feigned distress and hopped across the gravel path in front of the two boys, hoping to lead them away from a nest it had concealed somewhere nearby.

"Think we should follow it?" Timmy asked in a tone that suggested he found the idea about as interesting as trying to run up a tree.

"All I can think of is the pond," Pete muttered. "We could go fishing."

"My pole's broken. So's yours, remember?"

Pete nodded. "Oh yeah. The swordfight."

"That *I* won."

"No you didn't."

"I sure did. I snapped yours first."

"No way," said Pete, more alive than Timmy had seen him in days. "They both snapped at the same time!"

"Whatever."

"'Whatever' yourself."

They walked in silence for a moment, the brief surge of animosity already fading in the heat. A hornet buzzed Pete's ear and he yelped as he flapped a hand at it. Timmy laughed and once the threat had passed, Pete did too. The echoes of their mirth hung in the muggy air.

They came to a bend in the path where the ground was softer and rarely dry even in summer. The passage of the construction crew had made ridges in the earth here, an obstacle the boys tackled with relish. This in turn led to a crude wooden bridge which consisted of two planks nailed together and flung haphazardly across an overgrown gully. Beneath the bridge, a thin stream of dirty water trickled sluggishly over the rocks and cracked concrete blocks the builders had tossed in to lighten their load.

Myers Pond — named after the doctor and his sons who'd built it one summer long before Timmy was born — had managed to remain unspoiled and unpolluted thus far. It was a welcome sight as the boys fought their way through grass that had grown tall in their absence.

The boy already sitting there, however, wasn't.

Pete paused and scratched furiously at his shoulder, waiting for Timmy to say what they were both thinking. They were standing where a wide swath of grass had been trampled flat, the slope of the bank mere feet away. A dragonfly hovered before the frail-looking boy on the bank as if curious to see what this new intruder had in mind, then zipped away over the shimmering surface of the pond.

Timmy looked at Pete and whispered: "Do you know that kid?"
Pete shook his head. "Do you?"
"No."

The pond was shared by many of the neighborhood kids, a virtual oasis in the summer if you were brave enough to stalk forth amongst the legion of ticks and chiggers, but few people swam there. The story went that when Doctor Myers built the pond all those years ago he'd filled it with baby turtles, and that now those babies had grown to the size of Buicks, hiding down where the water was darkest, waiting for unsuspecting toes to come wiggling.

Had it been another boy from the neighborhood, Timmy wouldn't have cared. But this wasn't any kid he had ever seen before, and while it was common for other children to visit their friends around here, they seldom came this far from the safety of the houses.

And this kid was odd looking, even odder looking than Pete.

He sat so close to the water they could almost hear gravity groaning from the strain of keeping him from falling in. He didn't wear shorts as the burgeoning heat demanded but rather a pair of long gray trousers with a crease in the middle, rolled up so that a bony ankle showed, the rest of his foot submerged in the slimy green fringe of the water, bobbing up and down like a lure.

His impossibly large hands – *adult hands*, Timmy thought – were splayed out behind him, whiter still than the chalky foot and even from where Timmy stood he could see those fingers were tipped with black crescents of dirt.

He nudged Pete, who jumped as if bitten.

"*What?*"

"Go talk to him," Timmy said, a half-smile on his face, knowing his friend would balk at the idea. Pete raised copper eyebrows and scoffed as quietly as he could.

Not quietly enough, however. For the kid turned and spotted them, his eyes like bullets gleaming in the sunlight as he appraised them. His hair was shorn away in patches, contrasting with the long greasy brown clumps that sank beneath and sprouted from the collar of his ripped black T-shirt. The exposed patches of scalp were an angry red.

"Who are you?" Timmy asked, stumbling out of his amazement and horror at the appearance of the stranger and composing himself, ready at a moment's notice to look tough.

The chalk foot bobbed. All three boys watched it and then the kid smiled at them. Pete actually backed up a step, a low groan coming from his throat like a trapped fly, and Timmy found he had to strain to avoid doing something similar. If someone had whispered an insult to his mother into his ear, he wouldn't have been any less disturbed than he was by that smile. It was crooked, and wrong. Something pricked his ankle. He looked down and hissing, slapped away a mosquito. When he straightened, the boy was standing in front of him and this time he couldn't restrain a yelp of surprise.

Up close the kid looked even more peculiar, as if his face were the result of a shortsighted child's mix-n'-match game. His eyes were cold dark stones, set way too far apart, and reminded Timmy of the one and only catfish he had ever caught in this pond. He wondered if there was something wrong with the kid; maybe he'd gone crazy after being bitten by a rabid squirrel or something. Stuff like that happened, he knew. He'd heard the stories.

The kid's head looked like a rotten squash beaten and decorated to resemble a human being's and his mouth could have been a recently healed wound…or a burn.

Instinct told him to run and only the steady panting behind him told him that Pete hadn't already fled. A soft breeze cooled the sweat on the nape of his neck and he swallowed, flinched when a bug's legs tickled his cheek.

The kid's eyes were on him and Timmy couldn't keep from squirming. It was as if his mother had caught him looking at a girl's panties. His cheeks burned with shame.

And then the kid spoke: "Darryl," he said in words spun from filaments of phlegm, making it sound as if he needed to clear his throat.

It took Timmy a moment to decipher what he'd heard and to realize it wasn't a threat, or an insult, or a challenge. The last thing he had expected from the creepy-looking boy was a simple answer. He felt his shoulders drop a notch.

"Oh. Hi. I'm…uh…Timmy." The moment the words crawled from his mouth, he regretted them. Without knowing why, he felt more in danger now that he'd revealed his name.

The boy stared back at him and nodded. "This your pond?" he asked, cocking his strangely shaped head towards the water.

Timmy's mind raced, quickly churning possible responses into something coherent. What emerged was: "Yes. No." *Aw crap.*

The boy said nothing but grinned a grin of ripped stitches and turned back to look out over the water. Pine and walnut trees clustered together on the far side of the pond and some distance beyond them lay the train tracks. Timmy found himself wondering if the kid had been traveling the trains and jumped off to see what trouble he could cause in Delaware. He sincerely hoped not and was all of a sudden very conscious of how far away from the houses they were. Would anyone hear a scream?

A sudden gust of wind hissed high in the trees and a twisted branch overhanging the pond dipped its leaves into the water as if checking the temperature.

The kid slid back down to his spot on the bank and returned his foot to the drifting pond scum. Out in the water, a red and white bobber rode the miniature waves: memento of a past fisherman's unsuccessful cast.

"What are you doing, anyway?" Timmy asked without knowing he was going to. He made a silent promise to himself never to argue again when his father told him he asked too many questions.

The boy answered without raising his head. "Feeding the turtles."

The gasp from behind him made Timmy spin in Pete's direction. Pete had a hand clamped over his mouth, his face even paler than usual, his freckles gray periods on an otherwise blank page. He pointed at the boy and Timmy looked back, expecting to see the kid had jumped to his feet again and was brandishing a knife or something worse. But Darryl hadn't moved, except for his foot, which he continued to let rise and fall into the cool water. Except this time Timmy watched it long enough, watched it come back up out of the water and saw that a ragged semicircle of the boy's ankle was missing, the skin around it mottled and sore. Blood plinked into the water as the boy lowered it again and smiled that ugly smile to himself.

Pete's urgent whisper snapped Timmy out of the terrible and fascinating sight of what Darryl had called 'feeding the turtles.'

"Timmy, *c'mon*. Let's get *out* of here. There's something *wrong* with that kid." He emphasized every couple of words with a stamp of his foot and Timmy knew his friend was close to tears. In truth, he wasn't far away from weeping himself. But not here. Not in front of the crazy kid. Who knew what that might set off in him?

He stepped back, unable to take his eyes off the boy and his ravaged ankle, rising and falling like a white seesaw over the water.

"We're going now," he said, unsure why he felt the need to announce their departure when the element of surprise might have suited them better.

The boy dipped his foot and this time Timmy could have sworn he saw something small, dark and leathery rising to meet it. He moved back until he collided with Pete, who grabbed his wrist hard enough to hurt.

As Timmy was about to turn, Darryl's head swiveled toward him, the frostiness of his gaze undeniable now. "See you soon," he said. Timmy felt gooseflesh ripple across his skin.

They didn't wait to see what might or might not be waiting with open mouths beneath the boy's ankle. Instead, they turned and made their way with a quiet calm that begged to become panic, through the weeds and the tall grass until they were sure they could not be seen from the pond. And then they ran, neither of them screaming in terror for fear of ridicule later when this all turned out to be a cruel dream.

CHAPTER TWO

That night, after showering and checking for the gamut of burrowers and parasites the pond had to offer, Timmy slipped beneath the cool sheets, more glad than he'd ever been before that his father was there to read to him.

Beside his bed, a new fan had been lodged in the open window and droned out cool air as his father yawned, set his Coke down on the floor between his feet and smiled. "You remember where we left off?" he asked as he took a seat just below his son's toes.

Timmy nodded. They were reading *The Magician's Nephew* by C.S. Lewis. He smoothed the blankets over his chest. "Queen Jadis turned out to be really wicked. She wanted to go with Digory and Polly back to their world to try to take it over but they touched the rings and escaped."

His father nodded. "Right." As he flipped through the pages, Timmy looked around the room, his eyes settling on the fish his father had painted on the walls last summer. They were tropical fish; brightly colored and smudged where the paint had tried to run. A hammerhead shark had been frozen in the act of dive-bombing the wainscoting. Here a hermit crab peeked out from the shadows of his sanctuary; there a jellyfish mimicked the currents to rise from the depths of the blue wall. A lobster waved atop a rock strategically placed to hide a crack in the plaster. Bubbles rose toward the ceiling and Timmy tracked them with fearful eyes down to the half open mouth of a gaudily painted turtle.

He listened to his father read, more comforted by the soft tone and occasional forced drama of his voice than the words themselves.

When his father reached a page with a picture, he turned the book around to show it to Timmy. It was a crosshatching of the fearsome queen, one arm curled behind her head, the other outstretched before a massive black metal door as she readied herself to fling it wide with her magic. Timmy nodded, indicating he'd seen enough and his father went back to reading.

Timmy's eyes returned to the crudely drawn turtle on the wall. It was bigger than any turtle he'd ever seen and the mouth was a thin black line twisted slightly at the end to make it appear as if it was smiling – his father's touch. The shell was enormous, segmented into hexagonal shapes and much more swollen than he imagined they were in real life. Was it something like this, then, that had been chewing on Darryl's ankle? The thought brought a shudder of revulsion rippling through him and he pulled the sheets closer to his chin. It couldn't have been. Even a kid as crazy-looking as Darryl couldn't have done such a thing without it hurting him. Perhaps the boy had been injured and was merely soaking his wound in the pond when they found him. Perhaps it had all been a trick, a bit of mischief they had fallen for, hook line and sinker. That made much more sense, and yet he still didn't believe it. The cold knot in his throat remained and when his father read to him of Digory's and Polly's escape from Charn and their arrival – with the queen in tow – at the mysterious pools in the Wood between the Worlds, he wondered if they had seen a boy there, sitting on the bank of one of those pools, his feet dipped in the water.

"Dad?"

His father's eyebrows rose above his thick spectacles. "What is it?"

Timmy looked at him for a long time, struggling to frame the words so they wouldn't sound foolish, but almost all of it sounded ridiculous. Eventually he sighed and said: "I was at the pond today."

"I know. Your mother told me. She tugged a few ticks off you too, I believe. Nasty little buggers, aren't they?"

Timmy nodded. "I saw someone down there." He cleared his throat. "A boy."

"Oh yeah? A friend of yours?"

"No. I've never seen this kid before. He was dirty and smelly and his head was a funny shape. Weird eyes, too."

The eyebrows lowered. "'Weird' how?"

"I-I don't know. They had no color, just really dark."

"What was he doing down there?"

"Just sitting there," Timmy said softly, avoiding his father's eyes.

"Did he say anything to you?"

After a moment of careful thought, Timmy nodded. "He said he was feeding the turtles." There was silence then, except for the hum of the fan.

Timmy's father set the book down beside him on the bed and crossed his arms. "And was he?" he said at last, as if annoyed that Timmy hadn't already filled in that gap in the story.

"I don't know. There was a piece of his foot missing and he was—"

His father sighed and waved a hand. "Okay, okay. I get it. Ghost story time, huh?" He stood up and Timmy quickly scooted himself into a sitting position, his eyes wide with interest.

"You think he was a ghost?" he asked, as his father smirked down at him.

"Well isn't that how the story is supposed to go? Did you turn back when you were leaving only to find the boy had mysteriously vanished?"

Timmy slowly shook his head. "We didn't look back. We were afraid to."

His father's smile held but seemed glued there by doubt. "There's no such thing as ghosts, Timmy. Only *ghost* stories. The living have enough to worry about these days without the dead coming back to complicate things. Now you get some rest."

He carefully stepped around his Coke and leaned in to give

Timmy a kiss on the cheek. Ordinarily, the acrid stench of his father's cologne bothered him, but tonight it was a familiar smell, a smell he knew was real, and unthreatening.

"Good night, Dad."

"Good night, kiddo. I'll see you in the morning." He walked, Coke in hand, to the door. "Have sweet dreams now, you hear me? Don't go wasting any more time and energy on ghosts and goblins. Nothing in the dark you can't see in the daylight. Remember that."

Timmy smiled weakly. "I will. Thanks."

His father nodded and closed the door, but just as the boy had resigned himself to solitude and all the fanciful and awful ponderings that would be birthed within it, the door opened again and his father poked his head in.

"One more thing."

"Yeah?"

"I don't want you going back to the pond for a while. You know, just in case there are some odd folk hanging around down there."

"Okay."

"Good boy. See you in the morning."

"See you in the morning too." His father started to close the door.

"Dad?"

A sigh. "Yes?"

"Do you think there are turtles back there? Like, big ones?"

"Who knows? I've never seen them but that isn't to say they aren't there. Now quit worrying about it and get some sleep."

"I will."

"Goodnight."

The door closed and Timmy listened to his father's slippers slopping against the bare wood steps of the stairs. It was followed by mumbled conversation and Timmy guessed his mother was being filled in on The Turtle Boy story. Her laughter, crisp and warm, echoed through the house.

Timmy turned his back on the aquatic renderings and stared at his *Hulk* poster on the opposite wall. As he replayed moments from his favorite episodes of the show, he found himself drifting, edging closer to the bank of sleep where he sat among ugly children with wounded feet and burst stitches for smiles.

CHAPTER THREE

The next morning, he called for Pete and found him in his sun-washed kitchen, hunched over a bowl of cereal as if afraid someone was going to steal it.

"Hi Pete."

Pete looked positively bleached. Except for the angry purple bruise around his left eye. "Hi."

"Ouch. Where did you get the shiner?"

"Fell."

"Where?"

Pete shrugged but said nothing further and while this wasn't unusual, Timmy sensed his friend was still shaken from their meeting with Darryl the day before. He, on the other hand, had managed to convince himself that they had simply stumbled upon some sick kid from one of the neighboring towns who had ventured out of his camp to see what the city had to offer. Pete's father had once told the boys about the less prosperous areas of Delaware and warned them not to ride their bikes there after sundown. He'd frightened them with stories about what had happened to those children who'd disobeyed their parents and ventured there after dark. They had resolved never to step foot outside their own neighborhood if they could help it. Of course, they couldn't stop people from coming *in* to their neighborhood either and after much musing, Timmy had decided that that was exactly what had happened. Nothing creepy going on, just a kid sniffing around in uncharted territory. No big deal. And though he'd been scared to stumble upon the strange kid with the mangled foot, the fear had buckled under the weight of solid reasoning and now he felt more than a little silly for panicking.

It appeared, however, that the waking nightmare had yet to let Pete go. The longer Timmy watched him, the more worried he became. It didn't help that Pete was accident-prone. Every other week he had some kind of injury to display.

"You all right, Pete?" he asked as he slid into a chair.

Pete nodded and made a snorting sound as he shoveled a spoonful of Cheerios into his mouth. A teardrop of milk ran from the corner of his mouth, dangled from his chin, then fell back into the white sea beneath his face. A smile curled Timmy's lips as he recalled his mother saying: "If you ever eat like that kid, you'd better be prepared to hunt for your own food. Honestly, you'd think they starve him over there or something."

When Pete finished, he raised the bowl to his lips and drained the remaining milk from it, then wiped a forearm across his lips and belched softly.

"So what should we do today?" Timmy asked, already bored with the stale atmosphere in Pete's house.

Pete shrugged but the reply came from the hallway behind them.

"He's not doing anything today. He's grounded."

Timmy turned in his chair. It was Pete's father.

Wayne Marshall was tall and thin; his skin brushed with the same healthy glow nature had denied his son. He wore silver wire-rimmed glasses atop an aquiline nose. Thick black eyebrows sat like a dark horizon between the sweeping black wings of his bangs. He was frightening when angry, but Timmy seldom stuck around to see the full force of his wrath. Right now it seemed he was on 'simmer.'

"What were you two boys doing back at Myers Pond yesterday?" he asked as he strode into the kitchen and plucked an errant strand of hair from his tie. From what Timmy had seen, the man only owned two suits – one black, the other a silvery gray. Today he wore the former, with a white shirt and a red and black striped tie.

He looked at Pete but the boy was staring into his empty bowl as if summoning the ghost of his Cheerios.

Timmy swallowed. "We were looking for something to do. We thought we might go fishing but our poles are broken."

Mr. Marshall nodded. As he poured himself a coffee, Timmy noticed no steam rose from the liquid as it surged into the cup. *Cold coffee?* It made him wonder how early these people got up in the morning. After all, it was only eight-thirty now.

"The new Zebco pole I bought Petey for his birthday a few months back, you mean?"

Timmy grimaced. "I didn't know it was a new one. He never told me that."

The man leaned against the counter and studied Timmy with obvious distaste and the boy felt his face grow hot under the scrutiny. He decided Pete had earned himself a good punch for not rescuing him.

"Yeah well...." Pete's father said, pausing to sip from his cup. He smacked his lips. "There isn't much point going back to the pond if you're not going fishing, is there? I mean, what else is there to do?"

Timmy shrugged. "I dunno. Stuff."

"What kind of stuff?"

Another shrug. His mother had warned him about shrugging when asked a direct question, and how irritating it was to grown-ups, but at that moment he felt like his shoulders were tied to counterweights and threaded through eyehooks in the ceiling.

"Messin' around and stuff. You know…playing army. That kind of stuff."

"What's wrong with playing army out in the yard, or better still in *your* yard with all the trees you've got back there?"

"I don't know."

The urge to run infected him, but his mind kept a firm foot on the brakes. He had already let his yellow belly show once this week; it wasn't going to happen again now, no matter how cranky Mr. Marshall was feeling this morning. But it was getting progressively harder to return the man's gaze, and although he had seen Pete's dad lose his cool more than once, he wasn't sure he had ever felt this much animosity coming from him. The sudden dislike was almost palpable.

Mr. Marshall's demeanor changed. He sipped his coffee and grinned, but there was a distinct absence of humor in the expression. His smoldering glare shifted momentarily to Pete, who shuffled in response. Timmy felt his spine contract with discomfort.

"Petey was telling me about this Turtle Boy you boys are supposed to have met."

At that moment, had Timmy eyes in the back of his head, they would have been glaring at Pete. He didn't know why. After all, he had told his father. But *his* father hadn't blown a gasket over some busted fishing poles, Zebco or no Zebco, and had waved away the idea of a ghost at Myers Pond without a second thought.

The way Mr. Marshall was looking at him now, it appeared he had given it a *lot* of thought.

"Yeah. It was weird," he said with a lopsided grin.

"Weird? It scared Pete half to death and from what he tells me you were scared too. Didn't your mother ever tell you not to talk to strangers?"

"Yes, but it was just a ki—"

"Don't you know how many children disappear every year around this area? Most of them because they wandered off to places they were warned not to go. Places like that pond, and while I don't believe for a second that either of you saw anything like Pete described, I don't want you bringing my boy back there again, do you understand me?"

"But I didn't—"

"I spent most of last night prying ticks off him. Is that your idea of fun, Timmy?"

"No sir."

"I told him not to hang around with you anyway. You're trouble. Just like your father."

Caught in the spotlight cast by the morning sun, dust motes seemed to slow through air made thick with tension.

Timmy's jaw dropped. While he had squirmed beneath his friend's father's angry monologue, this insult to his own father made something snap shut in his chest. Anger and hurt swelled within him and he let out a long, infuriated breath. Unspoken words flared in that breath and died harmlessly before a mouth sealed tight with disgust. He felt his stomach begin to quiver and suddenly he wanted more than anything to be gone from Pete's house. The departure would come with the implied demand that Pete go to hell in a Zip-Loc bag, the sentiment punctuated by a slamming of the front door that would no doubt bring Mr. Marshall running to chastise him further.

Fine, he thought, the words poison arrows in his head. *Let him. He can go to hell in a baggie too.*

"I gotta go now," he mumbled finally, and without sparing his treacherous comrade a glance, started toward the front door.

Hot tears blurred the hallway and the daylight beyond as he left the house and closed the door *gently* behind him. The anger had ebbed away as quickly as it had come, replaced now by a tiny tear in the fabric of his happiness through which dark light shone. He was dimly aware of the door opening behind him.

Pete's voice halted him and he turned. "Hey, I'm sorry Timmy. Really I am."

"Oh yeah?" The hurt spun hateful words he couldn't speak. With what looked like monumental effort, Pete closed the front door behind him. With an uncertain smile, he said: "My Dad'll kill me for this, but let's go do something."

"Good idea," Timmy said, aware that an errant tear was trickling down his cheek. "You can go to hell. I'm going home."

"Timmy wait —"

"Shut up, Pete. I *hate* you!"

He ran home and slammed the door behind him. His mother sat wiping her eyes, engrossed in some soppy movie. He waited behind the sofa for her to ask him what was wrong and when she didn't he ran to his room and to bed, where he lay with his face buried in the cool white pillows.

And seethed.

CHAPTER FOUR

That night, he dreamt he was standing at his bedroom window.

Down in the yard, beside the pine tree, a boy stood wreathed in shadow, despite the cataract eye of the moon soaring high in the sky behind him.

And though the window was closed, Timmy heard him whisper: "Would you die for him?"

He squinted to see more than just shadow, his heart filled with dread.

"Darryl?"

And then he woke, warmed by the morning sun, nothing but the distant echo of the whisper in his mind.

CHAPTER FIVE

Shortly after Mr. Marshall made his feelings known about Timmy and his father, he sent Pete to summer camp.

Although the anger and hurt had settled like a stone in the pit of his belly, Timmy missed Pete and hoped Mr. Marshall would realize his cruelty and allow things to return to normal before Timmy found himself minus a friend. Summer was only just beginning and he didn't relish the idea of trudging through it without his best buddy.

Early the next Saturday, he came home from riding his bike to find his parents grinning at him in a way he wasn't sure he'd ever seen before. It made his heart lurch; he couldn't decide if it was a good or a bad thing.

"What?" he asked. They were sitting next to each other at the kitchen table, looking fresh and content. His mother was looping a strand of her hair around her finger, his father nodding slowly. They almost looked *proud*. As soon as Timmy's eyes settled on the source of their amusement, he felt as if someone had forced his finger into a light socket.

Kim Barnes.

"What is she doing here?" he asked, pointing at the black-haired girl with the braces who stood in the hallway behind them. Her arms were crossed and she shifted from foot to foot as if no happier about where she had found herself than he.

His mother scowled. "Is that any way to talk to a lady? Kim's sister and her friend have gone to camp too, so she has no one to play with for the whole summer. Isn't that a nice coincidence?"

Timmy was appalled. "She's a *girl!*"

"No flies on him," said his father.

"But...she doesn't even *like* me!"

"Now how do you know that? Have you ever asked her?"

"I know she doesn't. She's always making faces at me in school."

Kim smiled. "I don't mean anything by it."

"You see," his mother said. "You have to give a girl a chance."

Timmy felt sick.

"I don't have to play with you if you don't want me to," Kim said in a pitiful tone. Timmy felt an ounce of hope but knew his parents, who melted at the sound of her feigned sorrow, would vanquish it.

"Don't be silly. Timmy would love to play with you, wouldn't you, Timmy?"

He sighed and studied the scuffed toe of his sneakers. "I guess so."

"Speak up, son."

"I guess so," he repeated, wondering how this summer could possibly get any worse.

His mother went to Kim. With maternal grace, she eased the girl into the kitchen. Timmy felt the color rise in his cheeks and looked away.

"Now see," his mother said. "Why don't you both go on outside in the sunshine and see what you can find to do. I bet you'll get along just fine."

I bet we won't, Timmy thought, miserable. With a heavy sigh, he turned and opened the door.

CHAPTER SIX

They were standing in the yard, Kim with her arms still folded and Timmy watching the bloated white clouds sailing overhead when she said: "I didn't want to come over here, you know."

Without looking at her he scoffed. "Then why did you?"

"Your mom called my mom and told her you were bored and lonely and—"

"I wasn't *lonely*. I was doing just fine."

"Well, your mom thought you weren't and asked if I could come over. I told *my* mom I didn't want to play with you because you are dirty and smelly."

Timmy gaped at her. "Really?"

She shook her head and he had to restrain the sigh that swelled in his throat.

"So I guess we'll have to do something for a while at least," she said. "What do you want to play?"

"Not dolls, anyway. I hate dolls." He watched a blue jay until it flew behind her. Tracking it any further would have meant looking in her direction and he wasn't yet ready to do that.

"Me too," Kim said, startling him, and he looked at her. Briefly.

"I thought *all* girls liked dolls."

He saw her shrug. "I think they're dumb."

"Real dumb."

"Yeah."

The silence wasn't as dreadful as Timmy had thought it would be. For one, she didn't like dolls and that was a plus. Dolls really were dumb. He hadn't said it just to annoy her. And at least she *talked*. By now he'd have grown tired of listening to himself talking to Pete and getting no answer. So, he guessed, she wasn't *that* bad.

But still, he didn't like the idea of being seen hanging around with her. No matter how cool she might turn out to be, if anyone at school heard about it they'd say he was in love with her or something and that they were going to have a baby. And that would be bad news. *Real* bad news.

"Why don't we go back to the pond?" she asked then, as if reading his thoughts.

Going back to Myers Pond was no more comforting an idea than hanging around with a girl, but at least there no one would see them together.

"I'm not allowed to go back to the pond," he said, with an ounce of shame. Admitting you were restricted by the same rules as everyone else seemed akin to admitting weakness when you said it to a girl.

"Why not?"

"I'm just not."

When she said nothing, he gave a dramatic sigh and conceded. "Pete Marshall's dad thinks there might be some creeps back there or something. He thinks it might be dangerous for kids. My dad doesn't want me going back there either."

"Creeps? Like what kind of creeps?"

He almost told her, but caught himself at the last minute and shrugged it off. "Just some strange kids."

She stared at him for a moment and he struggled not to cringe.

"Like The Turtle Boy?"

Now he looked at her and through the shock of hearing the name he had given Darryl, he realized she wasn't so ugly and stinky and everything else he associated with the chittering group she swept around the playground with at recess. Her eyes, for one thing, were like sparkling emeralds, and once he peered into them his discomfort evaporated and he had to struggle to look away. Her skin reminded him of his mother's soap and that conjured a memory of a pleasant clean smell. But still...she was a girl and that made him feel a strange kind of awkwardness.

"What?" she said after a moment.

Eventually he composed himself enough to croak: "You've seen him?"

"Yes. He's awful creepy looking, isn't he?"

"But...when did *you* see him?"

"The first day of summer vacation. My cousin Dale came to visit with his mom and we went fishing back there." She gave him a shy smile. "I'm not much good at fishing. I lost my bobber."

Timmy remembered the small red and white ball drifting in the water the day they'd seen Darryl and wondered if it was hers.

"Dale caught a catfish. It was ugly and gross and when he reeled it in, he raised it up in front of my face and tried to get me to kiss it. I ran into the trees and that's where he was. The Turtle Boy. He stank really bad and looked at me as if I had caught him doing something he shouldn'ta been. I was scared."

Timmy was confused. "But why do you call him that? Did he tell you that was his name?"

"No. I just...I don't know. I just remember thinking about it later and that's the name I gave him."

"That's weird. That's the name *I* gave him."

"I guess that is weird."

"Have you ever seen him around before?"

She shook her head. "Have you?"

"No, but I wish I knew why he was here and where he came from."

A blur of movement caught his eye and he followed it to a groundhog shimmying his way along the bottom of the yard toward the road. He looked back to Kim. "Did he say anything to you?"

"Yeah." She swallowed and the same fear that had gripped him when he'd seen Darryl's ankle was written across her face. It made him feel better somehow to see it. It meant he was no longer alone in his fear. With Pete it wasn't the same. Pete was afraid to ride his bike on the off chance he might fall and get hurt. He was also afraid of storms and dogs and pretty much anything that moved and had teeth.

"He said: 'They're hungry.'"

"When me and Pete saw him he was putting his heel into the water. There was a piece of it missing. He said he was feeding the turtles. What do you suppose it means?"

"There's only one way to find out," she said.

"How?"

Kim's braces segmented her mischievous smile but couldn't take away the appeal of it. A slight smile crept across Timmy's lips in response. He got the feeling that even though The Turtle Boy had frightened her, she wasn't easily deterred from any kind of adventure.

"We have to ask him, of course."

CHAPTER SEVEN

Rather than taking the regular gravel path back to the pond, a path that could be spotted from most of the houses, they cut across Mr. Patterson's field, pausing only to look at the large puddle, which was all that remained of the hole Timmy and Pete had been digging. A pile of earth like a scale-model mountain sat next to it.

"We were looking for gold," he explained.

"Did you find any?" Kim asked.

He shrugged, strangely ashamed. "No. We found some red clay though."

Kim smiled. "Maybe that would be worth something in some other country. Maybe some country where they have gold to spare and kids dig for red clay?"

He nodded, a silly grin breaking out across his face. He knew it was a foolish notion – he'd never heard of a place that had *too* much gold – but it was a nice fantasy, and he silently thanked her for not making fun of his efforts.

They carried on through the high grass, chasing crickets and wondering what kind of exotic creatures they heard scurrying at their approach. The field ran parallel to the gravel path, but the trees shielded them from view and they hunkered down, the grass whipping against their bare legs. Much to his surprise, Kim kept the pace as he raced toward the narrow dirt road leading into the pond. At times she drew abreast of him and, more than once – though he would never admit it – she began to inch ahead of him, forcing him to push himself until he felt his chest start to ache.

At last they reached the makeshift bridge. Kim, her legs braced on the wobbling boards, leaned over to catch her breath. She looked down at the stream trickling beneath them. "They've ruined it, haven't they?"

It took him a moment to realize what she was referring to and then he told her that yes, they had ruined it. The construction crews dedicated to tearing up the land they'd once played in seemed equally driven to foul whatever they'd been prohibited to touch. Gullies became dumping grounds for material waste, streams became muddied and paths cracked beneath the groaning and shrieking metal of their monstrous machines. Timmy joined her in a moment of mournful pondering at the senselessness of it all, then tapped her on the elbow and pointed up at the sky.

Shadows rushed past them, crawling through the grass toward the train tracks and spilling from the trees as the breeze gained strength. Over their heads, the sky had turned from blue to gray, the sun now a dim torch glimpsed through a caul of spider webs. All around them the trees began to sway and hiss as if the breeze were water, the canopies fire.

Kim nodded at the change and hurried to his side. She mumbled something to him and he looked at her. "What?"

"I said: my dad says they're going to fill in the pond."

Before Timmy had met Darryl, this might have hurt him more than it did now. Still, it didn't seem right. "Why?"

"I don't know. He says in a few years all of this will be houses and that the pond is only in the way. Apparently Doctor Myers's son sold this area of the land so they're just waiting for someone to buy it before they fill it in."

Timmy knew her father worked on a construction site across town and would no doubt be privy to such information. It was a depressing thought; not so much that they would be taking the pond away, but because he suspected that would only be the start of it. Soon, the fields would be gone, concrete lots in their place.

They carried on up the rise until the black mirror of the pond revealed itself. Timmy's gaze immediately went to the spot where he had seen Darryl, but he saw no one sitting there today. Kim walked on and over the bank and made her way around the pond toward the brace of fir trees weaving in the wind. She paused and looked back at him over her shoulder. "Are you coming?"

"Yeah."

But he was already starting to question the logic behind such a move. At least the last time he'd been here he'd had the escape route at his back; if The Turtle Boy had tried anything it wouldn't have been hard to turn and run. Going into those trees was like walking into a cage. You would have to thread your way through brambles and thick undergrowth to be clear of it. And even then, there was nowhere to run but the train tracks.

A quiver of fear rippled through him, and he masked it by smacking an imaginary mosquito from his neck. Overhead, the clouds thickened. With a sigh, he followed Kim into the trees.

On this side of the pond, dispirited pines hung low. The earth beneath was a tangle of withered needles, flattened grass and severed branches. The children had to duck until they'd cleared the biggest and densest stand of pines.

At last they emerged on the other side, a marshy stretch of land that offered a clear view of the train tracks but soaked their sandaled feet.

After a moment of listening to the breeze and searching the growing shadows around them, Kim put her hands on her hips and looked at Timmy, who was preoccupied with trying to remove sticky skeins of spider web from his face.

"He's not here," she said, stifling a giggle at Timmy's dismay.

He didn't answer until he was sure some fat black arachnid hadn't nested in his hair. When he'd cleared the remaining strands, he grimaced and looked around. "Sure looks like it. Unless he's hiding."

"Maybe he's gone."

"Yeah, maybe." It was a comforting thought. Behind them in the distance, the hungry heavens rumbled as God made a dark stew of the sky. "Maybe he caught a train out of here."

Kim glanced toward the tracks, which were silent and somehow lonely without a thousand pounds of steel shrieking over them. "Or maybe a train caught *him*."

Before Timmy could allow the image to form in his mind, he heard something behind him, on the other side of the pines.

"Did you hear that?"

Kim shook her head.

A twig snapped and they both backed away.

"It's probably a squirrel or something," Kim whispered, and Timmy was suddenly aware that her hand was gripping his. He looked down at it, then at her, but she was intent on the movement through the trees behind them. He ignored the odd but not entirely unpleasant sensation of her cool skin on his and held his breath.

Listening.

"Maybe a deer," Kim said, so low Timmy could hardly hear her above the breeze.

They stood like that for what seemed forever, ears straining to filter the sounds from the coiling weather around them. Timmy could hear little over the thundering of his own heart. Kim was holding his hand even tighter now. A terrifying thought sparked in his mind: *Does this mean she's my girlfriend?*

"C'mon," he said at last. "There's no one there."

She nodded and they both stepped forward.

Timmy was filled with confused excitement. Then, just as quickly, uncertainty came over him. Was she waiting for *him* to let go of *her* hand? Was she feeling uncomfortable and embarrassed now because he was holding her hand just as tightly? He tried to loosen his fingers but she squeezed them, and a gentle wave of reassurance flooded over him.

She wasn't uncomfortable. She didn't want to let go. His heart began to race again but this time for a completely different reason.

And she continued to hold his hand. Continued even when something lithe and dark burst through the pines in front of their faces and dragged them both screaming through the trees.

CHAPTER EIGHT

Timmy's mother opened the front door. Her look of surprise doubled when she saw the rage on Wayne Marshall's face.

She stood in the doorway, leaning against the jamb. "What on earth is going on?" she said, crossing her arms. The gesture meant to convey that she was prepared to dispense blame wherever it was due.

On the porch, Pete's father still had a firm grip on the collar of Timmy's T-shirt, but he held Kim by the hand. Timmy felt strangely jealous.

"Sandra, I found these two snooping around back at Myers Pond," Mr. Marshall said firmly, as if this should be reason enough for punishment. Timmy's mother stared at him for a moment as if she didn't think so. Her gaze shifted briefly to Kim, then settled on her son.

"Didn't your father tell you not to go back there?"

Timmy nodded.

"Then why did you? And I suppose you dragged poor Kimmie back with you, back into all that mud and sludge? Look at your sandals. I only bought them last week and you've wrecked them already." She shook her head and sighed. After a moment in which no one said anything, she looked at Mr. Marshall. "You can let them go now, Wayne. I don't think they're going to run away."

But he didn't release them and Timmy thought he could feel the man's arms trembling with anger. In a voice little better than a growl, he said, "Sandra, it's not safe for kids back there. I don't think I have to remind you what happened a few years ago. I know I certainly don't want Pete back there and it's becoming blindingly obvious that your son has taken the role of the neighborhood Piper, leading everyone else's kids back there to get into all sorts of trouble."

A hard look entered Mrs. Quinn's eyes. "Now wait just a second –"

"If you had any sense you'd send this little pup away for the summer like I sent Pete. It's the only way to keep them out of trouble. I mean, what was your son doing back there on the other side of the trees? With a *girl?* Is this the kind of thing you're letting him do behind your back?"

Timmy's mother straightened, her eyes blazing. "Just what the hell are you saying, Wayne? That because we don't shelter our boy and scream and roar commands at him around the clock that we're doing a bad job? Is that what you're saying? How about you mind your own business and let me raise my child how I see fit? Or would that be asking too much of you? He's eleven years old for God's sake, not a teenager."

"Just what I expected," Mr. Marshall said with a humorless smile. "All the time strolling around like you're Queen of the Neighborhood, better than everyone else. Well, I'm afraid your superior attitude seems to be lost on your kid."

"That's rich coming from you. At least Timmy doesn't live in fear of me."

"Maybe he damn well *should* live in fear of you."

"Watch your language in front of the children."

"*Fuck* the children!" He wrenched Timmy's collar hard enough to make the boy gasp. "You don't keep a watch on them. You don't care what happens to them. You let them wander and that's how they get hurt. It's bitches like you that make the world the way it is."

The trembling in his arms intensified, spreading through Timmy and making him queasy. He tried to pull away but the man held firm. When he looked up he saw that Mr. Marshall's face was swollen with rage.

"Let them go."

He didn't.

Timmy's mother took a step forward, teeth clenched. "I *said*, let them go, Wayne. Let them go and get the hell off my property or we're going to have a serious problem."

Mr. Marshall dropped Kim's wrist. Timmy felt the grip on his T-shirt loosen. They went to his mother's side. Mrs. Quinn tousled their hair and told them to go into the kitchen. As they did, Timmy heard Mr. Marshall mutter darkly, "We already have a problem. But I'll fix that. You'll see."

CHAPTER NINE

After Mr. Marshall stormed off, Timmy's mother made the kids some lemonade and ushered them into the living room. Timmy noticed the ice clinked more than usual as she set the glasses down on coasters for them, her smile flickering as much as the lights. She switched on the television and changed the channel to cartoons. *Spider-man* twitched and swung through the staticky skies of the city. Rain drummed impatient fingers on the roof. Kim scooted closer to Timmy and, though pleased, the boy guessed the image of Mr. Marshall's hands bursting from the trees was still lingering in her mind. Those hands had terrified him too. Even when he realized it was his friend's father that he was looking at and not the mangled squash countenance of The Turtle Boy, he hadn't felt much better. Or safer. Though Pete's dad had never been the friendliest of people, it seemed he'd become a monster since the start of summer.

They watched cartoons for a few hours until Timmy's father came home, cheerful though soaked from the hissing downpour. With a degree of shame, Timmy watched his father's good mood evaporate as his mother related the day's events. Kim shrank down further in her seat.

Eventually his father sat at the kitchen table with a fresh cup of coffee and called him over. His mother ferried a basket of laundry into the den and Kim watched with fretful eyes as he swallowed and slowly obeyed.

"Your mother tells me you were down at the pond today?"

"Yes, sir."

"Look at me when I'm talking to you."

Timmy felt as if his chin were the heaviest thing in the world. It was a titanic struggle to meet his father's eyes.

"Didn't we discuss this? Didn't I ask you to stay away from there?"

Timmy nodded.

"But you went anyway."

Timmy nodded again, his gaze drawn to his shoes until he caught himself and looked up.

His father stared for a moment and then shook his head as if he'd given up on trying to figure out some complicated math problem. "Why?"

"We were trying to find The Turtle Boy."

He expected his father to explode into anger, but to his surprise he simply frowned. "This is the kid you said you and Pete saw?"

"Yes, sir."

"Then you really did see a kid down there?"

"Yes, sir."

"Was everything you told me about him true, even the stuff about the wound he had?"

"It was horrible. He kept dipping it in the water. Said he was feeding the turtles."

His father nodded and poked his glasses back into the red indentation on the bridge of his nose. "It sounds like one of your comic book stories, but I believe you."

Timmy was stunned. "You do?"

"Yes. And I think the reason Mr. Marshall is so mad is because he's been drinking like a fish the past few weeks. It doesn't help to have you hanging around with his kid and making trouble."

"But I wasn't making tr—"

"I know, but the way he sees it you are. Wayne is going through a tough time, Timmy. His wife passed away, he started messing with...well, with bad stuff I don't really want to go into. He drinks too much and it's starting to get to him, to make him crazy, so I think it would be better to avoid him from now on."

This had never occurred to Timmy. His mind buzzed with possibilities. "But what about Pete?"

A sigh. "Son, I think it's time for you to start making new friends, like Kimmie there. Now wait — before you get upset. If you wanted to play with Pete I wouldn't raise a hand to stop you, but I found out that Wayne put his house up for sale this morning. And with the way things are developing around here, he'll have it sold in a heartbeat, especially at the low price he's asking for it. So I don't think they're going to be our neighbors for much longer."

Timmy was appalled. "It's not fair. Pete's my best friend."

"I know," said his father, clamping a hand on Timmy's shoulder. "And God knows he's not having an easy time of it either. It's not right what Wayne's putting him through."

"What do you mean?"

"Never mind. I'm going to ask you now to stay away from Pete's dad, and this time I want you to promise you'll do as I say."

Timmy was buoyed a little by this new alliance in the dark world his summer had become. "I promise. He scares me anyway."

"Yes, I'm sure he does. He had no right to speak to you or your mother like he did. I'm going to go over there and have a few words with him."

Timmy felt something cold stir inside him, an icy current in the tide of pride he felt at his father's bravery.

"Don't."

His father nodded his understanding. "He's a bully, but only with kids. He'll think twice before crossing me, I guarantee it. He owes all of us an apology and I'll be damned if I'll let him be until I get it."

"Are you going to fight?"

"No. That's the last thing we'll do. You know how I feel about violence, what I tell *you* about violence."

"But...can't you go over there tomorrow?" Timmy gestured toward the rain-blurred kitchen window where the storm tugged at the fir trees. "It's nasty out there. You'll get drenched."

"Don't worry about it. I'm not exactly bone dry as it is."

"But—"

"Timmy, I won't be long. We'll just have a little chat, that's all."

But Timmy wasn't reassured. The storm was worsening, buffeting the house and blinding the windows. Lightning flashed, ravenous thunder at its heels, the sibilance of the rain an enraged serpent struggling to find entry through the cracks beneath the doors. It was the kind of weather when bad things happened, Timmy thought, the kind when monsters stepped out of the shadows to bask in the fluorescent light of the storm, drinking the rain and snatching those foolish enough to venture into their domain.

And his father wanted to do that very thing.

"Why don't you wait until the storm passes?" he asked, though he could see the resolve that had hardened his father's face when he shook his head and downed the dregs of his coffee.

"Timmy, there's nothing to worry about."

Timmy didn't agree. There was plenty to worry about, and as he watched his father stand and steel himself against the weather and the things it hid, he felt his legs weaken. A voice, calling feebly to him from the far side of the sweeping desert of his imagination, told him that he would remember this moment later, that summoning it would bring a taste of grief and regret and guilt. And failure. It would etch itself on his brain like an epitaph, inescapable and persistent, haunting his dreams. He felt he now stood at the epicenter of higher forces that revolved around him in the guise of a storm, that this little family play was taking place in its eye, tragedy waiting in the wings.

"I want to go with you."

Shrugging on his jacket, his father shook his head. "It'll only agitate him further."

"But you said he should apologize to me too, remember? You can ask him to apologize to me if I'm with you and I'd feel safer with you there."

His father studied him for a moment, then a small smile creased his lips as he dropped to his haunches and drew Timmy close. He hugged him hard and the boy felt a comforting warmth radiating from his father, mingled with the smell of aftershave.

"Timmy," he said softly, "I love you. You have no idea how hurt I am by what Wayne said to you. If I had been there I'd probably have punched his lights out, so I'm glad I wasn't. Nobody has any right to speak to you like that and I don't want you to ever take any of it to heart. Wayne Marshall is a sick man, and a coward. Remember that. Your Mom and I love you more than anything in this world and we're proud of you. That's all you need to know."

He rose to his feet. The movement seemed blurry and strange through the tears in Timmy's eyes. "*Please*," Timmy whispered, but his father was already walking toward the door.

CHAPTER TEN

An hour passed.

Timmy sat in front of the television with Kim silent by his side.

His father had still not come home and the worry made him sick to his stomach. His inner voice chastised him for letting his father go alone, but he quelled it with forced reassurance.

And then the power went out, darkness thick and suffocating descending around them. Kim gasped and grabbed his arm hard enough to hurt. He winced but did not ask her to release him. He welcomed the contact.

His mother arrived downstairs following a candle she had cupped with one slender hand. The yellow light made her face seem younger, less haunted, and the smile she wore was as radiant as the flame she set on the coffee table before them.

"Don't touch that or you'll burn yourself, if not the whole house," she told them. "I'll set up some more candles so we can see what we're doing. I don't like the idea of losing you in the dark."

Although she said it with humor, the phrase stuck with Timmy. *Losing you in the dark*. Was that what had happened to his father? Had he been lost in the dark? He was now more afraid than he could ever remember. Even more afraid than when he'd seen The Turtle Boy. He struggled to keep from trembling, something he was determined not to let happen. At least not while Kim was touching him.

"When's Dad coming home?" he asked, and saw his mother stiffen.

"Soon," she replied. "He's probably managed to calm Mr. Marshall down and they're discussing things man to man." She didn't sound like she believed it. "Wayne probably broke out the beers and the two of them are sitting out the storm and having a fine time." She laughed then, a sound forced and devoid of hope. Timmy shivered.

"Why don't you call and make sure?" he asked.

She sighed. "All right."

He watched her, dread stuck like a bone in his throat as she picked up the phone and stared for a moment at the shadows parrying with the light. After a few moments she clucked her tongue and hung up.

"The phone's out," she told him.

Thunder blasted against the walls, making them all jump and Kim let out a little squeal of fright.

Mom sighed and set about placing pools of amber light around the kitchen. They made twitching shadows and nervous silhouettes of the furniture.

"I hope he's okay," Timmy mumbled and Kim scooted closer. She was now close enough for him to feel her breath on his face. It was not an unpleasant feeling.

"He'll be fine," she said. "He's a big tough guy. Much bigger than Mr. Marshall. I bet if they got into a fight, your dad would knock him out in a second."

Timmy grinned. "You think so?"

"Sure!"

"Yeah, you're right. I bet he'd even knock some of his teeth out."

"Probably all of them. He wouldn't be so scary without those big white choppers of his."

They both laughed and, as if the sound had drawn her, his mother appeared beside them and perched herself on the arm of the sofa. "You two going to be all right?"

They nodded.

"Good. I think I'm going to go see what's keeping your father. Kim, if you want to come with me, I'll walk you home. It's not too far and you can borrow an umbrella if you like. I'm sure your mother is worried about you."

Timmy's throat constricted, his skin feeling raw and cold at the idea of being left alone while his mother and Kim ventured into Mr. Marshall's house.

What would he do if they left him and never came back? What would he do if they left him alone and Mr. Marshall came looking for him? What if he lost them *all* in the dark?

"Okay, Mrs. Quinn," said Kim. She sounded as if leaving was the last thing she wanted to do. She stood and Timmy opened his mouth to speak but nothing emerged.

"Guess I'll see you tomorrow?" she said, with a look he couldn't read in the candlelight.

He tried to make out her eyes but the gloom had filled them with shadows.

"I'll go with you," he blurted, scrambling to his feet. He looked at his mother. "Mom, can I go too? I don't want to be by myself." He felt no shame at admitting this in front of Kim.

"No, Timmy. I want you to stay here. We won't be long."

"That's what Dad said and he *has* been gone long!" Timmy said. "Please, let me go with you. This house gives me the creeps. I don't want to be here alone while you and Dad are over there with Mr. Marshall. He scares me."

Again his mother sighed but he was already encouraged by the resignation in her expression. "Go on then, get your coat."

He raced to the mudroom and returned with a light blue windbreaker.

"You may need something heavier than that," his mother pointed out. "What happened to your gray one?"

"Ripped."

Timmy started moving toward the door. He waited while his mother cocooned Kim in one of her overcoats. She emerged looking chagrinned, lost inside the folds of a coat far too big for her. Timmy suppressed a laugh and then his mother handed them each an umbrella. They clustered by the sliding glass door, looking out at a blackness broken only by small rectangles of yellow light, and listened to the crackling roar of a storm not yet matured.

"How come the neighbors have got power and we don't?" Timmy asked.

"It happens that way sometimes. The lightning must have hit the transformer box on the side of our house. Let's go. Stay close to me," his mother said, and tugged the door aside.

They filed into the raging night, huddling against the needle spray of the rain. The wind thudded into them with insistent hands, attempting to drive them back; the air was filled with the scent of smoke and saturated earth. With the door closed and locked behind them, they bowed their heads and walked side by side to Wayne Marshall's house.

CHAPTER ELEVEN

Despite their fears – and Timmy was in no doubt now that they all shared the same ones – Mr. Marshall's porch was a welcome oasis from the storm. Timmy shuddered at the cold drops that trickled down his neck. Kim shivered, her hair hanging in sodden clumps like leaking shadows over the moon of her face. They snapped their umbrellas closed and his mother trotted up the three short steps to the front door.

It was already open.

His mother turned back to them, her face gaunt as she hurried them down from the porch and back into the rain.

"What is it?" Timmy asked, shouting to be heard above the shrieking wind. Sheets of icy rain lashed his face. Kim gave him a frightened look he figured probably mirrored his own. All he had seen as the door swung open had been a dark hall, broken at the end by the fluorescent glare from the kitchen. He was sure no one had been sitting at the table.

"Nothing," his mother called back. "Nothing at all. But I don't think they're here!"

Timmy felt as if his head had been dunked in ice water. His teeth clicked and an involuntary shiver coursed through him. Over their heads, a plastic lighthouse struggled valiantly to keep its wind chimes from tearing loose. The resultant muddle of jingles unsettled him. Mr. Marshall's weather vane groaned as it swung wildly from south to north and back again, adding to the discordant harmony of the turbulent night.

"Then where are they?" Kim shouted, her arms crossed and buried beneath the coat as she danced from foot to foot.

But Timmy knew the answer.

"The pond," he said. His mother turned toward him and put a hand to her ear.

"The pond," he repeated. Another chill capered down his spine, like a flow of icy water.

"That's absurd," she said. "Why would they go back there? Especially on a night like this!"

Timmy shook his head, but in the wind he heard his father: *I think the reason Mr. Marshall is so mad is because he's seen it too.*

It occurred to him then that The Turtle Boy – Darryl, or whoever he was – had come to Myers Pond not for Timmy, or Pete, or any of them. He had come for Mr. Marshall. And Mr. Marshall had been acting so strange, so angry because The Turtle Boy was tormenting him, *frightening* him.

But why?

It didn't make sense and the more he pondered it, the less likely it seemed. All he was sure of in that moment, standing in the pouring rain outside Mr. Marshall's house with the nervous white faces of his mother and Kim fixed on him, was that for whatever the reason, the men had gone to Myers Pond.

"I'm going to call the police," his mother said, already mounting the steps. "You two wait here and yell if you see them coming."

With that, she disappeared into the house, the door easing closed behind her.

Timmy turned.

"Hey!" Kim called and he looked back at her. She was a huddled mass of shadows, only a trembling lower lip visible through her hair. "Where are you going?"

"To the pond. I think Mr. Marshall is going to try to hurt my father. If we wait for the police it might be too late."

"But what are you going to do? You're just a kid! You can't stop a grown-up if he wants to do something bad. Especially a *crazy* grown-up!"

Timmy shook his head. If Mr. Marshall intended to hurt his father, he at least had to *try* to stop it. Chances were he'd end up getting hurt in the process, but that didn't matter. He remembered his father reading to him, hugging him in the kitchen and telling him he loved him. He remembered riding his father's shoulders through the cornfields and feeling like the king of the world atop a throne. He remembered the disappointment of being in his first school play without his father present, only to see him creep to a seat next to his mother halfway through. He remembered the nightmares, the dreams in which he lost his father. He remembered the fear, the horror at being left alone without his father to live with the ghost of his mother.

No.

He would try. It was all he could do and just maybe it would make a difference. Determined, he stalked through the curtains of rain, flinching when the sky cracked above his head. He squinted through the temporary moonlight of the lightning, the mud sucking against the soles of his shoes.

"Timmy, wait!" Kim cried and he faltered at the far side of the house.

After a moment, he called to her: "Just tell my Mom where I'm going and not to worry."

"You idiot, of course she'll worry!"

"Just tell her!"

"Tell her yourself," Kim shouted, the hurt in her voice ringing over the raging wind.

He walked on until the ground hardened and stones rolled beneath his shoes. In a flash of lightning that sent stars waltzing across his field of vision, he saw the gravel winding ahead of him, emerging like a pale tongue from the black mouth of the weaving trees. Then the shade of night dropped once more and he was blinded, walking on a path from memory.

CHAPTER TWELVE

Daylight.

Impossible and warm.

Mind numbing in its reality but most certainly there.

Eyes wide, Timmy stumbled and almost fell from the rain-swept night into a summer day.

This can't be happening. This isn't real.

But as he felt the sun start to warm his face, he knew it was real. The grass was dry against his ankles, the sky above the pond a stark, heavenly blue that bore no hint of rain. It was as if he'd stepped from real life onto a movie set, onto an authentic reproduction of Myers Pond on a summer day.

Timmy moved slowly, as if in a dream. Frogs croaked and toads belched in the reeds while dragonflies whirred over the unbroken surface of the water. Birds chirped and whistled, trilled and cawed and rustled in the trees. He glimpsed the rump of a deer, cotton-white tail twitching as it wandered away from the pond.

With his neck already aching from trying to take in all this magic at once, Timmy looked down to the bank where he had seen The Turtle Boy on that first day in another world. And there he was.

Darryl.

But not the scabrous, grotesque creature he and Pete had seen. No, this boy was smiling, fresh-faced and healthy, his skin pale but unmarked, devoid of weeping wounds and bites. His hair was parted neatly and shone in the midday sun, his gray trousers unsullied, the crease down the middle crisp and unruffled. His black t-shirt looked worn but not old. He did not seem to notice he was no longer alone, so intent was he in dipping his ankle into the cool water. Timmy watched as that ankle rose, expecting to see a glistening red wound, but the skin remained unbroken, unblemished. Pure. This, Timmy realized, was who The Turtle Boy had been before he'd changed into the malevolent, seething figure of decay and disease they'd found on the bank that day. This was Darryl before whatever had corrupted him had compelled him to feed himself to the turtles.

"Who are you?" Timmy asked softly, but received no reply. Darryl continued to smile his knowing smile, continued to dip his smooth ankle into the calm waters.

"Why are you here?" Timmy demanded. For the first time he noticed the small red notebook sitting next to the boy. He was almost tempted to reach down and grab the book, to read it, to search for the answers he could not get from the boy on the bank. But he didn't. Couldn't. For as the resolve swelled in him to do that very thing, he heard the gentle swish of grass being crumpled underfoot as someone approached from the opposite side of the rise.

Mom, Timmy thought with a sigh of relief, and wondered if she too would see this miraculous pocket of daylight and calm where there should be a storm.

But it wasn't his mother.

The man who came striding over the rise was longhaired and thickly built, his faded denim jeans ripped across the knees and trailing threads. He wore battered tan loafers, comfortable looking but tired and dying. A v-shaped patch of tangled black chest hair sprouted from the open neck of the man's navy shirt. He looked normal, except for one horrifying detail.

He had no face.

Beneath the brim of a dark blue baseball cap, there was nothing but a blank oval that twitched and shifted as if made of liquid. The flesh-colored surface darkened in places as if plagued by the memory of bruises and now and again, the suggestion of features—a dark eye, the twist of a smile—surfaced from the swimming skin. But otherwise, it was unfinished, a doll's face left to melt in the sun.

Timmy opened his mouth to speak, but the stranger spoke first, his words jovial and clear despite the absence of a mouth. "Hey there!" he said pleasantly. "You're Jodie's kid, right?"

Timmy frowned and backed up a step as the man continued to approach him. Darryl didn't seem perturbed by the faceless man, leading Timmy to believe they were not seeing the same thing.

"Yes. Who are you?" said a young voice behind Timmy, and he turned to see Darryl looking at him...no, not at him...looking through him to the stranger. Stricken, but feeling as though he had intruded on a conversation not meant for him, he stepped away so he could watch this bizarre interaction.

The stranger's eyes resolved themselves from the shimmering mass of his face— so blue they were almost white—then gone again. "I'm a friend of your uncle's. We're practically *best* friends!"

"Really?" said Darryl, sounding dubious.

"Sure. We chug a few beers every Friday night. Game of poker every other Thursday." He stepped forward until his shadow sprawled across the boy. "You ever play poker?"

"Yes, sir. Once. My daddy taught me before he left us."

The stranger nodded his sympathy. "Shit, that's hard. I feel for you kid. Really I do. Can't be easy waitin' on a daddy that might not ever come back."

Darryl's eyes clouded with pain. "Yes, sir."

"Hey, c'mon," the man said, hunkering down next to the boy. "Don't be so down. If he didn't hang around, that's his loss, right? Besides, you got people—good people—looking out for you right here."

"Like who, sir?"

"Well, let's see..." The stranger's awful blank face turned to look out over the water at trees so green they were almost luminescent beneath the sun. "Well, me for one."

Darryl shrugged. "But I don't know you."

"Ah that's okay. I didn't know you either. Least until now. Heck, we're practically best friends now, right?"

"You smell like beer," Darryl said, a quaver in his voice.

Though it was not there for him to see, Timmy sensed the stranger's smile fade. He couldn't understand why Darryl or the man couldn't see him and why Darryl wasn't seeing the man's face, or lack of one. Were they ghosts? If so, then what did that make the version of Darryl they had seen on the bank with the pieces missing?

"Yeah, I knocked back a few before I came over. So what? One of these days you'll be tipping beers like your old man, I'm willing to bet."

"My daddy doesn't drink. At least he didn't while he was with us. He said it was evil."

"Well, shit and sugar fairies boy, your old man sounds like a real party animal." He threw his head back and laughed. It wasn't a kind sound, the echo even less so.

He reached into his shirt pocket and produced a crumpled cigarette. He set about straightening it, then paused and held it out to the boy seated next to him. "You want a puff?"

Darryl shook his head and reached for his notebook. He was obviously preparing to make a hasty exit. The stranger stopped him with a gesture, a dirty fingernail aimed at the little red square in the grass between them. "What's this? A diary?"

"No sir." Darryl made to retrieve the notebook but the man snatched it up and switched it to the hand farther away from the boy.

"What have we here?" With one hand he flipped through the pages with a soiled thumb, his other hand snapping open a Zippo lighter and bringing the flame to the tip of the crooked cigarette, jammed low between lips that weren't there.

Darryl looked crestfallen and stared at his submerged ankle as he muttered, "It's a story."

"A story, eh? Like a war story?"

"No. A love story."

"Aw shit!" the man said, coughing around his cigarette and chuckling. "You a little fairy boy?"

Darryl shrugged. "I don't know what that means."

"Sure you do. You like boys?"

"Yes, sir. Some of them."

The man slapped his knee, knocking the ash from his cigarette into the water. "Shit, I knew it!"

It was clear by the expression on the boy's face that he didn't know just what it was the man 'knew' and wanted to leave so bad it hurt. Timmy, still paralyzed by disbelief at where and how and possibly *when* he had found himself, felt a pang of sorrow for the boy and wished the stranger would leave him alone.

But the man stayed where he was and flipped a lock of chestnut-colored hair from the ghost of his eyes as his laugh grew hoarse, then died. "I knew a fairy boy like you once," he said. A mouth appeared in the skin-mask as he attempted to blow a smoke ring but only managed a mangled S before the breeze snatched it away. "Couple of years ago back in college. He was like you, you know. Dressed real nice, spoke real good. Had no time for anyone he thought beneath him, if you'll excuse the pun, which meant pretty much everybody was beneath the sonofabitch. That cocksucker didn't get to me though. No sir. I fixed his goddamn wagon real good."

"I'd better go. Can I have my book?" Darryl withdrew his foot from the water. He braced his hands beneath him to lever himself up and that's when it happened.

Just as Darryl began to rise, the man, in one smoothly executed move, clenched the fist holding the cigarette and swept his arm hard beneath the boy's hands, dropping him hard on his back. Timmy heard the whoosh of the boy's breath as he lay confused and frightened. He saw the bobbing of the boy's Adam's apple as the fear registered. And then the man rose, his shadow once again draping itself over Darryl.

"Stop it! Leave him alone!" Timmy roared, but he felt as if he was locked inside a glass cage.

"Now why'd you have to go and get all impolite on me, huh? Weren't we having a good little chat, just the two of us? No women, no bitching, no bills, no bullshit. Just you and me having a fine time." His 'face' darkened. "What would your daddy think if he knew what you are? Or does he know? Are you queer because of him? Is that it? Shit, that's terrible. I mean, I feel sorry for you, man. I really do. No kid should have to deal with that shit. I mean, my father got drunk one time and tried to—"

Darryl ran. It happened that fast. One minute he was on his back, trembling like an upturned crab, and the next he was on his feet and running toward the trees.

And the stranger fell on him. To Timmy it seemed as if the man had hardly moved and yet he was there, lying across the area of flattened grass Darryl had occupied only a moment before, both hands wrapped around the boy's ankle, the cigarette forgotten and smoldering between them.

"Let me go!" Darryl cried and clawed at the grass. "Please, let me go!"

The stranger grunted and tugged the boy back toward him, flipped him over and struck him once across the face with his fist. It was enough. Darryl's cries faded to a whine, tears streaming down his face and scissoring through the dirt smudged there.

The man shuffled forward and sat down on the boy's legs, trapping him. Darryl regarded him with animal panic, subdued only by the threat of further violence.

"Aw Jesus," the stranger said as twin trails of blood began to run from the boy's nostrils. "Aw Jesus," he repeated, grabbing fistfuls of his long hair and tugging hard. "Look what you did. Look what you did," he said, over and over as if it was a spell to ward off consequences. "Look what you did. You're bleeding. You'll tell. You'll run and tell and they'll throw me in jail. All because you couldn't just be polite and sit and listen. No, you tried to run. You tried to run away and *look what you did!*"

"Please," Darryl sobbed beneath him.

A few feet away, Timmy wept too. He wanted to help, wanted to make this stop, somehow prevent what was going to happen because he knew, just *knew* in his heart and soul what was going to happen next.

He screamed then and looked away, knowing the scream wasn't entirely his own, aware his own vocalized pain was drowning out the anguished cry of the boy on the bank. Timmy saw the man's hands settling on both sides of the boy's neck and looked away. He moaned and fell to his knees on the edges of a killer's shadow as a sound like dry twigs snapping told him Darryl was dead.

An eternity passed before he looked up again. The killer stood there sobbing into his fist, but only for a moment. He quickly composed himself and set about tugging old rocks from where they had stood untouched for many years. He carried them to the inert body lying sprawled on the bank and stuffed the biggest ones under the boy's shirt and down his trousers. After wrenching Darryl's shirt into a crude knot to hold the rocks, he grabbed the boy's legs around the ankles. Darryl's head lolled sickeningly, the sightless eyes finding Timmy for the first time. Timmy felt sick, this new world of sunshine and murder seen through tears as he watched the killer step back into the water, the man's face swirling. He dragged the boy's body into the pond, held it in his arms for a moment, the water lapping at his waist, then let go and watched it sink, watched as bubbles broke the surface and the ripples fled.

Timmy wiped a sleeve across his eyes and sobbed, the tears hot with rage and horror. His temples throbbed. It hurt to think, to see, to bear witness to something so appallingly brutal. He knew he would never be the same again.

He looked up in time to see the stranger clambering onto the bank, his jeans darkened by the water, streams trickling from beneath the cuffs. He was weeping mud-colored tears, muttering beneath his breath, cussing and batting at the air over his head as he slipped and fell, then hurried to his feet. He almost forgot the book, but then turned and scooped it up and jammed it into his inside pocket. He looked around and, for one soul-freezing moment, his gaze found Timmy's but then continued to scan the surrounding area for signs that he'd been seen or that someone had heard the boy. Satisfied that he was alone, he cast one final glance back at the water before heading back toward the rise, his head bowed.

After a moment, Timmy got to his feet and moved toward the bank. A dewdrop of blood glistened on the sun-baked grass. A hush fell over the pond, so noticeable that Timmy looked up at the sky. A raindrop smacked him on the forehead and he jumped, startled.

Something in the pond made a sucking sound and his gaze snapped down to where the surface of the water was starting to heave.

The air hummed. There came a noise like the sea heard in a conch shell and the hair rose on Timmy's arms. Lightning fractured the sky and normality returned with a sound like heavy sheets of glass shattering. The boy staggered back a step. The rushing sound grew louder.

And then day exploded in one deafening scream into night. And rain.

Timmy tottered forward. The rain hammered against his skull, soaking him. He almost lost his footing. He regained his balance and squinted into the thick dark. In the distance, someone called his name. Lightning strobed again; the shadows crouched around the pond flinched. Another cry, from somewhere behind him.

He turned and a figure rose up in front of him. "It's all your fault," Mr. Marshall sobbed. He drew back his fist and a darkness darker than night itself swept itself on wings of sudden pain into Timmy's eyes and he felt the ground pull away from him. A moment of nothingness in which he almost convinced himself he had dreamed it all, despite the stars that coruscated behind his eyelids, and then an immense cold shocked him back into reality. He thrashed his arms and felt them move far too slowly for the weight of his panic. An attempt to scream earned him nothing but a mouthful of choking water and he gagged, convulsed and tried to scream again. *Oh God help me I can't swim!* His mind felt as if it too were filling with water and suddenly he ceased struggling, his throat closing, halting its fight against the dirty tide flowing through it. His heart thudded. One more breath. Water. Then a blanket of soothing whispers, a sheet of warmth draped over him and he no longer felt the pain of his lungs burning. It was as if he was feeling the pain in a separate body, a body he could ignore if he chose to.

And ignore it he did as he sank and drifted on waves of peace that carried him away. Until a sharp pain drove the resignation from his brain and his leg twitched, spasmed, and he was jerked from the panacea of death's reverie. His eyes fluttered open. Darkness, but darkness he could feel between his fingers. Another bite and his heart kicked. Agony. Water. Something was gnawing on his foot. A self-preserving panic like liquid fire swelled in him and he kicked, struggled, pushed himself up to where the water moved with purpose and rhythm, shifting to the sound of the storm.

More pain, needling between his toes, and his head broke water, panic rattling his skull as he drew a breath and went under once more. He struggled against the heaving water, his tongue numb, cottoned by the acrid taste of the fetid depths. The water fell below his neck and he sucked greedily at the air, aware for the first time that the storm vied for dominance with the sounds of human violence. Men yelled, women screamed and someone called his name.

This time he stayed above water, his frantic paddling halting abruptly when his foot connected with something hard, something unmoving. He could stand and did so falteringly, his chest full of red-hot needles as the water shifted around him, trying to reclaim him. It rushed from his stomach, his lungs, his mind and he vomited, vomited until he felt as if his head would explode, then he staggered in the storm-induced current, his face raised to the rain.

A splash behind him. Timmy turned, blinking away tears, rain, pond water and trying to focus on something other than his own lingering blindness and trembling bones.

The Turtle Boy stood before him, unaffected by the tumultuous heaving of the water. He looked as he had when Pete and Timmy had found him, his face mottled and decayed. He wore a coat now and the coat moved. Timmy stepped back, the bank so preciously close and yet so far away.

"You saw it," Darryl croaked, the shoulders of his coat sprouting small heads that sniffed the air before withdrawing. "You stepped behind The Curtain and you saw what he did."

Somehow Timmy could hear him over the storm, over the churning of the water, though Darryl did not raise his voice to compete with them. He nodded, not trusting his voice.

"You don't know who did it. When you do, remember what you saw and let it change you. There is only time to let one of them pay for his crimes tonight."

"I don't understand!" Timmy felt dizzy, sick; he wanted to be home and warm, away from the madness this night had become, if it was really night at all.

"You will. *They'll* explain it to you."

"Who?"

"People like me. The people on The Stage."

Darryl swept past him and in the transient noon of lightning, he saw the coat was fashioned from a legion of huge, ugly turtles, their shells conjoined like a carapace around the boy's chest and back. Wizened beaks rose and fell, worm-like tongues testing the air as Darryl carried them toward the bank and the figures who fought upon it.

From here, Timmy could see his mother and Kim, huddled at the top of the rise, his mother's hand over Kim's face to keep her from seeing something. He followed their gaze to the two men wrestling each other in the dark.

Dad! Possessed by new resolve that numbed the flaring pain in his feet and the throbbing in his chest and throat, he thrashed to the bank and reached it the same time Darryl did. They both climbed over, both paused as the storm illuminated the sight of Wayne Marshall punching Timmy's father in the face—

Just like he punched Darryl before he killed him

—and stooped to retrieve something he'd dropped as the other man reeled back. Over the cannon roar of thunder, Timmy heard his mother scream his name and resisted the urge to look in her direction as he slipped, slid and flailed and finally tumbled to the ground between her and where his father was straightening and bracing himself for a bullet from the weapon in Wayne Marshall's hand.

In the storm-light, Mr. Marshall grinned a death's head rictus, his skin pebbled with rain. He raised the gun. Timmy's father cradled his head in his arms and backed away.

Mr. Marshall pulled the trigger.

And nothing happened.

He jerked back his hand and roared at the gun, fury rippling through him. "*No, fuck you, NO!*"

He thrust the gun out, aimed it at Timmy's father's head and pulled the trigger.

Nothing.

Again and again and again, nothing but a series of dry snapping sounds.

"God*damn* you!"

"No!" Timmy yelled, then realized it hadn't come from his stricken throat at all. It was Darryl and his cry had not been one of protest. It had been a command.

And it was heeded.

The ground beneath Timmy's hands moved, separated into ragged patches of moving darkness, slick and repulsive against his skin. He jerked back and rose unsteadily, eyes fixed on the moving earth, waiting for the lightning to show him what he already knew.

The turtles. An army of them. All monstrous, all ancient. And all moving toward where his father had his arms held out to ward off the bullet that must surely be on its way.

"Timmy...son, stay back," he said, risking a quick glance at his son. "Just stay there."

"Dad!" This time Timmy knew from the pitiful croak that it was indeed his own voice.

He ran, halted, drowning again but in fear, confusion and the agony of uncertainty as the creatures Doctor Myers had introduced to his pond all those years ago trudged slowly but purposefully toward their prey.

"Darryl," Timmy cried, scorching his throat with the effort to be heard. Darryl looked toward him, the coat slowly shrugging itself off to join its brethren. "Darryl, please! Make them stop!"

Another shadow rose from the pond.

Timmy felt a nightmarish wave of disbelief wash over him. Even after all he'd been through, was *still* going through, he felt his mind tugging in far too many directions at once.

But there was not enough time to dwell on it.

He looked away from the new shadow and ran, skidding to the ground before his father. Darryl turned to look at him.

The turtles slowed.

"You'd die for your father?" Darryl asked, his voice little more than a gurgle.

"Yes!" Timmy screamed, without hesitation. "Yes! Leave him alone!"

"Why?"

"Because I *love* him. He's the best father in the world and I love him. You can't take him away from me. *Please!*"

"Maybe he deserves to die."

"Don't *say* that. He doesn't! I *swear* he doesn't!"

The storm itself seemed to hold its breath as Darryl stared and the impatience of the turtle army stretched the air taut.

A gentle pulse of lightning broke the stasis.

Darryl turned to regard the shadow standing in the water next to him. Pointing to Mr. Marshall, he asked the same question: "Would *you* die for *him?*"

Even Mr. Marshall seemed intent on the answer the shadow would give.

But it said nothing. Instead, it gave a gentle shake of its head.

"No!" Wayne cried as Darryl turned back to face him.

Slowly, Timmy's father lowered his hands and after a moment in which he realized Wayne Marshall's attention was elsewhere, he moved away into the shadows of the pines, his face a pale blur of horror as he saw what had his neighbor's attention.

Darryl turned back to watch the turtles advance. The first of them found Mr. Marshall's leg and after a moment of stunned disgust, he aimed his pistol downward and in his panic, tried the weapon again.

This time the gun fired.

A deafening roar and the gun let loose a round that took most of Mr. Marshall's foot away with it. He shrieked and dropped to the ground, then realized his folly and scuttled backward on his hands. The dark tide moved steadily forward.

Timmy's father burst from his hiding place and ran the long way around the pond, through the pines, the marsh and along the high bank until he appeared through the weeds on the far side of the rise. His wife released Kim at last and ran to him.

Multi-colored lights lit the sky in the distance, back near the houses. Timmy guessed the police had arrived and were now searching for the woman who had summoned them. He silently begged them to hurry.

A guttural scream was all that could be heard from the shadows as the tide of turtles progressed ever onward and engulfed their victim.

A single flicker of lightning lit the face of the shadow in the water and Timmy felt a jolt of shock.

The dead and bloated face staring back at him was Pete's.

Oh God...

Someone grabbed Timmy's shoulder and spun him roughly around. He looked up into the frightened face of his father, noticed his swollen eye and crushed nose, and almost wept again, but there was no time. The sirens were growing louder, drowning out the shrieks and snapping sounds from beneath the pines. Timmy let himself be led and almost didn't feel Kim's hand slipping into his own. He smiled at her but it was an empty gesture. There was nothing to be cheerful about and, head afire with unanswered questions, he looked over his shoulder as they descended the rise as one huddled, broken mass. Pete was gone. The earth still crawled and among the seething shadows The Turtle Boy stood, unsmiling in his victory.

CHAPTER THIRTEEN

Timmy slept for days afterward, speaking only to his parents and Kim and occasionally a police officer who tried his best to look positive. Timmy saw the horror in the man's eyes, a horror that began on a warm sunny morning at the start of summer.

What he learned, he learned from his father, the papers and Kim who in turn had heard it from her own parents—apparently too shocked to be discreet in their gossiping.

They had pulled three bodies out of the pond. One was a young boy, little more than a skeleton cocooned in algae. According to the medical examiner's report, he had been there for some time and had died as a result of a broken neck, sustained it was assumed, by a fall from an old tire swing that had hung for a brief time above the pond back in the late seventies. They had identified the body as Darryl Gaines, nephew of the second decedent, Wayne Marshall. Apparently, Marshall's nephew had visited him back in 1967 while his mother was being treated for drug abuse. Marshall was drinking in his backyard with friends and poking fun at the boy (according to Geoff Keeler, an ex-buddy of Wayne's) and the kid had run off in a sulk. They'd never seen him again. Divers had searched the pond and come up empty ("apart from some big <bleepin> turtles" one of them stated on the news, obviously relishing the attention of the camera). Shortly after, Darryl's mother, Joanne Gaines was institutionalized. She committed suicide a month later.

The third body filled Timmy with a wave of grief he was afraid would never leave him. Every time he stared up at his bedroom ceiling; every time he glanced at a comic book or thought about the red clay in Patterson's field, he saw Pete's face.

Pete had never made it to summer camp. His body had shown signs of chronic physical abuse, culminating in a broken neck sustained—according to the evidence obtained from the Marshall house—from a fall against the edge of a marble fireplace. It was assumed Wayne Marshall had killed his son by accident, in a fit of alcohol-fueled rage.

Panicked, Wayne decided to dump his son's body in the pond (perhaps so he could claim later that the boy had run away) and was readying himself to do so when Timmy's father arrived on the scene.

"I just stood looking at him," Timmy's father said. "I couldn't believe what I was seeing. Wayne, with Pete in his arms…I didn't want to believe he was dead, couldn't believe Wayne would kill his own son. I watched him lay the boy down on the grass. That's when he pulled the gun on me. That's when I saw his eyes and knew he was lost. Jesus, I should have *known*, should have done something sooner."

Timmy only smiled through the tears when he thought of what Darryl's turtles might have done to Wayne Marshall.

Wayne Marshall, the faceless man Timmy had seen at the pond, murdering his nephew and leaving him beneath the water to feed the turtles.

The visitors came and went, attempted to soothe Timmy with words he couldn't hear and through it all, through the mindless passage of feverish recollection and the debilitating agony of loss, The Turtle Boy's words returned to him again and again, nagging at him and begging to be decoded: You don't know who did it. *When you do, remember what you saw and let it change you.*

Maybe he deserves to die.

Three weeks later, they filled in the pond. They'd been trying for years but somehow mechanical difficulties had always kept them away. Timmy thought he now knew what had caused those problems.

CHAPTER FOURTEEN

Summer ended, and as per the rules of the seasons in Ohio, there was no subtle ushering out of the warmth; the weather dropped in temperature and the earth darkened on the very day the calendar page turned.

Spurning all attempts his father made at trying to come up with something fun for them to do on what might be the last Saturday of good weather for quite some time, Timmy took a walk.

Fall was already setting up camp on the horizon, prospecting for leaves to burn and painting the sky with colors from a bruised pallet.

He wanted to forget, but knew that would never happen.

There were three reasons why the fear would always be with him, dogging his every step and making stalkers out of the slightest shadows.

First, the reporters. In the months since Pete's and Mr. Marshall's deaths, the newspapers had played up the ghost angle, delighting in the idea that an eleven-year-old boy had helped solve a murder through an alleged conference with the dead. There were phone calls, insistent and irritating, from jocular voices proclaiming their entitlement to Timmy's story.

They were ignored.

But this only led to speculation, and Timmy's face ended up in the local newspapers, topped with giant bold lettering that read:

11-YEAR-OLD BOY RESURRECTS THE DEAD, SOLVES MURDER!

Then the curiosity seekers started showing up, some of them from the media, most of them just regular folk. Their neediness frightened the boy. *We just want to touch him*, they said. Others wept and begged his mother to *let the boy see if he can bring my little Davey/Suzy/Alex/Ricky/Sheri back*. And they were still coming to the house, though not as much as they had in the beginning.

The second reason was that even if Timmy managed to dismiss the calls, the desperate pleas of strangers, the newspaper reports and the occasional mention of his name on the television, there were still the nightmares. Vivid, brutal and unflinching. In his dreams, he saw everything, all the things he had been able to look away from in real life. All the things he had been able to run from.

Every night, he drowned and ended up behind what Darryl had called 'The Curtain.' In the waking hours, the name stayed with him, conjuring images in Timmy's mind of a tattered black veil drawn wide across a crumbling stage. He imagined a whole host of the dead crouching behind it, waiting for their chance to come back, to find their own killers. And perhaps they would. Perhaps also they would only be successful if they had someone to draw strength from, as Timmy was sure Darryl Gaines had drawn strength from him and Pete.

Or perhaps it was over.

Believing that required the most effort.

Because the final reason, the last barrier stopping him from releasing the dread and shaking off the skeins of clambering horror was the recollection of something else The Turtle Boy had said: *You don't know who did it. When you do, remember what you saw and let it change you.* He had mulled over this every day and every night since the discovery of the bodies. It would have been simpler to forget had he not realized something about the murders, something that came back to him weeks later—Wayne Marshall was Darryl's uncle. The story had it that Darryl had been visiting his uncle and that's why he was there in the first place. But Timmy had been there, however it had happened, standing on the bank of the pond when the big man had come strolling over the rise. Among the things he'd said had been: *I'm a friend of your uncle's. We're practically best friends!* Which meant Darryl's murderer had not been his uncle.

But every time it got this far in Timmy's head, heavy black pain descended like a caul over him and he had to stop and think of nothing until it went away. It was too much. Maybe in the years to come it would make sense. For now, it would hang like an old coat in a closet, always there but seldom worn.

Maybe he deserves to die.

His walk took him back to the pond, to where bulldozers stood like slumbering monsters next to a smoothened oval of dirt. They'd drained the pond and ripped away the banks. The telltale signs of man were everywhere now, the animals quiet. Despite his relief at having the dark water gone, Timmy couldn't help the twinge of sadness he felt at having the good memories buried beneath that hard-packed dirt, too. All around him the land was changing, becoming unfamiliar.

He sighed, dug his hands in his pockets and walked on, unsure where he was heading until he was standing staring down at the railroad tracks. A cold breeze ran invisible fingers across his skin and he shivered. A quick glance in both directions showed the tracks were deserted. No trains, no funny tireless cars with flashing yellow beacons.

School would begin soon, and he hoped it would be the distraction he needed from the crawling sensation he had been forced to live with, the sense of always being watched, of never being alone.

It'll pass, son, his father had told him, *I promise.*

Timmy prayed that was true.

Because even now, with not a soul around, he could feel it: a slight thrumming, as of a train coming, the air growing colder still, the sky appearing to brood and twist, the hiss of the wind through the tall grass on either side of the rails.

And a droning, faint at first.

A droning. Growing.

Like a machine. Or an engine.

Pete's voice then, disgruntled, whispering on the wind: *They were stupid to ride that close to the train anyway.*

Not an engine.

Muscles stiffening, Timmy drew his hands out of his pockets, held his hands by his sides. He felt his knees bend slightly and knew his body had decided to run, seemingly commanded by the small fraction of unpanicked mind that remained. He looked to the right. Nothing but empty track, winding off out of sight around a bramble-edged bend.

He looked to the left.

The wind rose, carrying the stench of death to him and he felt his heart hammer against his ribcage. A child, limping, trying to prevent himself from toppling over, all his energy focused on keeping the mangled dirt bike—and himself—upright.

I wish that kid hadn't been killed up there.

The bike, sputtered, growled, whined. Or perhaps it was Danny Richards making the awful sounds—Timmy couldn't tell.

The child's bisected mouth dropped open, teeth missing, as he lurched forward, the weight of the bike threatening to drag him down and Timmy bolted, ran for his life. The wind followed him, drowning out his own screams, thwarting his attempts to deafen the mournful wail coming from the stitched-together boy hobbling along the railroad tracks.

"*Where's my sissssssterrrrrr?*"

Timmy stopped for breath by the memory of the pond. He could still see the boy, a distant figure lurching along the tracks—a pale, bruised shape against the dark green grass.

Something's wrong, something's broken. Timmy knew it then as if it had been delivered in a hammer-strike blow to the side of his head. He sobbed at the realization that the They Darryl had mentioned, the They who would show him what he needed to learn, were the dead. He would see them now. Again and again.

Everywhere.

And there was a truth he had missed, a truth he was not yet ready—not yet able—to figure out on his own. All that was left were questions:

Why did he want to hurt Dad?
Why did he ask me if I'd die for him?
Why did he say maybe he deserved to die?

As he straightened, struggling not to weep at the thought of what might yet lay ahead of him, he flinched so hard his neck cracked, a cold sheet of pain spreading over his skull.

A voice that might have been the breeze.

A whisper that might have been the trees.

And a face that peered over his right shoulder, grinning.

Timmy choked on a scream.

"*Mine, now*," said Mr. Marshall.

BOOK TWO
The Hides

"All the world's a stage,
And all the men and women merely players;
They have their exits and their entrances,
And one man in his time plays many parts"

— *As You Like It*, William Shakespeare

CHAPTER ZERO

The man on the porch seemed to have brought his own clouds. They peered over his shoulder like busybody aunts, grumbling and stabbing each other with swords of lightning.

Sandra stood at the door. Knox smiled.

"Hi Sandra…" He seemed uncomfortable addressing her by her first name. Jack Knox had lived in the house at the top of the hill longer than Sandra had lived here, but they had spoken only rarely, she being of the opinion that Knox was a peculiar sort and not the type of man she would ever call a friend. She did however, feel a small twinge of sympathy for him. He'd lost his boy only a year before.

"Mr. Knox." She looked at the road behind him, then up at the rumbling sky. "What can I do for you?"

Knox had adopted the pose of a child scorned for sticking his tongue out at a girl on the playground. If he'd had a cap, she thought he'd have wrung it, completing the Dickensian impression of a scolded waif. Though to call Knox a waif was akin to calling a rhino an ant. He was enormous.

"Is um…is your boy here?"

Sandra stiffened and tried to widen herself to block all access into the hallway beyond. The hall led to the living room where Timmy was playing chess with his father, and no doubt listening intently.

"Yes he is. Why?"

But of course she knew why and it made her throat go dry. Knox at that moment might be considering how best to put his request but he mightn't have bothered had he known he was far from the first to make it. She didn't know who had spread the word to the papers all those years ago – some loose-lipped rookie cop or one of the paramedics she supposed – but now she damned them for what they'd set in motion. Their house had fast become a hot zone for the morbidly curious.

And the hopeful.

"I was wondering if I could maybe…" He scratched his balding pate, flakes of skin coming away under his nails and looked down at his mud-caked shoes. "If maybe I could talk to him about something?"

She didn't move, even though his stance suggested he'd said enough to permit him entry.

"About what, exactly?" Though she knew, and felt drawing it out of him was being needlessly cruel, her frustration at how often people abandoned their faith in favor of the belief that her son was the answer to all the misery in their lives, kept her expression cold. Their hope was misplaced and it was all she could do to keep from screaming that into their faces every time they showed up blubbering and pleading and looking lost on her front porch.

He took a step back and for a moment she thought he was going to turn and lope back to the small red Honda parked outside her gate. But he lingered, still scanning his shoes, only occasionally letting his small green eyes meet hers.

"I know you folks have had a hard time of it and really I don't mean to intrude…"

Like hell, she thought.

"I remember reading about it in the papers all those years ago. Terrible thing. Must have been hard on all of you." His sympathy was not convincing, merely a delay tactic while he hovered around the point. "Thing is…if what they said about your boy is true. If he really can…you know…do those things…"

Sandra folded her arms and restrained a sigh of impatience. "What things?"

"You know—"

"What things, Mr. Knox?"

"Help the...um..."

"Yes?"

"Help the..." The next few words were rendered unintelligible by a sudden stutter. Knox, visibly frustrated, took a breath and looked her squarely in the face. "Help the dead."

When Sandra didn't comment, he continued. "The papers said he can see them. Make them come back."

A bitter smile. "Is that so?"

"Yes Ma'am."

"If I recall, you didn't hold much stock in that being the case six years ago."

His expression registered pain. "I didn't have a need to I guess."

"I see."

"I know how it must—"

"Did it ever occur to you they might have got it all sideways?"

Some of the hope leaked from his face at that and Sandra felt another twinge of guilt. *I hate this,* she thought. *God forgive me I hate doing this to people.*

Knox shifted his stance. His hands were trembling.

"I need to tell you this," Sandra said abandoning the anger and feeling a tremor of her own jerk at her stomach. "And believe me I wish the truth could be different, but what Timmy has...what Timmy can do is nothing that could benefit you. I'm sorry." After a moment's consideration, she stepped onto the porch and put a hand on his shoulder. He looked at it as if it were some kind of rare venomous spider and she let it fall to her side. Knox licked his lips.

"Jack," she said, loathing the helplessness she felt at having to explain this yet again, at having to pinch the weak flame of hope from another person's candle. "Timmy can *see* them. We don't know why or how, but that's all he can do. Believe me we wish he couldn't. But wishing doesn't make it so and the same applies to you. He can see them because they show themselves to him. What he *can't* do is bring them back."

A flicker of a smile crossed Knox's lips, his eyes scanning the windows of the house, finally settling on the window above the door. There were no tears and for that Sandra was thankful.

"Maybe if I could just talk to him," Knox persisted when his gaze finally returned to her. "Maybe if he could just come over and walk where my Harlan walked."

When she started to protest, he raised a hand, calloused and red. "No wait, please. I-I know he can't bring my boy back. I know that. But he might be able to tell me where he went, you know? They never did find him, Sandra. They never did find him and all's I want is to know if he went wherever he went smiling...or..." He cleared his throat and gestured uselessly. "...or not."

Alarmed to find tears gathering at the base of her own throat, Sandra shook her head and back-stepped into the hall. "I'm sorry," she whispered. "I truly am sorry. But there's nothing he can do for you."

"Sandra..."

She waited a beat for him to say something further. When he didn't, she closed the door.

Knox didn't move for a very long time. When finally she saw his silhouette lumber away, heard the gate squeak shut and a few seconds later, the growl of an engine, only then did she allow the tears to spill down her cheeks.

And when her vision cleared and she had composed herself enough to face her family, she found it one short.

"Where's Timmy?"

Her husband Paul, who was sitting alone at the chess table, nodded out toward the stairs, the expression on his face negating the need for words.

He heard, it said.

* * *

"Mr. Knox?"

"Who is this?"

"Timmy Quinn from down the r—"

"Timmy, yes, yes, of course. Did your mother tell you I stopped by?"

"Kind of. Will you be at home this evening...say around four?"

Silence.

"Mr. Knox?"

"I'm sorry. Yes I will. I'll be here."

"Okay. I'll see you then."
"Thank you. You don't know how much this means to me."
"I can't promise anything…"
"Of course, of course. I understand. Thank you so much. Thank you."

* * *

Sandra grabbed his elbow firmer than she'd intended. Paul was in the living room, pretending to read his newspaper, no doubt glad she'd elected to handle the situation.

Ha! As if there could be any handling *this*.

Timmy had just hung up the phone and when he turned to look at her, there was none of the anger, none of the irritation expected of someone his age. Just a kind of withering understanding.

"I knew Harlan," he said quietly. "Not well. He wasn't a friend, but I knew him. He sat across from me in English. Hated poetry and had a horrible habit of picking his nose and examining whatever he found." He dug his thumbs into the pockets of his jeans. "But that's not reason enough for him to stay lost. To have no burial and to leave his Dad wondering."

He stared at her hand until she removed it.

"I have to try," he said, then turned and opened the back door.

And that was enough. Anything she might have said would have fallen on deaf ears. She knew from experience.

"Just be careful," she told the door as he closed it behind him.

Only the thunder responded.

* * *

It was raining hard by the time Timmy reached the Knox farm. Winded from the hike up the hill, he took a moment to catch his breath, his eyes on the tall, narrow house towering over him.

He had long thought that houses reflected the emotional state of its occupants and the Knox house was a prime example: sagging gutters choked with leaves from another season, missing shingles, scabrous paint, peeling wood, untended yard, old work boots by the front door wrinkled so badly by the elements they would never see feet again. The building seemed to slump toward him, eager for a shoulder. To the left of the house with its peaked roof and dormer windows, green fields rolled away, the too long grass devoid of the livestock it had once used to keep it trimmed. The strengthening wind combed through the field with pale strokes.

Timmy headed up the blocky concrete steps set into the hill.

Wind chimes played a mournful tune on the stoop and he ducked his head to avoid disrupting the song.

Jack Knox was waiting for him, door wide and looking like he hadn't slept in days. The clumps of gray hair over his ears stood straight up as if statically charged.

"Timmy. So good of you to do this. Honestly. Why don't you come in?"

Timmy felt awkward. He always did at times like these. In the past six years, he'd had people offer him ridiculous sums of money to give them the correct answer and threaten him with physical violence when he hadn't given them the peace they'd so desperately sought. In one case, an old woman hoping her philandering, and recently deceased husband, wasn't still hanging around his old work shed had suffered a mild heart attack at the news that not only was he there, but he had a woman with him.

Others viewed him as a freak, though they tried to hide it. They asked what it felt like: *is there electricity, bright lights, a feeling of closeness to God or just a sense of dislocation?* Most of the time he lied, gave them what they wanted to hear. But the truth was he felt nothing. Not a thing. When the dead appeared it was just that, nothing more. Just some restless dead folk stepping from out behind The Curtain, as a dead boy named Darryl Gaines had called it once, just prior to demonstrating why they came back.

The interior of the Knox house was even more forbidding than the outside. The gathering storm seemed to weigh heavily against the roof making the whole house creak and groan. Knox led him through a narrow hallway crowded with coats and muddy boots into a dimly lit kitchen with dishes piled high in the sink and a smell of sour milk in the air. The lemon colored paper was starting to peel away from the wall.

Knox indicated a chair at the table in the center of the room and Timmy took it. He kept his hands off the plastic tablecloth. It was a museum of past meals.

Knox poked his head into a cupboard and emerged with a bottle of Wild Turkey and a single glass. He paused, looked back at Timmy.

"You're sixteen, right?"

"Seventeen."

"You drink?"

"No, but thanks anyway."

Knox nodded, closed the cupboard door and took a seat across from Timmy. He filled a tumbler almost to the top and set the bottle aside. Timmy noticed the insides of the man's index and middle fingers were yellow from smoking.

"I appreciate you being here, son. It means the world to me."

Timmy nodded. "As long as you understand that nothing might come of it. I'll only see him if he wants me to. If I don't, it could mean he just doesn't want me to see him or that he's moved on. Either way I may not be able to give you the answer you're looking for."

Knox shrugged. "Well I've lived without answers for a year now. If you don't get any, it won't change anything. Right?"

"Right."

Knox sighed, then brought the glass to his lips and the whiskey disappeared. Stifling a belch, he offered Timmy a feeble grin.

"I expect you'd like to get started before the worst of the storm hits? Too much rain might dampen the scent right?"

Timmy had no idea what he was talking about, but nodded anyway.

"You didn't bring a jacket?" Knox asked.

"No. I thought I might beat the rain."

Knox frowned. "Boy of your age should know better."

"Yeah, I guess so."

Knox nodded and rose from his chair. "I'll get you one of Harlan's slickers if you don't mind wearing it."

Timmy did, it felt ghoulish, but agreed to avoid offending the old man.

Suitably protected against the elements, Knox led the way out the back door, through a yard with a rusted pickup truck leaning on three wheels in the corner, past some low red barns with white trim and up a muddy trail which ran through a slight rise in the field, the rain pelting them all the while. An old grain silo, shedding its paint, towered over a ramshackle barn at the far side of the field. The barn was long, the roof dipping almost low enough on one side to meet the grass. Strips of wood were missing here and there, making it look as if the building was smiling a gap-toothed smile.

"He was out here," Knox said, standing close so he could be heard over the wind. He was wearing a yellow slicker, the hood pulled up, rain dripping from his bulbous red-veined nose. "Last I saw of him. Playing in the barn though he knew he wasn't supposed to."

Timmy said nothing, but made his way through the high grass and around the barn until he came to a wide open space in the rear of the building. From where he stood, he could make out vague hunkered shapes in the gloom. He looked over his shoulder at Knox, who was wheezing beside him.

"Did you bring a flashlight?"

"Oh yeah, sure. Sorry." Knox produced a slim cylinder from his inside pocket. It was no longer than a pencil, and only slighter thicker. He handed it to Timmy. "I can get a bigger one if you like."

"Nah, this will be fine. Thanks."

Timmy clicked on the light and a thin beam skewered the gloom.

"Do I need to do anything?" Knox asked, voice shaky.

"No, you're fine." *Just don't go crazy if nothing happens*, Timmy wanted to add.

A sudden gust made the barn rattle, dust sifting down in dirty threads from the gaps of gray light in the roof. Pigeons fluttered in alarm and then were quiet.

Timmy swept the narrow beam over the interior of the barn.

Rusted log chains hung from the roof, shifting and clicking lazily in the filtered breeze that managed to poke through the gaps in the walls. Old windows were stacked in a row in the far corner, glass besmirched by time and the intricate labors of insects. Beside them, a variety of saw blades different in size, united in rust. A column of flowerpots had fallen over and scattered themselves around the dirt floor, some broken, most not. Timmy let the beam linger on a bicycle wheel with pine cones clustered between the gaps. It was clear nothing but animals used the barn now. He let the beam move on, over shredded black plastic bags clutching greedily at the dirt in their folds, mud encrusted traffic cones, pulverized concrete blocks, loops of baling and chicken wire tossed carelessly aside to take root in the floor, an old fire extinguisher propped against the wall beside a fence stretcher, crushed beer cans, a wrinkled baseball glove folded in on itself like a dead spider.

"That was Harlan's," Knox said eagerly, but Timmy kept the light moving. He was not psychic as most people assumed. Picking up the glove would get him nothing but dirt on his hands. No flashes of the boy tossing a baseball against the wall of the barn, or sitting here swapping cards with his friends. Nothing. Inanimate objects remained just that.

In the middle of the barn stood a pair of battered workhorses, bent nails poking out from their elbows. An old rowboat took up the most space even though it had been shoved sideways against the wall. The light revealed a couple of half-cut plastic milk cartons strung together with braided black twine. Timmy felt a mild surge of unease at the sight of them. He had never used them, but knew all too well what they were for. Turtle floats. The memories this tried to bring to the surface were quickly dismissed, and he quickly jerked the beam away to fall on a tangle of old bicycles.

"Anything?"

Timmy shook his head, and kept the beam moving along the floor. It was junk, all of it, from the cracked table lying on its side to the leaning faucet in the corner, trailing a bridle from its neck. Dust, pea vine, creeper and burdock had claimed this place as its own and it gave off no hint of the lurking dead. It was a place for forgotten things. Not lost children. But before he could break the bad news to the anxious man shadowing him, a series of dull thuds rattled across the roof. Timmy swept the beam up through the haze of dust to where a penny-sized hole in the corrugated metal allowed him to see the darkening sky.

Knox moved closer. "What was that? Squirrel or something?"

"I've never heard a squirrel that big before, have you?"

Knox didn't answer, but Timmy felt the shrug. The man was close enough now for his acrid breath to be offensive. Timmy looked up at the low roof.

He could no longer see the sky through the hole that had just moments before showed dull gray clouds. He moved the flashlight, the beam now revealing the obstruction.

An eye had filled it.

Jesus. Fear thrummed through him but he quickly overcame it. Years of practice and still it gave him the creeps every time they showed themselves. He turned; the weight of the runner made the roof sag. Timmy followed the sound with his eyes, every thud marked by a fall of dust and looked out past Knox to the opening.

Just in time to see the boy leap from the roof, tumble to the ground, then shoot to his feet and race off through the high grass, a pale blur in the green.

"Shit!"

Knox jumped as if struck. "What? *What?*"

"It's Harlan," Timmy said, "He's here, and he's running."

He didn't wait for Knox's reaction. Instead, he ran from the barn, imagining the path Harlan would have left in the grass had he been a living, breathing boy. A path that wasn't there for a boy long dead. With Knox shouting at his back, Timmy ran on.

* * *

He crossed two fields in pursuit of Harlan's fleeing form, snagging his jeans on barbed wire and falling flat on his face more than once after mistakenly assuming the ground was level beneath the waist-high grass.

Now he stopped by the railroad tracks that bisected the farmland, bent over with his hands braced on his knees and waited for the acidic pain to leave his lungs. He waited, slamming the doors of memory closed when it tried to remind him of what he'd once seen on these tracks. The mangled boy, searching for the sister who'd survived the accident that had cost him his life.

Where's my sissssssterrrrr?

And at his back, the house, standing atop what had once been a pond. A pond that had coughed out his best friend and later, his father, who might have killed him there and then if he hadn't run until his legs gave out.

Mine now, he'd said before Timmy had fled for his life.

Now Timmy shuddered, straightened, and raised his face to the rain, washing away the memories, then looked across the gravel slope upon which the tracks criss-crossed. In the field beyond, Harlan was still running.

Where is he going?

I think you know.

And he did.

He was being led.

He looked over his shoulder and saw that Knox had only just

reached the edge of his own property, apparently in no hurry. Timmy supposed age, weight and grief had robbed him of all energy. No matter. He wouldn't be able to see his son anyway unless the boy wanted him to.

Timmy sucked in a breath, checked to make sure a train wasn't barreling its way toward him through the rain and jogged across the tracks and into the next field.

Thunder roared; lightning flared. The earth shook, the trees around him leaning in deference to the wind. And as Timmy drew closer, he saw that Harlan had stopped by a mound of earth and was waiting for him.

* * *

Time and the overgrowth it brought with it had hidden the old well from view. Until he was almost upon it, Timmy had puzzled over what might have caused the earth to rise in a tangled mound in the center of an otherwise flat field. And then he remembered. The McKay's had had a well before they boarded it up and moved to Kansas. Right around the time the papers had made a minor celebrity out of Timmy. They weren't missed, especially by Timmy's parents, who saw their departure as an end to all the anonymous hate mail and phone calls brimful of Biblical quotations they'd received after the news broke.

They'd thought Timmy was the Devil himself.

As he trudged through mud, corncobs, and their flattened stalks, Harlan's face resolved itself from the sheets of silvery rain. Timmy stopped close enough to touch him, but dared do no such thing.

To an observer, Harlan might have looked like a kid in need of a good meal and nothing more. Closer inspection however, would have had them wondering why he wasn't screaming in pain. He wore only one sneaker and it faced back toward the well while the bare foot, purplish and bloated, pointed at Timmy. Bruises ran down his neck like birthmarks, disappearing beneath a white T-shirt Timmy had mistaken for bare skin. Apart from the smudges of dirt and dried blood, it was the same color.

Hollow black eyes fixed on him and, as always, he felt a cold greasy wave flood over him. *Beetle eyes*, he thought and shuddered away the invasive feeling.

Harlan's nose had cracked across the bridge. A bloodless wound gaped.

His head lolled atop a broken neck. Timmy could hear the bones grinding together and couldn't restrain a wince.

And then the dead boy spoke.

"There's a rabbit down there. I never killed one before. Damn sure killed me one now though, didn't I?"

The wind sprayed rain into Timmy's face and he wiped a hand across his eyes. The words he had come here to say seemed absurd now. *Your Dad wants to know if you're okay...*

It was clear that Harlan was far from okay.

It was clear that Harlan had fallen down the well and had never left it.

And it was clear from the raging malevolence that seethed from his carapace eyes that someone had helped him to the bottom.

"His belly's shot out," Harlan continued. He twitched, his head rising slightly with the sound of a door scraping over a nub of coal and Timmy was immediately aware that someone was behind him.

"Do you see him?" Knox asked, his eyes mere wrinkles beneath the yellow hood. "You do don't you? Is he all right?"

Lightning stabbed the earth in the corner of Timmy's eye. He swallowed.

"Wanted to make you proud Papa," Harlan whispered and despite the wind, Timmy heard it.

Knox was shivering, the thick fingers of his right hand clenching and unclenching; the fingers of his left gripped tightly around the wooden handle of a dull-edged sickle.

"If you can see him Timmy," said Knox, desperation making his voice rattle, "Tell him I'm sorry. Tell him I love him and that it was an accident. He got me riled up is all, like he always used to whenever he did that pussy shit about being afraid to pull the trigger. I just got mad. Tell him that. Tell him I didn't mean it and that he needs to stop..." He held his free hand out, palm up as if the words he needed might come down with the rain.

Timmy finished the sentence for him. "...Haunting you."

Knox's sigh emerged as thunder. "Yeah. Go on, tell him that."

Timmy turned back to the well. And almost screamed. Harlan was standing right before him, close enough for him to smell the foul stench of ancient well-water and to see the thin blue veins mapping the boy's skin. His eyes were not merely black. They were gone.

"Tell him about the rabbit," Harlan sneered and Timmy nodded furiously.

"He says to tell you about the rabbit."

It was Knox's turn to step closer. Fearful, Timmy glanced over his shoulder. The big man loomed.

"I know about the fucking rabbit." Spittle flew from his lips. "He nailed it to the goddamn *door!*"

Timmy flinched, ripped down his hood and sidestepped. He dared a few more steps backward where the air was purer and the threat of harm less. Both father and son turned their heads to look at him. Knox was trembling furiously. Harlan was grinning.

Behind them, the wind wrenched the trees into a feverish dancing. Puddles were gathering where once there had only been footsteps in the mud.

"Tell him to leave me alone!" Knox demanded, raising the sickle to waist height. "You tell him now or so help me…"

Harlan's neck sounded like someone snapping a fistful of dry twigs as his head whipped around to glare at his father. Timmy took another step backward. Something was going to happen. He could feel it. It vied with the ozone in the air for dominance.

"I called for you," Harlan said, still whispering that wind-drowning whisper. "Called for you every night until I had to pretend the moon was your face smiling down on me."

Timmy heard it all, but when the large man's face suddenly paled beneath his hood, he realized this time Knox had heard it too.

He left him there…

Another step back. The sickle raised an inch higher, the fingers stark white around the handle, and trembling violently.

He left him there alive!

"Tell him to leave me the hell—" was all Knox managed before a spindly leg of blue-white lightning slashed through the trees behind them. In the sudden explosion of light, Timmy saw Knox look up, Harlan make a clumsy lurch forward, mouth open and shrieking. The air hummed with static electricity.

As Timmy ran, slipping and sliding through the muck, white spikes lancing his vision, he dared not look back. But he was weeping, as he always wept when the dead found satisfaction. He wept and ran, slipped and skidded his way back toward home, until the hoarse screams mingled with the howling wind and were devoured by the storm.

* * *

Later in dreams, there was sunshine and birdsong.
In the field there was corn.
In the well was a boy who played with a rabbit.
And next to him, a proud father watched.

CHAPTER ONE

Summer light danced in shimmering pools beneath the swishing canopies of leaves. Cicadas rattled high in the trees. The air was warm and buzzing with insects.

The girl on the porch was playing with a strand of her jet-black hair, her attention fixed on the magazine propped against her upraised leg. Her bare feet were braced against the porch railing. Timmy paused a few feet from her house, a half-smile on his lips.

Kim. The girl who had always been the one to make it better.

The smile faded, replaced with a heaviness in his chest that threatened to reduce him to tears. Again he thought of telling her nothing, just leaving without a word. But he couldn't. She deserved to hear it from him. After all these years of her chasing away his shadows, he owed her that much.

"Hello stranger."

He brought out his best winning smile and gave her a half-hearted wave. "Hey."

She dropped her legs and sat up, scooting over on the porch swing to make room for him. "Where've you been?"

"Working mostly." He sat down beside her and felt that familiar tingle as she let her hand rest on his thigh. "The rest of the time acting as mediator for my parents."

Her emerald eyes studied his, searching. "Things that bad?"

Timmy nodded. "They're getting divorced."

"Shit, are you serious?"

"It's been heading this way for a while now. I doubt having to deal with me and the lovely dead folk I keep running into has helped either."

Kim scoffed, her hand giving his thigh a gentle squeeze. "Don't be ridiculous."

"I'm not. This thing I can do—whatever the hell it is—has made life tougher for all of us. I think rather than hating me for it they turned on each other."

She sighed, her small breasts pushing against the fabric of her T-shirt. Timmy felt a rush of warmth.

"Look," she said, "your 'gift' has been hard on all of you. Christ, it's been hard on *me* with all the narrow-minded jerks we have around here. But I don't care because I love you and I know your parents feel the same."

He nodded, the sadness boiling inside him. *Tell her, tell her, tell her...*

"I love you too," he said, then turned to face her. She smiled. Gripping her hands in his, he rubbed her fingers. "But I have something to tell you."

"Uh-oh. Is it *Jerry Springer* time? Should I call my redneck cousins to come kick your ass for sleeping with my mother?"

"No," he said and saw the levity leave her face.

"What is it?"

"I'm leaving."

"Something I said?"

"No. My grandfather died a few weeks ago. Dad's worried about my grandmother. He's not sure how she's handling it."

Kim shrugged. "And he wants to go see how she's doing right? He's taking you with him to Ireland? Is that all? Christ Timmy, there's no need to look so—"

"Wait," he told her, squeezing her fingers tighter. "It's not all. My mother's selling the house."

"What?"

"And my father already has a job lined up over in Ireland. This won't be a vacation."

Kim frowned. "So don't go."

"It's not that easy."

"Why isn't it?"

"Delaware is dead, Kim. Mr. Vernon's going to be shutting down the bookstore in about a month then I'm out of a job, and he was one of the few people willing to give me a chance without fearing I'd see his dead dog loping around the store. Businesses are closing down, left, right and center. There's nothing here."

"So try for work down in Columbus. Just because Delaware is a hole doesn't mean you have to leave the country!"

She was flustered now, her cheeks red.

"It's not just that. You're going to Penn State soon, so we'd hardly ever see each other anyway."

"Well it would be nice to have the option." She turned away, folded her arms.

"Kim...it's only temporary. A trial run at best. My parents think I could use the change in scenery and you know what...they're right. I can't look in any direction without remembering something awful that happened here. I look out my window, I see the path that used to lead to Myers Pond. I hear the trains I think of Harlan Knox and Danny Richards. I need to do this."

Tears shimmered in her eyes, trapping the sunlight. "Oh? And you think it'll be any better for you in Ireland? Do they have some kind of rule over there that insists the dead stay quiet?"

"Kim—"

"No," she said, standing and sending the swing shuddering back to bang against the wall, "You're telling me that it's over, that your running away from everything. How am I supposed to deal with this?"

"Look, if I don't like it, I come home."

She threw her hands in the air, exasperated. "Oh. Great. If you *don't like it* you come home. Not, 'if I miss you Kim'. Jesus. What have we been doing together all this time?"

He stood and went to her. At first she resisted, then melted into his arms, sobbing. "Don't go," she said.

"I have to. I can't handle this place anymore. But I'll be back, I swear. I'm not leaving you." He stroked her hair, felt tears of his own gathering. "I just need to clear my head in a place where no one knows me, where there are no funny looks or people knocking at the door searching for the dead."

"You'll call?"

"Every day."

"I don't want you to go."

"I know and I don't want to leave you."

"What if I put off college for a year and come with you?"
"Then you'd be screwing up your life."
She let out a shaky sigh. "I love you, Timmy."

CHAPTER TWO

They flew into Shannon airport two weeks later, after a shuddering descent through thick gray clouds. The land beneath their wings was a patchwork quilt, the material a study of greens Timmy had never seen before. Threads of gray held those patches in place, which he knew from reading were crude yet effective stone walls dividing one field from the next. It looked like a lush vibrant land, strangely devoid of the soaring towers he had expected from a life spent in America.

"Beautiful, isn't it?" His father nudged him as the plane bucked a current. Timmy's stomach rolled. He nodded and looked back out the window, watched the airport swell in size from a pale gray shoebox to a sprawling outpost of lights and machinery.

They had promised each other that the tension and constant fighting—which had begun at the mention of relocation six weeks after the Knox incident and had continued up until they left for Columbus airport—would cease as soon as they were on the plane.

New life, new beginning, his father had said. *I know you're not thrilled about this idea but I appreciate you having the guts to give it a shot.*

But to Timmy, it was less about guts and more out of fear of his hometown. It had stopped feeling safe, and even though he had agreed to the move, he was still, even now, not sure he'd done the right thing by coming here.

When the plane thudded to the runway, he waited until it drew to a halt and the other passengers began mumbling before sighing with relief.

"Welcome to Ireland," his father said, eyes bright and clear for the first time in months. The look was assisted by the fact that he'd recently forsaken his glasses for contacts. They made him look ten years younger. Timmy tried to grin but gave up. He was glad to have landed, but beyond this airport lay the road to a beginning he wasn't sure he really wanted. Furthermore, his father's apparent refusal to consider that fact irritated him.

After enduring the frustrating customs ritual, they emerged at the gate where Timmy's grandmother was waiting, hands clenched to her breasts, eyes scanning the crowd. He had only met her once before, when she had on impulse taken a flight to the states to spend a week with them. Timmy had been thirteen at the time but although she'd aged, there was no mistaking the grim set of the mouth or the hard narrow blue eyes. He had spent his life with a man who possessed those same features.

She spotted them and her eyes widened. Timmy's father broke into a grin and rushed to greet her, arms wide. She wept joyful tears and stroked Paul's thick black hair for a long moment, then wiped her eyes and stepped back to appraise him. Timmy waited, feeling awkward, lost in the crowd and glad of it.

"My God it's good to see you," she said to Paul and squeezed his hand. "It feels like it's been forever."

"It has," he said then seemed to remember he hadn't taken the flight alone. He nodded at Timmy. "You remember Timothy, of course."

She gasped and waved a hand in front of her face as if to wave farewell to all hope of her not crying. "Oh..." She took a few tentative steps toward Timmy, then paused. "You probably don't even recognize me," she said.

"Of course I do. How are you Grandma?" he said, then set his bags down and went to her. Although he was nervous and in no mood to be civil to anyone, reason and manners intervened. This was his grandmother; a frail old woman he doubted had played any part in orchestrating this upheaval in his life. And she was a widow, still grieving.

Her embrace was tight and Timmy could feel her small body trembling against him. "It's so good to see you, Timothy," she sobbed.

"It's good to see you too." And it was. The stories his parents had regaled him with over the years had left Timmy with a permanent sense of admiration for Agatha Quinn. She was a hard woman, her thick-skin acquired thanks to her husband Aldous's decision that her only virtues were cook and punching bag. She had traveled extensively before settling into Hell with her husband, but it was on those travels Timmy's parents had focused when relating tales of her exploits. Agatha had always wanted to be an archeologist, even as a kid, but had never pursued the qualifications needed to make it a financially viable endeavor. So, she had simply saved her wages from her job at the council office, then quit to travel to world. Somewhere in a dusty box in Delaware, Ohio were grainy pictures of that explorer, youthful and beaming before various backdrops Timmy had only seen in movies: The pyramids of Egypt, the rainforests of South America, Stonehenge, the Coliseum in Rome, the Taj Mahal, The Eiffel Tower.

And here she stood, not an adventurer, but a fragile old woman. The torment of her life was written on her face in thin lines, but now they wrenched themselves into a smile that melted his heart.

"We have so much to catch up on," she said, tapping a cool hand on his wrist. "But let's get you both home and settled first. You must be exhausted."

Outside, the air was heavy and cold, those clouds he had seen from above now coiling smugly and whispering of rain.

Agatha's car was a scabrous yellow Volkswagen Beetle he didn't trust to get them out of the airport parking lot never mind the two-hour drive to Dungarvan. It did, albeit chokingly, taking them through many low huddled towns and down painfully narrow roads. Here and there crumbling castles watched him from a distance, Gothic churches soaring high enough to snag the clouds on their spires. He was overwhelmed by the impression of timelessness and the sense that they were meandering along routes previously traveled by Vikings and Norman invaders. Timmy knew little about the country's history, only what he'd been able to read in the travel guide Mr. Vernon had given him as a going away present, but it was clear that each dilapidated schoolhouse, staggering chapel, stumbling lighthouse and toppling wall that crawled past his window was hundreds if not thousands of years old. In contrast, the modern buildings wore garish coats, as if eager to distinguish themselves from their archaic neighbors. Some of the towns, both rural and suburban, were so old they almost creaked and the more he saw, the more unsettled Timmy became. This country was ancient.

"I'll bet this is all a bit of a culture shock for you, Timmy," Agatha said, startling him. Her eyes were like ice chips in the rearview mirror.

"Yeah, it is. It looks so old."

"You're right there," she said, "The first Irish settlers were traced back to 8000 BC."

"Wow."

"And we have a burial mound in County Meath called Newgrange which is thought to be the oldest manmade structure on earth. Built somewhere around 3200 BC."

It wasn't difficult to believe. He had never seen anything like the towns they passed through. They seemed possessed of a singular type of shadow, the turbulent clouds only adding to the anachronistic aura. He almost expected to see dust roll from the mouths of the people on the streets.

"Feck it anyway," Agatha said then and both Timmy and his father looked at her. She gave Paul an apologetic look and nodded at the windshield. "See it?"

He shrugged. "See what?"

"There's a crack in the glass," she said. "Small but there, down in the corner near the wiper."

"Oh. It's not bad enough to worry about though, is it?"

"Not yet it isn't. After you've been on a couple of these roads though, you'll see why it's best to take care of them sooner rather than later. When the government gets enough complaints and start fixing the motorways, the workers leave gravel lying around for weeks. A crack like that can turn into a split windshield in a heartbeat. It wouldn't bother me so much but our local mechanic Dave Mulcahy is a bit of a con artist. He'd make you take out a second mortgage just to fix the dome light."

Timmy's father smiled and patted her arm. "Don't worry about it. I'll fix it for you."

"Would you? Do you know how?"

"I worked at an auto shop for four years, Mom, remember? Lifelong ambition and all that."

"That's right. I'd forgotten." Her eyes moved to the mirror again. "And you have a fine strapping lad to help you!"

Timmy smiled but it never reached his eyes. His yearning to be with Kim, to be back where things were familiar and not immersed in a strange alien culture overruled any sense of adventure he might have felt had this been a mere vacation. The flare of hope he'd kept tended thus far had already started to wane now that he was on solid ground. Nothing about the move felt temporary and with no idea what lay ahead of him, anxiety manifested itself as a cold hand stirring his innards. He doubted it seemed as foreign to his father, who had grown up here, leaving at the age of eighteen to work in the states, where he met and married Timmy's mother. He was returning home.

With a sigh Timmy sat back and listened to his father and grandmother talk about the old times and the future, until jetlag smothered him in its warm embrace.

Sleep brought fleeting images of pale faced crowds gathered in graveyards, whispering...

He jerked awake some time later to his father's declaration: "We're here, Timmy," and his grandmother's proud announcement: "Welcome to Dungarvan!"

CHAPTER THREE

Dark heaving stretches of water on both sides of the long low bridge they crossed into Dungarvan impressed Timmy. In the distance, tall dark green hills stood sentinel at the borders of the town. Agatha turned the car off the bridge and onto a small road which meandered between a quaint firehouse and a monolithic town hall. The shadows sprawled across the road made gooseflesh ripple across his arms. When an old man with a twisted black cane shuffled in front of them, Agatha was forced to stop abruptly to let him pass—something he seemed in no particular hurry to do; he even cast them a sidelong glance laced with derision, as if they were inconveniencing him by being there.

"Paddy Kiely," Agatha said with a sigh. "He used to be a cook out at the Gaelic college until some guys jumped him on his way home from the pub, stole his money and beat him to a pulp. He was never right again after that."

Timmy watched the old man reach the curb and mount it with caution, a twinge of sorrow in his chest. It baffled him how anyone could summon up the callousness necessary to attack such a helpless creature. Comfort came in the thought that when the old man passed away, he might choose to come back and 'visit' his attackers.

The road rose slightly then and the Volkswagen shuddered. So intent was Timmy on the fibrillations of the car, he failed to notice at first the panorama that had unveiled itself before him.

They drew to a halt at an intersection. To Timmy's right, the road led past a post office, bank and hotel into a town square teeming with life. To his left, another bridge, humpbacked so he could not see where it led. Ahead, fenced off from the harbor by intermittent black poles, a narrow road stretched to form a dock; overseen by those same multi-colored buildings he'd seen before. Beyond the fence, the mercurial mass of the Atlantic heaved, multicolored fishing vessels clanking and swaying. On the opposite side of the harbor, a stone wall kept the water penned in and away from a crowd of houses before it threaded its way down and widened to allow the water out into the sea. There, a slender sandy arm of land reached almost full across the mouth of the harbor in an attempt to keep the tide inside.

"What do you think, Timmy?" Agatha peered at him over her shoulder. "Not quite Ohio, is it?"

"No," he admitted, "Far from it."

"I think you'll like it here," she said with such confidence Timmy couldn't help but be infected by it.

"Looks exactly as I remember it." His father spoke in a voice barely above a whisper, as if despite the familiarity, the view had knocked the breath from him too.

Agatha put the car in gear and angled the Volkswagen toward the humpbacked bridge. "Good things seldom change," she said, with confidence.

* * *

His grandmother's house turned out to be one of those he'd seen huddled behind the harbor wall from the intersection. It was a simple, narrow affair, a lemon box in a spectrum of similarly built houses. Flowerpots filled with marigolds sat atop chocolate brown windowsills; lace curtains made the windows stare like opaque eyes across the water. The street itself was wide, but the row of cars parked end to end on either side made it seem more suited to cyclists than drivers. Despite the parade of vehicles, there was a small space right outside Agatha's front gate. It was the only one. "They know better," she told Timmy by way of explanation.

The anxiety that had clenched Timmy's guts all the way from Shannon airport receded a little as she keyed the front door open and stood aside to let them in. The aroma of stew permeated the air in the hallway and though it was dark, the house radiated a sense of comfort. When Agatha clicked on the lights, Timmy found that he was facing the stairs leading to the second floor.

"I'll get our bags," his father said and edged his way back outside. Agatha patted Timmy's shoulder and made her way into the kitchen.

"It'll all be a little strange for a while," she said, gesturing for him to follow. "No-one ever went to live in a strange place without feeling as if their world had come to end for just a little while. But we'll have some good times, you and I. I missed a lot of years I'd like to have spent with you and I intend to make up for them starting right now."

Timmy smiled and leaned against the kitchen doorframe, watched her fuss around the kitchen.

"You'll make friends," she said. "There are some good spots around here for people your age. We have a local sports team in both hurling—it's like field hockey—and football. There's golf, tennis, anything you might want. And if you like to read, we've got a pretty good library that doubles as a museum. 'Books on the ground floor, bones on the first,' as old Ms. Ryan—that's the librarian—likes to say. I promise you won't get bored."

She set three plates down on the table, paused, then hurried over to him. With a quick glance over his shoulder as if to check they were alone, she said: "And another thing: I know you have a girl back home. Kim, isn't it?"

Timmy nodded.

"Well, calls to America are ridiculously expensive from here but I took the liberty of changing my calling plan, so you just feel free to call your sweetheart whenever the mood takes you. If your Dad starts getting suspicious, leave a ten-pound note on the phone table as if you're paying for the call. I'll take it and return it to you when he's not around. How does that sound?"

He smiled. "It sounds good. If you're sure you don't mind."

"Mind? Of course I don't mind. I want to try and make this… relo*cation* as easy for you as possible. So as far as I'm concerned this house is yours now too. If you respect it as I would yours, then we'll be cool as cucumbers."

"Okay."

Paul huffed and puffed his way in the door laden with bags and

Timmy rushed to help him before they dragged him to the floor.

"Timmy, your room is the first one on the left at the top of the stairs. Paul, you can take your old room. The bathroom is next to Timmy's room if you guys want to freshen up," Agatha said, with a wink. "Supper will be ready in about a half hour."

They thanked her and took the bags upstairs. At the threshold to his room Timmy paused. His father turned, face a pale smudge in the gloom and laid a hand on his shoulder.

"How are you feeling?"

"Okay I guess. A little tired."

"Yeah, me too. By the way I never thanked you," he said.

"For what?"

"For coming with me."

Timmy tried to think of a response to that, but his father didn't wait to hear it. Instead he shuffled off to his room, whistling.

Timmy's bedroom was roughly three times smaller than the one at home. The wallpaper was sky-blue with clowns on bicycles kicking up their heels and chasing balloons everywhere. Had he been ten years old it might have held more charm. The bed was dressed in sheets the same lemony hue as the house and topped by an expensive-looking mahogany headboard. Above it, a small window peeked out over the backyards of the other houses on the street. Against the opposite wall stood a full-length mirror, a blue card table and matching foldout chair.

He sighed and dropped his bags to the floor. Unpacking could wait. He collapsed heavily onto the bed and felt exhaustion overcome him in a welcome black wave. He dozed—

—And dreamed of a faceless man stalking over a riverbank, his step not quite sure, his gait caught somewhere between confident and dazed. On the bank sat a boy, his bare foot dipping into the water, sending gentle ripples across the clear mirror of the pond. Trees leaned over the water studying their reflections; bullfrogs eyed the passage of dragonflies and the world was hushed but for the soft susurrant breeze of summer.

The boy looked up. A smile surfaced like a black thread from the featureless surface of the man's face, but in this dream where no time applied, that smile faded, became a rictus as he knelt over the boy, tolerating the screams, but only for a little while. With a grunt, he wrenched the boy's mouth into silence.

"Timmy, c'mon. Let's get out of here. There's something wrong with that

kid."

Timmy found himself standing on the bank, his best friend Pete at his side, looking nervous as always. It's so good to see you, *he thought and felt warmth flood through his body. Just him and Pete, like the old days, before the world grew teeth and bit them both.*

His happiness was short-lived however for while the man was gone, the boy...the boy was still there. Still dipping that slender foot into the water, but he was dead now, a ragged piece missing from his ankle and as Timmy and Pete looked on in horror, horror Timmy could feel even beyond the borders of dreaming, the boy—Darryl Gaines— turned and grinned at them.

"What are you doing?" *Timmy asked and wished he hadn't.*

Darryl's eyes began to darken until they were the color of pond scum and when he opened his mouth to speak, something small, green and hard-shelled began to crawl out, tiny feet probing a maggot white tongue.

"Feeding the turtles," *the Turtle Boy said.*

He woke what felt like hours later though he quickly realized the light seeping in the window hadn't changed. The delicious smell of stew still filled the house. He shook off the lingering skeins of confusion and sat up, neck and shoulders aching.

It had been years since he'd had the dream and now he struggled to forget it, glad when a sudden scratching at the window distracted him.

He spun around on the bed and looked up, expecting to see a bird of some kind peering in at him. But there was nothing there. The sound came again, from the other direction this time but he couldn't place it.

Getting spooked already, he thought and rubbed a hand over his face. He swung his legs over the side of the bed, decided he needed a shower to slough away the feeling that he'd been run over by a herd of buffalo. A foul taste clung to his mouth, head throbbing as if it had swollen in his sleep. From his father's room came the familiar sound of whistling. He stretched.

Then stopped when the scratching came again. He cocked his head, trying to trace the source of the noise, imagining tiny claws on glass. After another moment, it ceased.

Then someone cried out.

Timmy flinched, stood. Listened to the frantic thumping of his father's feet along the landing, the *thudthudthudthud* of him descending the stairs.

Like Harlan Knox's feet along the roof...

After a second of confused paralysis, he raced to the door, the hall, the stairs and stopped at the kitchen door, breathless.

Agatha and his father were at the sink. His grandmother was hissing air through her teeth.

"What's wrong?" he said, then noticed the shattered pieces of a bowl on the floor. Around it sat puddles of gravy and chunks of meat. Little drops of scarlet led to the sink.

"Are you all right?"

"Yes," she said then yelped.

"Easy, there's still some in there," Paul told her.

Timmy felt some of the tension drain from his shoulders. "What happened?"

"I was ladling some stew into a bowl and the blasted thing just exploded! I've never seen anything like it!"

"Oh."

His father grimaced in sympathy at the jerk of Agatha's shoulders. "She's got some pieces stuck in her fingers, but she'll be in good shape once we get them out."

"Anything I can do?"

Agatha nodded. "If you could clean up that mess, I'd very—ow! *Gentle*, Paul!—I'd very much appreciate it."

Timmy dropped to his haunches and set about picking up the bigger shards of faux china. The soupy mess clung to his fingers as he rose with a handful of pieces and searched for the trashcan.

"This is a fine welcome for you two,' Agatha said disdainfully, "welcome to the home of an old biddy who can't keep her crockery from exploding."

"Don't be silly," Paul told her and plucked a sliver from her index finger. "We're glad to be here." Without looking away from her hand, he said: "Aren't we Timmy?"

Despite his warmth on the stairs earlier, Timmy detected a challenge in his father's tone that irritated him. *You know what to say boy, so say it.* He dropped the pieces into the trash and nodded. "Sure." Timmy hadn't been here a full hour yet but already he sensed this transition would be far from easy . And that brought a crippling weight to his shoulders. The last thing he needed was his father forcing him into it.

He grabbed a dishcloth from the sink and began to mop up the muddy puddles, scooping the meat onto the unbroken half of the bowl.

Paul finally taped up the cuts on Agatha's fingers (they turned out to be less severe than they'd all thought once the blood stopped flowing) and they took their designated places at the table while she made another attempt at serving the food. Waving away offers of help, she managed to get all the bowls filled and sat down with visible relief.

"Not exactly an auspicious start, is it Timmy?" she said, rolling her eyes through the steam that rose from her stew. He smiled and sampled the thick meaty broth. It was delicious and his stomach growled with anticipation. As he ate, he pondered Agatha's question. The only answer to present itself was: *Damn right it isn't.* He was starting to feel as if he had made a huge mistake in coming here, a fear that grew every time he glanced out the kitchen window at the darkening sky.

CHAPTER FOUR

Agatha's living room looked like a maritime museum. The cream gold-flecked wallpaper was suffocated beneath heavy gilt-framed sepia-toned pictures of trawlers, schooners and old sailing ships. In some of them, men stood shoulder-to-shoulder smoking or grinning toothless grins around their pipes. Their caps were pulled down so that arcs of shadow swept beneath their eyes. In another, a mast rose like a splintered ladder from the depths of the sea, rescue boats rising against frozen black waves that had already sealed the fate of the sunken craft. And where there were no pictures, or newspaper clippings depicting great storms or greater tragedies, there were seashells, conch, mussel, clam and cockle speckled about as if Timmy had entered a flooded room after the tide had gone out. All that was missing was seaweed and even so, he felt if he looked hard enough he might find it. The very air smelled of salt and sea-washed wood, of damp wool and strained wet ropes winding round capstans. Even the floor was bare and polished: an imitation deck. He half-expected it to roll at any moment, sending him crashing into the mantelpiece and its framed grinning folk who might yell at him to secure the sails before the squall tore them free…

A disorientating feeling, but not a threatening one.

The stew had settled in his stomach, warming his skin from the inside out. He craved a cigarette but had none and no idea where to get any without being totally obvious about it. He'd already resolved to tell his father soon about the habit but dreaded the inevitable war that would cause. Now more than ever he needed the rush tobacco provided and if there was any justice, his father would realize condemning such a common vice now, when they were a thousand miles from home, would be inviting trouble.

As he drew closer to the picture of a scowling man with a wild, clambering beard and a clay pipe jutting from the corner of his wrinkled mouth, Agatha entered the room. "Your father's gone to bed," she said. "Poor fella was exhausted."

"I know the feeling."

"You might want to consider bedding down yourself. It's almost eleven o' clock."

"You're right. I'll go soon."

She cocked her head. "Admiring our miniature version of the Louvre?"

"It's great. Who is this?" he asked, pointing at the portrait.

"That's your grandfather," she replied in a neutral tone. "A man you're better off never having known."

He studied the man's eyes. Even blurred by dust, his glare held power. Timmy thanked his good fortune that glass and time prevented him from being the true receiver of it.

Agatha drew level with him and folded her arms. "A wicked man," she said, her voice firm, "got more pleasure from watching people fail than anyone I've ever known."

"How come you married him then?" Timmy asked, before he realized he was going to, but she didn't take offense, merely sighed and drummed her fingers on her arm. He was only marginally interested, but felt obliged to listen to her story, reasoning that, living alone, it was probably one she hadn't told too many times before. Weariness made his eyelids heavy and he rubbed them with the heels of his hands.

"He wasn't like that when I married him," she said. "Nothing like that. He was a kind and handsome man before hatred twisted him, made him cruel and abusive, before he looked upon the world and everything in it as if they were out to get him."

"What made him change so drastically?"

"I think it was a number of things. He was a fisherman, a sailor, went straight from the navy to the trawlers."

"Trawlers?"

"Fishing boats. He worked them all year round. If he wasn't out with Frank Daly and his crew, he was repairing the nets or fixing the boat. I didn't mind all that much. I mean, if I wanted to see him, all I had to do was look out your father's bedroom window, or take a trip over to the dock. And I did both, quite often. If the weather was fine, we'd eat lunch right there on the pier wall, talking and laughing as the seagulls dive-bombed our sandwiches. Until the day he told me he'd tie me up in the nets and drag me across the bottom of the harbor if I bothered him at work again."

"My God."

"Nobody was more surprised than me, I can tell you that. But the man I met on the dock that day wasn't your grandfather. He was mean, and drunk and it only got worse from then on. He stopped going to work which meant I had to take a job at the post office. He didn't speak to anyone and spent much of his time in this very room drinking whiskey and staring out the window."

Timmy studied the thick red drapes. They were drawn, but a single wedge of yellow light from the streetlights outside bled through. He wondered what the old man had seen out there, what had kept him fascinated. Regret? Sorrow? Or had he seen anything at all other than his own hate coruscating across his eyes?

"It got so bad I couldn't have visitors," she said, clearly pained by the memory. "Not without fearing that Aldous would come stumbling in, cane raised, shrieking and cursing like a madman. Which I have no doubt he was by the end.

"Occasionally in his extremely rare lucid moments he'd tell me he was sorry, that everything was his fault and that he just wanted to die and be done with the hurt. On those occasions I would try to comfort him but he'd lash out and quickly become violent. I learned my lesson the night he hit me across the face with his cane." She raised her face to the small light above their heads. Timmy saw the small white upturned crescent on her cheek and winced.

"I learned not to care anymore," she continued. "And that in turn led to grief. I grieved for him long before his body died because I was able to convince myself that the Aldous I'd married had been lost at sea and never came home. What I'd lived with had been a bad replacement, the sea's attempt at a consolation prize. So when the cancer got him at last, I had no tears to shed for his passing."

"And you never figured out what made him change?"

Agatha looked thoughtful for a moment, then smiled. "I discovered certain things over the years that might have explained it, but they're not the kind of things you can tell a young man without him fearing his dead grandfather's madness was contagious."

"Hey, I won't think you're crazy. I promise. I could tell you some odd stories myself."

The look she gave him was a curious one. "Could you?"

He nodded.

She raised a hand and shook her head and it seemed enough to dispel whatever mood had temporarily taken hold of her. "All just stories, and not the easiest ones to ponder at the best of times. I miss the old man in that picture. No matter how horrible he was in those later years, he was still a part of me." She took him by the arm. "Come Timmy, you're forcing me to embarrass myself with these tales of woe. You haven't even been here a night yet and these horror stories can wait for some other time. This is Dungarvan, not Transylvania." She led him into the hall, then paused, hand still on his arm, skin smelling of primrose. "I hope you learn to like it here, Timmy. This house can be awful empty at times. I sometimes talk to myself just to break the silence, and that's not the healthiest thing to do. I'll never try and force you to stay here, but do me a favor and give it a chance. I think all of us stand to benefit from the arrangement."

Her eyes held his, dissuading argument with their intensity. Timmy smiled a sheepish smile and nodded.

"I'll do my best."

She nodded and looked away as if she knew his words lacked conviction, were merely recitations prompted by her need to hear them. When she reached the stairs, it was as if, just like Aldous, something had suddenly changed her. The vibrant, spirited woman who had just released his arm had vanished, and there now stood a very old woman, faded and worn, the light in her eyes fading like melted candles.

"I'm tired," she said, her voice low. "I think all the worrying about you and your father making it here in one piece has finally caught up with me." The smile she aimed in his direction was weak. "Goodnight, Timmy."

"Goodnight." He watched her walk up the stairs, one liver-spotted hand clamped around the banister until he could only see her black slippers and then they too were gone. He waited, still listening without knowing why, until he heard her bedroom door squeal closed.

His hands began to tremble. A frighteningly child-like thought led a wave of tears up his throat: *I don't want to be here.*

What he didn't know was why. So far, nothing had threatened him and yet he *felt* threatened as if at any moment the walls might lift and reveal a crowd of ghosts watching him with malevolent glee.

Stupid.

With tears in his eyes, he crossed the hall, quietly cleared his throat and picked up the phone.

CHAPTER FIVE

"Timmy, is that you? Oh I'm so glad to hear you guys made it there in one piece. Eight hours is such a long flight and anything can happen. I suppose I shouldn't say that. I'm sorry, but at least you're safe! How's your father doing? Did he—?"

"He's fine, Mrs. Barnes. Is Kim there?" Timmy hated being rude to Kim's mother, but even back home she was somewhat legendary in the neighborhood for her ability to talk until people felt like running away screaming into the night. If he'd let her ramble on, not only would the phone bill reflect his humoring of her, he'd have ended up with an earache as a reward for his patience. And he needed Kim. Badly. Every second she kept him on the line was a second less he'd have to talk to her daughter.

But as it turned out, it didn't matter.

"Sorry Timmy, she went to the Buckeyes game with a few friends. She'll probably stay with one of them down in Columbus tonight. You know how it is."

He didn't know how it was. At all. He didn't know why she wasn't there waiting for his phone call. His heart sank. Suddenly the house seemed a vast cavernous thing ready to swallow him whole.

"Please tell her I called. Can I give you this number?"

"Sure."

The number was written on a notepad tacked to the wall above the phone. He waited for her to get a pen, then relayed it to her. "Got it?"

"Uh-huh, but it's unlikely she'll call. It costs a fortune to call over there. I remember—"

"Just tell her I said—"

"—when your Mom and Dad vacationed in Ireland, back in...'80...maybe '81, she asked me to look after your dog Pele. Remember little Pele?"

He rubbed his eyes and sighed. If she heard, she ignored it.

"Of course it had to go and get sick on me, so I called and you wouldn't believe—"

"Mrs. Barnes, my time's up, I have to go. Sorry."

"Oh, okay. Well, just make sure you—"

He hung up.

* * *

The stairs became a thing of nightmare, endless and dark. Timmy was tired, eyelids heavy from the exhaustion, both physical and mental.

Images of Kim floated through his mind.

Kim. At home.

Home. Where right at that moment, she was probably on her way to a club, dressed in her red and white Buckeye sweater with the large 'O' embroidered on the breast. She would be smiling, showing off those perfect teeth and talking football with her friends. She might be chewing on a lock of her jet-black hair and mulling over the highlights of the game.

Which meant she wouldn't be thinking of him. The conversation would keep to sports and away from guys who were cursed with peculiar abilities.

Seen any dead folk lately?

The thought brought exhaustion to the edge of the abyss and danced with depression on the rim. He had to sleep. It had gone from a necessity to a defense in a matter of moments. He was so tired in fact, so miserable and drained that when he opened the door to his room, he reached for where the light switch had always been in his old room in Delaware. Momentarily puzzled, he felt along the dark wall. And stopped.

There came a creaking, not a scratching as he had almost expected. A creaking, like an ancient door opening after centuries sealed. He listened and it did not stop, but continued on long enough to confirm that it was coming from inside the room. And then it changed, became higher in pitch but no louder. Changed from a creak to a scraping like nails on a chalkboard. Or nails on glass. He felt his stomach lurch in sudden fear. *Is there someone here?* Or worse: *something?* Maybe some kind of weird rodent indigenous to this country, free and scratching at the window for escape...

It stopped.

Timmy pushed the door open, swallowed. He waited for a moment, willing his eyes to adjust to the dark faster than they were. Standing there blind, he was a target.

Go downstairs. Sleep on the couch. But what would he tell Grandma and his father in the morning? *Sorry folks. Heard a big-ass rat in my room. Took the couch.*

Right.

He gave up trying to find the light switch and sidled into the room, wishing to God he had a weapon of some sort. Neither moon nor starlight deigned to seep in through the small bedroom window. Using his hands as antennae, he tried to remember how the room had looked in daylight. A chair by the wall, a desk...

A jab of something hard against his thigh confirmed he'd been right about that much.

The scraping sound came again so suddenly – a short sharp shriek – that instinct propelled him into a defensive posture. He crouched and cracked his knee against something hard and unyielding. He dropped to the floor with a silent howl of pain, hands cradling his knee and turned before the unseen attacker could chew his face off.

He froze, stopped breathing. Someone was standing right in front of him, a pale shape against the curtain of dark, shuddering and rising from the floor where he'd been hiding. He was no longer shrieking but Timmy thought he heard it giggling from inside the folds of its coat, an unpleasant stuttering sound. He stifled a cry and began to slowly rise and move away, though it was hard not to scream and run. For this thing, this intruder appeared to end at the waist now that he had drawn himself to full height. No legs, no way for him to be standing there trying not to laugh at Timmy's panic. But he was.

Do they have some kind of rule over there that insists the dead stay quiet?

It was clear now they had no such thing.

This was one of *them*. Not a ghost. Ghosts were merely spirits, residual images culled from the memories or fantasies of the observer. To claim a ghost was real was to beg the question: How do they come back clothed? Did clothes have spirits too? No. What Timmy could see and had been seeing since eleven years of age were nothing so simple. These things could touch, feel, and manipulate things. They controlled who could see them and used the witnesses for their own ends. These were The Dead, come from beyond a barrier few knew existed.

The Dead, just like Darryl Gaines, the boy who had come out of Myers Pond. Just like Harlan Knox, Danny Richards, Pete and his father, and all those in between.

But if this was another of them, then *who* was it?

And then it came to him.

This hadn't always been *just* Agatha's house.

He backed away when he should have been heading toward the door, but to do that he would have had to pass within inches of whatever was standing (*floating*) there. The idea of screaming presented itself; his brain already was, but when he opened his mouth, all that emerged was a dry click. His tongue felt like a scorched piece of meat. When something papery scratched against his back he almost died then and there. Instead he spun, fists clenched, fueled by adrenaline, and watched another pale shape resolve itself in the gloom.

A lampshade.

Light.

At first the connection missed, so intense was his terror, then he ducked low and scrabbled for the switch with sweaty fingers.

A click and the room flooded with warm yellow light. Shadows shriveled away into the floor. He turned, expectant, hoping, but the legless man was still there, standing and yet not standing by the door, baring his teeth and breathing heavily.

Timmy frowned, confused.

He was looking at himself.

He stood there, reflected in the mirror though for a moment he would not, could not believe it was anything so benign. Could not believe Aldous wasn't standing there leering, challenging him, eyes aflame with the rage of madness.

But in the absence of darkness, he realized what had happened and felt his bladder come dangerously close to letting go. His shoulders sagged; he dropped to the bed and sat there, still staring at the mirror.

It was broken; the lower half of the glass swung like a gate in the breeze, still connected to the wooden frame on one side, the edges grinding together and shrieking, then stuttering back with a hollow chuckle. He noticed the left side of the mirror was hinged; it opened to reveal a hollow wooden cabinet inside. Somehow the bottom half of the mirror had cracked and set the glass swaying, severing the legs of any reflection it contained and shrieking as the edges rubbed against each other.

For the first time that day, he was relieved to find himself alone.

Laying back on the bed, he thrust a hand across his sweaty brow and prayed for sleep. His pulse throbbed and soon became a metronomic lullaby.

* * *

He imagined, on the borders of consciousness, that the ocean had flooded the world and sent a woman, blue-skinned and dark of eye to his bedroom window. She floated there for some time, watching, hair weaving like seagrass, bubbles rising in the green tide around her, then swam away with a smile, leaving him adrift in the current of sleep.

CHAPTER SIX

In the paroxysms of imaginary terror, it had never occurred to Timmy that a simple mirror might be at fault, nor did it occur to him that this was the third time in twenty-four hours something had broken or cracked.

Agatha's windshield, the bowl and now his bedroom mirror.

The connection had been delayed by the fear that something was stalking him, but over breakfast the following morning awash in the sunlight streaming in through the window, he put all of it under the microscope.

"My God, Timmy," Agatha said as she descended the stairs, hoisting a basket of laundry. "What happened to the mirror in your room?"

So preoccupied was he with trying to overrule the faintest idea of a 'visitation', he had completely forgotten to tell her what had happened.

Knowing my luck, the mirror was probably a family heirloom, he thought.

He looked across the table at his father, who was peering at him over his newspaper. *What the hell did you do?* his eyes said and Timmy looked away.

"I'm sorry, Grandma," Timmy said. "I woke up last night and it was like that, the glass at the bottom just swinging over and back. Scared the life out of me."

"Oh." It was clear she didn't believe him.

Across from him, the newspaper dropped a notch further and he could feel the accusation heating the side of his face, but he wouldn't look at his father.

"I'm sorry," he said again.

Her face was scrunched up, brow furrowed as if trying to figure out either how such a thing could have happened or why he was lying to her. Suddenly he felt consumed by irrational guilt—he *hadn't* had anything to do with it—but the combination of Agatha's disappointment and his father's burgeoning irritation was enough to make him feel like he had.

He considered telling his father about what he thought he'd seen, but promptly rejected the idea. This was supposed to be a break from that life, even though Timmy thought they both knew such a thing was impossible. The location had never been the problem; Timmy had.

"Oh, that's all right," Agatha said, and descended the remaining steps. "I'm sure we can fix it."

"I'd be glad to fix it," Timmy said, then immediately wished he hadn't. It felt like an admission of guilt. *Damn it.*

His grandmother offered him a flicker of a smile and vanished into the laundry room. Timmy swallowed and glanced at his father. The newspaper was lying spread-eagled on the table.

"What did you do?" he said in a neutral tone that promised it wouldn't be neutral for long.

"I didn't do anything, I swear. I know it sounds crazy but it broke itself. One minute it was fine, the next the damn thing had split in half. Honest."

Conspiratorially, his father asked, "Was it one of *them?*"

"No."

"Then you get out there. Today. You get a job and you pay for that damn mirror."

Timmy frowned. "A job? For what? Dad, I'm telling you the truth. I—"

"You may be sulking about this move but if you think trashing your grandmother's house is going to make a difference, you're wrong. She's an old woman, Timmy. The last thing she needs is some punk with a hair up his ass giving her a hard time."

Now it was Timmy's turn to get angry. "What the hell are you talking about? I'm not giving anybody a hard time."

"It's your room, your responsibility. If something breaks in there whether by your hand or the hand of *God*, then you need to make sure it gets fixed."

"I already said I'd fix it, Dad. What's with the attitude?"

"It doesn't seem like I'm the one with the attitude here."

Timmy felt the anger surge up his throat. All the frustration, the pain and the protests he'd kept shut away over the years rode the wave of his temper.

"What do you expect, Dad? You give me about three weeks' notice before dragging me out of everything I've known. I don't know anyone here, I'll probably never see Kim again and I'll only be able to talk to Mom over the phone until either she visits—which is unlikely with *you* here—or until I have enough money to go back home on my own. I know why you brought me here. You got tired of the strange looks from the neighbors, the grieving people hammering at the door. So did I, not that you'd know. You just thought if you uprooted me and stuck me in a quiet little country like this, things would be different. Well I'm sorry to have to break it to you Dad but the thing you're trying to get away from is the very thing you brought with you.

"I know you needed to get away from everything and I went along with it. But now you're pissed because I mope around? For Chrissakes, wouldn't *you* in my shoes? I'm doing my best here. It's Day One, okay. I don't need this shit from you so lay off with the heavy hand. I need time. If you can't give it to me then let me go back home where I belong."

His father looked shocked and angrier still, but his mouth didn't seem sure how to shape the words he wanted to say, so he closed it. Then, his eyes moved to something behind his son and Timmy felt a quiver in his insides.

Agatha. He knew she'd be standing there before he turned around and immediately felt regret. Not because of what he'd said to his father, who damn well deserved every word of it, but because it shouldn't have been said while his grandmother was within earshot.

When he turned, she was facing away from them, looking at the clock on the wall above the window.

"I have some business in town," she said. "I'll leave you boys to your discussion."

"Grandma—"

She disappeared and returned wearing a thick brown wool-lined jacket. "I've left a set of keys for both of you in your rooms if you don't expect to be together all day. I'll see you later."

She was gone before an apology reached Timmy's lips and when he turned back to the table, his father was shaking his head.

"Good job," he said and stood, the chair scraping loudly against the floor.

He fetched his coat, shrugged it on and left the house, slamming the door behind him hard enough to rattle the windows.

* * *

"Mom?"

"Hey sweetie, you get over there okay?"

"Yeah."

"By the sound of your voice I take it you still haven't warmed to the idea of Ireland."

"Not yet, no. It hasn't been peachy so far."

"What happened?"

"Damn mirror broke in my room last night."

"Broke?"

"Yeah. I know how it sounds, but I didn't touch it. It just...broke. Of course no one believed that, then I got into a fight with Dad. Grandma overheard and..."

"Oh dear."

"Yeah."

"Well, things are bound to be a little rough at the start, Timmy. You knew that going in."

"Yeah I did, but I just have a bad feeling about the whole thing, you know. Something other than I expected. Something...else."

"Like what?"

"I don't know. I think something's wrong here."

"Well of course it is. It's strange. You don't know anyone there. It's all unfamiliar territory. That'd be threatening for anyone."

"No, Mom. I mean *wrong*."

"I don't understand."

"Wrong...as in *Darryl Gaines* wrong..."

A sigh rumbled over the phone. "Timmy...We went through enough with this. Don't torture yourself. You're there to forget."

Do they think I'm nuts? Timmy thought, suddenly alarmed. *Have they managed to deceive themselves into thinking all of this was my delusion? Jesus!*

"Timmy...I know things are rough. They're rough for me too. You've only been gone a couple of days and already I'm missing you. But you have to give it a chance. If you don't...if you look for excuses to hate the place, then you make it harder not only on yourself but on everyone around you. Where you are right now is a good place, trust me, and if nothing else think of it as a rest stop, a place for you to take stock of your life and see where you want it to go. Your father took you with him because he'd never survive without you. He loves you, Timmy. You're everything to him, but as we both know, he's not always the best at showing that."

"Yeah, you're right."

She scoffed. "Of course I am. I'm your mother. I'm always right. And don't think for one second I'd have let him take you over there if I didn't believe it would be good for you."

"Right."

"Will you be okay, honey?"

"I guess so."

"Good, well you call me if you need anything, all right?"

"I will."
"I love you Timmy."
"Love you too Mom."

She hung up and he stood there listening to the dial tone, running through the list of people he could call and came up empty. He decided he could spend the day drifting about the house until the boredom drove him crazy or get out and see exactly where this great 'life change' had deposited him. After a few moments deliberation, he sighed and grabbed his coat.

CHAPTER SEVEN

He made his way into town via the Causeway – a quarter mile stretch of road flanked by the sea on both sides. In the harbor, the boats tilted lazily, a yacht snoozing by the pier as morning sunlight struggled in vain to heat the world. Chimneys rose like upended cigarettes from the factories along the dock.

Along the Causeway black posts studded the pavement, linked by chains painted silver, presumably to keep the errant walker from stumbling into the tide below. The thought of ending up in that cold dark water reminded Timmy of things he had to struggle to dismiss. Huddled against the icy breeze, he jammed his hands into his pockets. He had never felt cold like this before. While Ohio winters could be lethal, this new kind of cold seemed to start on the inside and slice its way out.

Halfway to the bridge, teeth chattering, he glanced down at where the wall sloped a few feet to the detritus-riddled shore. A shopping trolley lay on its side in the sand, a shredded white plastic bag hanging from the center of its handle. Next to it, he saw what looked like an enormous rusted cage with a weighted bottom standing canted like a drunk pausing to get his bearings. Some of the bars were missing, snapped off by time or the sea. A smashed beacon stood atop the peak of the pear-shaped object. Tendrils of seaweed flickered in the breeze. Timmy stopped, stared and felt the cold infect him like a living thing.

It was a buoy. A corroded birdcage festooned with seaweed, trash and other gifts from the sea. A relic.

And there was a dead woman clinging to it.

He was aware of his breath licking against his cheeks in quick wet surges as he struggled not to panic. He could hear the gentle shushing of the tide around the base of the buoy and the cars droning past like bored hornets. A seagull screeched overhead. All was normal but for this.

It was a woman, a wispy ragged thing, blue-skinned and emaciated. She was clutching one of the rusted bars at the top of the buoy, the small bumps of the muscles in her arms tensing and relaxing only slightly as she struggled to clamber aboard. Her hair was the color of seaweed, her skin mottled and sagging and when she turned to look at him, when she finally sensed that someone was *seeing* her, he felt bile fill his mouth.

Her eyes held only the faintest suggestion of corneas. Ragged sockets rimmed marble white orbs. Beneath her right cheekbone was a gaping hole large enough to make a mockery of her mouth.

And as he stood there watching, she let go of the bars and dropped to the sand. Her feet sank just a little. Her hair, thick and matted, framed a face contorted with rage.

Timmy backed away as she began to walk toward the wall, toward where he stood trembling. And though he was sure her lips did not move, her voice filled his head as sudden and painful as a migraine.

Jealousy, such a wicked, wicked thing...

He clamped his hands to his ears, for all the good it would do and clenched his teeth. The intrusion of that slithering voice into his brain repulsed him beyond words, and yet she continued to whisper as she drew closer, taking careful steps, her bare feet puncturing themselves on shards of broken beer bottles and sharp-edged rocks.

Madness favors it, you see...

He backed away and moaned. The edge of the curb slipped beneath the heel of his shoe almost sending him toppling backwards. A car honked as it sputtered past but there was no time to acknowledge it. The woman had reached the wall, was climbing, her flat blue dark-veined breasts scraping against the concrete leaving skin behind as fingers with splintered nails found the cracks and pulled.

Should I forgive the wrongdoer, Timmy Quinn?

His heart jumped at the mention of his name, though he wasn't all that surprised. Subconsciously he'd hoped the distance would have made a difference to things, but it hadn't. They always called him by name.

The dead knew him.

Her hands slid over the top of the wall, clutching.

Will you help me, Timmy Quinn? she hissed in his ear and he felt the breath rasping from his chest, hands clenching and unclenching. Terror colder than the air and the sea and the dead woman spiked through his veins and he turned, swallowed and ran, his feet pistons against the pavement, her whisper curling into his brain like smoke from a snuffed candle.

Or are you an enemy?

Confused and puzzled faces swept past him in a blur. Someone tried to grab his sleeve and he yelled aloud, was still yelling, the cold gnawing on his skin as he found the bridge, slumped against it and turned, expecting to see her walking toward him, a slimy trail of brackish water running in rivulets from the rotting holes in her body, seaweed hanging in putrescent strings from her hair.

But she was gone. Pedestrians looked at him as if *he* were the threat, some lunatic planning on doing them harm. His cries faded to labored wheezes as he straightened, quickly composed himself and headed into town. His hands and knees shook.

What the hell is wrong with you? You should be used to this by now.

But he wasn't and never would get used to it; didn't want to *have* to get used to it.

* * *

He found a small store on the corner of the town square and bought a pack of cigarettes. The old woman behind the counter would have qualified as the most hostile he had ever encountered if the blue-skinned harridan hadn't already won that title by a country mile.

Next to the newsagent's stood a hardware store with an expensive looking bench out front. A small Day-Glo tag told him the cost of comfort was $300. Disregarding any policies they might have about such things, Timmy dropped heavily onto the seat and lit a cigarette. The first drag was enough to saw the edges off the chill lingering in his chest. His hands continued to tremble, though less severely.

He smoked three cigarettes in a row until his throat was so raw he had to return to the newsagents and buy a can of Pepsi. This time however, there was someone else sitting on the bench when he emerged, so Timmy crossed the street, past an amusement arcade riddled with lights and a shoe store with a meager amount of wares represented in the window. All around him, people chatted animatedly, making what had happened less than twenty minutes before seem all the more surreal, and unbelievable. But rather than draw comfort from the crowds, they made him feel more alone. None of them had a clue how close the Curtain was, that veil keeping the dead on their stage and out of the real world.

It had been his English teacher, Mr. Roberts who had inadvertently sown the seeds for Timmy's idea of what the dead world was. Mr. Roberts and Shakespeare to be exact. *All the world's a stage*, he'd said, quoting Jaques from *As You Like It*, and Timmy had thought: *Yes it is, but it's not the only one.* And as the teacher circled the class, delighting in his dramatic oration, *And all the men and women merely players; They have their exits and their entrances...* Timmy had felt as if the words were meant for his ears only, that somehow Mr. Roberts was giving him the definition he so badly sought. To compound the thought, he recalled Darryl Gaines' words to him as he stood on the bank of Myers Pond, deciding the fate of Timmy's father: "*They'll* explain it to you. The people on The Stage."

It was something that had stayed with him. Another world, reserved for the dead, a Stage and the Curtain keeping it from the eyes of the living. Most of the living anyway.

They need you to help them, I guess, his mother had said once, years before. *Maybe you're gifted that way, as crazy as it sounds. Some people are put here to fix cars for a living, others to fix broken bodies. Maybe your job is to fix the lives of those who've lost them.*

The prospect of always having to be on hand to solve the riddles of lost lives, to see them stepping out from behind the Curtain rattled him to the very core of his being. He wanted to grab the next person who passed by, to scream at them *Now! I've infected you. You do it! You deal with these goddamn things whatever the hell they are!*

But worse, if what his mother had said was true, then they would plague him forever. He would never escape them. The Dead were everywhere, hiding behind a curtain big enough to cloak the world.

As he stood outside a tavern, peering in at old men clustered around pints of Guinness, each one pondering his own mystery, a tall

shadow slipped beside Timmy's reflection in the window.
I can't do this.

His life had become a question of: *who's dead, who's alive?* And he didn't want to know anymore.

When a hand fell on his shoulder, he flinched so hard his teeth clacked together.

CHAPTER EIGHT

"Smoking?" his father said, nodding at the cigarette.

"Yeah, I am. You scared the hell out of me." Timmy's initial relief at seeing a familiar face in a town full only of unfamiliar and now sometimes *dead* people, faded with the realization that this was probably going to be a continuation of the morning's tête-à-tête with his father.

"Got one for me?" he said then and Timmy almost dropped the cigarette.

"What?"

"I could use one if you have some to spare." One side of his mouth turned up in the beginnings of a smile, but quickly passed. It was enough. Timmy reached into his pocket and handed him the pack. His father studied the small rectangle with the red splash across the front. "Carroll's? I don't think I've ever smoked one of these before."

"They're awful," Timmy said and watched incredulous as his father screwed one between his lips and lit it with a practiced hand.

"I quit smoking when your Mom was pregnant with you," he muttered. "After the thing with that boy at Myers Pond, I started sneaking one here and there. Lately it's been more here than there." He exhaled and watched the smoke tearing itself away from him, then looked from the cigarette to his son.

"How long have you been at it?"

A shrug. "About a year."

"I suppose Kim's doing it too?"

"No actually, she hates it."

"Good for her. Maybe she'll knock some sense into you."

"How? Unless she's telepathic." He couldn't help the bitterness. If anything, it was preferable to the fear of what he might see walking toward them through the crowd at any minute.

"You'll see her again. I promise." He smiled.

"You sound awful sure."

"Well the job is definite. I spoke to the boss this morning."

"You did? Already?"

He waved away the questions with feigned irritation. "I was going to tell you this morning before everything went to hell. You know I had a job set up before I ever bought the tickets to come over here but details were a little fuzzy. Well, they're not fuzzy any longer and the money's pretty damn good. I was on my way to meet with the manager. I was hoping you'd come with me."

"Can we get a coffee first?"

He glanced at his watch. "Sure. But we better be quick about it."

They began to walk. "So how did you find me?" Timmy asked him.

"I wasn't looking for you. Just killing time, but as you'll learn, if you ever want to find anybody in Dungarvan, you'll find them in The Square."

* * *

They went to a place called Maggie May's—a quaint if cramped café hidden away beneath an archway leading to the town's shopping district.

Timmy felt better after a steaming cup of coffee and a few more cigarettes. Though he didn't protest, his father did seem appalled at the sheer amount his son smoked in the ten minutes or so they were at the table. Timmy appreciated his restraint.

It occurred to him more than once to tell his father about what he had seen on the Causeway, but he couldn't get the words out. Besides, he was so obviously glad to be starting work that he didn't want to rain on his parade. Not just yet anyway. He knew sooner or later he would have to tell him. If only to have someone on his side.

"So how is Grandma?" Timmy asked after a long moment of silence.

A sigh. "She's okay. Now. I can tell you though that she won't be able to take many more of those arguments. She's been there, too many times to count and she doesn't need it now that Aldous is gone.

We're supposed to be security for her, not reminders of her misery."

"I'm sorry. I didn't know she was there."

"Yeah. But she understands too how hard this is going to be on all of us. Probably best we got it out in the open rather than letting it fester. And you're right. I did kind of shanghai you into this, so I've been thinking…I figure the work is good enough here, I'll be able to save some money. Then you can have the summers and the price of a plane ticket home if you want," he said, stubbing out his cigarette with a grimace. "If you get a job, which I hope you will, then you can save your own money and go back whenever you feel like it."

Timmy felt as if someone had wiped the dirt from a window, allowing him to see what lay outside. But he was not thinking *visits*, he was thinking *escape*, if indeed such a thing was possible. "That would be cool. Where is this job?"

"The leather factory."

"Yikes, doing what?"

"Not sure yet, but the boss didn't waste time getting in touch once he'd read my resume. I expect I'll be manning a variety of machines. It's ugly work. I knew a guy who did it in Akron, and it's pretty rough. But money is money and I don't mind getting my hands dirty. Besides, there isn't much construction work available around here. I'd have to travel and I'm through with that."

"So where's this factory?"

"Down on the docks."

That made Timmy hesitate, just for a split-second, but it was long enough for his father to notice. "What?"

He was picturing the woman hobbling toward the sea wall.

"Nothing. Nothing at all."

CHAPTER NINE

After at least twenty minutes spent navigating a labyrinthine system of side streets which led past a church, a castle wall and the crumbling castle itself, they found themselves standing in the cold shadow of a dilapidated warehouse. An eight-foot high sliding wooden door stood locked before them, long striations in the wood looking like battle scars, the edges tinged with ancient maroon stains.

As they watched, the wood thrummed to the tune of the thunderous roars bellowing from the machines within.

For a moment they didn't speak. Timmy didn't like it one bit. Now that whatever-the-hell-was-wrong-with-him had been activated again and he knew the dead were coming, were perhaps *seeking* him, he couldn't help but look on that enormous door as if it were the maw of a tiger. His gaze was drawn to the base of the door, where the erosion of frequent use had left a thin crack between the ground and the wood. Tongues of smoke lapped at the space and rose, dissipating before they reached eye level.

Beyond them, the machines roared like furious creatures.

"You'll go deaf working in there, Dad," he said, struggling to keep the tremor from his voice.

SomethingwrongSomethingwrongSomethingwrong—
But if they're coming…who are they coming for?

"Like I said," his father said, stepping close to the man-door, "I don't mind getting my hands dirty."

"It's not your hands I'm worried about," Timmy muttered, knowing he hadn't been heard.

He watched his father tug at the stained handle on the small door. The door shrieked open and a belch of dirty smoke rolled out to greet him. "Yikes," he said and looked back at Timmy. "You coming?"

He didn't want to; his mind had split in half, one side screaming at him to go, to grab his father and get as far away from the factory, the town, the country as possible, the other chastising his cowardice.

You can't go through life afraid to move because of these things, he told himself. *You'll go crazy.*

Bracing himself, he joined his father and stepped inside.

The smoke was nothing compared to the smell.

"Jesus." Timmy clamped a hand to his nose, eyes watering as he surveyed the inside of the factory. Thick wooden poles, some still dressed in bark, supported a gridwork of heavy oaken beams which held the low ceiling over their heads. The poles ran for about twenty feet on both sides of the room before the thick fog spewing from the machines swallowed them. Dim light bulbs, ineffective in the soupy gloom, dangled from bare cords and jittered from the vibrations.

"Yeah, it's bad," his father agreed and looked around.

It was the smell of death, or of what Timmy had always imagined brimstone might smell like. It was a smell of fear and decomposition and sickness.

As if his father had read his thoughts, he turned and nodded. "It's the chemicals. They put the animal hides in barrels of chemicals to treat them. And see over there," he said pointing at a series of large wooden drums spinning on belts and powered by a huge coughing motor against the wall to their left, "that's where this damned fog is coming from. They tan and dye the hides in there."

Timmy felt as if the noxious odor was invading him, clinging greasily to the insides of his nose and throat. *How the hell is Dad going to bear working here?* As he looked around, he noticed steam pipes dripping puddles onto the floor, wisps of white drifting from them like escaping ghosts, adding to the omnipresent murk.

And through the gloom, pale hollow-eyed men in white aprons moved.

At first Timmy thought he'd found the fear he'd felt at the threshold of this awful place. With such a quota of death, he fully expected to see or sense something amiss in here but when one of the figures emerged from the heaviest fog and winked in their direction, his father waved a short salute and smiled. Timmy relaxed. A little.

On the right wall stood a series of what appeared to be old-fashioned clothes wringers, only they were far longer and larger than anything the boy had ever seen. Another apron-clad man, sallow-faced with tousled red hair and a grim expression trundled a triangular wooden frame on castor wheels up to the machine, a pile of dark hides heaped atop it. He then proceeded to feed the uppermost hide from the stack into the machine, teeth clenched in determination as the wheels began to roll.

This is Hell. The thought came unbidden, and shook Timmy more than the constant thrumming from the machines could hope to.

"Paul Quinn, I presume!" a voice bellowed over the din and after a moment a pair of meaty forearms emerged from the fog followed by a portly man in a red cotton shirt and brown corduroy slacks. He grinned toothily and offered his hand. It was with great reluctance that Timmy unclamped his nose to shake it.

"Howya Paul. Name's Dan Meehan. We spoke on the phone," he said, but his eyes were on Timmy. "Who's this fella? Did you bring me another laborer out of the goodness of yer heart?"

"I don't think he's interested," Timmy's father told him. "The smell, you know?"

Meehan feigned hurt. "Sure that's only the sweet scent of the lime yard and the maggots in the drums. Perfume to the senses after a while."

"I doubt it," Timmy said, "for anyone other than sadists."

"So he came with you for moral support did he?"

"That he did."

"Jaysus that's nice. The only time my young fella bothers his arse to come see me at work is when he needs the feckin' car."

Paul laughed along with Meehan but a question had risen to the forefront of Timmy's mind and he asked before the nerve to do so left him. "Why hire a guy all the way from America? I mean Dungarvan's a pretty big place by Irish standards right? So how come you can't get someone local?"

His father shot him a piercing look, which Timmy ignored.

Meehan raised an eyebrow. "By God, Paul. Is he trying to lose you the job already?"

"I don't know what he's trying to do. I really don't."

Meehan looked around as if the answer was written in clues somewhere in the factory. At last he rolled his eyes and gave a dramatic sigh of exasperation. "It's not that simple."

"What isn't?"

"Getting people to work here. Take a look around you, boy. As you noted yourself, 'tis foul. The fumes from the chemicals tend to give you sore eyes for a week, the dust from the hides gets into your pores, like coal will a miner's. You need strong men for this type of work, or they'll get killed. Some of these machines are vicious. Like the one your father will be using. 'Tis called a slokum staker." Here he turned to Timmy's father and adopted a more serious tone of voice, as if instructing now, not merely entertaining a bothersome child.

"The slokum's a machine for softening the leather but 'tis a tough one, like playing tug-o-war with a crocodile. Has bladed jaws that clamp down on the leather when you feed it in. Your job is to hold the material at the other end and worry it around while the machine basically chews the hard leather soft. The trick is to leave a flap of the leather hanging down so you can pin it to the machine body with your hip. That way the jaws can't rip the leather out of your hands and send you flying. Happened to a fella here not so long ago. Robby Hennessy. He'd worked with that bloody thing for nearly ten years and one day he scratched himself at the wrong time and we ended up prying his lower jaw off the blades while he sat unconscious at the other side of the room. Never knew what hit him."

He turned back to Timmy. "As I said, 'tis'nt a job for everyone. Your Dad called me and I filled him in on what we'd be doing here and the kind of hours he'd be expected to work. He seems like a capable body, so he gets the job. We have openings here pretty much all the time. The careless don't last long. And do you know many people willing to live side-by-side with maggots? Add superstition to that and you have a job that stays at the bottom of most people's prospective employment list."

"Superstition?"

He nodded. "Old buildings like this attract that kind of thing. Like your regular haunted house."

"But why here?"

Something odd happened then. The thrumming in the floor stopped abruptly, then stuttered back to life, the lights swinging over their heads. Timmy's father shrugged, Meehan grinned, but Timmy didn't. Maybe it had only been a power surge, but to him it had been a sign, a voice, telling the factory manager *uh-uh, no tales today.*

And it had worked.

"Look, the day's getting on..." He looked at Paul for support and got it, but not without a cutting glance at Timmy for good measure.

"I guess I'll take off then," Timmy said, and no one objected.

He watched as Meehan clamped a hand on his father's shoulder and steered him into the swirling fog. The grind and clatter of the machines seemed to swell as they approached, then settle as the muddy clouds consumed them. After giving the men in the aprons a final glance, Timmy started to turn when a flicker of shadow caught his eye. It was just one of the light bulbs swinging, yet his skin crawled and the hair prickled on his arms. He moved toward the door, then stopped.

The light bulb...

Turning slowly he looked at the row of lights running along the center of the room, their amber glow fading as they reached the area where the fog was thickest. The machines rattled and grumbled, pounding in his ears like a heartbeat in stereo.

The bulb above his head was now the only one swinging.

But its shadow wasn't swinging at all.

Slowly, swallowing the fear, his eyes flitting from the light to the ghost-like men in the aprons, he moved away, back from the fog and the stench to the door. Then he was outside and slamming it shut behind him. He had taken two steps when bile flooded his mouth, doubling him over. He vomited his breakfast onto the street.

CHAPTER TEN

Timmy slammed back against the wall, the taste of vomit in his mouth potent enough to inspire another round. He breathed deep and felt smoke and sea-salt flooding his nose. It was not an altogether pleasant mix, but it was better than sickness. Rubbing a hand over his face, he saw that he had stumbled into an alley, the leather factory wall at his back leaking moisture that seeped through his clothes. Another tall ancient looking wall stood before him. Growing like mold across the brick were splotches of graffiti so old they had lost any hope of offense. At the far end of the alley, the path dropped away and trailed down to the sea. The sliver of headland out there had faded beneath low slung clouds.

Another breath, slow and deep and he stepped away from the wall, one hand clamped across his stomach, as if its presence could pacify the rebellious organ.

Something wet tapped against his shoe and he almost laughed. *Rain. What next?*

As further drops pattered on his shoulders, he frowned and looked back out onto the street. Pedestrians strolled by, oblivious to the sickly boy in the alley. Oblivious to the rain.

Drip, drip, drip...

The drops spattered his sleeve and he recoiled. It wasn't rain. And the drops were red.

A sound then, like a child's fingernail tapping a bell and the air shivered in faintly visible waves.

Creaking.

An airplane threaded through the clouds, stitching them together to form a storm.

Fearful, Timmy looked up, slowly, ever so slowly, relishing these few precious moments of ignorance. *Don't let there be one of them up there. Don't let...*

The clouds filled the narrow space between the alley walls with opaque skin. The windows of the leather factory were small, and high, closer to the roof than the ground. Some of them had been broken. And from one hung a dead man.

Timmy flinched and the man mimicked him.

He was a slender figure, his black suit and white shirt hanging in tatters. An old rope, hooked to the windowsill, was wound round his throat so many times it reminded Timmy of the African tribal women who used rings to stretch their necks. Only one pocket in the breast of his coat was undamaged and it was from this that he produced something that gleamed dully. With a crooked smile and a practiced hand missing most of its nails, he tossed the object down to Timmy.

It clinked against the cobblestones once and lay still.

Timmy watched the man sway for a moment longer, afraid to take his eyes off the hideous thing lest it should fall and land on top of him while his attention was elsewhere.

When at last he did risk a look, he saw what the man had thrown was nothing more sinister than a coin, albeit a peculiar looking one. Cautiously, he picked it up and studied it. It was about the size of a dollar coin, with a bull caught preparing to charge on one side, a harp on the other. Engraved below the bull in ornate lettering was the word: SCILLING.

A creak of the rope brought his gaze back to the hanging man. He spoke, a thunderous whisper: "Cut me down, I'll give yeh another."

Timmy dropped the coin and watched in horror as more blood dripped from the man's mouth. He was grinning widely now, rotten teeth stained red.

"C'mon, help me. There's so much I need to *show* 'em."

Timmy began to edge his way out of the alley.

The smile vanished, grew ugly, hating.

"Cut me *down* so I can show 'em what 'tis *like*, young fella," the man growled, his movements tightening the rope until the blood flowed down his body and began to pool on the cobblestones. Flesh began to lift as the noose twisted deeper. *Creeeeeak.*

"Aw Jesus," Timmy breathed, feeling his gorge rising again. He staggered out of the alley, the whispered threats from that bleeding mouth tangling with the wind.

CHAPTER ELEVEN

He walked in a daze for what felt like hours, colliding with people on the street and muttering apologies he wasn't sure could be heard.

The sun had reemerged briefly, then pulled the dark covers of the clouds up over its face, lending a monochrome aspect to the town that only deepened his despair. He stopped in the arched doorway of a boutique and watched the first raindrops fall, the passage of the pedestrians accelerating accordingly.

His thoughts were in a furious tangle. He needed to think, to get focused so he could lay out what little he knew so far, but it seemed someone had let him out in a blizzard and severed the lifeline. The sick feeling had infected his nerves.

He took a deep breath, then another, lit a cigarette and watched umbrellas blossom like flower buds on fast-forward as the rain became a steady downpour. Inside the boutique someone clucked their tongue and commented on how they'd never make it home now without getting soaked.

Timmy closed his eyes.

Someone hung a man from a window. Why? And who would he hunt down if cut free?

There is a dead woman and if past experience means anything at all, then she wants me to do something, to set in motion some chain of events that will help her achieve something. Revenge, most likely. But on who?

He took a deep drag on his cigarette, heard someone complain about the smoke from the kid standing in the doorway, and ignored it.

He watched a father tuck his collars up and make a dash for his car, his squealing daughter in tow as they splashed through puddles. It brought to mind his own father and the factory.

Something is in there. One of them. *And yet it doesn't feel the same.* The shadow swinging out of synch was a sign but even without it, he had sensed something in there watching as they stood talking to Dan Meehan. Something hiding in the smoke, in the steam, in the walls. Something far more dangerous, far more powerful than the hanging man, or the woman or anything he'd dealt with before.

Not exactly an auspicious start to your relocation, is it Timmy? Agatha had said after the incident with the stew bowl. But that minor cataclysm was far more preferable to the official greeting Dungarvan had given him today. He didn't know what it was the thing, or things in the leather factory might want, but until he knew he did not like the idea of his father being in there.

When the woman in the boutique cleared her throat far too loudly, he knew his smoke had outstayed its welcome. Which was fine. He had to move anyway. Whether or not anything would come of these 'visitations', he was gripped by a terrible urgency to act sooner rather than later.

As his father had always said: *Know your enemy.*

That seemed like the logical place to start.

He flicked the cigarette out into the rain and looked over his shoulder at the boutique owner. She was standing behind a waist-high counter, arms folded over a mammoth bosom, small dark eyes peering at him over her half-rim glasses.

"Can you tell me how to get to the library?" he asked her.

On the outside of the counter, a small squat woman, the woman Timmy presumed had been the one worried about her journey home, muttered *American*, as if that explained everything, and the boutique owner nodded. She pointed at the far wall.

"Keep going this way then take a right and you'll see it at the end of the street. A large white building. You can't miss it."

Timmy thanked her and left them to their muttering.

* * *

He followed the boutique lady's directions and within minutes had reached the library, a tall but narrow glass-fronted building with a peaked roof upon which a weathervane groaned and turned its back on the wind. Beneath the apex of the roof a small black circle contained the figures 1609 over the words OLD MARKET HOUSE. Above the main entrance similarly styled letters read: PUBLIC LIBRARY.

In the foyer, a crudely handwritten sign pointed the discerning traveler up the stairs to the left, where the museum was located. *Books on the ground floor, bones on the first,* Agatha had said. Timmy ignored it and continued on through the double doors into the library proper. The rain had graduated to a deluge and hissed against the small mullioned windows at the back of the room.

An old woman with sharp features and a widow's peak greeted him with a nod as he approached her at a desk laden with books. Her spinsterish appearance suggested a woman genetically bred to be a librarian. A bronze nameplate on the desk told him her name was Ms. Ryan.

"I was wondering if you could help me," Timmy began, suddenly realizing he wasn't sure exactly what it was he was looking for.

"Well I'll certainly try," she said, her face shriveling up into a grimace as she sniffed at the air. It might have been a haughty attempt at establishing superiority or a nasal affliction, he wasn't sure which, and was, at that moment, far beyond caring.

"Uh yeah...I was hoping to find some history on the leather factory."

Ms. Ryan seemed amused by the request. "Really? Now why would an American boy be curious about the history of such a horrid place?"

"College thesis."

"Ah. I wouldn't have taken you to be old enough for college."

His patience flagged. "I skipped a grade. Or two."

"Hmm." She lifted one spindly arm and let her pointed chin rest on her fist. "Well far be it from me to get in the way of such an educational endeavor. What exactly was it you wanted to know about the place?"

He shrugged. "Just its history. You know...whether anything of note ever happened there."

She smiled, but only just. "Well you don't need to go trawling through oodles of microfiche files or Dungarvan history books for that. I'm also the museum curator here, not to mention, a history buff. It helps when tourists ask questions if you actually know what you're talking about. Ask me what you'd like to know and I'll do my best to help you."

Sure, okay, he thought grimly, *Let's start with anything that might have produced a couple of not-quite-dead folk and take it from there, shall we?*

When he said nothing for a moment, she drew his attention with a cluck of her tongue: "How about the name of your thesis for starters? That might help us get the ball rolling."

It came to him then and he almost cheered. "Superstition."

"Oh my," she replied, "Well then you've certainly picked the right place to study."

"Really?"

"Yes, but I suggest you get comfortable if you want to hear the sordid details. Why don't you come around to the staff desk. I assume you brought a pen and paper for notation?"

Think fast. "Um...no, I was going to photocopy whatever I found here so..."

She smiled and shook her head, as if sympathetic to the plight of the ignorant. "Ah well, I'm sure we can find you something to scribble on."

She indicated the small Formica table pushed against the wall behind her. Three foldout chairs sat around it amidst the carts heaped with books. Timmy carefully edged his way through the unstable looking towers and chose a seat with his back to the main area of the library. With considerable propriety, Ms. Ryan lowered herself into the chair by his left hand. She had brought a small notepad and a stubby red pencil he imagined wouldn't let him get his name down before giving up the ghost.

"Now, where shall we start? A bit of background I suppose."

Timmy poised the pencil, even though he had no intention of writing anything down. If she said anything helpful, he'd remember it.

"That place has been host to a lot of different things and it consists of more than one building. I'm not sure if you noticed that."

He told her he hadn't.

"Well, there are a cluster of buildings, hardly connected, but all satellites of the same moon if you'll allow me the dramatic comparison. The oldest part of it was Barry's Store, now abandoned. It was used to house famine victims in 1847 and part of it dates back to the sixteenth century. When electricity was introduced to the town in 1920, the electric company used the factory as their headquarters. There were rumors prior to that that the building had been used as lodging quarters for British soldiers during the Irish War of Independence, so they could monitor the activity of, and receive supplies from, the ships in the harbor, but no one knows for sure. Although a number of bodies were discovered in the warehouse during that time and their identities never released to the public, which of course got everybody whispering, especially the reporters."

He nodded, his interest probably more genuine than she knew.

"Once the Black and Tans—British soldiers of a most bloodthirsty and vicious nature—had been driven out of the south and indeed the country, the townspeople began to rebuild, depending on outside financiers and governmental assistance to aid them. In 1923, a man named Vincent Morrison from Kilmahon—that's up near Cork—invested huge sums of money in the town and it wasn't long before he had a cluster of pubs, boarding houses, warehouses and factories vying for space along the dock. One of them was your leather factory—after the electrical company moved their headquarters into town proper—and it became a prime source of income for the town. And what better place for it? As soon as the leather was made, all they had to do was wheel it out to a ship and ferry it anywhere in the world for sale. Those were better days, but not necessarily for Morrison.

"You have to remember these were poor times for the Irish. And people who prosper in poor times tend to draw the envy of the suffering. And that was the case with Morrison and his family. Some of the townspeople felt the businessman had the town in a stranglehold. They couldn't prosper unless they worked day and night in his factories and yet without him they would surely perish. They saw it as entrapment, which might have been a little extreme but not when you consider that the town had lived through British attempts at occupation and the sight of German U-boats patrolling the mouth of the harbor almost daily during World War One. It was a delicate time for the people; trust was a rare commodity and crime was rampant.

"Morrison's workers began to protest the working conditions. More than one man had died at the hands of the leather factory machinery and many complained of breathing problems due to the thick clots of dust that rose from the hides. They demanded more wages and frequently showed up at Morrison's house, often vandalizing the place in a misguided attempt to improve their lot.

"Morrison was a fair man, but he also had a family to think about, so he did the only thing he could think of. He sold his businesses and a year later, with the deal closed and the paperwork filed, he and his family hitched a ride on a boat returning to Dublin, where Morrison's brother lived. But they never made it."

Timmy sat forward, chair creaking. "What happened?"

She smiled. "There's where your superstition comes in. The boat was found abandoned just beyond the Cunnigar—that's the little arm of land that juts out past the harbor. The cargo was still present and accounted for, but the skipper, and Morrison and his family, were gone. A regular *Marie Celeste*. A search was conducted but no bodies were ever found. The ship was brought back into port so an investigation could be conducted. Shortly afterward, the harbor earned the nickname "The Haunted Harbor" because of apparent sightings of ghostly figures walking the dock. All nonsense of course."

Of course, Timmy thought, wondering what she'd think if he shared with her a ghost story of his own.

"But like every tragedy, it soon gets forgotten in place of far deadlier things. In this case the Second World War shifted the focus of the town back out onto the water and the variety of ships, both allied and enemy that monitored the incoming traffic to our little port. While Europe tore itself apart, Ireland continued its struggle for true independence from the British. The violence here at home took precedence over any kind of imagined spectral activity attributed to the town.

"Eventually the war ended and people once again tried to rebuild their lives, seeking employment where they mightn't have sought it before. Dungarvan boomed, both from tourism and its own shipping and harbor business. If anyone remembered the mysterious disappearance of Morrison and the superstitious ramblings of some nervous locals, it didn't prevent them from taking work at the leather factory. As a result, the town prospered even while newspapers continued to bring the people reports of nationwide fighting and political deadlocks."

Here she took a break to process the literary bounty carried by two teenage boys and a middle-aged woman. When she returned, she was silent for a moment, then, "Am I boring you yet?" she asked and Timmy shook his head.

"Not at all. This is just the kind of stuff I'm looking for."

"Okay, good. I won't be able to keep you much longer anyway. I have to close in twenty minutes for lunch."

"That's no problem. I really appreciate this."

"Yes, Dungarvan's past can be fiercely interesting if only people would stop to look over their shoulders every now and again. Now where was I?"

"The town was prospering."

"Yes, it was," she said slowly, then her eyes brightened as she found her mental bookmark. "Right. Superstition. I mentioned it had been all but forgotten, yes? Well, one night in 1955, something happened that would resurrect all the old ghosts for the townspeople.

"Apparently, a handful of men agreed to work the night shift at the leather factory at the request of their boss, a man by the name of Hannigan. The boss had, it seems, received word from the owner of the factory that their numbers were down. Not wanting to instigate the ire of his employer (factory foreman was a pretty good job back then), Hannigan decided to call in some of his best men to work like lunatics for three nights over the weekend. His men showed up that Friday evening after the day shift had ended, punched in and set about their work. The noise of the machines and the hissing of steam echoed across the harbor until late Saturday night, when inexplicably, the factory fell silent. People coming home from the pubs reported seeing the lights go out shortly afterward but figured the boys had either shut down early or had blown a fuse or something. At any rate, the testimony of a few drunks wouldn't have held much muster for the authorities.

"But no one had been drunk the following morning when Hannigan showed up to find the factory completely deserted. After breaking down the front man-door (he'd instructed the workers to lock the place from the inside to dissuade thieves and vagrants), he discovered the workers' caps and coats hung in the usual places, lunchboxes tucked away beneath them, unopened, the food inside uneaten. Understandably confused, and more than a little irritated (this was more to do with him keeping his cushy job than anything else), he searched the factory top to bottom. No one was there. He called the workers' homes. They hadn't come home. He stormed the pubs he knew they frequented. Nothing. They were gone, just as Morrison and his family had vanished from the boat twenty-odd years before. The subsequent police investigation turned up nothing unusual, though one young Garda—that's what we call our police, the Garda Siochana, or Guardians of the Peace; it'll be a nice little touch for you to throw into your thesis—found a series of chemically-treated and maggot-farmed hides scattered about on the second floor. In Hannigan's haste, he'd run right over them, but even when it was brought to his attention, he didn't think much of it. The trolleys used to transport hides from machine to machine were not always reliable and sometimes tipped over, he said, which could explain the mess."

Rain sprayed like pellets across the front windows. Timmy wasn't too eager to get back out there but knew he'd have to. Not everything Ms. Ryan said had struck him as important, but some of it had. It was clear, whether she believed it or not, that he'd been right about the factory. Something was in there, perhaps the restless remains of Morrison and his family. He didn't believe they had just disappeared, no more than the factory workers had. Something had taken them. The woman he'd seen on the beach could have been Morrison's wife, or daughter. It wasn't much, but it was more than he'd had before.

"So they were never found?" he asked.

"I'm afraid not, but of course there must have been a logical explanation. Some said the six men had agreed amongst themselves to leave town and start up new lives elsewhere, tired of their wives and their lives in Dungarvan. Far-fetched as that is, it wouldn't have been the first time someone decided to jump ship without telling anyone. Another theory was that the men had brought alcohol into work with them, knowing they would not be supervised. So they got blind drunk and danced along the harbor, perhaps dared each other to dive in and got caught in the currents. All speculation, never proved or disproved."

"And you still don't think there's anything more to it?"

She sighed and let her hands rest on her knees, back straight as a board. "Young man I have been in this town for almost seventy years and have never seen anything to lead me to believe that anything other than bad judgment, God's will and the evil of man are the governing forces here. People do foolish things and sometimes it costs them their lives. Blaming misfortune on ghosts and ghouls is simply a method of deflecting the focus from the true culprits. Responsibility is a thing of the past, sadly enough, and as long as there are fools and wicked men, there will always be superstition to help alleviate the magnitude of our own shortcomings as a supposed superior species."

"So nothing strange has happened at the factory since then?"

"Nothing of note, no."

Timmy stood and extended his hand. "I can't thank you enough for your time, Ms. Ryan. You've really given me a lot to think about."

She gave him a gracious smile and took his hand. Her skin was warm and supple. "You should stop by the museum some time. You'll see some excellent pictures of the town in its various stages. Perhaps I could copy some of them for you."

"I will. Thanks again."

"You're most welcome. Please be good enough to let me know the results won't you?"

"Results?"

"Of your thesis?"

"Oh yes, of course."

He rounded the main desk and started toward the door, then stopped as a thought occurred to him. "Ms. Ryan?"

"Yes?"

"That boat the Morrison's disappeared from? What kind of cargo were they carrying?"

"Hides, if I'm not mistaken. Tons of hides."

"Thanks."

"Don't mention it. And do watch out for those ghosts now, won't you?" she said with a sardonic grin.

"I'll do my best," he called back and plunged out into the rain.

CHAPTER TWELVE

He ran through the downpour somewhat more bolstered. All around him, people with umbrellas for heads crowded together, jostled and pushed their way to shelter. Those devoid of protection clustered under marquees and awnings, staring out at the sky with contemptuous eyes.

A check of his watch as he splashed through puddles and dodged slow-moving cars told him he'd only been talking with the librarian for a half an hour or so. He wondered if that had been ample time for his father to finish the tour of the factory. He doubted it and decided to head home. Besides, whatever waited inside the factory would hardly do anything while the workday was in full swing which gave Timmy time to speak with his father before he fully committed himself to working there.

And you think he'll believe you?

He had to take the chance that he would. There wasn't much Timmy could tell him yet because he didn't know enough. But unlike a child afraid to tell his parents about the monster under his bed, he had experience as proof of his abilities to sense things. His father had almost died that night at the pond back in Delaware. He'd seen the boy with the coat of turtles and what it did to Wayne Marshall. Timmy was sure his father had seen other things over the years but if so, he was keeping it to himself, but Timmy knew that no amount of denial or drinking could make him forget them. The knowledge that they existed, those phantoms that forever haunted the corner of the eye, was a form of haunting in itself.

His father would believe. He would have to, or all was lost. Because the more Timmy thought about it the more he was starting to feel as if everything that had happened thus far had been orchestrated by something. That everything he did was as he was supposed to in the eyes of a puppeteer. The thought made his skin crawl.

He ran on, toward the bridge, his eyes avoiding the heaving gray tide, and kept going, head down until he was on the opposite side of the Causeway, and standing panting at the gate to Agatha's house.

* * *

Thunder grumbled in the roiling sky as he let himself inside. The hallway was dark and still smelled faintly of last night's stew. As he flicked on the light and watched the thick shadows recede he heard a sound from the living room, a kind of stifled groan that made him stop and listen.

"Grandma?"

No reply.

He made his way into the room and stopped at the door. The curtains were open and hazy light limned the edges of the mantle, the room's sole chair and the pictures on the wall. The armchair had been pulled around to face the fireplace so that it's back was to him, but he could see a mass of silvery curls slowly rising and falling.

Agatha. Asleep.

He lingered a moment, wondering whether or not he should wake her. Part of this was genuine concern for her comfort, being asleep in such a rigid chair. Another, more selfish part of him, didn't like being the only one awake in the house.

She stirred, gasped, then her head tilted to the side and for one panicked moment, he wondered if something had happened to her, if perhaps she had just died right before him. She was old; it wasn't impossible.

But then he heard the rasp of her breathing, saw her shudder and he let out a slow sigh of relief. *Just leave her be.* His nerves were frayed. Until this was over, assuming it would ever be, the most innocent situations would seem sinister.

He eased out of the room, carefully closing the door and wincing at the click of the latch. Turned.

Agatha was standing in the hall.

Icy needles paraded up his back but the thought of a scream was all he was permitted. His voice was gone.

Suddenly the air thickened, became a sickly yellowish haze as if the house had filled with mustard gas. His grandmother moved her head forward in slow motion, her inquisitive expression smeared across a jaundiced face, blinking like someone awaking from a deep sleep. Panic clamored inside him. It was like watching an old home movie, or being inside one of the dusty pictures mounted over the mantel, staring out at the world through time-blemished glass. He raised his hands up before him, watched them obey far too slowly, the fingers weaving and dancing like seaweed in a current, the clotted air shifting reluctantly around them. Shadows oozed down the walls, apparently unhindered by this new and terrible slowdown; they moved as fast as his pulse and just as rhythmically. He could hear the steady thumping, reminding him he was still alive, not dead nor dreaming, while outside of him there was no sound but a distant hushing, like stage whispers.

Stage whispers.

The Curtain.

And they were calling his name.

Fear spread through him and he shook his head to deny it. The motion only caused the awful new world of dust and shadow to blur further. With exaggerated slowness he clambered for a way out, for release. It was the frantic struggle of the suffocating, though he could breathe quite normally. Agatha was reaching for him, her fingers splayed and drawing closer by degrees, mouth opening and closing soundlessly, a leprous mime in an amber world.

Cold consumed him and he turned, slowly, slowly, drawn by the awareness of someone else's presence.

The living room door was open and wobbling, snatching at shadows and releasing them. He wanted to look up, to see that he was beneath a golden tide with the surface within reach, but knew he'd only see ceiling. There was no salvation here, he realized with numb resignation. Only death. On this side of things, he was an insect, a moth in a killing jar and could beat his wings as hard and as much as he liked. In the end, this was their territory and their rules. He was either a guest, or a victim.

Inside the room, the chair had been pushed back from the fireplace and now faced the window. Aldous's window. And there was someone sitting in the chair, a figure composed of jittering shadow, decay and disease. Timmy was suddenly glad for the liquidity of the air here; he was in no hurry to meet his host.

"Come inside," it said in a voice that rattled Timmy's bones and made his head ache. That voice filled the world and became it, the air shimmering around the passage of the words as if they were bullets.

There was no choice but to obey. He started to turn to see if Agatha was still there but the effort was too much. His neck muscles crackled like burning leaves.

After what felt like hours Timmy made it across the room, the floor like tar sticking to the soles of his feet, grasping at his every step. The walls did a serpentine dance with the shadows. The huddled figure looked up at him, face veiled in darkness.

It was a woman.

And she was monstrous.

"Will you listen?" she asked in that thunderous voice.

"Yes," Timmy said, his own voice like a whisper of wind beneath a door.

"Will you heed?"

"Yes, Grandma." For that was who it was, albeit decayed and exuding malevolence, her pretty blue eyes gone, replaced by tiny cerulean sparks, her skin desiccated and sloughing off, slipping like empty white gloves from the shadowy mass of her face. Her fingers were bare bone, resting on a black clad lap and as she breathed, though he knew she had no need to, the room shuddered in time with it.

Not Grandma, he realized. *The Stage's version of Grandma.* What she would become when the soul left her. Dark understanding washed over him. These things behind the Curtain were shells, husks, what the soul left behind when it moved on. Lost, vile things, corrupt imitations of the living. His masters.

The woman in the chair was an amalgam of every childhood terror he'd ever had before The Turtle Boy stepped from the Stage and shattered his reality forever. She was a witch, a boogeyman, a child-snatcher, the pollution of innocence all jumbled up in a tattered black cloak. Her lips moved apart like a gaping wound, amusement curling one bruised corner into a smile as she basked in his repulsion.

Instinct tried to drag him out of there; the floor held him firm.

"You can see," she hissed, "You can see the Stages. What a magnificent curse to bear. But I imagine it should be kept interesting, when a man can claim entry to two theaters, yes?"

He did not know how to answer, did not want to understand whatever it was she was telling him.

"When a man can see so many Players, he should be filled with a particular kind of elation, yes? Perhaps even a feeling of superiority over his brethren?"

He was afraid to answer.

"But curtains get old and when the curtain comes down for good, there will be nothing left to hold us, do you understand?"

This time she did not wait for a response.

"You will recognize the revolution for what it is, won't you, dear boy?" She leaned forward, shadows slipping from the folds of her. Her rank breath emerged like eels from her mouth and writhed in the gelatinous air, and he was suddenly struck with the awful thought that she was breathing only to mock him, that this parody of a human was just that—a foul dead thing fulfilling its role as 'Player' perfectly, mocking him by imitating the pitiful needs of its living counterpart.

"And the revolution," she said, with a horrendous attempt at a smile, "will recognize *you*."

Revolution?

She turned her head with the sound of wet ropes tightening. This time when she smiled her lower lip split like a rotten fruit. The resultant zipping sound brought more thoughts of running to Timmy's mind. "You are not as familiar with your own as you should be. They are not what you think," she said, her words cutting swaths through the haze. "And I will show you why."

The room and everything it contained froze. Then a burst of light shredded the shadows, inspiring a scream Timmy couldn't release. The rippling walls stilled again just as quickly, colors emerging, the shadows withdrawing and Timmy watched, stunned, as the air thinned and the real world living room grew around him once more. Polished wood and unblemished paint rose from beneath the scabrous cauls; picture frames cast off their cloaks. The miasmic stench of death dissipated, shredded by the fall of dust motes.

Diffused light crept through the curtains. It appeared the room had returned to normal.

And so had Agatha.

Almost.

"What...?" he began, surprised to find he could hear himself clearly.

The woman, no longer old, did not acknowledge his presence, and he was reminded briefly of that night back in Delaware when he had found himself standing in another time, another place watching a faceless man kill an innocent boy on the banks of Myers Pond. The scene that still haunted his dreams. A chapter of his life that had changed it forever.

And now it was happening again.

Before him was a different Agatha, a far younger woman, tanned and vibrant. The wrinkles were gone, her skin like ivory, blonde hair cut into a sensible bob, small pearls punctuating her ears and cinched around her pale, slender throat. The pictures Timmy had seen had not done her justice.

She was writing a letter, her brow furrowed in concentration. Every now and then, she raised her head and stared out the window, toward the dock, where she would appear to find her thoughts and write them down. During one of these instances Timmy followed her gaze and saw a cluster of old-fashioned masts lined like crucifixes along the dock. Old schooners were berthed in crowds, men milling about them as the sun cast broken glass across the waves. The last time he'd seen it look that way, it had been in black and white and locked in a frame.

A knock on the door brought his focus back to the room. Agatha looked up, her face impassive. "Yes?"

The door opened and a stunning woman with long brown tresses and hazel eyes slipped into the room. She wore a light blue dress, tastefully cut to give only the faintest hint of cleavage. Her beauty was marred only slightly by the uneasy expression she wore.

"Good morning Agatha, Father Kerrigan said you were looking for me. He made it sound urgent. I hope nothing's wrong."

A flicker of a smile passed over Agatha's face. "You know how holy men are, Lucy. If it's nothing to do with them or the church they think it's urgent. Please come in. I know you're a…busy woman…so I won't keep you long."

Timmy detected the sarcasm in his grandmother's voice and noticed her guest had too.

Lucy nodded and looked around for a chair but there was only the one Agatha occupied, so she remained standing.

"What was it you wanted?"

Agatha continued to write, ignoring her and Timmy watched, sympathizing with the woman's awkwardness as she studied the room, her gaze finally settling on a large gilt-edged mirror hanging over the fireplace. She studied herself, primped her hair, ceasing only when Agatha looked at her in amusement.

"You look fine, Lucy."

Lucy smiled. It was empty of humor. "I wasn't aware you were home from your travels yet," she said, trying to be nonchalant. "It must be quite a life, getting to see all those sights the rest of us only glimpse in pictures. I'd love to see the world someday."

"Would you?"

"I've never been farther than England myself, and that was for a funeral. These days it's hard to pay the bills, let alone travel the world on the kind of wages we're getting. Tell me…where have you been this time? You certainly have a good color wherever it was."

"Peru, actually. I went to see the Temples of the Sun and Moon in Trujillo."

"Oh. Sounds nice," Lucy said, shifting her stance. "Temples."

"Only if you're interested in that sort of thing. I think the heat was too much for me on this occasion, though. Such awful heat, and I won't even begin to tell you about some of the insects I encountered. They'd make your hair stand on end." She sighed. "I can't say I enjoyed my trip as much as some of the others. I expect it's because I'm getting older. In fact, Peru may actually be my last port of call. It's high time I settled down, don't you think?"

"Oh, I don't know. If I had the opportunity to do what you do, I'd keep at it until there was nothing left to see."

"I suppose, but on the other hand, I'd hate to feel like I'm neglecting my post here at home, letting poor Aldous fend for himself. It would kill me to come home only to find he'd grown tired of waiting and replaced me!"

"I'm sure that would never happen."

"Are you?"

Lucy smiled, a thin nervous smile. "Yes. He loves you."

"And how would you know that, Lucy? Declarations of love for an absentee wife hardly passes as acceptable pillow talk these days."

Lucy's smile vanished. "What?"

"Small town talk has been the downfall of more important people than you, dear."

Lucy paled. "I don't know what you're talking about."

Agatha sat back, arms resting on the chair, the pen tumbling over her fingers like a trickster's coin. "Don't you?"

"No."

"Mrs. Connor at The Moorings Inn is an old friend of mine."

"So?" But Lucy looked snared, caught in a lie that was almost certain to bite her.

"So she had the most interesting tale to tell about a man I might know and the harlot he brought with him for a night of rambunctious behavior and tawdry pleasures."

"I'm no harlot," Lucy sneered.

Agatha smiled. "Who said I was talking about you?"

"This is ridiculous, Agatha. I don't know what kind of fever brought this on but I'd rather not have to listen to it, if it's all the same to you."

"And I would rather you stayed where you are and shut your bloody mouth while I'm talking," said Agatha, taking the pen and a piece of paper and rising from the chair. Lucy was stunned into silence. "You see, I've had plenty of time to think since learning about your escapades, and I have to tell you my first instinct was to get some of those thugs from the dock to pay you a little visit, maybe put the fear of God into you by demonstrating what less considerate males will do when presented with a prime piece of skirt like you. And then I thought: too messy. The repercussions would almost certainly be worse for me than you. I even considered murder. Can you believe that? I've never hurt anyone in my life and here I was fantasizing about slitting your throat while you slept. Awful thoughts, but behavior such as yours can inspire such uncharacteristic fantasies in the meekest of people."

She held up the letter.

"In the end, I opted for a calmer, less violent alternative and put my creative energy into writing a letter. To your husband, who I believe is in Dublin fighting for our freedom right now, yes?"

Lucy took a step forward, the muscle in her jaw twitching. "How *dare* you!"

Agatha scoffed. "How dare I? Oh I think I'm perfectly entitled to 'dare' as much as I please. A more educated woman than you might have considered the benefits of discretion. After all, I would have thought it of paramount importance to you that your illicit trysts went undiscovered; who needs that kind of trouble? But not only did you conduct your affair with my husband in broad daylight, you *flaunted* it. Almost as if you wanted me to find out. Why was that?"

"I don't know what you're talking about, you mad bitch. All that sun must have boiled your brains."

If Agatha was offended by the slight, she didn't show it.

"Today," she continued, "I kissed my husband on the cheek before he went to work, and let me tell you how hard it was to resist the temptation to confront him—"

"He would have slapped you in the mouth," Lucy interrupted, with visible glee.

Agatha ignored her. "Then I had breakfast and thought this over. Naturally I was furious, heartbroken, tormented by feelings of betrayal etcetera, etcetera, but if I've learned one thing in all my years of traveling, it's that time wasting is the fastest way to the grave. So, rather than play the role of spurned lover and moon about the house pondering the futility of my life, or engineering methods of dispatching you I'd never have the courage to set in motion, I decided instead to come in here, Aldous's favorite room and write a letter to Phillip Conlon of the Irish Republican Army. Your husband. I imagine he must get bored of the same old recycled periodical tripe, so something new to read—a letter from home—would be appreciated, don't you think? Even if the address is not yours and the content somewhat disturbing. But I do think it's only fair that a man fighting for the freedom of our fair nation should be given a little freedom of his own, even if it comes in the form of separation from his whore of a wife."

"What your mouth," Lucy said, fists clenched. "You have no right to talk to me like that. I'll go to the Guards and tell them what you're doing."

Agatha laughed. "Will you? And what will you say? That the wife of the man you're having an affair with is harassing you? They'd laugh at you, pat you on the head and send you on your way. If that's what you'd like to do though, I ask only that I can come along to witness it. There's not nearly enough comedy in my life these days."

"What do you want from me?"

"Very simple. I'm not going to harm you or spread the word all over town that you're a slut—assuming that word hasn't already done the rounds. Instead I'm going to ask you to write a letter of your own."

Lucy glared, hands trembling. "To whom?"

"To my husband of course, from you. Finishing it. Either you write your letter or mine goes out in this evening's mail. A proposition simple enough for even someone like you to understand."

Lucy took another step closer. They were now little more than arm's length from each other.

"Let me tell you something. Someone like *me* turned out to be everything you're not. Do you think for one second Aldous would have ended up in my bed if someone like *you* had what it took to make him happy? You're a married woman Agatha and you should know your place. Instead, you take off trouncing around the world like some kind of self-proclaimed pioneer. You should have been here, cooking for him, cleaning for him, making sure he was taken care of after breaking his back working all hours of the day. But you weren't and when he needed someone, *I* was there. I looked after him. I gave him everything you weren't here to give him, and he loved me for it. Still loves me. So while I feel a little sorry for you having to find out you're a worthless wife, I'm not going to stand here and feel guilty about you losing a husband to a better woman."

Agatha smiled, but for the first time there was a trace of uncertainty to it. "I haven't lost him. A man is allowed a lapse in taste and judgment when he's desperate." She looked Lucy up and down. "Which he obviously was."

"You'd be surprised how close a man can get to someone who genuinely cares for him. If you ask him, he'll tell you."

"What are you talking about?"

"Why don't you *talk* to your husband for a change? I can tell you he had plenty to say on the subject while you were off working on your tan and poking around crusty old ruins."

With that, she lurched forward, hand outstretched, to take the letter from Agatha's hand. Agatha stepped back, her eyes wide with sudden fury.

"Give me the letter," Lucy said between clenched teeth. "Nothing you can do now will change anything anyway. So you send the letter. So what? Do you think I care about Phillip anymore? He's just like you, spending all of his time away and expecting me to be waiting with open arms when he gets back. Loneliness is a powerful emotion Agatha and it can crush the noblest of causes in a heartbeat. So to hell with you and your threats."

"If you don't care, then why do you want the letter?" Agatha's voice had lost some of its resolve. It was clear her plan was begin to fragment. Timmy stood there, by the window, casting no shadow and lost in the scene, everything limned with amber light as if unsure on which plane the scene belonged. He could sense what was coming—it hung in the air like a veil—but something, some barrier in his imagination, told him he was imagining it, that it would turn out all right.

Then why are you seeing it?

Lucy seemed to have stolen Agatha's composure. She stood proud and smiling bitterly, her words more forceful than before, while Agatha seemed to almost be retracting, drawing into herself to escape the thought of losing everything.

"If my husband has to find out how I get my thrills," Lucy said. "It won't be from a posturing bitch like you." She lunged again but this time Agatha took a step back and swung her hand around in an arc as if to slap Lucy in the face. "NO!"

And that's all it would have been had she not still been holding the pen.

The air froze, dust motes seized mid-fall. The light flooding through the windows seemed crooked, fading and Timmy felt the breath sucked from his lungs. *It can't have happened like this. It has to be trick*, he thought, desperate to believe it, but another part of him answered, *why? They never tricked you before*. And as horrible as that was to accept, it was the truth. No matter how hideous or unimaginable the visions had been in the past, they'd always proved to be reflections of a shadowed past.

Horrified, he watched Lucy fall sideways with a strangled gasp, her hands trying to fly to her face even as she collided with the arm of the chair, a spurt of blood painting a crooked Z on the fabric. She slumped to the carpet, moaning. Agatha loomed over her, hair wild, breath wheezing from her mouth. It was as if she'd been drugged. Even from halfway across the room, Timmy could see the red in her eyes—the color of rage.

"You see?" she said in a high-pitched voice. "You see what happens? See what you made me do!"

Without warning, another scene superimposed itself over the nightmare in the room: hunched-over trees growing from the walls, the carpet shimmering as a breeze passed over the surface of the pond it had suddenly become, tall grass brushing against Timmy's ankles, and a man, faceless and wailing as he bent over the prostrate body of a boy. "Look what you did. You're bleeding. You'll tell. You tried to run away and *look what you did!*"

It's always the same, Timmy realized, as the image began to fade back into the walls, the hidden projector giving up the ghost. *People die and their killers blame the victims.* He'd been holding his breath long enough to make his lungs hurt and exhaled slowly, tried to relax, to reassure himself that this was the past, that it had already happened and there was nothing he could have done to prevent it. But still...the wild-eyed woman now turning the fallen Lucy over on her back was his grandmother. A woman he had thought of as innocent, harmless.

"You silly, silly woman," Agatha said, grimacing at the sight of the pen jutting from below Lucy's cheekbone. It had driven deep enough so that Timmy could see it inside the woman's mouth and heard it clicking against her teeth. Lucy tried to speak, her hands raised to ward off further violence. Timmy had to restrain himself from rushing to help her. He knew it would be useless. Whenever he was allowed these images, it was for no other reason than to display for him the sins of murderers, a replayed scene from a past that could not be changed by the viewer.

His grandmother was a murderer.

After a moment in which Agatha's expression changed from disgust to panic to hate until finally settling on a mixture of all three, she reached down and grabbed Lucy's wrists.

Lucy choked, coughed a gout of blood all over her chin.

Agatha dragged her up into a standing position. "Mind my carpet."

"…gatha…hlees…hlees…gatha…hall octor…*hlees*," Lucy pleaded, her hands gesturing feebly in the air. Her mouth continued to bleed, staining her teeth red and pouring down the front of her dress. The wound was bleeding copiously, but only inside her mouth. The outside wound had folded in around the shaft of the pen.

Agatha dragged her to the mirror, propped the woman up so that she was leaning against the mantel and grabbed a handful of her hair. "*Look*," she raged, raising the woman's wounded face to the glass. "*Look at what you've done to yourself!* Do you think he'll find you pretty *now*? Do you? Do you think my bed will be cold for long with you looking like *this*?"

Lucy's eyes started to close, her consciousness ebbing away. Her skin was marble white, except where the blood had smeared her chin and throat. She weaved, Agatha struggling to keep her upright.

"Answer me!"

Lucy's eyelids flickered. "H'uvs ee," she murmured, the pen still sticking out of her cheek, the glass tube crossing under her front teeth.

"*What?*" Agatha seemed lost in madness. "*What did you say?*"

Lucy didn't answer, but then Agatha shook her hard and she moaned. "Uvs me," she whispered.

He loves me.

The resultant silence was ugly, the air sharp now and soaked with the promise of violence. Timmy told himself to look away, as he always willed himself before the climax of a scene in which an innocent was murdered, but found he couldn't stop watching. Watching, as Agatha shrieked and drove Lucy's head forward into the mirror, again and again and again until the glass was gone and the frame itself began to crack.

CHAPTER THIRTEEN

"Should have listened. Should have listened to me," Agatha muttered.

Fearing what might occur if she tried to pass through him, Timmy stepped away from the window as his wild-eyed grandmother crossed the room in three strides, gave a frantic look outside, and tugged the curtains closed. Darkness swept into the room and lingered, retaining the correct properties of shunned light only for a moment before everything changed again. The walls began to waver and Agatha's retreating form was torn asunder and claimed by the shadows like a flock of birds exploding from their roosts. In the chair, a pale form began to surface, a moon-white face emerging from the dark. Ragged breathing filled the air.

"Did you see?" the withered Agatha asked.

He nodded. It felt like moving his head through quicksand.

"Then go back into *life* knowing."

"Is that supposed to help?" He hadn't meant it as a challenge but as his words burrowed through the air toward her, he realized that's how they had sounded.

"Nothing helps," she thrummed, the blue sparks of her eyes boring through him. "Not here. Not out there. It all ends the same. But someone has already torn doorways into your world. Doorways where there shouldn't be any. Renegades. And a war will come. People like you, of which there are many, can sense those doors. Do what you can while you can. Soon, it won't matter."

He dared move closer, reached out a hand to touch her, even as every muscle in his body protested. He needed to see if they had bodies in here, just as he seemed to have abandoned his and become a ghost in their domain.

"I don't understand."

"You will."

His fingers brushed skin that sank beneath his touch. He recoiled and light flooded the room. The chair was empty but for a scattering of dust, a mangled whisper caught between worlds drifting away from him.

After a moment spared to regain his breath, he realized he was not alone and spun around, startling his grandmother, Agatha, the *real*

Agatha, as she was outside of other realms and visions. She was standing at the window, daylight making a silhouette of her frail body. "My God," she said. "Timmy, are you all right? What happened?"

The Curtain had fallen back and left him standing in 'life'—as the Agatha-thing had called it with marked derision. He considered celebrating his return until he realized he still had more questions than answers, and now a terrifying reality to face.

"Timmy?" She came to him, concerned.

"Stay away from me."

"What?"

"I know."

"You know what?"

"About you. About Lucy."

She smiled crookedly. "Lucy? Lucy who?"

"The woman you murdered years ago. You stabbed her in the face with a pen."

She jerked away from him as if he'd caught fire. "Timmy, you...you were in some kind of a daze...just standing there. Exhaustion will—"

He cut her off. "I *saw* it."

"Well then you've been imagining things." She flapped her hands. "For God's sake, *listen* to yourself."

He felt sick, as if everything inside him was going to come bursting out in a black torrent. He despised himself at that moment, despised himself for knowing what she had done, for being *able* to know it. "No," he told her. "*You* listen to *me*."

"Timmy, please..."

"She was sleeping with Grandpa. You found out and killed her. I know you didn't mean it—"

"Stop it." She was trembling so violently her necklace jingled.

"Gr—" He'd been about to call her Grandma but knew he'd never be able to use such a casual term with her ever again. "Agatha, I was there."

"You were where?"

"In this room. You were much younger. You...you threatened to tell her husband—Phillip Conlon—unless she wrote to Aldous breaking it off."

Agatha said nothing, but some of the confusion had fled her eyes.

Timmy didn't like what he saw in its place.

"Get out," she said, the shake in her voice not enough to hide the anger. "Get out of my house."

For the first time in his life, he was afraid of her. "If that's what you want."

"It is."

"But if I leave I'm going to Dad and telling him what I know."

She smirked. It made her look more like the woman who'd killed Lucy Conlon than the one who'd cried when she'd seen him at the airport.

"So tell him. He won't believe you."

"He knows what I've seen in the past. He won't want to believe me but he'll know I'm not lying."

It was as if someone had spun a dial in the old woman and for a moment he wasn't sure whether or not it was genuine. She shrank before him, her face collapsing into a grimace, tears welling in her eyes. The rage it seemed, had gone.

"Oh God. But..." She gestured uselessly. "*How* do you know?"

He wasn't sure exactly how much Agatha Quinn knew about his past, whether or not his parents had confided in her such an implausible secret. And if they had, then why would she ask them to come here? Surely she must have known what it would mean, what it meant now. "I think you already know that," he said and knew immediately by the way the helpless old lady act vanished that he was right.

"I'm not sure I believed it," she said. "But here you are airing my dirty laundry."

"What did you do with her body?" Timmy asked, maintaining a safe distance from her. The look on her face was frightening.

"The harbor," she said after a moment. "I dumped her in the harbor."

CHAPTER FOURTEEN

She wept, but Timmy felt nothing for her, couldn't be sure it wasn't just more play-acting to draw his sympathy. Although the images of Agatha as kind old woman and murderer were incongruous ones, they were still snapshots of the same person. He had to remind himself, as he watched her body shuddering sobs out of her, that knowing what she'd done had made him an instant liability and though she was old, the fire he'd seen in her eyes warned him that he shouldn't underestimate her.

"How did you get the body to the harbor without being seen?"

"I didn't do it alone."

"Who helped you?"

She wiped her nose with a tissue. "I've seen her you know. Felt her around me. Now that you've seen her, will it stop?"

"Who helped you?" Timmy said firmly, ignoring her.

She nodded up at the grim portrait of her husband. "He did."

"What? Why? If what Lucy said about him not loving you was true, why did he help you? Why not just turn you in and be done with you forever?"

"He didn't love her. She was a piece of trash, a worthless low-life bitch, and now she's haunting me. Ha! I thought at first it might be Aldous…"

"Agatha."

"…Coming back to make the rest of my life miserable. But no. It was her."

"*Agatha.*"

"What did you see, Timmy? Did you speak to her?"

He sighed. "I saw you kill her. That's it. Now answer the question."

"I'm so glad you're here, Timmy," she said and for an instant, he believed her.

"You talked my father into bringing me with him because he told you about what happened at home with all those people, all those *dead* people, right?"

She looked away, nodded.

"I think you wanted to see if I could protect you against Lucy with my Amazing Powers of Control over Dead Things. Which, by the way, is bullshit. Lucy has come back for you and I'm not sure I can do anything to stop that, just like I do nothing but *see* these things when they need me to. That's what you don't understand, what nobody ever understands—I draw the dead like a magnet, I see them, but I can't get rid of them. *They* use *me*. Just like you did."

"It's not like that."

"Oh no, then tell me what I'm missing, and, while you're at it, tell me why I shouldn't hate you for uprooting my life, dragging me here to face *your* sins for you?"

"You needed to get away. They said you needed to get away. I didn't know it was going to be the same here. I only hoped that your presence would be enough to chase her away. I'm sorry." She brought her hands to her face.

"You need to tell me," Timmy said, "why Aldous helped you when you'd killed a woman he loved."

Agatha looked up, glared. "I already told you, he *didn't* love her. Don't you dare say that."

And there it was again, the murderess come to visit. Timmy waited for the rage to fade from her. It did, but in dying it took with it any sympathy he might still have retained for the woman. *Good things seldom change*, she'd said when they arrived in Dungarvan. It was apparent now that bad things didn't either.

"Why did he help you?"

"He had to," she said, her voice even now, though her eyes were still wet. "He didn't have a choice."

"Why?"

She smiled grimly. "I threatened to turn him in."

"Turn him in?"

She nodded. "For his part in the disappearance of that family."

"What family?" Something cold twisted in his belly.

"The Morrison family."

"Everyone thought it was a big mysterious thing. Talked about ghosts and curses and all manner of nonsense. But it wasn't mysterious at all. It was cold-blooded murder, that's what it was. Morrison was a businessman, he'd been trying to leave town with his family, to get away from an increasingly hostile town. There had been death threats and vandalism. Someone even poisoned the family cat. They couldn't walk the streets without fear of attack. So Morrison hired a boat. As soon as they got out a safe distance from the harbor, the skipper, John Lehane, cut the engines and waited, feeding the family some excuse about water in the engine. Aldous had been paid a considerable sum of money to bring two IRA men out to stop Morrison's departure. Apparently Morrison had been helping to finance the British effort in Dungarvan because of a belief that the economy would improve under sovereign rule. When it became clear a lot of people would have to die first, Morrison tried to sever his ties with the organization. He might have succeeded too had not one of them been captured and interrogated. Among the names the man gave up was Morrison's. His death warrant was signed immediately. Aldous brought the IRA men alongside Lehane's ship and waited while they murdered Morrison and his family."

Timmy closed his eyes. "What did they do with the bodies?"

"They bound them up in some of the hides Lehane had as cargo and transferred them onto Aldous's boat. Lehane had been paid enough to get out of Dungarvan in a hurry and no one ever saw him again. Aldous helped the IRA men stash the bodies."

"Where?"

"Why do you care?"

"Goddamn it, *where?*"

"In the leather factory," she told him. "They left them wrapped in the hides and dumped them into barrels full of chemicals. The acid and the maggots took care of the rest."

Terror crawled up the nape of Timmy's neck. He glanced at his watch. His father had been gone for over two hours.

"No they didn't," he said and hurried into the hall. Frantic, all he could think about was the common denominator that linked the dead he'd encountered: Darryl Gaines, Harlan Knox, Danny Richards, Wayne Marshall, the woman in the harbor, the hanging man, the family…all of them had come back for revenge. But assuming the IRA men were dead and buried, and with Aldous already in the grave, what had the Morrison family come back for?

His mouth went dry as an awful thought occurred to him.

Aldous had cheated them and died before they could reach him. Maybe they were willing to settle for his son.

CHAPTER FIFTEEN

"Wait!"

Timmy paused at the gate, the sky the color of elephant hide, rain pouring down in a torrent. Lightning illuminated the cracks in the Heavens as he turned, already soaked, to look at Agatha standing in the doorway.

"I'll drive you. You shouldn't be out in this weather."

He almost laughed at that. Framed by the hallway light, she looked so small and frightened he wanted to pity her. Instead he turned away.

"Timmy, please! This isn't how I meant for things to happen."

Again he paused, angry with himself for doing so. "You say that like you had some kind of control over it."

"No. I didn't, but I never meant for you to see what I did. Never meant to drag you so deep into it."

"Yeah well..."

"Let me drive you. I don't want to be here alone. I don't know why she didn't come for me before now but..."

"She didn't because she needed *me!*" he shouted. "Just like they all do. They can float around and spook and scare the shit out of you all they like but until I show up, they can't come out from behind the Curtain. Don't ask me why and frankly, it doesn't matter. The fact is, they're here because of people like you and the bewildering penchant for murder that seems to run in my goddamn family!"

He had of course been referring to Agatha, and Aldous's complicity in the deaths of the Morrison family, and yet something nagged at the edge of his mind, like a muttered word he had to strain to hear. He dismissed it quickly before he lost his focus and because he wasn't entirely sure he wanted to know where it might lead.

"Are you coming or not?"

She didn't fetch a coat or close the door, just hurried across the path toward him. He opened the gate and let her precede him to the ugly yellow Volkswagen.

* * *

"It shouldn't have turned out like this," she said once they were inside the car, her knuckles white on the steering wheel. "I'm sorry. Truly I am. The way your father made it sound...If the past had only stayed in the past..." She trailed off, sighed heavily. "I'm sorry. You don't understand what it's been like."

A red traffic light smeared itself across the windshield. Timmy checked the intersection then told her, "Run it."

"What?"

"Run the light, there's no one around to see it."

"But—"

"For Chrissakes just *do* it!"

She jumped, startled and stamped down on the accelerator. Rain sluiced across the hood as the car bucked and whined, threatened to skid out until his grandmother yelped and wrenched it back under control. The Volkswagen tore through the light and onto the Causeway.

"I thought you could help me." She spoke in a quiet voice. "I thought you could make her go away just like you did that boy in the pond when you were a kid."

He scoffed. "I didn't make him go away. I helped him come back and that got people killed. Perhaps if you'd bothered asking me instead of assuming I could make your mistakes disappear I could have told you that."

"Timmy—"

"He was the first. I never thought there'd be more. If I had I might never have bothered saving myself from the pond."

"Don't say that." He ignored her.

"My best friend Pete Marshall and I found him down at Myers Pond. His name was Darryl Gaines. At the time we thought he was just some strange homeless kid, hanging around looking for somewhere to sleep. Or to hide. But we found out the hard way that he wasn't. He could control turtles. *Use* them. Maybe because they'd fed on him and parts of him were still inside them. He'd come back to get the man who'd put him there years before, a neighbor of mine. But in doing so, people got hurt. Innocent people. It almost got my father and me killed too." He turned to look at her, a bitter smile on his face. "*That's* what you wanted me to set in motion."

He looked out the window at the heaving gray mass of the sea beyond the chain-link fence. The sidewalks were deserted; there were few cars on the road save those parked alongside the curbs. In the harbor, bells on masts clanked loud enough to be heard over the grinding of the car's engine. The boats tipped their respect to one another as the sky above darkened further. Rain lashed down, rendering the windshield wipers ineffective.

"This is awful," Agatha moaned and Timmy couldn't tell whether she was referring to her own situation or the visibility.

A flash of lightning and a lithe figure slinked away from the harbor wall to his left, dark hair trailing after her. *Lucy*. Now she had a name. He glanced at Agatha to see if she had noticed, but her eyes were narrowed as she struggled to make out the road. He looked back, thought he saw the woman loping toward the tide, then vanishing into the angry surf, but couldn't be sure.

"If anything happens to Paul..." Agatha said, shaking her head.

"It won't," he replied firmly, and believed it. Had to. He rolled down the passenger side window and rain spat in his face. Squinting, he tried to make out the monolithic bulk of the leather factory squatting on the dock. He fancied he saw lights in some of the windows.

Good, he thought. He couldn't shake the image Ms. Ryan had given him of the factory shrouded in darkness. *People coming home from the pubs reported seeing the lights go out.* For Timmy, as long as there were lights, there was hope that he wasn't too late, that the Morrison family hadn't risen again to take the son of the man who'd helped see them to their graves and who had, unwittingly, walked straight into their lair. Or more appropriately: their *haunt*. That his father hadn't yet become another in a series of mysterious disappearances. But of course, they were no longer mysterious to Timmy. He believed those six men who'd vanished from the factory were now wandering behind the Curtain somewhere, milling around the Stage waiting for their chance to come back.

The Volkswagen rumbled over the humpbacked bridge and turned left, down to the dock.

Despite the rain and the rapidly darkening evening, Timmy found it odd that there was no one around. The dock was an industrial area—where were the workers, the fishermen, the people rushing to and from their jobs?

Agatha pulled the car to a halt close to the entrance to the factory, but kept the engine running.

Timmy cracked open his door, then looked back at her. "What are you going to do?"

"I'll wait," she said, still staring out through the windshield. He was about to leave her when a faint scraping sound drew his attention back inside the car. It was then he saw that she was not looking out at the storm at all, but at the crack in the lower left hand corner of the windshield.

Timmy watched, heart thudding as the crack grew longer and longer still, zigzagging its way toward Agatha's side as if someone unseen was using a glasscutter to split the windshield.

"Go," she said tonelessly.

And after a moment's hesitation, he did.

CHAPTER SIXTEEN

Timmy didn't look back. What he'd told Agatha about his 'abilities' hadn't been a lie. Nothing so far had given him any indication that his role in these situations was as anything other than a battery, the missing part of the equation necessary for the dead to pass from their dank, twisted waiting room into our world. And yet every answer left him with more questions. Such as: If those things were dead, or shades of them, then how was Agatha behind the Curtain? Did everyone have dark versions of themselves?

He figured he'd find out sooner or later. Prayed he wouldn't.

As he opened the door to the factory, he was relieved to hear the reassuring hum and clatter of machinery. The noxious odor he had smelled earlier rolled across the floor to greet him. When the lights flickered he restrained himself from looking up to see if their shadows were moving in synch.

"Dad!"

In the thick waist-high fog skulking about the floor, the now familiar sight of pale-faced apron-clad workers emerged, following stacks of opaque and blue-veined hides. The skins dripped milky liquid and exuded a stench far fouler than the wretched stink already permeating the place.

"Hey!" Timmy called, moving further into the factory. A ramshackle shed of corrugated iron he assumed served as an office of some sort stood to his right. Yellow light leaked out from beneath. He tapped a knuckle on the door. "Mr. Meehan?"

There was no reply. He nudged the door and it swung inward, revealing a cramped office overflowing with stacks of paperwork, old magazines, a small foldout chair and a radio. A black and white picture of a topless model had been tacked to the far wall. There was no one here.

Back outside, he watched the silent workers going about their business.

Some of these machines are vicious. Like the one your father will be using. It's called a slokum staker. Of course, if his father was trying out the machine, chances were he wouldn't have heard anyone hailing him. As Timmy walked into the thickest of the fog, the feeling of being watched grew stronger, until the hair on his neck prickled. One of the men swished past, almost colliding with him, the fog swirling in his wake. And yet he did not acknowledge Timmy's presence. Another trundled a trolley laden with hides toward the spinning drums, his face contorted with effort. Timmy moved among them, almost gagging at the smell. Still another swept by, his somber passage announced by the clanging of a steel bar against the pipes on the wall. Confused, Timmy turned to watch him and noticed after only a moment that ahead of him the floor was darker and tumbling, moving, squeaking.

He's driving out the rats.

Shuddering, Timmy used the support poles along the center of the work floor as a guide and slowly made his way toward the far end of the factory, grimacing when his feet came down on something that squelched and gave way. The coiling fog seemed to stick to his skin, trailing behind him as he moved and the deeper he went, the more he felt the presence of something enormous in the factory with him.

Through the billowing clouds he made out a set of crude wooden steps leading up to the second floor. Relieved to escape the fog and whatever it might be hiding, he bolted for the stairs. The rise was short and when he emerged on the second level, he found himself in a room half the size of the one below, one side open with a balcony overlooking the factory floor, a row of mullioned windows on the opposite side.

He was relieved there was no rope lashed to the windowsill. No creaking. And no dead men asking to be cut down.

A single man occupied this room. Even with his back turned Timmy recognized his father. He was shuddering, the muscles in his arms tensed as he fought with the chattering blade of the ungainly machine.

"Dad!"

The machine crackled then recommenced its assault on the leather splayed across the surface. As instructed his father had one corner of the hide pinned to the machine with his thigh so it couldn't pull it out of his hands. Fine black dust rose from the material and clouded the air in front of his face like a vicious army of gnats. The machine blade rose and fell, quickly snapping closed to chomp on the skin and Timmy winced every time the jaws clamped shut. It looked a little too much like a guillotine for his liking. One slip, one wrong move, one distraction could mean disaster so he quit trying to get his father's attention and waited instead. For now, he was relieved to find his father unharmed.

Finally, Paul shut off the machine and the rat-tat-tat dwindled to a solitary bark, then nothing. The room was quiet.

"Damn thing," his father said, brushing dark dust from his arms. When he turned around, he looked like Al Jolson in blackface, his surprise at seeing Timmy only adding to the effect. At any other time it might have been funny.

"Dad..."

"Timmy...what are you doing here?"

"We have to go."

"Go where?" He rubbed his hands together; dust rained down on the floor.

In his panic Timmy hadn't considered how much there was to explain. There was no time to do it now.

"We have to get out of here."

"What?" The rubbing stopped. His father's eyes were like chalk circles on a blackboard. He swallowed.

"There's a lot we need to talk about but *please God*, don't think I'm doing this to get you to bring me home. I'm not. This is just like Darryl Gaines and all the others but much, much worse. Grandma's involved too. I'll explain it all later but right now we need to get as far away from here as we can before..."

"Before what?"

"Before whatever's here tries to kill us."

He stood silently, a dirt-caked figure, his eyes radiating the kind of confusion Timmy recognized immediately.

"Dad...I swear to you, this is not a joke. Something's here and I know it's a lot to take in but you were there at the pond that night. You saw what happened. I'm asking you to trust me now, to believe me. If I'm wrong you can kick my ass. But just trust me for now. Please." He was alarmed to find himself on the verge of tears. His father walked close, then veered away and reached up to a coat hook mounted on the wall. Shrugging on his jacket, he nodded. "Okay,

Timmy. Okay. Let's go." His own voice was shaking.

Timmy almost slumped with relief. "Thank God."

"Got a smoke?"

"Yeah," Timmy said with a nervous smile as they headed toward the door. Before they reached it, he paused, looked toward the balcony.

"What is it?"

Timmy froze.

"Timmy?"

"Listen," he whispered.

"I don't hear anything."

"Exactly."

The machines had stopped.

"We need to go now and *fast*," Timmy said, pushing past him to the stairs.

Three steps down, he saw something slip away into the fog. He stopped, tried to imagine what the shape might have been, but the glimpse had been too fleeting.

"Shit!"

"What?" Timmy found a peculiar sense of comfort in his father's fear, comfort that he was not the only one afraid.

"There's something down there."

"Something? What kind of something?"

"I don't know."

He started to move again, eyes fixed on where memory told him he'd seen the pale shape disappear.

"Come on, Dad. Stay close."

He did. Timmy could smell the mingled odor of sweat and hide-dust from him.

Halfway down the stairs, the lights went out.

CHAPTER SEVENTEEN

"Timmy, you okay?"

"Yeah, you?"

"Spooked. I suppose if I were to guess that we just experienced a natural power outage you'd tell me different."

"Yeah I would."

"Thought so. What now?"

"We keep going."

"Right. Forget the cigarette. How about just a light?"

It was not total dark, the fog beneath them seemed to radiate a curious phosphorescent glow, but it was not nearly enough to see by. Timmy withdrew the cigarette lighter, flicked the wheel and the flame rose, sending their shadows sprawling away from them. They proceeded slowly down the stairs.

"Pretend I have an overactive imagination," Paul whispered. "Cryptic information could lead a man to all sorts of horrible ideas about what you think is after us. So how about a hint here?"

"I'd give you one if I could, but I don't know what it is."

"How do you know *anything* is here then?"

They were almost at the foot of the stairs.

"Let's just say it's been an interesting day. I sensed there was something here earlier. A few people helped confirm it."

"People like who?"

"Like Grandma."

His father grabbed a fistful of Timmy's shirt. "Is she all right?"

"Let's just keep moving."

His voice raised a notch. "No. Is my mother all right?"

It didn't hit Timmy until then the enormity of what Agatha's deeds meant. He had been so consumed by anger he'd almost managed to dismiss the effect it would have on her son. His whole world would be shattered. Timmy felt his wall of resolve crumble, imagining how he would feel in his father's place.

"Dad," he said. "Later."

"No, damn it!" He pulled Timmy back so hard the boy almost lost his footing and ended up slamming into the railing. The flame sputtered but thankfully stayed alight.

Paul's face was invisible in the gloom.

"Tell me."

"She's fine. At least she was when I left her."

"Left her where?"

"Outside in the car." Timmy grabbed his father's arm as he made to move. "Wait! There's something you don't know about her. About Aldous too. They...they did some things that may have damned them, and us too. It's what triggered this whole thing, the shattering glass, the woman in the dock, whatever the hell's in here with us...all of it!"

His father's arms trembled like live wires beneath his grip.

"Dad, look...things have gone to hell, but we need to get out of here. Then we can try to figure out what to do next. We'll be no good to anyone dead."

Paul said nothing, but pushed past and hurried down the last few steps, fear forgotten. Once out onto the factory floor however, he stopped.

Timmy followed and stood by his side. They surveyed the room.

It was deserted. The lighter's flame only reached a few feet around them making the darkness beyond it that much thicker.

Timmy felt the fog seep into his shoes. "Where did they go?"

"Who?"

"The other workers."

"They went home hours ago. What are you talking about?"

Timmy frowned. "Well, who was here with you?"

"Just Meehan."

"So where's he?"

His father shrugged. "Went to get a cup of coffee at Maggie May's. Why?"

Timmy thought of those sallow-faced men, mentally counting off how many he'd seen.

Then Mrs. Ryan's voice replayed in his head, studious and focused as a teacher's, telling her tale of the six men vanishing from the factory.

And six came back.

"C'mon. We need to go."

They began to move, the fog snaking around their ankles. The lighter flame fluttered, went out. Frantic, Timmy lit it again.

And stepped in something like a bundle of wet newspaper. He recoiled, thought about checking his shoe but instead moved back, colliding with his father who had been following close behind.

"What is it?" he asked.

"Listen."

There was silence for so long Timmy began to wonder if he'd imagined the sound. Not even the pipes hissed at them. And then it came again, a soft but tortured gurgling, as of someone drowning. Then silence.

"Shit, what *is* that?"

Again he hushed him.

It seemed to come from all around them, someone trying to scream for help with lungs full of water. It was a terrible sound. The strangled pleas rose to the rafters, echoed off the walls and fell to the floor.

The air grew denser; the factory walls closing in on them.

"*Wait...*" Timmy whispered, so softly he wasn't sure anyone but himself had heard it.

Rain speckled the roof, distantly. The wind probed the cracks in the huge building and continued on unsatisfied.

Silence but for their breathing.

Silence but for Timmy's heart pounding in his ears.

"Look," his father whispered then, reaching a trembling finger out in front of them.

The fog had begun to separate as water will separate around a dropped rock. They moved back toward the stairs. The gurgling grew hollow, the pleading throat swollen. The shadows which had, until now, been content to dance around the walls to the rhythm of the meager lighter flame, abandoned all pretense and began to ooze from the walls like tar. Just as they had when the Curtain had opened at Agatha's house.

No...

"Timmy?"

The gurgling grew louder but it was no longer a solitary plea. It was joined by another voice, then another as the floor began to thrum and the fog continued to swirl around an apparent vortex in the middle of the room.

Run, something inside Timmy urged, but the floor might as well have been quicksand for all the use his legs were.

"We should go back upstairs," Paul said.

"No. Then we'll be trapped for sure."

There came a shriek of bending metal and they clapped their hands to their ears.

"What's happening?"

Timmy could only shake his head in response.

A creak like rusty bolts being tightened and the drums on the wall to the right exploded with a noise like machine gun fire. Timmy and Paul dropped to the floor, hands over their heads, but frightful eyes raised to watch as a gory cocktail of chemicals and animal hides burst from the drums.

"Jesus *Christ!*"

The pale fleshy spray hit the floor with wet smacking sounds, some of the hides clapping against the brick and sliding messily to the ground. Along the opposite wall the pipes cracked and ruptured, sending plumes of steam whistling into the air. The room shuddered and groaned.

Time was running out.

"Someone must have heard that!" Paul yelled.

"No. It wouldn't *let* it be heard."

"It?"

Timmy shook his head.

"Could we run?"

"We'd never make it."

"But we can try, right? There isn't a whole hell of a lot else we can do. Unless we try and get out the windows upstairs."

The windows upstairs. It was an idea. But then Timmy remembered seeing the building from the outside when the hanging man had appeared. The windows were roughly twenty feet above the ground, with nothing between them and the concrete below. Suicide, in other words.

He started to tell his father this when something began to rise from the fog.

"Oh shit."

It was perhaps the best way of expressing the horror that blossomed in his belly and soared upwards hard enough to halt his breathing. As the fog rolled towards them in waves displaced by the surfacing of the monstrous thing in the middle of the factory floor, he tried again to make his legs move. It was no good. Though he dared not look away, he could sense his father was paralyzed with the same total shock that held Timmy rooted in place, and all his illusions that they were facing the vengeful husks of a murdered family vanished. What stood before them was nothing less than a walking, breathing, living representation of every unjust death, every ounce of hate and pain that had ever been loosed within the factory walls rolled up into one glistening nightmare fusion of animal skin and black rope.

"Oh my God." The dust on Paul's face was fading, washed away by rivulets of sweat.

The Hides. Timmy knew its name, knew it *wanted* him to know it. As he stood there, muscles twitching with the thought of action, adrenaline spiking in his veins, heart pounding for release against the prison bars of his ribcage...he sensed its contentment that he'd understood. The Hides. The sickening genesis of it flooded his senses, almost knocking him to the ground with the blue waves of its torment.

Sixty years of shrieking terrified animals dragged to their deaths, the confusion, the pain, the scent of death as the hammer fell, the blood and maggots, the decay, the pungent tang of lime, the human bodies stuffed in barrels, the children still alive and trying to remember how to scream, the vengeance, the man hung from the window for speaking out against the corruption of his comrades, the treachery, the covert meetings of the IRA in the loft, the missing people turned to sludge in the sodium sulphate containers so their silence could be guaranteed, the midnight trysts between unfaithful lovers...on and on and on it went, the sins, the horror, the evil of man. And here it stood now before them.

It swept out of the shadows, moving with a grace that belied its hulking frame, the fog wreathing itself around it. Amid the nest of shadows, ill-formed faces shrieked from its chest. Animal, human, all contorting like flies in a spider web, struggling to be free. The Hides' 'body' was hairless, nothing more than a roughly stitched together series of blue-veined animal skins, the head a shapeless knot of waste skin and discarded animal pelt someone had tied in a ball with rough black twine, errant hairs poking at the ceiling. Rough cut holes served as its eyes, a series of hollow elliptical slits cut into the body, the chest, the arms, the legs, with no particular pattern in mind. At first they'd looked like hand-sized leeches. Now that they were open and staring, Timmy knew different. He could feel them on him, probing, testing.

It stood over ten feet tall, and wide...so wide Timmy knew they had no chance of trying to run around it to the door. Its chest rose and fell with the sound of saws digging into wet wood, the mere presence of it offending the eye, bullying the imagination into accepting that it was there even as reality screamed that it couldn't be.

For Chrissakes Timmy, RUN!

The inner scream jolted him out of inaction. He turned, grabbed his father, who was almost absently trying to wipe the sweaty dust from his face, eyes wide and locked on the creature.

"Dad, c'mon!" Timmy pulled at him. In that instant he saw, reflected in his father's wide stare and illustrated by the shadows on his face, something erupt from the back of The Hides. Hissing filled the air but Timmy did not turn. Instead, he jerked his father almost off his feet until he staggered, blinked, then nodded.

"My God Timmy…"

They ran back toward the stairs, the smoky air behind them suddenly teeming with malevolent and deadly life.

CHAPTER EIGHTEEN

Outside, the wind rattled the buildings clustered along the harbor. Thunder crackled in a bruised sky, pierced by swords of cobalt light.

From the warmth and safety of their homes, people watched the curious glowing fog streaming from the doors and windows of the old leather factory. They stared in silence as the storm heaved the sea into waves that slammed against the harbor walls and tossed the boats, felt a twinge of unease as the lights in the factory flickered. They did not recall the last time such a thing had occurred, did not talk about the thunder that was not thunder, the animal roar that sent vibrations running through the earth to shake their beds.

And when they saw the factory lights go out, shrouding the harbor in darkness, they shivered and whispered thanks that they were safe at home.

CHAPTER NINETEEN

They raced up the steps and burst into the room gasping. Below the balcony came the stuttering hiss from whatever had sprouted from the creature's back, then the ear splitting crack of old boards being rent asunder. Dust barreled up from the stairs and spread across the window directly opposite, splinters and bigger shards of wood bouncing off the wall and falling to the floor.

"There goes the stairs," Timmy said miserably.

Paul spun around, his eyes darting from the windows to the creature to the machine shoved against the wall. He whirled and indicated it with a tilt of his head. "What if we can snap the blade from this thing? It'll at least give us some kind of weapon."

From downstairs, a roar, then the gruesome sound of enormous soggy feet slapping down on bare wood. It was coming.

Timmy shook his head. "How the hell is that tiny blade going to do anything against something that size? You'd be dead before you got close enough to use it."

He ran a dirty hand through his hair in frustration. "I can't believe this is happening. What *is* that thing?"

"Everything bad that ever happened here," Timmy told him, alarmed at how casual he sounded.

"How do we stop it?" He waved his hands in the air. "Forget that. How the hell do we get *away* from it?"

Thunderous footsteps; the huffing of a giant. Timmy looked over toward the balcony and black ropes snapped away like children caught peeking over a wall.

"I don't know."

His father spun again, desperately seeking something to defend themselves with and Timmy felt the hope ebb away. Coming here he had known they might be facing something hideous, but nothing like this. In his head he saw Dan Meehan returning to find the hides scattered on the floor with no sign of Timmy or his father ever having been here, just like Hannigan had back in 1955.

He had survived thus far with scraps of knowledge about the things that had crossed the threshold into this world, but about this creature he knew nothing save for the events leading to its conception. Few of the dead had meant him harm. The Hides meant to kill them both.

Whipcord ropes cracked at the air, knocking him from his frenzied thoughts and forcing his father to abandon his search for an escape route.

"It's almost on top of us," Timmy said.

Paul, breathing so heavily his son could hear him wheeze over the bellowing of The Hides, suddenly clenched his teeth and looked at Timmy, his eyes afire with renewed resolve. "Help me," he said and rushed to the bladed machine by the wall.

"What are you going to do?"

"Help me pull it," he said, spreading his legs apart and grabbing the sides of the machine. He pulled, the muscles in his neck standing out like ropes beneath canvas. Timmy rushed around to the back of the slokum staker, dug his fingers in between machine and wall and heaved. The machine weighed a ton, but staggered a few inches out before catching on the floor.

"Okay, again," his father said, "One-two-*three!*"

This time, despite its screeching protest, the machine moved out a good five feet. But it was still too far from the balcony.

"He's coming," Timmy cried, though it wasn't necessary. The cacophony of liquid movement and hissing was so close he expected the snake-things to come slithering over the balcony to grab them at any second. The air filled with a noxious odor more overpowering than anything they'd smelled in here before. The lights flickered on like a surge of hope but then just as quickly died. But in the brief flash, Timmy had seen enough of the monstrosity to double his efforts.

"Again!" Paul roared.

Timmy slid around and, digging his heels into the floor, pushed with all the strength he could muster, while his father pulled and wrestled from the other side. They dragged it the rest of the way to the balcony, exhausted and terrified, both of them soaked with sweat and breathing ragged gasps of air that tasted of death.

The Hides appeared at the balcony railing. The creature had mounted the carts, machinery and towers of animal skins stacked beneath the balcony, rising like some foul long dead thing from the surface of the ocean floor. Metal shrieked and groaned.

The fog swirled, as lasso-like, the black ropes swung round and shot out through the haze toward their faces.

Timmy screamed and tumbled back, colliding with the edge of the slokum staker so hard he thought for a moment he'd cracked his spine.

"Timmy? Are you—?"

Groaning, Timmy fell to the floor and looked up in time to see one of the black writhing appendages split at the end to form a gaping bone-toothed mouth that latched onto his father's face. Paul screamed and began to flail wildly, fists beating at what Timmy could now see was an appendage formed from charred hide.

"Dad!" He scrambled to his feet and grabbed his father's shirt.

Blood spattered his hands and the surface of the machine but he would not look up. He pulled, tugged, screamed loud enough to drown out those of his father.

"Goddamnit, let him go you fucker!" he roared and yanked back with all the strength he had left. There was a sucking sound, like a vacuum being popped and suddenly he was falling, his father on top of him. Timmy tried not to see what the snake-thing might have taken away in its mouth.

When they hit the floor, Timmy struggled out from beneath his father. "Dad?"

His face was bloodied, but his eyes were open, blinking. Timmy felt an immediate swell of relief.

"Jesus," he said, almost blubbering. "You're okay?"

He knew he wasn't, not really, but well enough so that the ring of ragged bite marks circling his face didn't mean the end of him. At least not yet. God only knew what might have been left inside the wounds or how deep they were beneath the flow of blood.

"*Cold...*"

"Can you stand?"

"*Get down,*" his father said through clenched teeth.

Without thinking, Timmy ducked, felt something rough and wet graze the back of his neck as air whooshed past. To his right another ropy thing vanished back down below the balcony railing.

"We have to do something. Can you stand?" he asked.

A grimace, then a nod.

Timmy helped him up so that they were leaning against the machine. A sudden booming sound rocked the foundations.

At first he thought the creature was attempting to knock the place down around their ears, but then Timmy remembered the man with the pipe, the *dead* man he had seen herding the vermin earlier.

"He's trying to make us run," he said with a bitter smile. "Like rats."

His father groaned, the blood from his face pooling in the open throat of his shirt. "C'mon, help me lift this." He moved forward and grabbed the edge of the slokum staker once more. Timmy went to him and mimicked his posture, grabbing the ledge of the machine and pulling. They managed only to tilt it forward, then it caught against the banister and thudded back to the floor, sending dust pluming up from the cracks.

He cursed, Paul kicked the machine in frustration and they waited, desperate but out of ideas for The Hides to come tearing through the floor. Timmy wondered whether it would be a simple thing, if they would just cease to exist when it consumed them or if they would join those wandering things behind the Curtain. Would there be pain or just a sensation akin to floating in the ether? He didn't want to find out, but the only escape route had been the stairs and The Hides had ripped it to pieces.

Paul gave the machine another shove. This time Timmy didn't help. He knew it was useless. Even if they did manage to get it tipped over the balcony, he didn't see the impact doing much to stop the creature below.

Then his father straightened, frowned and looked down at the floor.

Another roar and the floor shook hard enough to make them stagger.

And yet Paul kept staring at the floor. As Timmy watched the blood trickle, he shouted at his father in a voice wracked with fear and pleading.

Dust sifted down from the rafters.

The Hides bellowed, the black rope-things lashing at the air and tumbling up toward them again. Timmy heard their skins rasp against the wooden railing and his shoulders sagged.

This was it.

The End.

He almost had strength enough to resign himself to it.

He followed his father's eyes, reasoning that if the man could induce his own catatonia to escape the horror, perhaps he could do the same.

And saw that Paul wasn't just looking at the floor.

He was looking at a square section cut into the wood. The creature's battering had loosened the dust caking the gaps, revealing it.

"A trapdoor." Timmy's voice cracked. But he was not yet ready to allow excitement to overcome him. For starters, the square cut out of the floor was not nearly big enough for either of them to fit through, even if it did lead to escape, which was doubtful. He hadn't studied the underside of the floor from below, but he was sure there hadn't been any passages or extra spaces attached to it.

"Dad," he said and rocked as The Hides slammed something into the balcony with enough force to shatter the windows, sending glass raining down onto the street. "Shit!"

Paul dropped to a crouch and hurried to the trapdoor on all fours. "Give me a hand!"

Timmy joined him in clearing away thick clots of grime. There was a small brass ring in the center of the panel, made stiff by the rust of disuse. He tugged. It didn't budge. His father nudged him aside and, with a knee on either side of the door, he grabbed the ring and pulled, the muscles in his arms straining against the sleeves of his shirt.

The door groaned, then burst free, sending him sprawling. Quickly, he scooted back to the hole and Timmy peered down into a shallow enclosed space. It was barely big enough for a cat to navigate and to his dismay he saw there was nothing inside but some old bottles. He thumped his fist against the floor in frustration and thought The Hides might have chuckled in response.

But his father was smiling.

"What?"

The creature let out an earth-rumbling roar and more glass tinkered to the street from the shattered frames. Lightning seared the sky through them.

Paul reached into the small space and withdrew the bottles. One. Two. Three. Four. He inspected the hand drawn labels and turned them around so Timmy could see what had inspired the smile.

All the labels were the same, written in faded black and slapped onto dust-clouded bottles: SHELLAC.

"What is it?"

His father looked to the railing, at the writhing shadows, then back to his son. "It's a corrosive, flammable liquid. They use it on the sheep hides. These days it comes in barrels but I'm guessing back in the old days they brought up bottles to save them having to hoist the drums up here. God bless 'em."

It took Timmy a minute to catch on, but when he did, he felt a giddy twinge of excitement in his stomach.

"We torch the bastard," Paul said and wiped blood from his cheek.

CHAPTER TWENTY

Doubt dogged the heels of hope. *How do you even know it'll burn?* And: *Do you think it will* let *you burn it?*

Timmy didn't, but in the absence of other options, it was worth a try.

As Paul removed his blood-spattered shirt and tore it into strips, Timmy grunted with the effort of trying to remove the caps from the old bottles. They worked silently and quickly, a job made all the more difficult by the creature thrashing at the balcony and thumping the floor beneath them, sending some of the shellac sloshing onto the floor. The pungent aroma stung their nostrils.

As Paul jammed the ragged strips that had once been his shirtsleeve into the bottles and turned them to soak the material, The Hides slammed down on the railing, splintering it and sending Timmy sprawling, his belly across the trapdoor opening.

The bottle danced from his father's grip. He cursed, snatched it mere inches from breaking and turned to look at something behind Timmy.

The Hides had started to tear the balcony down. *I'll huff and I'll puff...* One gnarled fist, tendrils of steam threading between its knuckles, animal countenances shrieking from beneath its opaque fingernails, had grabbed onto the railing and was peeling it away from the first floor like a wet bandage.

Timmy felt a thump on his shoulder and almost lashed out at it in panic, afraid he'd missed the sly approach of one of the snake-things. But it was his father's fist and now it opened in front of him like a blossoming rose, grim resolve darkening his features.

"The lighter," he said. "Now!"

Timmy straightened his legs and fished the lighter from his front jeans pocket, almost dropping it down the hole beneath him more than once before Paul snatched it from his grip. His father swallowed, looked up at the railing vanishing before his eyes and flicked the lighter wheel.

Nothing happened. Not a flame, not a spark.

"C'mon c'mon *c'mon...*"

Shnick! Nothing.

Timmy began to back away from the hole, suddenly aware that with nothing solid between the ground floor ceiling and himself, The Hides could break through and drag him down before he'd have any idea what had happened.

"Dad…"

Paul's face was contorted with concentration, bottle held sideways in one hand, its red and blue checked cotton streamer trailing down to the lighter in the other. *Shnick! Shnick! Shnick!*

A massive crunch from beneath and the floor bucked. Timmy cried out and rolled sideways, saw the lighter flare and the bottle jump from his father's hand at the same time. Splintered wood flew like arrows. The floor had buckled, planks popping and somersaulting through the air as the structure of the first level ruptured and strained the beams holding the room in place.

Recovering quickly, Paul grabbed the bottle, flicked the lighter again and smiled briefly at the long orange blue-tipped flame that resulted. Timmy felt a vicious tug on his ankles and for one terrifying moment wondered if the creature had crunched off his feet, remembering the stories he'd heard about swimmers only feeling a painless jerk when sharks removed their limbs. But when he looked down, his feet were still there, albeit only barely visible under the thick black ropes coiling upward. He counted three angular black heads, bone-teeth exposed in wicked grins as they wound their way up his body, spitting at him and each other.

"Dad!" he screamed but his father's attention was elsewhere.

Namely on the eyeless nub of bone and animal skin that was The Hides' head. The crooked ball grinned but had no mouth; glared but had no eyes. It needed none of them, the apertures in its body saw all it needed to, and it was drawn to Timmy and his father like a moth to a flame. Timmy could feel it and with such ferocity he knew his father felt it too.

One of the snakes reared up like a cobra, stealing a glance back at its master before it turned and shot forward, sinking its teeth into the skin of Timmy's wrist. Cold, stinging pain drilled its way up his arm. He knew the thing had been aiming for his face but instinctively he'd raised his hand up to protect himself. More cold spots bloomed in his thighs and stomach. Bites. Instantly he could feel ice leaking into his veins, freezing the blood and thought, with a curious absence of panic: *Poison. They're poisoning me.*

The Hides cast aside what little of the railing remained with no more effort than a man backhanding a fly. Timmy was dimly aware of the sound of wood clattering off the factory floor and then a sudden crackling of heat. He turned his head, felt more ice picks stabbing his chest and throat, convulsed once, twice, and there was his father looking like a stranger, his eyes wild with ragefurymadnessfear, still kneeling, holding the sputtering flame in his hand like some insane parody of Lady Liberty at war, teeth bared, face crimson and snarling. He touched the flame to the cotton. It lit immediately.

The Hides reared up, snakes snapping at the air as the monstrous hybrid of restless dead and stitched animal skins, of hate and loss, fury and hunger rose and drew back its arms with a creaking sound like a house about to collapse.

And then it spoke its first and only word: "*Quiiiiinnnnnnn.*"

With that, it lurched forward with blinding speed and Timmy saw his father jerk in surprise, the snakes rushing toward him mouths agape.

With a defiant roar, he dropped the lighter and threw the bottle.

And as the snakes encircled him, tearing him off his feet and cinching around him, Timmy closed his eyes.

To get away from the pain infecting his mind.

To get away from the sight of his father screaming, those leathery mouths opening in The Hides' body to accept him.

And to get away from seeing that bottle with its fiery comet tail burning shadows as it sailed up, up and smacked into the creature's chest only to bounce back and smash on the floor a few feet away from where Timmy lay.

* * *

Screaming.

The screaming drew him back and out of a cold sleep and as he lay there shivering he promised himself that when he opened his eyes he would stare at the floor, stare at the remaining bottles, at the walls, at anything but what the creature was doing to his father to make him scream.

And then Paul called his name.

Even as the screaming continued.

The cold shifted but did not leave Timmy, despite the blooming fire to his left. He shuddered.

"Timmy!"

A dream. Had to be.

"Timmy, please God, *wake up!*"

He tried to lift his head. Felt as if it had been glued to the floor.

The screaming changed. He squinted, saw stars supernova in the mud of his vision.

"TIMMY!"

His father hung before him, the snakes binding him like a mummy, his eyes and mouth all that could be seen through his new glistening black shroud. The Hides was turned away from the balcony, his feeding delayed as the black ropes held Paul aloft over the factory floor. Something had distracted him. Timmy tried to sit up, felt his brains run like icewater down his skull and throat.

"TIMMY FOR *GOD'S SAKE!*"

Timmy sat up with monumental effort, now wondering if the screaming was only inside his head, if the cold poison was even now rending apart his mind with a gleeful shrieking.

And then even The Hides flinched as the screaming became a wail and the sliding doors at the front of the factory exploded inward. Debris flew through the air, stippling The Hides with wooden darts.

Paul's eyes were wide and imploring. *Help me Timmy, don't let it get me...*With hands trembling so violently he was sure his vision had trebled, Timmy lunged for the shellac, dragging the bottles away from the licking flames and clambered blindly for the lighter.

The sound began to fade. The creature turned and looked down at something Timmy could not see and roared, the bodies beneath its skin straining to see what was happening.

He grabbed one of the bottles, teeth chattering and struggled to get the lighter in his grip. Thumbed the wheel and was rewarded with a gout of flame. Small, but enough.

He raised the bottle and lit the cotton, then heaved himself up on his knees. He could not feel the floor beneath him, but the fire was raging at his back, sucking on the air blowing through the rents the creature had made in the wood and the shattered window. Dazzling pain coruscated through his head as metal screeched, the screaming came again and something sent tremors running through The Hides' body.

Not a scream. A car horn.

"Ti—" his father began to shout until a black cord filled his mouth. He began to convulse, eyes ready to burst from their sockets, and, with a prayer on his tongue and ice in his eyes, Timmy shuffled sideways, aiming away from the creature, and threw the bottle towards the drums from which The Hides had come.

He saw the confusion in his father's eyes, the terror as he realized Timmy had condemned him to death and then the bottle smashed an inch shy of the drum.

The Hides still had its back to Timmy, but now that loathsome nub of a head swiveled to where blue flame was licking toward the drums. Timmy saw his father's eyes change.

The chemicals ignited. The snail trail of sodium phosphorus, acids, solvents, resins and shellac The Hides had left behind became a path of fire through the fog. Immediately the faces which had until now been pleading for release, sank back into the skin of the creature and fell silent. The knot of waste material twisted around at an impossible angle to look at Timmy and he felt pure seething hatred burst from it in tangible waves.

Clever boy...

The serpents reared up and released Paul, dismissing him in favor of outraged cries. As he fell, he dug his hands into the creature's chest for purchase but the skin gave way like wet wallpaper and his fall continued until he was gone beyond Timmy's line of sight.

The Hides did not scream, or bellow as the cerulean flames rushed up its glistening chemical-soaked body. It did not attempt to douse itself or run. It simply glared as it began to peel like a rotted fruit, shuddering as the flames consumed it, the shed skin reverting to the inanimate animal hides they had been before the dead had used them for a costume.

Smoke billowed upward, halting at the ceiling and spreading out like the ghost of an upside down waterfall.

The Hides continued to shed, the fire licking greedily at its chest as the skin sloughed away. Inside were shadows, lithe and knuckled, and unlike the monster they had controlled, they were not silent, but screamed in utter torment and fled, pouring like oil down what remained of their host.

Timmy watched, cold tears streaking down his face, hair singed atop a frozen skull until the ice inside him began to melt. The flames all around him drowned out the screams of thwarted shadows as The

Hides staggered once, glared at him then toppled and fell in on itself.

Timmy turned away and hobbled toward the stairs, weeping, shivering and praying that the sound of his father's voice was not just in his head.

CHAPTER TWENTY-ONE

He found him huddled in a corner beneath a broken steam pipe, the steady dripping aimed at a smoldering piece of his leg. From a blackened shred of his jeans emerged a glistening shard of bone. His hands were burnt and shaking, his face ringed with cuts.

The fire was spreading fast.

"Are you all right?" Timmy asked as he limped toward him, circumventing the crackling mountain of hides and the shadows that leaked from it like whipped dogs to scurry away into the fog.

Paul grimaced. "I will be," he said hoarsely. "Couple of busted bones but nothing terminal. You?"

"I'll be fine."

"Mom...My God, she was here. Go see if she's all right." His face wrenched into a sob. "Jesus...the car..."

Timmy had almost forgotten. The honking of the car horn, the exploding doors. Agatha. His grandmother had been here, trying to help them. Trying to *save* them.

"Timmy. Go see if she's hurt." He flinched with pain and gritted his teeth, both hands sliding toward the jutting bone in his leg but stopping short. "Please."

"Not without you."

"Come back for me."

"No." With a nod, he indicated the yellow and blue flames crackling their way along the rafters overhead. The whole building seemed to slump; puffs of dirty black smoke rising and sending black specks of soot sailing through the air. There was fire overhead and fire around them. In minutes the place would be an inferno.

"Okay, damn it. Help me up."

Timmy swallowed, edged his way through the smoke and fog and grappled with his father until he had him standing. Paul's clothes were sticky with blood and the unspeakable ichor from The Hides.

His arm was bleeding and clamped tight around his son's shoulders. Timmy prayed he had the strength to support him. The fire surged up the walls and somewhere behind them a drum ruptured with an ear-splitting report that elicited startled cries from both men.

"C'mon," Timmy said, grunting with the effort and they started to move. With the chemicals The Hides had trailed all over the place, the amount of kindling scattered everywhere and the noxious fumes permeating the air, he knew he'd have to move fast or they'd all die anyway. The factory had become a tinderbox.

"Did we kill it?" his father asked as they bowed their heads against a sudden drift of choking dust and smoke. Timmy waved his hand in front of them and hacked a cough.

"No," he replied. "Just ripped its costume."

Paul called out for Agatha, using his free arm to guide them through the blinding murk while Timmy wrenched his shirt up over his nose. The air was growing thinner by the second. Even now, it felt as if every labored breath drew in nothing but fumes.

A section of roof tumbled down and a moment later, they heard the cacophony as the balcony followed suit, wood clattering as it fell, sparks dancing like fireflies through the gloom. Timmy heard the bottles of Shellac shatter, then a *whump* as the liquid caught. He tried to move faster. It wasn't easy, his father's weight seemed to increase with every step.

When Paul rammed his uninjured knee into a solid metallic surface, Timmy knew they'd found the car. His father cut an involuntary howl of pain short when they realized the front end of the Volkswagen had accordioned in on itself. The windshield, which had held that ominous growing crack, had been obliterated completely, shards of glass scattered over the crumpled hood. Timmy left his father leaning against the car and continued around it alone, poked his head inside and squinted through the smoke, dreading the horror that might resolve itself from the gloom at any moment. But there was no one inside, the driver side door swinging open with a muted groan.

"She's not here."

"Okay..." Paul coughed into his fist then jammed the heels of his palms into his eyes. "Okay, let's keep moving. Maybe she went outside."

Timmy returned and circled an arm around his father's waist. They moved on into the fog, following the cool night air blowing in through the obliterated entrance. He was all too well aware that it would also be encouraging the flames behind him and whispered a silent prayer. His throat felt raw, scorched.

Another explosion made them duck, heat singeing their hair and Timmy looked over his shoulder, sure a tower of flame would be rearing up to pounce on them. But though the far wall was ablaze and the air blackening fast, they were for the moment, safe.

"Timmy..." He turned to see his father bent double, dark spit trailing from his mouth as he tried to keep his balance. It did not look like he was going to succeed. "Dizzy," he moaned. Timmy had just slung Paul's arm over his shoulder and started forward when one of the apron-clad workers stepped in front of them.

Timmy stopped, realized by the lack of tension in his father's body that he had lost consciousness. The weight increased. He was slipping.

The worker's eyes were jet black and leaking. Reddish hair curled atop his head like painted fire. He was smiling and dirty smoke poured from between his teeth.

Can't be afraid. Not now. "Let..." Timmy began but felt his throat itch and coughed once, then again. "Let us through."

The worker said nothing, his smile widening.

"Goddamn it, let us through."

At first he thought there'd been another explosion, but it was too muted, too distant and just as he became aware that the worker was not alone—he glimpsed a wicked grin here, an apron there; they were all around him—their heads all turned as one, looking at a point over Timmy's shoulder.

The explosion came again, but now there was a tone to it.

It was a voice and it carried a command.

The heat soared across Timmy's back and he jerked forward. A support beam collapsed, a shower of sparks rained down on their heads. Paul moaned, slipping further, making the muscles in Timmy's arm quiver.

The apron man tipped an invisible hat, his smile a little less broad and stepped away into the fog. It consumed him.

They were ordered to let us be, Timmy thought. *Why? And by whom?*

There was no time to wonder. He rushed forward, breath held until cool night air whipped the fog from his eyes and he almost wept with relief. He shook his father, slapped his cheek and Paul's head lolled, his eyes open but unfocused.

"Dad?"

Through the shattered doors he could see the harbor, the heaving sea.

Agatha was sitting with her back to Meehan's shed, apparently unharmed, but pale and shivering.

"Grandma?"

It took her so long to acknowledge his presence that he began to fear his initial diagnosis had been wrong. But then her eyes focused, her head moved and she offered him a wan smile. There was no humor or welcome in it. Had they not just been through Hell, it might even have been frightening.

"She didn't come," she whispered, her small frail hands smoothening out the smoke-stained wrinkles in her skirt. "She didn't come to get me." Her eyes narrowed then, grew dark with accusation. "*Why?*" Her upper lip curled into a snarl. "You know why. *Tell* me."

Timmy felt the strength run from his body, the fresh air filling him to the point of nausea. The flames reared close behind him. His skin stung. "Dad's hurt," he told her. "We need to go."

Her furious gaze bored into his skull as he stumbled out into the rain.

* * *

The night was a rage of colors.

There would be questions, Timmy knew. Endless streams of questions from the stark-faced gathering on the pier.

Police cars formed a barricade around the burning building; a fire truck crawled down the dock, blue lights flashing and chasing shadows.

A flustered Dan Meehan hurried along the street, his peaked cap flying off and forgotten, arms out as if hoping to part the flames like Moses had the Red Sea. He was stopped a good distance away, his protests aimed at a policeman's pacifying hand. He called out to Timmy's father but was ignored as Paul was helped to a waiting ambulance. As they loaded him onto a gurney and strapped an oxygen mask over his face, Timmy saw him smile around it and squeezed his hand. *We made it*, that smile said. *Son of a bitch we made it.*

Again. He winked and was gone, ferried into the ambulance leaving his son thankful it hadn't been a hearse. It drove away, only to be immediately replaced by another.

Agatha remained a silhouette at the door, the flames leaping high behind her even as more drums and chemicals detonated inside. Timmy hurried to her aid but a policeman intervened and two masked firemen assisted. The rest of the crew were busy aiming streams of gushing water into the factory. While the wind worked against them, the rain was welcome.

Agatha let herself be led but collapsed a few feet from the ambulance. The crowd assembled beyond the police cordon gasped as one. A policeman who looked only a few years older than Timmy approached him with a notebook. A paramedic tugged at his arm. Dan Meehan hailed him from the other side of the barricades. Timmy ignored them all, only giving the fireman who patted him on the shoulder his full attention when he noticed the crack in his visor.

He watched.

And it grew longer.

Agatha smashed Lucy's face into the mirror. She watched herself die. The glass cracks when she returns...

He remembered the scratching sound in his bedroom: the mirror breaking. It hadn't been an appearance, but a sign. A warning.

Lucy through the looking glass.

"Grandma..." He pushed away the fireman and saw Agatha look at him.

Someone cried out and the faces of the assembly turned toward the dark heaving sea behind Timmy. It was as if someone had dropped a slab of concrete into the water from a great height. A plume of foamy water reached ten feet into the air eliciting confused murmurs from the crowd.

They never thought to look up.

Nothing had been dropped into the water.

Something had come out of it.

The cry for Agatha was out of Timmy's mouth and winging its way to her only slightly ahead of his limping run, his eyes raised to a point just above the smoking roof.

Where the dead woman was descending.

It didn't take long for the gathering to see what had sprung from the harbor, even less time for them to start screaming and running while the policemen shouted commands that were ignored.

They can see her.

Lucy Conlon landed feet first on top of the ambulance, caving in the roof as if it were no more than a pale blanket. The windows burst outward, spraying glass into the faces of the few remaining observers, who'd been too shocked to move, but now were dancing in horror and slapping at the shrapnel. The dead woman's impact had knocked the paramedics on their backs where they still lay, arms over their faces and screaming in terror.

Agatha lay sprawled on the hood of a police car a few feet away, ignoring the panicked attempt at ministration by the young officer, her eyes wide and fixed on the thing climbing down from the crushed ambulance.

Timmy staggered to a halt right in front of her and she mouthed a silent 'no', her eyes wide and pleading. He turned. Lucy, her mouth stretched into a smile that split the sides of her face and widened the already gaping wound in her cheek, dropped from the crumpled ambulance and moved to stand in front of him, water running from her naked rotten body, the breeze shoving the scent of her decay into his face.

The police were no longer shouting. In his peripheral vision, Timmy saw them retreat ever so slowly, arms spread as if they might attempt to fly should the dead woman set her sights on them.

Lucy cocked her head.

"Are you my enemy, Timmy Quinn?" she asked in a voice like a broom sweeping across a dusty floor.

He swallowed, heard Agatha's whispered pleading at his back and the ambulance sirens dwindling into the night. His father was safe. Could he save Agatha too? Did she even *deserve* to be saved?

Lucy raised one blue hand to her face and began to probe the wound in her cheek. The resultant sucking sound sickened him, his heart beating a tattoo against his chest.

"I see her," Agatha whispered. "Oh God, I see her."

From the wound, Lucy withdrew a long, thin coral-encrusted tube. It took Timmy a moment to connect the rotten thing to the pen Agatha had used to stab her.

Terror spread like a cold rash across his insides.

If he saved her, or tried to, it might cost him his life, and all things considered, would that be bad? It would be the escape he'd longed for since the day at Myers Pond, and the years since, when he'd come to realize the truth about what had happened there and his world had become a much more dangerous place.

A boy had come back for his killer. A killer had died. But not the right one.

"Yes," he told Lucy and watched, terrified, as she swung the pen around in an arc to penetrate his skull, mimicking the act that had preceded her own death.

"Then you're a victim," she said.

He felt the thud but none of the pain, and when the darkness came it was as if a curtain had been draped over his mind.

A single plea followed him down. Agatha, begging for her life.

CHAPTER TWENTY-TWO

They never found her body.

Witnesses claimed a 'banshee' had dragged the old woman over the harbor wall and into the cold green depths, but none of the statements colluded and so were quickly (and with considerable relief, Timmy guessed) dismissed.

After weeks of questions and a search of the harbor, the police left Timmy and his father alone, their dissatisfaction clear. The fire in the leather factory was ruled an accident—something to do with a buildup of heat in one of the drums and a long-overdue safety inspection. Dan Meehan took the brunt of the blame for leaving a new employee unattended in a factory full of dangerous chemicals and lethal machinery.

Most of the questions centered around Agatha's disappearance and how her car had ended up sitting in the middle of the factory floor. Gossip offered a secret drinking problem as a viable excuse. Agatha had been drunk when she'd driven through the factory doors, setting off the explosion that had incinerated her and almost killed her son and grandson.

Though this theory was full of holes and more than a little implausible (Agatha had never been a drinker), the newspapers pounced on it and eventually so did the police, content to have an explanation devoid of flying banshees.

Timmy's injury, they surmised, had been sustained as a result of flying debris. Testimony to the contrary from the paramedics and firemen was put down as a hallucination as a result of smoke inhalation and chemical poisoning.

Life in Dungarvan went on, Agatha's disappearance soon forgotten, though to a select few, it became a ghost story.

* * *

"Kim?"
"Oh my God, Timmy. I heard what happened, are you all right?"
"Yeah, I am. I miss you."
"I miss you too. When are you coming home?"
"I'm not sure yet. Soon, I hope."
"I'm worried about you."
"Me too."
"How is your Dad?"
"As well as can be expected I suppose."
Silence.
"Timmy…"
"Yes?"
"Please come home, baby."
"I will, I promise."
"I don't want anything else to happen to you over there."
"It won't. It's over."
"Over? How? These things are everywhere, aren't they?"
A sigh. "Yeah. Yeah they are."
"How is your—"

* * *

"Dad?"
Paul looked up from the smooth gray pebble he'd been studying and offered his son a feeble grin. "Hey." He was sitting atop the stone wall that separated the sea from Abbeyside church, the closest one they'd found in relation to Agatha's house. The ruins of an old Augustinian priory still clung to the back of the newer building, ancient tombs and crumbling crosses replacing worshipers within its nave.

The day was bright and cool.

Timmy's father sat facing the calm ocean and the morning sun, his legs dangling over the sand a short drop below. He was wearing a black suit, his tie loosened around his neck. Dark circles ringed his eyes, ageing him. His cane rested against the wall.

Mourning.

Further up the beach a fisherman cast his lure out into the placid water and waited.

Timmy folded his arms on the wall. It was a beautiful scene, the glittering sea, the slender arm of land stretching across the bay, the lighthouse sitting atop a cliff on the headland, their appreciation marred only by the circumstances that had led them here.

They had come to visit Aldous's grave, or more accurately, the marked but unused plot next to it.

"It doesn't matter you know," Timmy said.

"What doesn't?"

"That she's not lying there with him."

His father tossed the pebble; it plunked into the tide, startling a feeding heron. "Oh yeah?"

"Yeah. I don't put much stock in the whole burial thing anymore. Not after what I've seen."

Paul looked down at his hands, a frown on his face. It was clear he wrestled with the concept, wanting desperately to believe it but unable to for now. Grief had made him angry, frustrated at everything.

Timmy continued. "I think there's either peace or not. The restless come back, those at peace don't. They go on. No middle ground."

"I hope you're right."

Timmy sighed. "I know I am."

"It just seems so wrong, you know. I can't see her hurting anyone. Christ, I mean, back then even Aldous was a good man. It's just..." He waved a hand in exasperation. "I doesn't gel right in my head, you know?"

"You can't dwell on it," Timmy said. "If you do it'll drive you nuts. Better to just remember them as you knew them. As they were after you were born."

His father nodded. "It won't be easy. My father was a tyrant in his later years but still, I miss him. Now this..."

They watched the sunrise in silence, its reflection in the waves a fractured golden path stretching the length of the bay. After a shuddering sigh, he looked at Timmy, eyes watery.

"I didn't mean for any of this to happen."

"I know."

"I shouldn't have forced you into coming here."

"You didn't. I needed to come here, or at least I thought I did. This whole disaster just shows that no matter where I go, I'll never be able to get away from these things. I'm going to have to learn to deal with it. Make some changes."

He squeezed his father's arm. "I'm just sorry so many secrets had to come out because of it."

"It's probably for the best. I can at least hope that because those skeletons came out, my parents got a chance at redemption wherever they ended up."

"I think they probably did." Timmy's tone was sincere though he was not altogether sure the words were. He didn't want to think about where Aldous and his grandmother might be now.

"I can't help but feel responsible though Timmy, that if maybe I'd paid more attention to things over the years…caught the little glances, the black tempers…that maybe I might have realized…"

"Dad…look, it's too easy to blame yourself. Believe me, I've been doing it since Pete's death all those years ago. But you can't. It suffocates you and you end up curling into a little ball waiting to be kicked again. Jesus, I mean, every time one of the dead comes back because I can see them, someone usually ends up getting hurt. I blamed myself for that for a long time until I realized that I didn't make it happen, *they* did. I'm the one being used as a lifeline and even if I locked myself in a room for the rest of my days, all that means is that murderers go unpunished." He exhaled heavily. "Besides, I doubt I'm the only one who can see them."

"Can I ask you something?" his father said in a tone of voice that suggested he hadn't heard Timmy's last speech.

"Of course."

"Do you think I'll see her again? Agatha, I mean. You feel anything?"

Timmy felt an unpleasant tightening inside him and instantly grappled for an answer other than the one which immediately came to the fore. *Yes, you probably will.* Instead he cleared his throat and, avoiding his father's stare, said: "I don't know."

But of course he did. Since his time spent behind the Curtain, he had been unable to rid himself of the other-Agatha's words. They echoed around his skull like a taunt: *You will recognize the revolution for what it is, won't you dear boy? And the revolution will recognize you.*

As he raised his head and watched a gull ride a thermal, he found it impossible to fathom the enormity of the message those words conveyed. He sensed the closeness of that accursed Curtain — the air was tight with it and yet he maintained the hope that dead time did not run parallel to theirs. That an imminent threat might still be millennia away. He had to hope this much or live in the shadow of threat forever.

"I don't know what to think anymore, Timmy," his father said shakily.

Timmy nodded in silent agreement.

A revolution was coming, the many tears and rips in the fabric of the Curtain combining to make it fall, letting the dead run free. And what would happen then?

The dead woman had said that day was close.

A revolution was coming. He prayed he'd be long gone before it did, and that being gone would make a difference.

Suddenly, he jolted as if struck, his hands clenching of their own accord, nails digging into the crumbling stone of the wall. Panic thrummed through him.

"Dad!" he hissed through clenched teeth.

"What?"

It was there reflected in his father's eyes, a sudden inexplicable fear.

The wind rose. The church bell creaked. A quick glance to the left showed the fisherman had gone, his pole drifting in the shallows.

"Oh no…"

"Timmy?"

He shook his head, unable to answer. Turned.

And cursed himself for not thinking, for not expecting them.

Here of all places.

"Dad…"

"What?"

"Something…"

Tears leaked from his father's eyes as he joined him in watching, reached for his cane and slipped from the wall to face the church. "I know. I see them."

Timmy swallowed. "Don't look for her now. Please don't. She isn't here. I promise. Don't look at any of them."

His father didn't respond and Timmy knew it was too late. Hope had trapped him.

Kim's voice in his head: *Do they have some kind of rule over there that insists the dead stay quiet?*

They were not quiet now.

He began to tremble.

"Timmy," his father said, softly. "There's something I never told you."

Timmy nodded. "I know. And so do they."

And on the air came the smell of carrion as the crowd in the graveyard began to whisper of murder.

BOOK THREE
Vessels

"A little learning is a dangerous thing;
Drink deep or taste not the Pierian spring;
There shallow draughts intoxicate the brain,
And drinking largely sobers us again."

— Alexander Pope

CHAPTER ONE
"Bless Me Father, For You Have Sinned"

The interior of the confessional smelled faintly of Old Spice and older sin. The solid oak walls had proudly withstood the barrage of dark secrets foretold within their confines for almost a century now, and they would hold a century more. Tim Quinn stood on the threshold, the door held open in one clammy hand, a haze of dust dancing around him, spotlighted by the single shard of afternoon sunlight streaming through the arched stained-glass window at his back, upon which St. Peter's eyes were ruby-red from weeping over a mosaic rose.

An old woman coughed into her fist at the head of the church and the sound staggered back through the rows of empty pews to reach him. Prayers were offered up to the vaulted ceiling in frantic whispers.

Tim hesitated. Inside the confessional a small red cushion—meant only, it seemed, for the knees of young children—was shoved snugly against the right wall so that the face of the penitent could reach the wooden hatch, through which the priest would listen and pretend not to look. It was dark in there, as if nothing so pure as light would be welcome in a room reserved for sin.

But Tim was not here to confess. Not today. Today he had come to listen, and the thought of what he might hear, what he would *have* to hear, almost sent him hurrying toward the exit.

"Are you going to stand there deliberating all day?" There was a scraping sound as the hatch inside the confessional was drawn back.

"You've made it this far, you might as well come inside." A small square of murky light had appeared in the darkness. Through it, a face, made sinister by the poor light and the wire screen, peered out at him. It looked aged, withered, much like the faces Tim had seen emerging from behind the dreaded Curtain for much of his life.

"Timmy," the priest said. "Come inside. Please."

A hiss from the nave as a match was struck and touched to a candle, igniting the wings of grief and illuminating a soul for as long as the light would last.

The rattle of beads thumbed by shawl-shrouded women, their faces upraised to the dimly lit effigy of eternal agony suspended over the altar.

The faintest trace of smoke as a soul was extinguished by a draft from the entrance.

Tim stepped inside, and closed the door.

"Thank you for coming," said the priest.

Tim didn't respond. Already he felt awkward. With nothing but a narrow pew there was nowhere to sit, and to remain standing in a confessional felt oddly disrespectful to forces higher than the priest behind the screen, despite Tim having abandoned his faith years ago. With a sigh, he knelt on the pew's hard cushion and placed his elbows on the small ledge beneath the screen. He did not, however, raise his head to study the priest.

"Why now?"

"You promised sanctuary," Tim replied, coldly. "And I need it."

"You risked a lot in coming here. Did you see any of them on the w—"

"It doesn't matter," Tim interrupted. "You said you know some place. Tell me where it is and we can be done."

"Just like that?"

"Yeah."

He didn't want to meet the priest's gaze but he could feel the man's stare boring through the top of his skull, spreading out across his mind with furtive fingers, searching for an ounce of pity to fuel the feeble hope that this meeting might lead to a reconciliation.

"It's a place called Blackrock Island," the priest said, after a deep sigh. "Just off the coast of Dublin."

"Ireland?" Something dark and unpleasant crept up Tim's throat at the thought of what had happened the last time he'd been there.

People had died, and his father...

"Don't worry. It's not a heavily populated area. There are roughly forty people living there, most of them fishermen. There's a daily ferry service if you need to visit the mainland, or if you decide you need to leave. There's one bar, a chapel, a small school, a police station, and not much else. The locals are clannish, as you might expect given their distance from proper civilization, but they shouldn't give you any trouble."

Tim looked up, only enough to see the small pamphlet the priest had slid under the screen. On the front of the brochure was a colorful picture of a rugged cliff towering over the tide that had eroded it. In another, smaller picture, a cloudless azure sky spun vertiginously out over the slumbering peaks of a series of low hills, in the shadow of which dark green fields were separated by gray stitches of old stone. Small cottages with thatched roofs huddled together at the side of a narrow meandering road. It looked quiet, which was precisely what Tim was looking for.

Before he looked away, he caught a glimpse of silver light bouncing around inside the priest's side of the confessional, reflecting off something held in the man's hand. A crucifix, no doubt. The irony of it filled him with bitterness.

"Have you been there?" Tim asked.

"A long time ago."

"Then it could have changed. It could be a miniature New York now for all you know."

"I called, checked everything. You'll be safer there than anywhere else I can think of."

"Famous last words."

"There wasn't much information available on the mainland about the history of the place, but it is, and apparently always has been, relatively crime-free."

"Relatively?"

"No murders on record. Accidental deaths, mostly. Fishermen lost at sea; children wading out too far and drowning; people falling off cliffs. The kind of things you'd expect on any island."

"But you can't say for sure that there haven't been any murders."

"No, I can't." A rasp as a hand was rubbed across stubble. "Blackrock has a fair tourist trade in the summer. It wouldn't be in their best interests to promote past murders, assuming they had any, now would it?"

"So in other words all you know is what the brochure and your own undependable memory tells you?"

"Unfortunately, Timmy—"

"It's Tim. Just Tim now."

"Tim. I haven't been able to spend the last ten years researching remote locations in the hope that every single murder ever committed there will be clearly advertised. Every place has its secrets. I don't need to tell you that." Another glimmer of silver. "I can't conjure up a sanctuary for you. You have to find it, or let *it* find *you*. And if your haven turns out to be a hell, then blame whoever made it that way, not me for being unable to read minds."

Tim felt anger surge through him. "That's not good enough."

"Oh?" The priest shifted in his chair. "Then why don't you tell me exactly what it is you *want* me to do for you? What superhuman feat can I pull off to finally make you forgive me? Or do you intend to make me pay for my sins forever?"

At last Tim looked up, and almost gasped. The man looking back at him was not someone he knew, and it made him falter, the sea of anger forced abruptly back as if by the hand of Poseidon himself.

He swallowed. The priest was old. No, more than old—ancient. Bags of wrinkles hung around his eyes as if intended to collect tears; deep lines radiated from the sockets, stretching out almost far enough to infiltrate the thinning field of silver hair that cradled the gaunt, bony skull. No man could have aged so much in ten years, not without suffering.

"What happened to you?"

Crinkled lips fashioned a smile. "Didn't you ever wonder about that day in the churchyard? Why they didn't kill me there and then? It was, after all, what they'd come back for, wasn't it?"

Tim nodded.

"I murdered a child," the priest said, visibly pained by the memory, or the long-delayed confession of it. "I didn't mean to, but I don't need to look at your feelings for me to know that doesn't cut it. It's still murder, still a heinous sin no matter what way you look at it. That I wasn't in full possession of my faculties means nothing. It happened, and you knew it that day at the pond when that dead kid came back, when he asked you if you'd die for me. You knew he'd come back, to kill me and set things right. But he didn't, and all those years later the others came to try again. But again, I survived."

Tim remembered: the sudden cold breeze at their backs, the whispers of murder. Remembered turning, dread in his heart, and seeing them all, a legion of the dead, staring with malevolent eyes at the man who had killed Darryl Gaines, a boy Tim had come to call The Turtle Boy. He remembered the slow deliberate movements as they drew closer, the air shimmering around them as they emerged from behind the Curtain. In one terrifying moment, Tim realized how successful he'd been in repressing the obvious truth about what had happened in Delaware. His father had murdered a child and let a dead man take the blame. And in that cold gray churchyard, the Curtain had parted again. They had come to exact revenge on behalf of that child.

But they were stopped by a voice.

For the second time in Tim's life, something unseen had spoken, turning the crowd away, their frustration seething from them in tangible waves, their eyes burning with hate. Tim and his father had been left unharmed, and with the disturbing realization that their survival would forever depend on the intervention of whoever or whatever it was that had such awesome power over the dead.

"They left me to my own guilt," the priest said now. "And it was...*is* worse than anything they might have done to me. Worse than that, you knew what I'd done, *accepted* it, and the moment you let the truth in, I stopped being your father."

Tim frowned. "You didn't help anything by running away."

"What else was there to do? You of all people should understand the need for escape, the need for solitude, the need to be away from anything that might hurt you, the need to be away from people you love who might get hurt *because* of you."

"And it brought you here, to Los Angeles, and an all-cleansing collar?" Tim made no attempt to hide the disdain in his voice. "How has the holy life helped your soul, Dad? Did you find the penance you were looking for? Handful of Hail Mary's and an Our Father and you're golden?"

"You don't understand."

"Fucking right I don't."

"Watch your mouth."

Tim stood. "I think I'd better go before I start saying all those lovely things I swore I wouldn't when I finally faced you. Thanks for the brochure." He snatched up the leaflet and jammed it in his pocket.

"I'm still your father."

"You're still a *murderer*."

"Listen to me, Timmy."

The anger burned within him now, a hot tide pouring from old forgotten fissures. "God*damn* it. It's Tim. *Tim*. T-I-M! 'Timmy' was a dumb old kid who didn't know any better than to trust you."

"Please..."

"This was a mistake. You think that costume absolves you from anything? From all the pain you've caused?"

"No, I don't."

"Think it makes you innocent?"

"No."

"Then what good is it? What good is any of this?" he demanded, gesturing at the dark walls of the confessional. "But another way to fool people into believing you're worth a damn. Like you fooled me and Mom."

"Wait..."

"No, I won't. I'm sorry, Dad. Really, I am. I'd love to be able to give you the peace you're looking for, but I can't. I won't. It's too late, for both of us."

Insides in turmoil, Tim yanked open the confessional door and stormed out into the church, narrowing his eyes against the shaft of sunlight and ignoring the worshipers, who had turned in their seats to scowl at him. No doubt they'd heard the last few words he'd said to their beloved priest.

Despite the rage, despite the disgust that had colored his view of his father for so many years that he couldn't remember ever having felt any different towards him, he slowed his pace and waited for the sound of the confessional door opening, waited for a voice to disregard the reverential quiet of the church and hail him. Waiting.

You're being ridiculous. When are you finally going to give up on him?

At length, with the cloying scent of incense offending his nose and the narrowed eyes of the annoyed worshipers still on him, he continued toward the door, firmly resigned to the fact that he would never see his father again.

If he was honest with himself, the thought saddened him, and he felt more than a little guilty at how today's meeting had gone, but over time, he had mastered the art of suppressing his emotions. In a week or so, maybe less, this would all be just another bad memory to be added to the collage in his head.

His fingers touched the front door's cold brass handle and a sudden inexplicable draft made the candles behind him flutter. An odd, slow, grinding click turned him around. Sour faces continued to regard him. Gnarled hands counted off prayers on dark beads. His imagination suggested it was the latch on the confessional door he'd heard and he waited a beat, eyes fixed on the oak box nestled under the gallery alcove at the rear of the church.

For the briefest of moments, the perfect quiet was allowed to settle around his shoulders, smothering the foolish notion that his father would sacrifice his pride to come try to talk sense into a son who hated him.

But then that quiet was shattered by the sound of a single gunshot, deafeningly loud even with the heavy oak door of the confessional trying to keep it contained.

CHAPTER TWO
"Swaddled In Her Verdant Finery, What A Seductive Witch She Makes..."

The endless ocean surrounded him on all sides, except where the low dark green hills rose to obscure it from view. But even when it was out of sight, he was conscious of it—a thing of monstrous power, a shape-shifting creature with an awesome command over mankind, a great leveler deceptive in its complacency, capable at any given moment to rise up and erase the blemish of humankind from the earth. He feared its secrets, the spawn of tragedies that might swim beneath it, the remains that might be waving up from the depths, desperate to catch the eye of just one living thing or caring god. It was a massive womb, a vault of secrets, and today, it had delivered a boat to the shore.

Tim had never seen a craft quite like it. It was closer to a kayak than a regular rowboat, clad in a skin of dark-colored hides, prow raised to saw through the tides. The inside was latticed with bowed wood, vaguely intestinal in color, and, coupled with the dark oily hide, made Tim think of a dolphin shorn in half. Brackish water and clots of seaweed had pooled in the bottom.

This, he assumed, was the boat he'd heard the locals refer to as a *curragh*.

It drifted up to the shore on a remarkably sure course, as if guided by knowledgeable hands, but it had only the wind as a master until the wet sand stalled it a few feet away from where Tim stood. He expected it to tilt, to list until it lay on its side, but it did not. It stayed upright, a queer aura of expectancy surrounding it.

He shivered. It was if he'd summoned it himself, as if he'd donned the role of lost soul waiting for the ferryman on the banks of the river Styx. When he tried to scoff away the thought, it persisted. His eyes roved over the prow and down into the guts of the boat. It was empty but for a single oar.

He looked along the beach, at the dark craggy cliffs, the gulls trying to balance the air beneath their wings, the curving shore steadily vanishing beneath hungry waves that swelled at the thought of a storm. The houses, small and silent, huddled along the cliff-top, houses that had not appeared in the brochure his father had given him. As he'd suspected, much had changed over time. The brochure was no longer an accurate guide, but that didn't matter. There was peace here and Tim had been basking in it for two months without a sign of a disturbance.

But the boat made him uneasy.

He aimed a gentle kick at it, the resultant hollow thunk swallowed by the thickening air. A glance upward showed bruised clouds tumbling restlessly, the light dimming as the sun was smothered beneath their skins.

As he turned and hunched his shoulders against the wind, Tim told himself that the crimson buttons of color he had seen on the oar of the curragh had been nothing but old paint.

* * *

Despite the sparse population on Blackrock, Tim had discovered that solitude was not easy to obtain. But he managed as best he could, avoiding the well-trodden paths and sticking to the fields for his daily walks. The reticence of the islanders aided him in his cause. On the few occasions when he did encounter one of them, they seldom acknowledged his presence, and that suited him fine, negating the need for conversation he was ill prepared and unwilling to initiate.

But as he ascended the concrete steps set into the cliff-face, one hand clamped around the steel rail to quell the vertigo, he felt a twinge of unease at the thought of entering Madigan's Inn. There would be people there. He suspected the fishermen confined to shore by the coming storm would be gathered around their drinks, laughing and discussing things incomprehensible to Tim. On some distant level, he missed the fraternity of it all, the security companionship provided, but the reality of the dangers friendship brought with it quickly dissolved all regrets.

The inn was a short walk from the top of the cliff, but there was time enough for him to consider, not for the first time, veering off and over the fields to his own small cottage and forgetting all about the boat. But he reminded himself that if the craft was valued by any of the island men and he left it to the tide, he might be held accountable, particularly if someone had seen him from the cliffs. And while he cared little for whatever opinions the islanders might hold of him, he didn't want to needlessly provoke them or engage their animosity. Such things could only make living on the island that much harder.

The inn was built of sturdy, whitewashed stone, the thatched roof tarred to keep out the rain, of which there was plenty, all year round. Small mullioned windows with imitation casements gazed blankly out over the ocean, and, as Timmy drew close, he could see his own hunched over ghost in the glass, the curious faces of the somber-looking patrons staring out from his reflected chest. He opened the door, wiped his feet on the mat (even though the muddy footprints on the wooden floor inside testified that it was a seldom-practiced ritual), and the ill-lighted faces around the bar turned to regard him. Conversation did not so much halt as fade to murmurs, which was almost as bad.

Tim offered them a flicker of a smile and let the door groan shut behind him.

Pipe smoke hung heavy in the bar, twisting and writhing in the draft like the satellite image of a storm. Fuzzy, capped silhouettes grunted and tended shots of iceless amber fluid in the corners. A duo of wild-haired men with threadbare coats watched him approach, while a middle-aged man in a uniform consulted with the ruddy heavyset bartender at the far end of the bar. Their stares were not hostile; wary perhaps, but Tim instinctively felt the lack of welcome. He nodded once for whoever might require such a thing and stepped up to the bar.

"The phone's busted, lad, if that's what yer here fer." The bartender stayed where he was, with the policeman he'd been talking to watching intently.

Heads turned back to muttered conversations, but Tim knew he still had their interest. "No. I don't need to use the phone, but thank you. I appreciate it." Someone muttered *Yank*—a not altogether flattering term for Americans—but Tim maintained his composure. "I was on the beach just now. I saw a boat on the shore...drifting. I thought it might belong to someone here."

Madigan raised his eyebrows as if to say: "*Did* you now?"

Tim considered ordering a drink to wet his parched tongue then thought better of it. It would only delay his departure, his *escape*, from this place. "I just wanted to let you know in case it goes back out with the tide and breaks up on the rocks or something. Looks like it's getting rough out there." He shrugged. "That's all."

"Good lad," a voice said as Tim turned to leave. It was the policeman, who had moved away from his perch and was now approaching him, a solemn expression carved on his stony face. "Thanks for bringin' it to our attention." He clamped a meaty hand on Tim's arm and squeezed. Then he turned to address someone in the bar.

"Joe, tell Ned Looby when he comes in at noon that his skiff is dancin' with the tide again, would ya? Least I'm guessin' 'tis his. That eejit never knew how to tie a boat. And if tis'nt his, then take a buncha lads down there and try to find out who owns it, like a good man."

A huddled figure with a hawkish countenance raised a hand over his pint of Guinness and saluted. "Will do, Michael."

"Grand." The policeman released Tim's shoulder and appraised him with dark eyes set too close together. "Would you mind if we had a bit of a chat?" he asked.

Tim did mind, and summoned what he hoped was a genuine smile of apology. "Some other time, maybe. I'm in a bit of a rush."

"Oh? To do what, if you don't mind my askin'?"

"I have an important call to make," Tim lied.

The policeman grinned broadly, exposing large crooked teeth. "And here I thought you'd said twasn't the phone you were lookin' for at all." He nodded. "This will only take a moment. Cross my heart."

He led the way outside. Tim muttered a curse, stowed his hands in his pockets and followed.

"Name's Sergeant O' Dowd. At least that's what the official name is. The islanders know me as Michael."

He offered his hand.

Reluctantly, Tim shook it. "Tim Quinn. Nice to meet you."

"Likewise." O' Dowd reached into the breast pocket of his navy uniform and produced a hand-rolled cigarette which dribbled flecks of tobacco. He screwed it between his thick lips and cupped a hand around a Zippo lighter. The flame seared half the cigarette, but O' Dowd didn't seem to care. He dragged deeply and studied the dark rolling clouds above the small weed-choked parking lot.

"I called to yer house the other day," he said. "To give you the official 'Welcome to the Island' speech. You weren't home."

"I was. I just didn't answer."

"Oh?" If the policeman was offended, he didn't show it. "Busy, were you?"

"Yes. As I am most of the time." He made a show of looking at his watch, hoping the policeman would take the hint.

He didn't.

"I see. Well, that's to be understood. Few visitors come to Blackrock lookin' for a party."

Tim said nothing.

"In fact, to tell you the truth we don't get many visitors at all; at least, not many who come here to live. That's why you might have felt a little like a deer in the headlights in there," he said, jerking a thumb over his shoulder. "A stranger always arouses curiosity among the locals. Everyone wants to know the stranger's story."

Tim nodded. "Right."

"So…?"

"So what?"

"So what's yer story?"

"You ask all newcomers that?"

"If I feel I need to."

"Part of your 'Welcome to the Island' speech?"

O' Dowd grinned. "I just like to know who we have living with us. 'Tis a small community. Nice and peaceful. Everyone knows everyone else. No one knows *you* though," he said. "And I think t'would be better for my—and for the community's—peace of mind if you were honest about yer intentions here."

Tim scoffed, aware he was being defensive but unable to help himself. "I'm not marrying the island, Sergeant. I'm retiring here."

The policeman frowned. "You don't look old enough to be retirin'. What age are you? Thirty?"

"I'm older than I look, trust me."

"Well that's just it, you see, I can't trust you. Not until I know somethin' about you other than the obvious fact that yer American."

"Is that going to be an issue?"

"What? Trust, or your nationality?"

"Take your pick."

O' Dowd laughed. "Ah Jaysus, no, lad. We're not all narrow-minded bigots here, you know. Of course, there are a handful who'll take an immediate dislike to you based on yer accent, but I expect you'd get that anywhere you go." He puffed on his cigarette. "We have a tendency to think of Americans as flamboyant, boisterous loudmouths, because once the summer rolls in, that's all you'll see around here. So when a quiet one shows up, it knocks us for a loop, y'know? Goes against all our expectations. Makes us immediately suspect he can't be a savory type."

"I see."

"Whereabouts in the states are you from?"

"Ohio."

"Ohio," O' Dowd repeated, and "Ohio" he said again, as if tasting the word. Tim waited, growing more irritated by the second, until the policeman squinted at him and said, "Nasty scar you have there." He tapped a finger against his temple to show what he was referring to.

"Yeah. Are we finished here, Sergeant?"

"What happened?"

"Can't remember," Tim lied, "Happened during my wild teenage years." And that last was the truth, but he knew O' Dowd would never believe the rest of it, even if he chose to tell him. *A dead woman came out of the sea and stabbed me with a pen, Sergeant. Damndest thing.*

The policeman smiled, but there was no humor in it. "We're a tidy little community here, Mr. Quinn. That's the message I was tryin' to get across, nothing more. 'T'wasn't said to offend, or to make you feel unwelcome. We're just a little wary of troublemakers here, as any close-knit community would be." He shrugged, "it's just one of those things. But the bottom line is: the more I know about you, the easier it'll be for me—for *all* the islanders—to sleep at night."

"So in other words, I don't get the key to the island unless I bare my soul for you, is that it?"

O' Dowd waved a hand. "Ah, no. Not at all."

"Well, I'm sorry, but I don't think I'm obliged to tell you anything about my business on this island, Sergeant," Tim said stiffly. "And I'm struck by the sneaking suspicion that you, and everyone else on this rock, have already made up your mind about me, so why you're demanding reassurances is beyond me."

"Now I've upset you," the policeman said, with a cluck of his tongue.

"I really have to go." Tim started to leave.

"I hope to see you again," O Dowd said.

Tim paused. "You're a cop. If you need to find out about me you have your own way of doing it, right?"

"That I do."

"Then I guess I'll be hearing from you soon."

CHAPTER THREE
"They Call My House A Place of Saints, But Sinners Beg To Differ"

Tim made his way home, annoyed at the grilling O' Dowd had subjected him to. It inspired him to compare the policeman and his cronies at the bar to vultures—ugly, dull, dimwitted creatures, with little point to their existence but to watch and wait for carrion to pick apart. And Blackrock in the off-season had little carrion. As a foreigner, Tim would be fair game. Worse, in his irritation he'd goaded O' Dowd into digging up his past, and he sorely regretted that now. What the man would find—and it wouldn't take much looking—might very well close the doors on Blackrock Island for Tim, and he could ill afford to so casually guarantee his expulsion from any haven, as rare as they had become. But that was almost certainly what he had set in motion. As soon as the islanders discovered the truth, they would treat him like a freak, a charlatan, or a lunatic. They would avoid him as if his perceived moral deficiency was contagious. But it would not be long before they changed their minds. Their nocturnal imaginings would beget hope, reigniting the light grief had snuffed out and it would lead them to his door like whipped dogs, that dreaded question on their lips: *Can you really bring them back?*

A vicious gust of frigid air froze him in his tracks and tugged him from his thoughts. He wrenched the lapels of his overcoat together and winced as the wind raked icy nails across his cheeks. He ducked his head and continued along a winding gravel path, which would forever lead the way through dark green, magnificently featureless fields before meandering its way up a steep incline to his cottage. Thunderous clouds rolled over the hills ahead, sending a deep shadow over the barren, unremarkable land and down to where Tim had stopped, his head bowed, eyes staring forward.

The chapel.

Until now he'd avoided it.

He looked at the small stone building squatting at the side of the road. It was ancient, worn, built not for beauty but to protect its worshipers against the harsh island weather, and nestled in the shadow of hills that seemed to be leaning conspiratorially towards one another. A single candle fluttered behind a sole window, but it failed to bring life to the ugly sandstone mass. A rusted spire jutted crookedly out of the heavy slate roof, giving the building the appearance of a golem felled by a sword. Unruly grass formed a cushion around the base of the structure, the main door messily recessed into the stone as if pounded back by the fist of a giant.

There was someone inside. A hunched shape, distinguishable only as a paler wedge of darkness through the glass, moved closer to the window, blotting out the candle.

Tim stepped away, his mouth suddenly, inexplicably dry.

It's nothing, he told himself, but didn't believe it.

The sky rumbled; the grass sighed softly beneath the heavy hand of the wind. Rain began to fall, pattering on Tim's shoulders with impatient fingers.

At the window, the shape pressed twin white starfish against the pebbled glass.

Hands.

It's just someone praying. Someone who heard me out here.

The fingers, bone white strips, separated and spider-walked up the glass.

Just someone praying.

But he knew he was deceiving himself, prescribing to thinking of the wishful kind—something he had long ago realized was treacherous. The twisting of his nerves and the fluttering in his stomach was all he needed to know that this was not a normal situation, that this was yet another *visitation*.

A squeak as a nail scratched the glass and then the face moved into view, a fuzzy oval masked with shadows. Tim knew without a doubt that its eyes were trained on him. He felt them, but couldn't move away. He wanted to, but fear had severed the link between brain and limb. So he watched. Watched as those thin-fingered hands crept up the glass to cup the distorted face. The window was now completely blacked out, but for the misshapen theater mask and the long white hands framing it.

Raw need penetrated the glass and rolled in invisible but tangible waves across the short distance between Tim and the chapel, and he was suddenly enveloped in a cold black shadow, a manifestation of utter hatred and the desperate desire for revenge. It crawled through him, probing his innards, tearing at his skin, but still he didn't move. There was no pain, just the dull but terrifying sensation of being violated, of an outside force invading his senses, stirring his guts. It had happened before, too many times to count, but it was never the same. In this place, this island of supposed safety, they had found him, or rather he had found *them*, and again he was reminded of the futility of trying to escape a realm that forever had him surrounded. The only thing more potent than the invasive cold at that moment was the crushing realization that he would never be free of the dead, never be free of their hunger for vengeance, never be able to crawl out from beneath the shadow of *their* world. All that was ever needed, wherever he went, was sin—a murder—and his presence, for that dreaded Curtain to part.

Dad was wrong, he thought miserably, but then another possibility occurred to him, infinitely more chilling in its inherent implications. *He wasn't wrong; he* lied. But he couldn't think about that now.

The thing at the window lifted one hand away from the glass, to beckon to him. The air between them shimmered and the ugly feeling inside Tim dissipated. There was the faintest sound of a bell he knew no one else would hear, and suddenly he was walking, slowly, calmly, toward the chapel door.

You can still run, he reminded himself. As the rain pelted down with renewed force, washing the color from the world around him, he looked at the path twisting away from the chapel, a trail that would lead him to the cottage, to light, safety and warmth, away from whatever nightmare waited inside the brooding old building. A short run. He could be there in minutes.

But knowledge of escape did not make escape possible. This was his calling and he knew, from past attempts at flight, that it would find him, draw him back until he gave them what they wanted.

The chapel door was opening, ever so slowly, ever so slightly.

The path seemed to call to him, one last feeble cry. *It's not too late!*

Then it was.

The sprawling shadow of the building slid over his shoes like tar.

The door opened a little wider, and without warning he was lost in darkness deeper than any he had ever known, about to flail blindly at whatever untold horror might be waiting for him in its folds, when a sudden flicker drew his attention, and feeble strains of amber light fluttered across the walls.

He was inside.

Rain drummed on the roof, the sound dulled by thick oak rafters and layers of slate. The flame danced atop the candle. Tim quickly turned to his right and scanned the far side of the room, his gaze lingering on the spot before the window where he'd expected to see whoever had been peering through it, but there was no one there.

A whisper.

He spun and peered into the gloom over the pews, which ran ahead of him to the altar, but no further. Three wide marble steps led to the pulpit, a splintered oak affair that looked as if it would fall under the weight of the Bible. There was no priest in attendance, no patrician gentleman fussing over sin's remedies. Only Jesus Christ himself presided over the altar from his cross upon the wall above the tabernacle. It was a life-size effigy, but time or poor craftsmanship had blunted the figure's features, making His face oddly blank, as if he were wearing a hood. Unlike most of the representations of the crucifixion Tim had seen, this one looked fake, but in a chapel so devoid of aesthetic value from the outside, he realized he shouldn't have expected the interior to be any different.

The whisper came again

"Let him know I love him."

Tim squinted and moved down the narrow aisle between the pews.

"Tell him I'll love him always."

He stopped as a huddled figure resolved itself from the gloom.

"Tell him I'll be with him again."

It was a woman, sitting in the first row, closest to the altar. Her shoulders were hunched forward, over what Tim guessed was an open prayer book or a bible on her lap. Her face was hidden from view by a scarf she had wrapped around her head—a common look for the island women. Gnarled hands were clasped together in fervent worship. Despite his anxiety, Tim suddenly felt like the invader, as if by eavesdropping on the woman's prayers he was negating them, robbing their power, contaminating them. With a slight shake of his head, he started to move away. The whisper stopped. The woman's head turned slowly, not enough to allow her to see him, but enough to let him know his presence had been detected.

He stopped. Waited. Then, "I'm sorry if I disturbed you," he said softly.

"You didn't," she said. "I'll be out of yer way in a minute."

"No, that's all right," he told her, flooded with relief that she was just a woman and not some malevolent clutching thing sent forth from that Other Place. "I just...I followed someone in here. I thought that's who you were."

She turned in her seat to look at him. The gloom allowed him to make out nothing but the deep trenches in her face and the sorrowful curve of her brow. "There's no one here but me."

He feigned relief, even as his eyes studied the thick shadows hanging in rotten veils around the nave. "Sorry, my mistake."

"You're that fella who lives in the old Thompson cottage," she said. "American?"

"Yes."

"Ah, I see. Haven't seen much of you about the island."

"I keep to myself."

"Probably sensible with all the fools we have on this island, of course that only makes them more eager to know yer business, doesn't it?"

He allowed himself a slight smile at that. "Yeah, it does." He moved to the end of the pew in which she sat. "Do you mind?"

When she shook her head, he slid in and sat down a few feet away from her, close enough to smell the sickly sweet scent of her perfume. He also saw that he'd guessed right — a heavy bible lay open on her lap.

"Tim Quinn," he said, proffering his hand.

She shook it, her grip weak and cool. "Agnes Noonan. And should I ask what brings you to the island or would that be makin' me a fool too?"

He shrugged. "The peace and quiet, mostly. The last few years have been hard."

"Must have been somethin' awful to bring you all the way out here."

"Yeah," he said, feeling her eyes on him in the gloom. "It was."

"I expect the venerable Sergeant O' Dowd has already given you the third degree?"

"That he has."

"I wouldn't think too much of it. He gives every newcomer the same going-over."

Cold fear held Tim in its tight embrace, but he managed another plastic smile. Whatever was in here hadn't yet shown itself, and that bothered him. They had always seemed so eager to reveal themselves in the past. Imagining it in the pools of darkness, watching him with the old lady made his skin crawl.

Where is it hiding?

"Are you cold?"

He looked at her. "What?"

"You shivered."

"Oh, no, I'm fine."

What is it waiting for?

"We had a big power failure on the island a few weeks ago. 'Tis storm season, you know. The chapel isn't always this dark."

"Right."

"So how long are you stayin'?"

Not long, was his answer, now that he knew the island was as condemned as anyplace else he'd sought out for its promise of a reprieve, but saying as much would only be begging for more questions so he said, "I haven't decided yet. Until my head clears I suppose."

She breathed a little laugh. "Then you might be here forever."

"Have you always lived here?" he asked her.

"Yes. Seventy years now."

"Did..." *Be careful what you say*, he reminded himself. "Has anything strange ever happened on the island?"

"Plenty," she said grimly.

"How about in here?" he asked, indicating the chapel.

"That's a peculiar question to ask. Why do you want to know?"

"I'm interested in old buildings, and supposed hauntings. It's something of a hobby of mine."

"Ghosts," she said, amused.

"Do you believe in them?"

"There's only one spirit I believe in," she said quietly and nodded up at the crucifix. "But to answer yer question: somethin' did happen here. Not that long ago either..."

As she said this, Tim followed her gaze up to the crucifix, and jolted in his seat, an involuntary gasp escaping him. A pulse of fear raced through his guts and he stood.

"What on earth's the matter?" Agnes asked, startled, leaning forward to get a look at his expression.

He couldn't tell her. Didn't know how.

The figure of Jesus Christ was gone from the cross, but the longer Tim stood staring, heart thumping painfully against his ribs, he realized that the effigy had *never been there*, that from the narthex the figure had struck him as odd-looking because something else had been mimicking Christ's pose, mocking the messiah's death. A figure in a hood, arms akimbo.

Waiting.

CHAPTER FOUR
"The Hangman Is No Friend, For He Always Lets You Down"

"What's wrong?" Agnes asked. Then, in a vain attempt at humor, "It's not one of yer ghosts, is it?"

Yes, Tim thought, *that's exactly what it is*. "You need to leave," he told her, and reached down and took her by the elbow. She resisted for a moment, eyes widening in fear, but his persistence won out, perhaps aided by the fear in his voice.

"What are you doin'?" Her bible slid to the floor with a thump as she rose. She made a half-hearted effort to retrieve it before leaving it there and allowing herself to be lead into the aisle, where she stood, her sizable bosom rising and falling rapidly in the gloom. "Yer not going to hurt me, are you?"

He shook his head. "No, but you need to get out of here."

"But why?"

"Someone else is here. Someone who *will* hurt you."

"The person you were followin'?"

"Yes."

"I can't see anyone," she whispered. "Are you sure he's here?"

The lone candle guttered and spat.

Tim tore his gaze from the cross to lead Agnes toward the door. "I promise you. He's here. You have to go. Quickly."

The candle went out. Shadows reached across the room, and now only the weak gray daylight filtered through the windows.

"Should I fetch O' Dowd?"

A voice sliced through the dark: *"Your father says 'hello,' Timmy."*

He stopped dead, forcing Agnes to do likewise until she jerked her elbow away and stared at him. "What on earth are you *doin'*?"

The voice came again. *"And if you look real close at those shadows in the corner, you'll see a little wooden box, the receptacle for all the island's sins. Not big enough to stand up in, but quite suitable for a man on his knees. Appropriate, wouldn't you say?"*

The voice was coming from behind him. It was clear that Agnes couldn't hear it. This was nothing unusual. The dead always decided who could or could not hear or see them.

"Get out," he said, nodding at the door straight ahead. Thunder roared and hissed rain at the roof. The windows darkened.

Agnes said nothing, but worry and distrust were written in the furrows of her brow, as if it had just occurred to her that he might be the real threat, and not the unseen antagonist he claimed was hiding in the shadows.

He did not try to assure her as she backed away toward the door. If her fear of him quickened her flight, then all the better.

"I'll summon O' Dowd," she said, but there was no conviction in her voice. "I'll tell him yer here."

"He's so awfully sorry, Tim. So frightfully sorry for his sins, but of course," said the voice at his back, *"it's much too late to repent for them now."*

"Who are you?" Tim said under his breath. Agnes was still watching him, but she looked less afraid the closer she got to the door.

"Depends on who you ask. To some I'm Edmund Brennan. To others, I'm The Scholar. And then of course, there were the disparaging names people would only use behind my back. I'm sure you know what I mean." A hoarse chuckle like wind soughing through the eaves. *"Timmy the Freak. The Wicked Quinn Boy. The Devil-Child. How cruel people can be when they don't understand what you can do for them."*

A hand crawled like some kind of diseased crab over Tim's shoulder. He restrained the urge to cry out. Instead he turned, slowly, to face the thing hovering in front of the altar. He was dimly aware of the sound of the door opening, the rage of wind and rain that whipped itself into the church as Agnes prepared to leave, and a small part of him relaxed. She would be safe now.

"Tell me," said The Scholar. *"Just what is it that you do?"*

He had once been a priest, Tim saw. He still wore the long black cassock and dusty white collar, which was cinched around his throat just beneath an oily stretch of rope that had been tightened around the base of a pale pillowcase hood almost enough to sever the head from the body. The rest of the rope curled away over the priest's shoulder, writhing like a serpent up into the shadows where it coiled atop the head of the crucifix on the wall. Portions of the hood had been torn or had rotted away but in the pale light, Tim could make out little, even if he'd wanted to. The moving rope held the priest suspended a few feet above the floor and though he did not move, occasionally the umbilicus would tug at him and he would shudder, eyelids closing as if it gave him pleasure.

"All I can do is see you," Tim said, in reply to The Scholar's question. "It's a curse."

The priest waggled a chiding finger at him. *"Now, now. Until you've been ground down into oblivion by hateful hands only to awake in a place of infinite dark, you can't possibly know the meaning of the word. Death is the curse and there is no lifting it. All you can do is strive to set the balance right."*

Tim braved a glance into the shadows nestled in the corner to the right of the altar. After a moment, his eyes adjusted and he fancied he could make out the corners of a narrow box. A cold finger traced a path down his spine.

"You said my father was in there."

"Yes."

"Why?"

"Isn't that a question you should take up with him?"

"He couldn't have gone behind the Curtain. He wasn't murdered."

"Oh? Then you don't consider suicide self-murder?"

He did, and had worried about the consequences of his father's actions even through the horror of watching the paramedics removing the bloodied corpse from the confession box. His fears were exacerbated at the funeral, when the polished oak casket had been laid in the ground through air a little too thick and a little too fragile, as if the body was being laid, not in the ground, but into the hands of something worse.

"But you only come back to settle scores," Tim said, his voice frail, ready to crack under the weight of fear, not of The Scholar, but of what might be waiting in that impenetrable darkness in the corner of the chapel. "He has no score to settle with anyone but himself."

The Scholar cocked his hooded head and the rope around his neck cinched tighter. *"If you are your own killer, how do you find peace?"*

"But why come back at all?"

"Would you not surmise that the damned belong in Hell?"

"Yes."

"Well," the priest said, spreading his hands. *"Here we are then."*

"Damn it." His head pounded with the strain of trying to understand. "But he didn't *die* here."

"It doesn't matter. Just as I'm tethered to this accursed cross, so is your father tethered to you."

Invisible hooks tried to drag Tim toward the confessional, but he stayed himself, drawing upon the rage he'd felt in the days after his father's death, when the abject hatred he'd kept locked up inside came flooding out of him. Alone, the poisonous torrent had had nowhere to go but his own mind, where memories of his father cavorted through the veils of grief.

"No," he said aloud, then quickly glared up at The Scholar. "Why are *you* here?"

"You already know."

"Who is it?"

"'Who are they?'"

Tim ran a hand through his hair. The hooks tugged. He closed his eyes. "I won't do this. I can't. Not anymore. Find someone else."

There was the sound of a rope scything the air and he looked up in time to see the dead man hurtling toward him, the speed of the priest's passage causing the hood to lift, exposing bleached white skin and a cruel black slash of a mouth. With no time to move, Tim braced himself, waiting for those hooked hands to savage him.

Then a crack and a strangled gasp as the rope snapped taut. The Scholar, arms still outstretched, hands scrabbling at the air, was jerked back to slam into the altar like a dog on a choke chain, tar-like clots of liquid spattering the floor from the dark ring around his throat as he struggled against his snare. He writhed, snarled and spun until he was facing Tim once more. Through the rotten fabric, silver eyes glowed with rage. He moved slowly, liquidly, to hang in the air in front of the altar.

"You know as well as I do that you don't have a choice," he said. *"The moment you set foot in this chapel, you accepted the task. You followed your senses, you watched the Curtain part, and you came here to see who had stepped out from behind it. Well, I stepped out. It's my turn to set things right, to tear the hides from my executioners, and you will help me. You'll cut me down and return me to my parish so I can root out the sinners."*

Tim swallowed. Looked from the coiling dark in the corner to the priest. *"You'll do it,"* the priest said, his tone brimming with threat. *"Or you'll suffer."*

"Maybe I *should* suffer. Maybe the only way to end this torture is to let you kill me. But of course, you can't do that, can you? Because then you'd be wasting the only chance you might ever have to get your revenge on whoever strung you up there."

"Death would be a merciful punishment for you. There is so much else, so much worse that can be done before the life is coaxed from out of that hollow vessel

of yours."

Although fearful of taking his eyes off the seething priest, Tim glanced at the patch of shadow hung like a drape in the corner. The confessional. *Only a few steps*, he thought. *And I'd see him again. Wouldn't it be worth it, just to know?*

Like a punch in the gut, he snapped out of his thoughts.

The Scholar rose as far in the air as the rope would allow. *"I'm warning you..."*

Tim turned quickly, and ran down the aisle toward the door. Again he heard the snap of the rope as the priest tried to reach him. The door was only a few feet away now. Lightning painted the windows neon-blue.

Almost there...

A swish of frantic movement behind him. He started to look over his shoulder and—

Something snagged the collar of his jacket and he was wrenched backward, his feet flying out from under him. "Shit!" He slammed down hard on the floor, the air knocked out of him.

"You can't run away. You never could."

Panicked, he tried to rise. Then something cold and hard thudded against the back of his head and pain burst like scalding liquid across his skull leaving him lying on his side on the floor, dazed and winded, the darkness speckled with pirouetting stars.

"You'll do as you're told, you little bastard."

Tim rolled onto his back and looked up. *He can't kill me*, he reminded himself, even as his vision wavered. *He won't.* The Scholar's rotten hood edged into his vision as the priest floated above him, struggling against the noose. In one upraised hand, he held an object, the spine facing down toward Tim's eyes.

It was Agnes's bible.

Tim tried to bring his hands up to shield his face but it felt as if lead weights had been tied to his wrists. "Don't," he said feebly.

When the tome came down, it brought merciful darkness with it.

CHAPTER FIVE
"Cast Me Ashore, So I May Weep With the Tide"

On the shore, the restless tide washed salt into the wounds of the boat and heaved it further onto the sand, receding only when a single drop of blood pierced its watery hide.

It drew back with a hush as if chastened.

For a moment, the air stilled despite the burgeoning storm. Not a breeze, not a gull, not a roar of thunder.

The boat was bleeding. And from its belly came a sigh.

CHAPTER SIX
"The House of Drowning Sorrows"

"He's awake, Mike."

Tim awoke adrift in a sea of faces. They peered at him beneath heavy brows tattooed with shadow, even as curves of soft amber light traced their grizzled cheeks. Dark eyes glimmered; work-roughened hands hovered in uncertainty over where he lay immobile, all his energy focused on holding their stares, dissuading their intent. His heart was a lonesome drumbeat, tended by a musician unsure of his tempo.

"Give him some air, lads."

Slowly, Tim turned his head toward the voice and noted as he did so that he was lying on a wooden bench or a table. Men surrounded him, blocking his view of anything but the scarred edges of its surface. The smell of alcohol and pipe-smoke rolled from their heavy coats and woolen sweatshirts.

Now that consciousness had returned, it came armed with pain that blazed across his scalp. He winced and brought a hand to his skull. The men shuffled aside to allow the speaker access to the table and Tim glimpsed the long poorly lit bar behind them. *Madigan's*, he realized.

"Didn't take you long to find trouble," O' Dowd said, with a smirk.

"It never does. How did I end up in here?"

"Agnes Noonan came in about a half hour ago, scared half to death. She was concerned that we might've let a lunatic onto our island. Said she'd met him up at the chapel. She even gave us a very competent description considerin' the lack of decent lightin' up there."

"I hope she made me sound handsome."

"So," O' Dowd continued, ignoring the remark, "I sent a few of my lads up there. I guess in the States you'd call them my *deputies*." There was a soft rumble of laughter from the men. "And lo and behold what do they find but our American friend panned out on the floor bleedin' like someone had tried to crack his head like an egg." He leaned close, his voice lowered to a conspiratorial whisper. "We don't like people bleedin' in our chapels, Mr. Quinn. Unless it's stigmata, it tends to scare off the tourists."

More laughter.

"Why did you bring me here. Why not my place?"

O' Dowd shrugged. "Well, we have all the tonics a wounded man might require to steady himself right here. We didn't know how badly you were hurt."

As Tim struggled to sit up, the pain intensified and he clasped his other hand to his skull as if the mere contact would be enough to dissuade the throbbing. O' Dowd muttered something to one of the gathering and a moment later Tim flinched as an icy cold compress was shoved into his hand. He nodded his gratitude and brought it to his scalp. The skin beneath felt encrusted and swollen.

One of the gathering, a stick-thin elderly man with a pronounced limp and a sneer too grotesque to be anything but the result of past physical trauma, broke away from the rest of the men and shuffled his way toward a pair of narrow doors set slightly apart at the back of the bar. Each door held a small placard adorned with Gaelic script—'Fir' on the left and 'Mná' on the right. Bathrooms, Tim concluded and watched which one the old man took in case that information proved useful later.

"I don't suppose you'd care to tell me what you were doin' up there?" asked O' Dowd, but Tim didn't look at him until the old man had eased open the door marked 'Fir'. Then he replied, "I have a thing for old buildings."

"Have you a 'thing' fer frightenin' old ladies too?"

"I wasn't trying to frighten her."

"Well, you did. She said you were convinced someone else was in the chapel with you. Someone who intended to do you harm, and Agnes too, if she hung around."

"I was overreacting."

"To what?"

"Shadows. Sounds." He sighed. "My father was a priest. He killed himself in the confessional of a church in Los Angeles about four months ago. I guess I haven't dealt with it as well as I thought."

Uncertainty passed over the faces of the men. O' Dowd suddenly looked uncomfortable. It was clear they'd gathered for a sentencing and hadn't been prepared for the discovery that their quarry was human, or that he was the son of a holy man. And while that might not elevate him much in their eyes—after all, he was still an outsider, and therefore guilty by default of any charge thrown his way—it certainly gave them pause for thought. For Tim's part, he hadn't planned on telling anyone on the island anything about himself, but since meeting O' Dowd, he'd felt as if he was digging himself deeper and deeper into a hole and waiting for the sides to collapse. Frightening Agnes Noonan had only accelerated things, to the point where he was forced to offer the lynch mob a part of himself in the hope that it would sate them for a while.

"I'm sorry to hear that," O' Dowd said, actually managing to sound as if he meant it. "But I would have thought such a thing would have kept you away from chapels fer good. What was so fascinatin' about ours?"

"I don't know," Tim said. "I was drawn to it."

O' Dowd stared hard at him for a few moments, then broke his gaze to look at the men. "All right lads, go back to yer drinks while this fella gets his head together." The command was greeted with the expected groans of disappointment, but though slow to obey, the men eventually returned to their seats. Tim slid his legs over the edge of the table and blinked away the dizziness that threatened to drop him like a stone to the floor. The dull glow from the lanterns strung around the bar floated like fireflies across his eyes.

"Jesus," he hissed, wincing.

"We don't have a doctor on the island," O' Dowd said. "He passed away last summer and we've all but given up tryin' to lure a replacement out here. So, we cleaned yer wound ourselves. It doesn't look too nasty, but it mightn't hurt to catch the ferry in the mornin' and have a doctor on the mainland check it out. You might have a concussion."

Tim nodded. It felt as if someone was holding a saw against the top of his head. "I was hoping to get the ferry sooner than that." He stood and the room started to pull away.

O' Dowd caught his elbow, steadying him. "Last one's come and gone fer the day. There won't be another until dawn. Why, may I ask, are you suddenly so eager to leave?"

"Why do you care? Isn't that what you want?"

"I want to know why yer here, but I'll make do with the truth about what happened to yer head."

"Low ceiling."

O' Dowd exhaled through his nose. "Agnes said you looked fairly convinced there was someone else in the chapel. She said you told her whoever was there might hurt her. That sounds like an awfully funny way to talk about shadows."

Tim nodded pointedly at the compress before tossing it on the table. "Thanks for that, and for getting me out of there." He turned and started toward the door. O' Dowd stepped up behind him and grabbed his arm.

"Before you go, allow me to tell you what *I* think," the policeman said.

Tim sighed and O' Dowd released his grip. Everyone was watching, still caught like hungry fish on the hook of intrigue.

"I think you came to Blackrock to get away from somethin'. Maybe yer in trouble with the law on the mainland, or Stateside. If that's the case, it won't take much to get the story. So why don't you save me some hassle and tell me what's goin' on. What are you runnin' from? Drugs? Murder?"

"Nothing you'd understand."

"That's not an acceptable answer."

"I don't have one that is."

"Try."

Tell him, Tim thought then, resigning himself to the reality that it might be better to come clean and be thought a lunatic than say nothing and be thought a murderer, or worse.

"I need rest," he told O' Dowd, and that was not a lie. He felt stiff and sore all over, his head a nest of wasps that stung the backs of his eyes every time he moved them. "Call by my place tomorrow morning. I'll tell you what I can. Then I'll gladly take the first ferry off your island."

O' Dowd straightened and gave a satisfied nod. "Fine." He cleared his throat. "I'm sure you think I'm an ogre, Quinn, but you'd do the same thing in my position."

Tim gave a smile that felt more like sneer. "Maybe," he said, turning back toward the door. "Or maybe I'd realize that there are some things I'd rather *not* know."

CHAPTER SEVEN
"She Whispers To Me In My Dreams"

The storm had rolled like a black tarp over the island, silvery threads of lightning dancing on the horizon as the wind drove the rain in vertical sheets. The swollen sea roared, the sound of it carrying across the length of the island. Jacket pulled over his head, Tim found himself wondering if the men had taken in the boat or left it to be dashed to pieces against the cliffs, then decided at this point, he didn't much care. As he hurried on through the maelstrom, every step on the stony earth felt like a fresh blow to the wound in his scalp.

Directly ahead of him stood the chapel, but this time, he did not so much as spare it a passing glance despite the nauseating magnetic pull he felt tugging at him from within its lightless recesses. He kept to the grass, avoiding the path entirely for fear it would bring him close enough to the chapel door that The Scholar could influence his resolve.

Lightning flashed, turning the rain to mercury, and thunder rolled in its wake.

For the first time since coming to the island, the cottage felt like home. Until now, it had represented little more than another prison, chosen for its isolated location, keeping him safe behind its walls and away from harm. And while it had become devastatingly clear that there indeed *was* harm to be found on Blackrock, he was too exhausted and sore to think of anything but the warmth, and the whiskey, that awaited him at the cottage.

Tomorrow, he promised himself, as he blinked rainwater out of his eyes. *Tomorrow I'll leave.* But instead of making him feel better, that promise only filled him with an immense, crippling hopelessness, for the truth was that there was no place left to go, no place that would protect him from the dead, nowhere on earth devoid of the secrets and sin that kept *them* coming back again and again and again. It would never end. Even suicide, a thought he had entertained so many times over the years, had been revealed as nothing more than a means of joining those vile things behind the Curtain, of coming back to sit in a dark box suffering forever more.

The thought conjured up an image of his father, dead but not gone, and he tried to resist wondering what he looked like now, what he might say if Tim summoned the courage to face him again. Would he be a hate-filled creature like all the others, or a pitiful thing, trapped in a cage of his own despair?

The lightning revealed the cottage sitting alone in a wide uneven field just ahead. The lamp burning in the living room window was like a beacon, drawing him from the violent night, the rain trying to smear the brightness down the glass. A thread of smoke was torn from the chimney and tossed to the storm.

There has to be a way to stop this, he thought. *Some way to stop seeing them, to stop them from getting through. But how?*

As he neared the cottage, almost losing his balance as an explosion of rain and wind battered against him, something dawned on him. It was not an idea, not the solution to the nightmare he'd been hoping for. Rather, it was a fragment of seemingly insignificant memory that had risen the moment he'd looked at the cottage. And now that he had focused on it, it stopped him in his tracks, teeth bared against the pummeling of the storm. He wiped rain from his eyes.

The lamp was on. He had left it on, unsure when he might return and growing ever more accustomed to the island's capricious light.

He looked up, at the smoke tugging itself from the chimney.

He hadn't lit the fire.

There was someone in his house.

* * *

It was a ghost.

Standing inside the cottage, the door held open in case he should need to flee, the wind raging around it, Tim had to fight against the shock that threatened to steal the air from his lungs and the strength from his legs.

"Jesus, Timmy, close the *door!*" she said, and he obeyed before he even knew he was going to. The wind moaned against the wood, the high bright flames fluttering in the fireplace as it tried to come down the flue.

It was a dream. It had to be. The blow to the head must have jarred something loose, dragging images and memories from the past and assembling them to make the hallucination he saw standing smiling before him. Because she couldn't be here. She couldn't have found him, not after all this time.

"Aren't you going to say something?" Her smile faltered the longer he stood there staring. He willed himself to reply but worried that acknowledging her presence, or the presence of what was most certainly an illusion, would only serve to inflame his madness.

Kim Barnes.

"Holy shit," he breathed and put a hand against the door to steady himself. He couldn't take his eyes off her. It had been more years than he could remember since he'd left her behind, broken her heart by forcing her to believe he no longer loved her, and she hadn't changed at all. Her long black hair might have been a little shorter than he remembered, her face a little leaner, but otherwise it was as if she'd stepped out of the photograph he'd taken of her a decade ago and which now stood on his nightstand. She stood next to the fire, her eyes wet with tears, arms folded across the small swell of her bosom, and returned his stare.

"Say something, Timmy. Please."

As much as he hated the name 'Timmy' these days, he couldn't imagine her calling him anything else, didn't want her to call him anything else because just hearing her say it reminded him of a time in his life when he hadn't been alone, when she had stood by his side even as the dead stepped forth and commanded him. She had seen them too, and had never run away.

"How did you find me?" he said, but didn't move from his place by the door. "Nobody knows I'm here."

"Your father knew you were here," she said softly. "He told me to come find you."

For one heart-stopping moment Tim thought she was talking about whatever now occupied the confessional in the island's chapel, but that didn't make sense.

"How?" he asked, confused, his skull aching more than ever. Rainwater gathered in puddles at his feet, but he didn't care.

Kim dropped to her haunches and began to rummage in a purse Tim hadn't noticed until now had been sitting by her feet like a loyal cat. Nor had he noticed the suitcase set on the sofa, so distracted had he been by its owner's presence.

At length, she straightened and unfolded a piece of paper. Then she stepped around the sofa. Tim's heart began to race and he moved back until he collided with the door. She halted a few feet away from him, visibly hurt by what must have appeared to have been revulsion on his part, and after a moment, held the letter out to him.

Tentatively, he reached out and took it, a tingle coursing through his fingers as they brushed against hers. Her skin was cold despite the fire. He peered at the letter, a pang of sorrow rising in him at the familiar sight of his father's handwriting. The letter wasn't dated. It read:

Dear Kim,

If you're reading this, then I guess things didn't work out the way I wanted them to between Timmy and me, and I've most likely taken the cowardly way out. For that I apologize, as I have in other letters to other people who still won't know how to forgive my selfishness. But I had my reasons, and lets just leave it at that.

I'm writing to ask you to do something for me, and for yourself too. Enclosed you'll find a brochure and a key to my son's cottage on Blackrock Island. I've included directions and the price of a return ticket to Dublin. A ferry will take you to the island.

You'll find him there, where I sent him, looking for peace. Chances are he won't find it. I think you know that too. You also know that I let him down as a father. I tried to make amends so that it might help him. Again, I failed. The only other person who can help him now is you. I know you love him, and no matter what he says, he loves you too. Go to him. Find him, and don't listen when he tries to tell you to leave. He has his mother's stubborn streak, but then, you have your mother's tenacity, so I don't doubt you're up for the job. Stay with him, please. Don't let him be alone again.

You're his angel, Kim. Help him find the strength he needs to survive this hell.

God be with you,

Paul Quinn.

His hands trembled as he handed the letter back to Kim. "When did you get this?"

"A month after he died. His attorney delivered it to my Mom's house. I don't live there anymore, so she forwarded it to me. Took me some time to get my own affairs in order before I could come."

"You shouldn't have," he said. "It was a mistake."

She nodded slowly. "Maybe, but I'm used to making mistakes and I'm here now, and I went to the trouble of warming up the place, so the least you could do is pour me a drink before tossing me out in the rain."

"Kim...You can't be here. You must have known that."

She nodded.

"Then...why did you come?"

"You're father asked me to." She sighed heavily. "And because I wanted to."

Her smile was uncertain and it broke his heart to see it. It was wrong that she was here; he knew that without a shadow of a doubt. He'd left her so she wouldn't ever have to see the things he'd seen again or deal with the strain they'd bestowed upon him. He'd turned her away so she might yet have a chance to live in the real world, the world of light, and to forget about the Curtain and everything it concealed. So she'd be safe. And now he wanted her to leave, to run while there was still time, to go back to whatever she called a life now.

But he couldn't. Not again. The words lodged like a bone in his throat, and the thought of only getting the briefest of glimpses of her beautiful face after all these years of imagining it, kept them there. The thought of seeing her go, perhaps never to see her again, ripped a hollow in his stomach he wasn't sure would heal quite so well this time.

No. I can't. For so long he'd been hiding inside a shell designed to protect everyone but himself, to stop them from getting close enough to see the horror in his eyes, to stop *him* from discovering what *they* might be hiding, that he had forgotten what it was like to crave another's company.

And no company had he ever craved so much as Kim's.

Now she was here; she had come to him as he'd often dreamed she would, and though it might be the beginning of a nightmare for them both, that didn't matter right at this moment, in this room in the middle of nowhere, because she was *here*, and he loved her still.

He approached her and saw her eyes widen slightly, her hands dropping to her sides, as if preparing to defend against an attack, though he had never struck her in all their time together, only shattered her heart. She tensed and swallowed, fresh tears making shimmering crystals of her eyes.

"I'm sorry," he whispered, on the verge of tears himself at the impossibility of her presence, almost afraid to touch her for fear she would vanish, but then she was in his arms and sobbing against his chest as he held her. "I missed you so much," he said.

She said nothing, but continued to weep as he stroked her hair and whispered to her, the wind still teasing the flames in the hearth.

CHAPTER EIGHT
"Love Is A Many Splintered Thing..."

"Your mother misses you," Kim said.

"I miss her too. You see her much?"

"Before I moved to Wisconsin I saw her almost every day. Made it a point to drop in on her. Even after the move I called her often."

"I appreciate that."

"It wasn't any trouble. We were friends, your Mom and I. She's a lot stronger than you give her credit for. She knows why you're doing what you're doing too, but I know she still hopes you'll come see her someday."

"Maybe I will."

They sat close together on the sofa, facing the fire, drinks in hand, and although the awkwardness of time and pain and distance still clung to them, the heat and the alcohol had melted the ice from their reunion. The storm maintained its assault on the island, but Tim could no longer hear it, only see it orchestrating the music of the flames as they sparked and crackled and hissed. Their talk covered a range of topics while often touching on the past and their relationship, though both were careful not to drag up reminders of things they were supposed to forget. All of that changed when Kim told him: "I almost got married you know."

Tim gaped at her. "You're kidding?" And while he made sure the question sounded neutral in tone, he was more than a little hurt by the revelation.

She avoided his gaze. Instead, she stared into the fire, the amber light giving her back the natural healthy glow the travel had stolen. "The guy next in line after you," she said. "Nice guy, too. Ex-jock. Your polar opposite, which is what I thought I was looking for if for no other reason than to make it easier to forget you."

"So what happened?"

"Oh, we did the usual courtship dance. He moved into my apartment and once settled decided he'd earned the right to stay out all night every night with his drinking buddies. I let it go for a year or so, until I couldn't take any more. So I waited up for him one Friday night. He staggered in at about..." She waggled her hand in the air, "I guess about three a.m. I asked him where he'd been, told him we needed to talk, made him some coffee...and then he punched me in the face and raped me."

Tim felt his guts clench. *"What?"*

She smiled grimly. "Yeah. Thing that gets me is, he'd never laid a hand on me before. Even in bed he was..." She flashed him a quick glance, as if realizing she was entering territory he didn't want to hear about, but then shrugged off the concern. "'Not given to violence,' shall we say. The morning after, he acted as if nothing had happened. So much so, in fact, that he almost managed to convince me I'd dreamed it all. Told me I must have rolled out of bed and banged my eye against the bedside table during the night."

"And the rest of it?"

"He said he got a little carried away."

"Asshole. Did you call the cops?"

"Nope. Stayed with him for another six months and cried like a baby when we broke up."

Tim had no response to that and after a moment, gave up trying to find one. Instead, he put his arm around her shoulders and pulled her close. She nestled herself against him, her head on his chest.

"I got over it," she said. "Told myself it could have been worse. He could have killed me, or beat me every time he came home drunk. Still, I learned my lesson."

"To avoid alcoholics?"

"No." She put her hand atop his. "To avoid anyone who wasn't you."

His heart leapt. "Kim—"

"Don't say it."

"You don't know what I'm going to say yet."

"Yes I do. You're going to tell me that as much fun as my sob story has been to listen to and as good as it is to see me, I can't stay because I'll only be putting myself in danger being here with you."

He sighed. "Well, it's true."

She sat up and swiveled around to face him. "I know all that," she said after leaning over to set her glass on the floor. "But you want to know something? I'm no safer out there than I am here with you. We broke up because you thought I would be, and look what happened? I'd rather be afraid and have you there to tell me it's all right than be scared on my own." She leaned closer, their noses almost touching. Her hands rose to frame his face. "I love you, Tim. I always have, and if you tell me you don't feel the same I'll smack the living shit out of you."

He couldn't help himself, he smiled. It didn't last long. "Look," he told her, putting his hands on hers and removing them from his face. "I do love you, but you wouldn't like what's happened to me, what I've become."

She frowned. "For Chrissakes, Tim. You're not the Incredible Hulk."

"I'm not saying that. But...listen, I lost Pete, my best friend, because of this."

"You lost Pete to his psycho father, a flesh and blood monster, not because of anything that came waltzing out of that Curtain of yours, so don't try that shit with me, I was *there*, remember?"

"Yes, you were, and you saw what happened next. You know they killed Pete's father and then he came after me. It's an endless cycle and I just don't..." His voice cracked and he closed his eyes, took a breath.

"What?"

"I just don't ever want to see you coming to get me. Not you."

She returned her hands to his face, but this time she leaned in and kissed him, slowly and softly, before breaking away and staring deep into his eyes. "I've already come to get you," she said. "And if you don't run me off I'll never have to come get you again."

He stared at her, at the determination on her face, and it summoned another smile. No, she hadn't changed. Even the crow's feet at the corners of her eyes couldn't dilute the effect that expression had on him. He remembered seeing it one summer a million years before, when he'd been without his best friend and forced to spend his afternoons with a girl he didn't even know. *This girl, who used the same expression she wore now to convey her emotions back then. Don't mess with me, kid, it said. 'Cuz I can be just as mean as you if I want to be.* And yet he wanted to argue with her, wanted to convince her that she was wrong, that she *had* to go, even as the need to have her stay swelled within him. The conflict tore him apart, brought tears to his eyes, pushed the words up his throat and into his mouth, but when he opened it to let them out, her lips were once more pressed against his, her tongue erasing all need to do anything but respond in kind.

* * *

In bed, the initial awkwardness that had hampered their conversation was also present in their lovemaking. The fluid symbiosis they had once been had atrophied over time, been tainted by mutual hurt, and so they moved slowly, with gentle caresses and whispered reassurances, both adapting to the new methods of an old lover.

Afterward, they lay together, no longer afraid to talk about old wounds and old times. They laughed until Kim fell asleep, her hand splayed across Tim's chest, her hair tickling his cheek. For now, he was glad she'd stayed and hadn't listened to his protests. He needed her, he realized, and my God how good it felt not to be alone after so many years.

He ran his hand over the curve of her hip and watched her shiver in her sleep. He dared not believe he would see her in the morning when light filled the house, but it was true. This was real. She would be there with him for as long as he wanted. As surreal as it felt, he was willing to bask in it for as long as he could.

He closed his eyes and drifted, a smile on his face.

But when at last sleep came for him, it was a thing of nightmare.

He was awake and yet not, and tracking the progress of a patch of mildew on his bedroom ceiling as it changed shape, ran liquidly and settled into the shape of a woman's shrieking face that, without warning, pushed forth from the plaster as if it were no more substantial than a thin sheet of plastic. As an unvoiced scream surged up his throat, the plaster split and gave birth to a dead, bloated face that kept pushing outward until its body began to follow, wriggling free, forcing the plaster wider and wider until with a sickening splash of fluid, the dead woman lunged free and fell headfirst, her milk-white eyes level with his own as she dropped toward where he lay paralyzed with fear.

He raised his arms to stop her, waiting for the impact of slick dead flesh against his fingers, and felt only the wind. Heard only a hush.

This isn't a dream, he realized then as he looked around at the breakers rolling into shore beneath the star-studded canvas of night, the sand soft beneath his feet. He was standing more or less where he had been when the boat had drifted ashore, and now it was coming again. Except this time, it wasn't empty.

The curragh was an oily wedge of darkness as the sea eased it onto land. A woman, dressed in dark clothing, sat within, one hand raised in greeting, sleeve rolled back to expose a slender arm. Before Tim thought to raise his own hand in response, he realized there was already someone else waving back. To his right stood a man, dressed in black but for a square of white at his throat. He wore a hat, pulled low over his eyes, hands joined behind his back, long fingers flicking each other, counting off the seconds, or the beating of his heart.

The boat rode the white shattered-glass path of the moon and the beauty of the woman was revealed. Her skin was flawless and glistening from the sea spray, her eyes dark and round, long auburn hair tangled by the wind. Her lips, soft and pink, creased into a smile as the boat scuffed its hull against the sand.

And then she was out, and running, arms held aloft.

The priest returned her smile, but to Tim, the man's breathing sounded odd. It seemed that it was not anticipation that forced the breath from the priest in half-grunted gasps, but something else. Tim could feel it, a powerful surge of emotion that set alarms ringing in his head.

The woman stumbled in the shallows, the surf caressing her ankles, seaweed snagged between her perfect toes. Then she straightened with an endearing smile of apology and continued toward him. She drew closer, the excitement visible on her pretty face.

Then she faltered, her smile hanging crooked. "Edmund?" she said.

The Scholar, Tim thought.

"My love," said the priest, with no love at all.

The smile vanished. "What's wrong?"

"You cunt."

Horror washed over the woman's face. She raised a hand to her mouth, perhaps to feel the scream that shock had robbed of volume.

The priest lunged forward.

Though lithe and fragile-looking, she was quick, the confusion on her face turning to panic as she turned and fled back toward the boat.

His hands tangled in her hair, then pulled, and for a moment those hands belonged to Tim. Horrified, he loosened his grasp and found himself floating over the priest and his terrified victim. The rage, which had never been his, began to subside, cooled by cold fear and the frustration of impotence. For a moment, he had stepped *inside* the priest and the intensity of the man's anger had frightened him. It was not something he wanted to feel ever again.

The woman gasped as the hands wrenched her head back. She flailed, her lips spread wide in a grimace of pain, and then the hands were gone and she was free. But it was freedom she hadn't expected and it conspired with gravity to send her sprawling forward. Her scream was abruptly cut off as her head smashed into the wood, the prow's point connecting with her right eye. Blood spurted. With a strangled gasp she tumbled sideways into the water.

Like an animal with wounded prey, the priest pounced on her, still grunting. His hands plunged into the dark floating mass and grabbed the woman's shoulders, forcing her down beneath the waves. Her one good eye opened wide, the mercy of unconsciousness fleeing, as her struggle for air and the instinct for self-preservation kicked in. She thrashed, the water foaming as the priest dropped to his knees and put all his weight on her. The cross around his neck hung beneath his chin, glimmering in the moonlight. The woman's eye, bleached coral in the blue, stared at him from beneath the water, the plea rising unspoken from the depths. The bubbles spewing from her mouth grew smaller. She convulsed, screamed the last of her air at her murderer, kicked once, then again. Her final convulsion was almost powerful enough to heave the priest off of her, but it was too late for it to have made a difference. The struggling stopped and the woman moved only at the tide's request.

The priest stood tall, the waves lapping against his thighs. He trudged back into the shallows. There he waited, watching as the incoming sea delivered his victim at his feet. He started to lean forward, then paused, as if he had heard a sound behind him. Tim watched the man's head start to turn, panic rising in his chest. *He's going to see me.*

No, he remembered, *he can't. It's not a dream; it's his memory. I'm not really here for him to see.*

Maybe so, another part of him countered. *But he can feel you.*

The shadows scaled back from a hawk-like nose as the eyes, lost beneath the brim of the hat, sought him out.

Wake up, Tim demanded. *Wake up, now!*

The man had turned around, was scanning the beach. Any second now he would—

Tim woke with a jolt. After a moment reserved to ensure he was not on the beach, was not sharing it with a priest who had just murdered an innocent woman, he sat up and ran his hands over his face.

Fuzzy gray light was beginning to bleed through the curtains. With a wince, he massaged the heavy bar of pain at the back of his neck. His skull ached, his muscles sore.

Kim...

He half-expected her to be gone, feared the night before really had been a beautiful dream, or that she'd awoken to the clarity only morning can bring and decided to go back to her life where there was only black and white, no gray.

But she was there, sleeping soundly, the sheets drawn down around her, exposing the soft skin of her shoulders, the small mole beneath her right shoulder blade. Her hair obscured her face from view and he brushed it aside just long enough to kiss her. She didn't stir, but smiled slightly in her sleep.

He sighed. Maybe things would be better now.

Maybe.

He got up and headed for the shower.

The sun was rising on Blackrock Island.

CHAPTER NINE
"And Though I Hide Behind My Hands, I Fear I See Them Still"

Tim was sitting at the table with a cup of coffee, staring out the window at the cloudless sky when Kim finally appeared at the kitchen door, her eyes still blurry from sleep. She wore one of his shirts and nothing else, her hair tousled, mascara smudged around her eyes. Tim's breath caught at the sight of her. How could he ever have—*left her*—let himself forget how truly magnificent she was, even first thing in the morning? His heart swelled, hands shaking slightly with the excitement of having her here, of knowing at last after all the crazy doubts, that this was real.

"Why'd you let me sleep so late?" she asked, coming to kiss him on the forehead.

"I figured after all the travel you'd need it."

"Well, thank you. I can't remember the last time I slept so well, even if I didn't have a clue where the hell I was when I woke up."

He watched how the shirt rode up to reveal her naked rear as she reached for a cup from the cupboard. A thrill rushed through him and he quickly looked away, his face hot. She'd kept herself in good shape over the years. He wished he could say the same. All the traveling, the searching, the fear—it had hollowed him out inside, drained his spirit and made a soulless wanderer of him. Kim's presence was like a beam of light in a hopelessly dark room. He was drawn to her, as he always been, but after his countless years of resisting the light, Kim had come into the dark to find him.

"So what's on the agenda for today? You going to show me this pretty little island of yours?" she asked as she searched for the sugar bowl.

"Maybe later. There's something I have to do first."

She looked over her shoulder and raised an eyebrow. "Are you making it sound ominous on purpose?"

"No. I made a somewhat foolish agreement with the local lawman last night. I agreed to tell him what I saw up in the chapel yesterday, then if he still wanted me to, I'd leave the island."

"And what did you see up at the chapel? Nothing good I assume?"

"You assume right, but it's not something you need to hear about."

She stirred her coffee, then brought it to the table and sat across from him. Fingering a lock of hair out of her eyes, she sipped the brew, sat back and gazed levelly at him. "If we're doing this," she said gesturing at the kitchen around them, "then it's all or nothing. I've seen them before, Tim. They changed my world as well as yours. So don't shut me out." She scooted her chair closer. "Now, how bad is it?"

After a moment's consideration, he told her. When he was finished she let out a long sigh. "And this dream—"

"It wasn't a dream," he corrected her. "It was just like all the other times. I was there, stepping behind the Curtain and into someone else's memory. I've figured out over the years that these memories are what normal people think of as ghosts, the emotional residue left behind, the last breath, so to speak. But the things that step into our world from behind that veil, they're not ghosts. They have physical presence, they can touch things, and they can hurt you. They come back for the sole purpose of making their killers answer for their crimes. That's it, and they won't hesitate to hurt anyone who gets in their way."

"But wouldn't that make *them* killers too?"

"I guess, and who knows what kind of cosmic retribution befalls them as a result."

"So this priest—Brennan—you think he murdered the woman you saw?"

"Yeah. And someone saw him, or found out somehow and hanged him from the cross in the chapel."

"And he wants you to help him find his killer."

"Right."

"So what are you going to do?"

"The only thing I can do, I suppose. Find out who put him there, and find out who his victim was."

"I could probably help you there."

"How?"

She straightened her back so that her breasts strained against the fabric of the shirt. "Sometimes people can be convinced to tell a woman things they won't tell a man."

He grinned. "Great, so you're going to whore yourself out?"

She scowled. "Easy, chief. I'll just turn on the charm and see who knows what, that's all."

His grin faded suddenly as he remembered something The Scholar had said. "There's more."

"Okay."

"Brennan told me my father was waiting for me in the confessional."

Kim paled. "You don't believe him do you?"

"I don't know."

"He was probably just taunting you, weakening your resistance."

"Maybe."

She reached across the table and took his hand, squeezed it. "Hey, listen, what happened to your father was awful, but it wasn't your fault, so don't you go thinking that he's going to come back for you. God knows you have enough to deal with." She smiled. "Your father's at peace, Tim. You have to believe that."

He nodded. "I do."

"And he died in L.A. Why would he be anywhere near this island even if he did decide to come back?"

"You're right."

"Of course I am."

A sudden rapping on the front door made Tim jump, his coffee sloshing over the rim of his cup. Irritated, he set the cup down and brushed the brown beads of liquid from his sweatshirt. "That'll be our friendly neighborhood policeman."

Kim stood quickly. "I'd better make myself decent."

"Okay, but I'll probably be gone by the time you're done." Tim rose, making his way to the front door.

"To hell with that, I'm coming with you," Kim called back, the slam of the bathroom door cutting off any argument he might have considered making.

***

"You've been keepin' things from me," O' Dowd said as he stepped inside. "I had no idea we had a celebrity on the island." He held a small sheaf of paper in one hand.

"There's a big difference between celebrity and notoriety, Sergeant."

"Not anymore. You know there's even a bloody website about you?"

"No, I didn't." Tim was genuinely surprised, and more than a little uncomfortable with the idea. "How much do they know?"

"A lot more than I did. Like this, for instance." He held out a sheet of paper so Tim could see it. It was a web page printout, the address *www.timmyquinn.com/* written at the top. The picture that took up the majority of the sheet was a reproduction of a newspaper cutting Tim knew all too well, even though it had been years since he'd last seen it. Above a black and white picture of a freckle-faced boy—a grainy version of a picture his mother used to keep on the sideboard in the hallway—the headline read:

11-YEAR-OLD BOY RESURRECTS THE DEAD, SOLVES MURDER!

O' Dowd stared. "Well?"

"Well what? I assume you've read it?"

"I have," he said, with a tight smile and returned the page to the top of the sheaf. "May I sit down?"

Tim shrugged and led the way to the kitchen table. "Excuse the mess."

Before the policeman sat, Tim saw the brief flash of surprise on his face at the sight of an extra breakfast setting. "Company?"

"An old friend," Tim replied. "Here for a visit."

O' Dowd nodded slowly, clearly unhappy at the idea of another invader on his precious island. Then he glanced toward the bathroom door, from which the faint sound of the shower running could be heard. With a sigh he gave an almost imperceptible shake of his head and set his stack of paper on the table, absently brushing crumbs away with his little finger. At length, he placed his hand atop the sheaf of printouts and said, "Do you expect me to believe any of this?"

"You can believe whatever you like."

The policeman leafed through the papers on his lap and fished out a facsimiled report. "Says here that in 1979, the remains of a child named Darryl Gaines were found at the bottom of Myers Pond, a short distance behind yer house. You, yer mother and father and ah...Kimberly Barnes—is that right?—allegedly all saw the boy come back fer his murderer." He read the next line and looked up with a sardonic grin. "'The turtles ate him,' you said at the time.

"And this..." he said. "Dungarvan. Right here in Ireland. There was a fire in a leather factory. Yer grandmother went missin'. You and yer father barely made it out alive. One witness said she saw a dead woman come out of the tide..." He chuckled in disbelief. "Are you honestly goin' to sit there and not deny any of this?"

Tim shrugged. "You've already made up your mind about it, so what point is there in my arguing with you?"

The policeman read on: "An incident in Germany at a youth hostel where you stayed for a brief time; a man and a woman you spent time with burned to death in their home in Cornwall; an elderly fisherman killed on an Alaskan fishin' boat in the Bering Sea on which *you* were the greenhorn. Jesus, this just goes on and on. I'm amazed yer not locked up already."

"I was," Tim said. "For a time, until I passed on a message to the warden from a teenage girl he'd had murdered."

"And how did you get yer hands on that, or is that a silly question?"

"At this point, I think so."

O' Dowd set the papers aside and produced a flask from his inside pocket. "Crazy people give me a dry mouth," he said with a rueful shake of his head.

"I'm not crazy."

"You'll have to work hard to convince me of that." He drew deeply on the contents of his flask and smacked his lips contentedly. "Tellin' me yer a magician, a fraud, a con man, a bit of a chancer, would be a good start. That you threw bundles of money into convincin' the media you were legitimate, then made it all back by chargin' the grievin' a fee fer showin' them their dear departed...by using special effects or somethin'. Anythin' along those lines would be good."

"Then I'm going to have to disappoint you."

O' Dowd met his gaze and held it, even as he patted himself down in search of a cigarette. Tim withdrew his own pack and handed him one. The policeman seemed surprised by the gesture, his eyes brimming with distrust as he leaned forward and aimed the tip of the cigarette at the lighter in Tim's hand. He sat back and puffed out a dirty blue cloud.

"You won't make much money on an island this small. We're quite content to let the dead rest. The people won't be easily fooled."

"I'm not here to fool anyone. I don't travel around capitalizing on people's grief. I see the dead because they show themselves to me. And even then it's only people who have died at the hands of others. I didn't come here with bells and whistles on, Sergeant, did you notice? There were no flyers announcing my amazing powers to resurrect the dead."

"Is that what you claim to be able to do?"

"If you've read those," Tim said, nodding at the papers, "then you already know the answer to that."

When O' Dowd rolled his eyes and took another draw from his flask, Tim leaned forward, "Hey, *you* wanted to know. *You* pushed and probed and went looking for answers. If you hadn't, we wouldn't be having this conversation right now because you'd still be in the dark. That's how I wanted it."

"Yer right," the policeman said. "But no one ever expects this kind of lunacy when they check up on someone." He dragged deeply on his cigarette, then mashed it out in the seashell ashtray in the center of the table. "So tell me..." He looked at Tim through the drifting skeins of smoke. "What is it you claim to see on my island?"

CHAPTER TEN
"The Shadow They Cast Does Not Fall At Their Feet"

"A priest died in that chapel," Tim said. "Father Brennan." He expected O' Dowd to be surprised to hear that he knew, but the policeman simply crossed his arms and stared, as if waiting for something truly worthy of his interest. Tim decided to give it to him.

"Hanged for the murder of a young girl."

Something did flicker across O' Dowd's face then, but it passed too quickly to be identified.

"Am I correct?" Tim asked.

"Yes." He shrugged it off. "So you did a bit of research. 'T'isn't hard to dig that kind of information up."

"So who did it?"

"Did what?"

"I'm assuming capital punishment doesn't exist on this island, so who hanged him?" He waited while the policeman coaxed another cigarette from his pocket, lighted it, then exhaled slowly.

"No one knows."

Tim found that difficult to believe, and told him so. "It's a small island, Sergeant, and from what I've seen you tend to be persistent. Are you telling me you found out nothing about what happened? No clues, no leads?"

O' Dowd smirked. "This isn't one of yer television programs, Quinn. In real life, the police don't always get their man."

Tim opened his mouth but Kim chose that moment to emerge from the bathroom. Both men looked in her direction. "What?" she said, with a playful smile. "Am I interrupting?"

She was wearing his robe, which led him to wonder if she'd brought anything of her own at all. And though it was cinched tightly around her waist, the sight of the exposed V at her throat, the skin beaded with water, together with her damp crimpled hair, was enough to stir something within him.

"You're dripping on the carpet," he told her as she approached O' Dowd, who was quickly rising from his chair, a polite smile on his face. It was the friendliest Tim had seen him look since they'd met. "Sergeant O' Dowd, this is Kim Barnes. An old friend of mine."

"Watch it with the 'old' remarks." Kim extended her hand.

O' Dowd shook it. "Pleasure, Miss Barnes."

"So you're the guy who's gonna run Timmy here out of town?" she said, with a slight grin.

"It's not quite as simple as that. We're just tryin' to get clear on what it is that he's doing here."

"Hasn't he told you?" Kim crossed her arms, feigned bewilderment contorting her pretty features, and looked at Tim. "You haven't told him?"

He shrugged, even as a laugh surged up his throat that he had to trap with his teeth.

"Why he's come to dig up buried secrets, just like he always does. I've often told him he should have followed in his late grandmother's footsteps and become an archeologist, because he doesn't just unearth things, you see, he excavates them."

O' Dowd was disappointed. "So you believe in this nonsense too?"

"I was there, Sergeant. I've seen them."

"Them?"

"The dead."

He looked from Kim to Tim and back again, frustration and disbelief giving him a manic look. "Do you hear yerselves? This is outright madness. If someone had told me a week ago that I'd be standin' in the old Thompson place listenin' to an American couple tellin' me they'd seen the dead struttin' around, I'd have laughed my arse off. But here I am."

Kim nodded, her smile broadening. She was clearly enjoying herself and, Tim noted, doing a far better job of handling the policeman than he had. "Tell me," she said. "Are you a religious man?"

"What does that have to do with anythin'?"

"Maybe something, maybe nothing. Are you?"

"I used to be."

"Did you believe in God?"

"Yes."

"In Jesus Christ?"

"Yes. So what? Did you see *Him* too?"

"No, but didn't he rise from the dead?"

The policeman said nothing for a moment. Instead, he looked around the kitchen, at the ghastly paisley print wallpaper crinkling on the walls, to the brown shag carpeting that looked at least four decades out of date, his gaze settling on the pink tasseled lampshade above the table. Tim knew what he was thinking because he'd thought it himself the day he'd moved in—whoever owned this house before him, they must have been colorblind, or into hallucinogenic drugs, or both. Finally, O' Dowd let out a heavy sigh.

"You believed in something you couldn't see. You believed he existed in some invisible celestial realm and influenced men's lives by walking among them?"

He wouldn't look at her now, a new blush on his face, this one fueled by irritation and the first strains of temper. "So?"

"You believed because you had to."

O' Dowd shook his head in exasperation.

"Why, then, do you have such a hard time believing what Tim is telling you?"

"Because it's insane," the policeman protested. "Only a fool would believe any of it."

Kim straightened. She was no longer smiling. "Some might say the same about religion."

"Great. Very dramatic, Miss Barnes, but I'd like to get back to my conversation with yer friend here if you don't mind."

Tim nodded slowly, then looked at Kim. "Why don't you get dressed? We'll wait for you in the car."

With a wink, she was gone.

O' Dowd began to pace, clearly pushed about as far as he could go before he lost his cool. Tim decided he'd rather avoid that. "Look," he said, rising from the table. "I know how it sounds. No matter who I tell—and believe me I try to avoid telling anyone, but there are always people who must know—it always sounds like some fantasy I conjured up, but I swear to you it's the truth, and the only way I can possibly convince you of that is to show you."

"Show me what?"

"The Scholar."

"I told you I don't believe in ghosts."

Tim smiled. "Then I envy you, because you've obviously never had to live with regret."

* * *

The sunshine was short-lived. As soon as they set out from the cottage, rain began to speckle the windshield.

"Does it ever stop raining around here?" Kim asked disdainfully from the back seat. She had dried her hair and tied it in a ponytail, a look that made her look more like the girl he had taken to his high school prom, if not for the lines and the awareness of pain that creased the corners of her mouth. She wore a pair of black denim jeans and a thick gray OSU sweatshirt, the kind of clothes she might have worn to do the laundry. She looked incredible.

"How do you think the grass stays so emerald green over here, Miss Barnes?"

When she didn't answer, Tim filled the silence. "What happened to me last night, at the chapel, it wasn't an accident," he said, one hand clenched around the door handle, the other braced against the dashboard as the policeman tried to keep the patrol car from sliding off the uneven gravel road. "Brennan hit me with Agnes' bible when I tried to leave."

Kim was quiet in the back seat, but he could tell she was unnerved. She was gripping the headrest on O' Dowd's seat as if it were a lifeline, knuckles white.

"Yeah," O' Dowd said, grinning. "Angry old ghost then, is he?"

"He's not a ghost."

"Well what is he then?"

Ahead, a small crooked spire scratched at the belly of the shale-colored sky. The sun was a silver coin beneath the gray.

"These things...they're more substantial than that, more tangible. They have physical presence, which is how he was able to pick up that book."

"Oh, I see," O' Dowd said, without even the pretense of belief.

"It's complicated," Tim told him. "There's a veil that seems to separate the dead world from ours. Imagine it as a theater, with dead people as the players. But that veil, or The Curtain, has holes in it, made by those who need to come back. And they can, but only by way of a conduit, a power source."

"And that would be you, I suppose."

"Yeah."

"Quite a story."

"I wish that's all it was, believe me."

"So you saw Brennan?"

"Yes. He said they used to call him The Scholar."

"And what was he doin' when you saw him? Sayin' mass and tryin' not to clank his chains too loudly?"

"Not exactly," Tim replied. "He was trying to get free."

O' Dowd groaned. The green hedges whizzed past the window, a verdant blur. They hit a dip in the road so suddenly Tim thought the car was going to flip over. His stomach lurched; Kim gave a grunt of surprise, but a moment later, the car was still on the road and weaving its way toward that ever-growing shadow up ahead. "So pretend I believe you," O' Dowd said with admirable calm, as if they all hadn't nearly gone through the windshield. "How do you know he'll show up again?"

"I don't. I don't even know if you'll be able to see him if he does. But you'll feel it."

"Aha."

The spire rose ahead of them, dragging the chapel up from the hills. As they pulled abreast of it and drew to a halt, brakes screeching, Tim noted that the front door was closed, the candles lit within. As he watched, rain pebbling the windshield, a sinewy old man dressed in a faded checkered shirt and worn jeans emerged, a slate colored cap pulled low enough on his head to cast his eyes in shadow. He saw the car, squinted, and his face twisted into a grin of recognition. He raised a hand in salute to O' Dowd, blessed himself with a hurried sign of the cross and shuffled away.

"Bernie Lohan," the policeman said. "Watches out fer the ferry; you probably met him when you arrived. A good fella fer gossip. If yer wild story ever gets out, you'll have him to thank."

Tim nodded, then looked over his shoulder at Kim. She mimicked a sigh of relief and rolled her eyes. "You want to stay in the car?" he asked.

"No, I'll come along. Been years since I went to church."

He grinned. "This one mightn't be the best place to start."

She shooed him with a hand and the three of them stepped from the car into the rain. O' Dowd made to hurry toward the chapel but Tim grabbed his arm. The policeman jerked away from him. "What are you doin'? We'll get soaked."

"I saw him from out here at first," Tim explained. "Going inside isn't a good idea. It'll be safer out here. Even strung up like he is, he can still hurt us."

O' Dowd sighed. "Wonderful." He turned up the lapels of his raincoat and cast a wary glance up at the sky. "I can't believe I'm standin' here in the pissin' rain waitin' to see a ghost. It would appear Mrs. O' Dowd raised a fool after all."

"It's not—"

"All right! Jesus," the policeman said, disgusted. "What*ever* it is."

Tim walked a few paces until he was in line with the door, but closer to the car, should fleeing in a hurry become a necessity. He looked back at O' Dowd.

"What was Brennan's story?"

O' Dowd shrugged. "He was a priest. Priests don't have stories."

Kim came to O' Dowd's side and leaned against the car next to him. "Look, you don't have to believe in any of this, but trust me, whatever you know about Brennan might help Tim. Forewarned is forearmed and all that jazz."

O' Dowd scoffed. "You really think somethin' is going to happen in there, don't you?"

"I'm sure of it."

"That's pretty sad." He looked away. "Rumor had it he got himself involved with a woman," he said. "When she turned up pregnant, rumor became conviction and Brennan hanged himself. One of the altar boys found him on a Sunday mornin'. Made a mess of his life too, I imagine."

Tim studied the chapel door and the single crack of shadowy light flickering beneath it. What O' Dowd had said didn't make sense. If Brennan took his own life, then why was he here?

Then you don't consider suicide self-murder?

And who had he come back for?

It's my turn to set things right, to tear the hides from my executioners, and you will help me. You'll cut me down and return me to my parish so I can root out the sinners.

He turned back to O' Dowd. "Did he leave a suicide note?"

"No." O' Dowd stared at the church.

Thunder crackled overhead. Moments later, the rain hissed down in a torrent.

Tim was still standing close to the front door, but nothing had pressed itself against the glass; the Curtain hadn't rippled open. For now, there was nothing here.

"Great. Do I have yer permission to come back and haunt you if I die of pneumonia?" O' Dowd said with disdain, and checked his watch.

Kim, oblivious to the rain, strode toward Tim. She looked once over her shoulder at the scowling policeman then said, "What are you planning to do?"

"I'm not sure."

"He might not see anything."

"I know, but as much as I want to run away again, I can't. I have to put the pieces together, if not for my sake, then for the sake of all the people Brennan might kill if I don't give him what he wants. And," he said, nodding at O' Dowd, "I have to hope he at least feels the Curtain move. If he walks away from here unimpressed, then I'm off the island."

"*We're* off the island."

"Right."

"He's probably holdin' out for whoever's in there to leave," O' Dowd called out to them, chuckling. "Doesn't want to ruin the effect."

"What?"

"There's someone still in there." The policeman nodded at the church window. Tim followed his gaze.

His guts turned to ice water.

One by one, the candles were being extinguished, pinched out by unseen fingers.

The air began to shimmer.

"Shit. Move back a bit," he said, hackles rising, and jumped when cold skin suddenly touched his own. But it was only Kim's hand, her fingers locking with his.

"Is it him? Brennan?"

"I think so." He dared to turn around, but only long enough to tell O' Dowd to get on the other side of the car.

The policeman looked nonplussed. "Why?"

"I think he's here."

"How do you know?"

"Just move back."

"Do as he says," Kim said forcefully.

O' Dowd looked at them as if they'd gone mad. Or madder than he'd already assumed they were. But the urgency in their voices compelled him to obey. He skirted around the car until it stood between him and the church, and smirked. "Now what?"

The chapel doors exploded outward. Tim instinctively shoved Kim aside, wincing as wooden needles stippled his skin. She screamed and dropped to a crouch, arms over her head. O' Dowd's startled cry dwindled as he sank down behind the car. Tim's concerns that the man was seriously injured were allayed by the sudden roar of "What the sufferin' fuck was *that?*" which immediately followed.

Tim dropped his hand, shattered oak still raining down around him.

The door was completely gone, broken hinges stabbing at the darkness inside the frame. And from that darkness, a pale face leered.

It was Brennan, Tim saw, no longer wearing the pillowcase hood. A split-second later and he noticed something else; something that sent bolts of fear racing up his spine. The Scholar was holding up what looked like a dead snake.

Oh Jesus. "Kim!"

She looked up, but her eyes were immediately drawn to the thing in the doorway.

"*Kim.*"

"What?" She blinked and tore her gaze away from Brennan.

"Get O' Dowd in the car and get out of here. Now."

"What? Why?"

He looked back to Brennan, and the shredded section of rope dangling from his gnarled hand. "He freed himself somehow. You have to get out of here. I'll meet up with you at the cottage."

"But—"

"Just *do* it."

"I'm not leaving you here alone." She rose and absently brushed at her sweatshirt. Her eyes were wide, filled with the kind of fear he had seen in them far too often.

"We don't have time for this. He'll hurt you if you stay, now *go*."

A moment's hesitation, then she gave him a look that said, *I hope you know what the hell you're doing*, and jogged toward the car.

"O' Dowd. Do you see him?" Tim called over his shoulder. The ground began to vibrate. The sneering visage before him writhed. Bloodshot eyes, seemingly held in their cracked sockets by will alone, swiveled and found O' Dowd. "*See.*"

Tim looked over his shoulder in time to see the policeman rise up from behind the car, his face alabaster in the rain.

Brennan's predatory grin scythed through the gloom. "*Dune var fore.*"

"Quinn...tell me this isn't happenin'."

"Get in the car."

"But what the hell is that thing?"

"I already told you what it is."

Dead white eyes moved back to Tim. "*There is someone here who wants to see you.*"

"Quinn..." O' Dowd said, fear tightening his voice.

"Get in," Kim called from inside the car. "While we still have the chance."

A second later, a car door slammed shut. The patrol car's engine roared as Kim aimed it up the hill. The thunder soon swallowed the sound of their retreat.

Tim was alone.

Almost.

Brennan turned. "*Come, my child*," he said, with obvious delight.

Before he knew he was going to do it; before his mind had a chance to protest, Tim stepped through the Curtain and into the chapel.

* * *

Brennan's face was a parody of human physiognomy. Though there were no candles left alight inside the chapel, occasionally the lightning would fill the windows and send echoes of electric fire in through the open door. In those brief flashes, Tim saw swatches of diseased flesh hanging from glistening bone, mildewed eyes catching the light and absorbing it, so that they gave off a faint blue glow. Filaments of hair poked from his otherwise scabrous dome of a skull, broken teeth crammed into a septic grin.

"*You know the way*," he said. "*Or would you like me to take you by the hand?*"

"No." Panic sped along his nerves. He should not be here. The Scholar was loose which meant everyone on the island was now in mortal danger. But what could he do about it? The only course of action available to him was to find whoever had strung up the priest, and sooner rather than later, and even that meant someone would die. But Brennan had not brought him here for that. He had brought him here for confession. He had brought him here to meet whatever the Curtain had made of his father.

He felt sick.

"How did you get free?"

Brennan, little more than a shadow against the dark, moved up the aisle toward the altar. "*Your father understands, it seems. In return for my bringing you here, he cut me down. I envy the shred of empathy he has retained in death.*"

Tim was suddenly struck by the thought that perhaps it had been his father's presence he had felt, and feared, outside this place. After so many years of dealing with the dead, of helping them find justice, of helping them to murder their murderers, he knew he should not still be so terrified of them. But if even on a subconscious level he had suspected his father might be waiting inside the chapel, it would justify the overwhelming dread he'd experienced standing in the building's shadow. There were things he did not need to see, nor want to. His father was one of them. But now that he knew The Scholar—who could just as easily have killed him and commenced his hunt—was telling the truth about what was inside the confessional, he was overcome with a desperate need to see his father, just once more, in the dark where he wouldn't have to see death's work. Perhaps all the regret and guilt that had festered inside him could be put to rest after all.

The wind raged through the door, pulling him from his thoughts. He could see nothing now, not even the lurching shape of The Scholar and it unnerved him, being in the dark with the dead man.

"Where are you?"

There was no answer. Arms held out before him, fingers testing the dark for obstacles, he walked a few steps and rammed his knee into the hard edge of a pew.

"Jesus Christ!"

A flare of lightning and he jerked away from the decayed face that was suddenly inches away from his own. The rotten flesh writhed with rage. "*Do* not," he said, "*Take His name in vain.*"

The lightning pulsed again as Brennan moved away. More strobe like flashes followed, and Tim used them to find his way between the aisles. He almost slipped on a mat of wet leaves the wind had blown in through the shattered doorway, but caught himself in time. Ahead, The Scholar, who had already returned to his place by the altar, waited with tangible impatience.

The walk up the short aisle took an eternity, the distance lengthened by the darkness and the thought of what—who, he corrected—waited in silence in the confessional.

At last he reached the altar, the lightning allowing him the briefest of glimpses of the cross, which would be bare now that The Scholar was free.

Except it wasn't.

In the momentary light, Tim thought he saw the figure of a man, torn and bloodied, dark wet hair hanging lankly over his face. He might have stirred, or perhaps the lightning had made the shadows nestled in the folds of his shirt twitch, he couldn't be sure, and was about to ask Brennan, but the priest spoke first.

"He's waited long enough for you. Don't prolong it."

Tim turned to face the confessional door. In the dark, the small box looked endless, as if it extended back through the wall and into infinity. As he steeled himself to enter, deja vu whirled through his mind. He'd felt no less afraid standing before the confessional door in Los Angeles, with thoughts of what his father might say, or look like after all these years, keeping him hovering on the threshold.

He reached out a hand, fumbled in the dark.

Lightning.

Unsaintly shadows fled from the tarnished brass handle, then all was dark once more. The metal was ice-cold against his skin as he tightened his grip on the handle and pulled, heart ramming against his ribs and pulsing in his throat. Rain scratched against the stained glass. Another flash of lightning revealed a vast dark emptiness inside the sinner's side of the confessional.

Get out of here, Tim told himself. *Just get the hell out of here. Do it! You keep squandering the chances you get to avoid this nightmare. This time, just run. Get out of here and off this island. Somewhere there has to be a safe place.*

"There isn't," said a voice from inside the box and Tim almost screamed aloud. "There never was."

CHAPTER ELEVEN
"Heaven Is An Orchard Though Its Roots Wind Down To Hell"

"Are you going to stand there deliberating all day?" They were the same words his father had used on that fateful day four months before, but the voice was different now. It was the voice of a man whose body still lay in a cemetery plot in Delaware, Ohio, lifeless and decomposing. It was the voice of a soulless thing, existing only to exact revenge on his murderer—himself—a quarry suicide had ensured he would never run down. To Tim, such an irresolvable conflict was the vilest form of torture imaginable—to be trapped inside your own murderous self forever, with mercy always so tantalizing close, yet impossible to grasp.

"Come inside," his father said, his voice a hollow whisper.

After a moment, Tim obeyed, despite knowing he shouldn't, despite knowing that all that separated him from whatever death had made of his father was a flimsy mesh screen. If the Curtain had corrupted his father, warped him into a malevolent thing, then Tim had just stepped inside the tiger's mouth.

Yet...

It was still his father, and there were things he hadn't said, things he'd wanted to say but had swallowed at anger's request that day in Los Angeles. Things everyone thinks of saying when it's too late to say them. But now...now he had a chance to set things right.

There was a small wooden stool in the corner of the confessional, tactfully placed so the confessor did not have to look the priest in the face. Not that it mattered now. Tim sat heavily and exhaled, his eyes darting at the specks that danced across the dark in his vision, afraid they might be the eyes of something wicked, watching him. His stomach ached.

"Dad?"

"Tim." The tone was flat. "You came."

"How...how are you here?"

"You know."

Tim said nothing. Even though he couldn't see, he looked in the direction of the screen and the voice that slithered through it. His imagination conjured up dreadful images of the countenance light would reveal peering in at him, but he pushed them away. *Still my father; still Dad,* he reminded himself. But the total dark and the dry, cracked whisper from the thing behind the screen tugged at his nerves.

"You've often wondered if the dead are anchored to their places of death, despite the evidence you've seen that proves otherwise." His father paused. "They used to be...but, no more. Things are changing. Now, we come and go as we please in a world that's full of gates and doors and other things."

Thunder outside, rumbling overhead.

"Why did you come back?"

"That, you also know." A hint of irritation had crept into the voice. "So why ask?"

"But you can't restore the balance. You took your own life!"

"True, but if I'm condemned to linger, I can at least help you understand." A rattling sigh. "And maybe someday you can tip the scales a bit in *your* favor."

"How?" Tim's insides writhed with sorrow. The situation seemed impossible, even with all the experience he'd had with the dead. He wasn't entirely sure his mind would be able to deal with the strain of sitting there listening to his dead father speaking to him through the confessional screen.

"All those times you nearly died. All those times the dead came for us...they were turned away. We never knew how or why. But now I do. It was simply a matter of timing, nothing more. It wasn't the right time. Everything that happened and will happen to you is predestined, Tim. Everything. And nothing is allowed to interfere with that. *He* won't allow it."

Despite the crawling fear that still rippled beneath his skin, Tim leaned forward, elbows on his knees. "Who is 'He'?"

"He's like you. He can see through the Curtain; he can bring the dead across into the living world, but his abilities are far more powerful than yours. Something happened to him when he was alive, something that altered him, and now not only can he see us, he can control us too."

Us. The word hit Tim like a bullet between the eyes. Quickly, he sat back.

"You know what you are?" he asked, carefully.

"He never lets me forget."

Instinct and the struggle to understand forced Tim's eyes to close, and now the dark was tinged with red.

"Someone *living* is controlling the deadworld?"

"Yes."

"But why...I mean, for what purpose?"

Lightning flickered beneath the door. "Because he knows the Curtain will soon fall. When that happens, he will bring us into your world, *all* of us, and everything will change."

Tim's head began to hurt. A web of pain spun itself around his brain. "The revolution," he murmured.

"A war." There came a rustling, followed by a faint moan.

Tim looked up. "Dad?"

"No." A note of pain diluted the harsh whisper. "Not anymore."

Panic sang through Tim. *Is he talking to me, or is someone hurting him?* "Dad?"

"You lost your father."

"Then what are you?"

"The detritus they couldn't squeeze into his coffin."

"I don't believe that." *I don't want to.*

"Doesn't matter. Entertaining false hope is about all you have left anyway. What difference will more of it make?"

"How do I stop this?"

"Stop what?"

"So far everyone who has come back because I acted as the battery they needed to do so, has come back to be put to rest, to have their vengeance sated. There must be something I can do to end this for you."

A gurgled laugh took Tim by surprise. "Oh no, there's nothing you can do. There never was. The minute I snapped that little fucker's neck at Myers Pond, I'd sealed my fate. Everything else was just filler."

"But he didn't kill you when he came back. Why?"

"He didn't need to. He knew how all of this was going to end."

"Do you know?"

No answer.

"I know you suffered because of what you did. I know it killed you inside, and I know I didn't make it easier by refusing to forgive you." Tim's voice cracked and he cleared his throat before continuing. "For that I'm sorry."

Silence.

"Dad?"

"Stop calling me that."

"Why?"

"Your Dad's in the ground, in a deep dark hole where he belongs."

Tim had no response to that. He knew arguing might only enrage his father, so he rubbed his hands over his eyes, then left them rest there for a moment while he tried to sift through the maelstrom of his thoughts. At length, a sob made him look up. He started to say *Dad* again, but stopped himself. His scalp prickled. It was a dreadful sound that tore through the screen—violin strings plucked in anger.

He stood, took a moment to compose himself, to assure himself that no matter what the dead man said, he was still his father and would never hurt him.

He stopped abruptly when something wet hit his cheek. He raised a hand and was surprised to find he was crying, the tears fat and warm as they trailed down his face. The tortured staccato sobbing, however, had not come from him. He stepped a little closer to the screen.

"Heaven is an orchard though its roots wind down to Hell."

"What did you say?" He squinted, demanding the dark retreat so that he could catch a glimpse of his father.

"I am where I belong. Grieve for the man in the grave, not the man on the Stage."

"You're trying hard to convince me there's nothing of you left, and I don't believe it."

"Then you're a fool."

"What does it do, this place you're in? What does it make you?"

"Angry."

"At what?"

"The living."

Tim felt his skin go cold. "Why?"

"Isn't it obvious? Because they have what we desire. All we do is seethe and regret, and hate. It's much easier than sitting around in this hell pondering what you would do if you had another chance, another stab at life. We have nothing but hate and a maddening thirst for vengeance. It eats at us, consumes us until we go mad—yes, even in death the mind can be lost. So we stand in the dark, dank, dripping halls behind the Curtain waiting for a chance that might never come, envisioning the horrors we will visit upon those who condemned us to the Stage." Again that peculiar scratched string sound. "And even if that chance comes and you get the justice, the revenge you so desperately need, you have nothing but oblivion to look forward to."

"What about Heaven?"

A snort. "Heaven? Heaven's roots begin in Hell and only a fool would think otherwise. Why else would there be so much evil out there? Why else would a man be permitted to build his own version of Hell and populate it with strangers who have no choice but to wait for their chance to snatch the lives of those who snatched theirs? On and on and on it goes, and when it stops, the whole world dies."

"The Stage is man-made?" Tim felt his bowels turn to ice. It couldn't be true...

...And yet it gave him hope, for if the Stage and its shield—the Curtain—were little more than remarkable and terrifying products of man's mad race to transcend and shatter reality and its dimensions, it meant there was someone out there who might know how to stop it, to end this insanity once and for all, to lay the dead back in their graves, their souls free to...

To what?

Heaven's roots begin in Hell and only a fool would think otherwise, his father had told him, but he couldn't believe that. Not now. Not when so much depended on his having faith of some kind, of any kind, to carry him through a lifetime of nightmare. Still, hope persisted, for no longer was he floundering in a seemingly endless sea of dead things—now there was a face, featureless for now, looking down on him, watching his every move.

A living face.

A face that could be reasoned with.

Or a face that could be destroyed.

"This man who created it, is he the same one who controls you?"

"No."

"There are *two* of them?" Tim's pulse quickened. After all these years he was almost afraid to believe what he was hearing. Real people pulled the strings behind this horrifying place. For now it didn't matter how they did it. What mattered were their identities.

"Who are they?"

"One of them is dead. The creator."

"The other?" *They died*, he thought, *and took their goddamn secrets with them*.

But then his father said: "Peregrine."

"What does that mean? Is that his name?"

"Yes."

"Where can I find him?"

"That should not be your immediate concern."

The air grew taut as razor wire. Blue light once more lanced the dark beneath the confessional door. "What do you mean?"

There was an interminable spell of silence; so long that Tim feared his father was gone.

"Dad?"

When the response came, it was not the cracked whisper Tim had been expecting, and he almost dropped to his knees in shock. It was a voice he knew all too well and it summoned a tortured moan to his throat, where he trapped it and brought his hands to his face.

"Forgive me," said the man who had once carried him on his shoulders through a summer field of swaying corn. The man who Tim had watched dancing with his mother to no music but his own humming, the two of them trying desperately not to erupt into fits of childish giggling as they stumbled over each other's feet.

"Please *forgive* me," sobbed the man who had spanked his son only one time in his life then silently wept at the kitchen table when the boy came to say sorry. The man that had painted marine creatures on Tim's wall and read *The Chronicles of Narnia* to him at bedtime. The man that had loved him and didn't mind saying it. As he knew he loved him still.

"We made a bargain. I wanted him to bring you to me. So desperately. I cut him down, but that wasn't enough."

Tim lowered his hands from his face. "What are you saying?" The walls of the confessional seemed to be closing in on him, the air thickening. Fiery dust whirled in his eyes.

More hideous silence. Scratches on violin strings. Lightning beneath the door.

Then the presence behind the screen made his final confession, and Timmy knew his father, the father he had known before death, was gone. There was no sorrow, or remorse in that voice now. Only glee.

And hate.

"He's going to kill Kimmie."

CHAPTER TWELVE
"The Sand is My Pillow, The Wave My Shroud"

The moon pulled the tide away like a silken sheet from a sleeping woman. The curragh had tilted, leaning on its side in the sodden sand like a smiling mouth, darker than the moonlit night.

Now and again, a curious wind would nudge the boat, then meander on, content to leave the abandoned craft a mystery.

And the woman, slowly forming like a dark stain inside the vessel, wept for its passing.

CHAPTER THIRTEEN
"I've Been Looking For Blossoms And Found Only Weeds"

He fled the confessional, the suffocating dark and the wicked thing that thrived on it, and felt his way blindly through the pews. If The Scholar was here, he was not making his presence felt, but Tim feared the priest was long gone. *Please let her be okay.*

In moments, he was across the chapel and hurrying through the open door. A cannonade of thunder sent vibrations through the earth, lightning dancing with spindly legs through the oily gray clouds as he raced up the gravel path toward the cottage.

Please...I can't lose her.

When the cottage rose into view, his stomach sank. The door was open, and there was no sign of O' Dowd's car, unless he'd parked it around the back of the house, but there was no reason for him to do so. Seized by unshakeable dread, Tim felt the energy drain from his body, but forced himself onward. Closer, and he could hear the front door's rusted hinges screeching as the wind battered it, the gusts ebbing and flowing like an invisible tide.

"Kim!" He broke into a run he was barely able to maintain. Everything in him demanded he just crumple into a heap right there on the path and sleep until the nightmare ended. But he knew better than to believe there was an end to this. He had lived in its shadow too long to entertain such delusions. He carried on, heartsick.

"Kim!"

Then he was inside, crossing the threshold and frantically searching the house, absurdly wishing it had more rooms so he wouldn't have to abandon hope so early. But after a few moments of panicked yelling for her, and with every inch of the small cottage covered, he put his hands to his face and rubbed away the notion of weeping. *Can't give up. Not yet.* But she was supposed to be here, he knew.

But she didn't know when you'd be back, another part of his mind countered. *Maybe she got bored and O' Dowd brought her to Madigan's?*

He didn't believe it, but it was infinitely better than any alternative theory he could come up with, so he steeled himself and headed back out into the turbulent evening, his nerves torn to shreds, tears burning in his eyes despite his best efforts to deny them. She'd be fine. She'd be all right. She'd be with O' Dowd.

If she wasn't...

If she wasn't, then maybe he'd have no choice but to join his father in Hell.

* * *

The police station was a lonesome tower of granite, a composite of the jagged rocks and boulders that surrounded it in ever decreasing circles. A road ran next to it, weaving its way between foxgloves and fern before ducking behind it to sneak back to the village. Like everywhere else outside the central hub of the island, it looked forlorn and forgotten. Ancient. The tower itself looked as if it had once been connected to a castle, which the hostile terrain had devoured, only to spit up the rocks that punctuated the dark green field around it.

There were a series of small recessed windows at the base of the tower, the sills painted a garish red as if to make it known to the observer that the building was more than a ruin. No sign hung above the door. Tim supposed that might have been seen as more of a blemish on the character of the tower than the lipsticked windowsills.

He continued on until he found the entrance, a dark oak weather-beaten door, and tried the handle.

Locked.

"O' Dowd?"

A chill breeze fussed its way through the grass at his back and caressed the hair on the nape of his neck. He shivered.

From inside the tower, silence answered.

There was an ornate cast iron handle on the door. Tim gripped it—it was ice cold—and depressed the latch with his thumb. The door shifted, but only slightly.

He walked around the building and peered in through the

windows. The glass was in dire need of cleaning, but Tim could make out a cluttered office with a large table dominating the room inside. Piled atop the desk were reams of paper, a cluster of old mugs, an old black rotary phone, and other standard office paraphernalia. A small winding staircase hurried out of view through a narrow alcove.

It was obvious there was no one here, so Tim, cursing under his breath, moved on.

He walked the length of Blackrock in just under an hour, quizzing the few wary locals he met, but no one had seen Kim, or the policeman. Tim wondered if they'd have told him even if they had. Outside what passed as the island's post office, however, Bernie Lohan—the elderly ferryman he had seen at the chapel earlier—seemed only too pleased to talk to him.

"She's missin'?" he asked, lips tight as his rheumy eyes took in Tim's anxiety.

"I'm not sure yet. She's just not where she said she'd be."

"That's women for you though, isn't it?"

Tim composed a smile. "I guess. Have you seen her?"

"Not since she stepped off the ferry, I'm sorry to say. She's a real looker though. Yer a lucky 'oul sod if 'twas you she came to see."

"Yeah, it was, but it looks like I've lost her."

Bernie scratched the silver stubble on his chin. "When did you last see her?"

"A couple of hours ago. She was with Sergeant O' Dowd."

"That eejit. Never liked him much." The old man grimaced, as if he'd said something prohibited by island law. "Sorry," he added. "I shouldn't be sayin' anythin' at all about the poor divil. He's had it rough enough without people talkin' about him behind his back."

Despite the frantic urgency that hammered against his insides, Tim's curiosity was aroused. "How has it been rough?"

"He lost his wife, the poor fella. So 'tisn't right for me to be wishin' him ill fortune, even if I do think he's a bit of a horse's arse."

"His wife died?"

Bernie nodded. "Very sad time indeed."

"How did it happen?"

"She was a beautiful woman. Very popular among the islanders. Then weeks went by without a sign of her. Word spread that she'd contracted cancer. O' Dowd supposedly took her to the mainland and that was the last anyone saw of her. Fishy, if you ask me." He rolled his shoulders. "But then, I've always been the suspicious type. I blame it on all them 'oul American cop shows." He winked.

"And no one asked O' Dowd what had happened?"

"Nobody thought it proper, I expect. We just assumed he'd talk about it when he felt like it."

"But he didn't."

"No."

Tim offered the old man as genuine a smile as he could muster, then thanked him and headed for Madigan's, where he felt sure he'd find O' Dowd. He hoped Kim would be with him, maybe relaxing as best she could in the unwelcoming atmosphere, with a drink in hand. Tim had a feeling his own welcome was about to expire too—as soon as he asked the island's policeman if he had murdered his wife.

CHAPTER FOURTEEN
"You'll Find Me, My Friend, Where The Spirits Are Quiet"

At Madigan's, he found O' Dowd slouched over the counter, nursing a tumbler of whiskey. To his dismay, Tim saw that Kim wasn't with him. The veil of smoke suggested the bar had seen a few patrons already today, and recently, but they were gone now. The policeman was alone. Even Madigan had deserted his usual post behind the counter. Tim crossed the room, his boots clacking on the floorboards and stopped next to O' Dowd.

"Where is she?" he asked. He was scared now, and didn't care if O' Dowd heard it in his voice.

The policeman did not look at him. Instead, he raised his glass and swished the contents around. His face looked sunken. Dark circles ringed his eyes. "Where's who?"

"C'mon, knock it off. *Kim*. Where is she?"

"How should I know?"

"You went with her to the house. What happened after that?"

"I left her there."

"So you saw her go in?"

O' Dowd frowned, irritated. "I suppose so, yeah. So what?"

"She's not there now."

"Well, I'm sorry to hear that. Maybe she got sense and left."

"I don't think so, but she *is* missing, which makes it a job for you. I want you to help me find her."

O' Dowd smirked, and it made him ugly. Tim found it hard to believe he was looking at the same man who'd grilled him outside this place only yesterday, the same man who'd accompanied him to the chapel and watched as a dead priest stood in the doorway. Had the fear done this to him?

"I know what you saw was upsetting…"

"Yes it was." O' Dowd ran a tongue over his lower lip, then gulped the rest of the whiskey down. "It certainly was upsettin'."

"…but we need to figure this out. We need to find out what happened so we can get rid of Brennan and whatever his death brought back."

O' Dowd raised his empty glass to the bar. "Ah, a fine and noble gesture."

"You're drunk," Tim said. "How long have you been in here?"

The policeman shrugged. "Not long enough apparently. I'm still findin' you fuckin' irritatin'."

"Be that as it may, I need—"

"Who gives a shit what *you* need?" Spittle flew from O' Dowd's lips as his head snapped around, eyes glassy and unfocused. His skin had turned a raw red hue. "You don't know the first thing about what you dragged me into, you bastard."

"And you do?"

"I told you we're not all country bumpkins here, Quinn. In fact, a few of us might even be smarter than you are."

Alarm bells began to ring deep down in Tim's brain. His muscles tensed. "What does that mean?"

O' Dowd's smile looked pasted on with clumsy hands. Tim watched his man's eyes drift to something near the entrance and followed his gaze.

They were not alone, after all.

Panic, already racing through his system at the thought that Kim was in trouble, increased a thousand fold.

There was sudden movement in the shadowed corners of the room. From a door behind the counter, Madigan appeared, looking grim-faced, but there was apology in his eyes and that scared Tim more than if he'd been carrying a loaded gun. He risked a glance over his shoulder and saw a man in a raincoat tugging the front door inward, scissoring off the meager light from outside. Another man was standing a few feet away from Tim. He was heavily bearded, his eyes wide, large hands by his sides. He appeared rigid with tension. But of them all, not one looked like they wanted to be here.

Tim thought he understood that.

He turned back to O' Dowd, who had not moved from his chair.

"I guess this is the long-delayed Welcome to the Island party, then?"

O' Dowd shook his head. "No. This is the official Get the Fuck Off Our Island party. In yer honor."

"Why?" Tim asked, feeling adrenaline searing through him. It was a ridiculous question, little more than a stalling tactic.

"Give me another one. Fer the road," O' Dowd said to Madigan.

The barman hesitated, then said, with visible discomfort: "Why don't you wait until yer sober, Michael? Deal with this when things are a little clearer."

The policeman's response was to slide his empty glass closer to the barman. "Things are clear enough. Fill it," he said.

Madigan, being careful to avoid looking at Tim, did as he was told.

"You don't belong here." O' Dowd snatched the drink and drained it one gulp. His eyes watered; he hissed air through his teeth.

"And why is that?"

"Because you came here to raise the dead and I'm not the only one who'd rather they stayed where they were."

A shuffling from behind him made the hair on Tim's neck rise. Phantom pain spread like ice across the back of his head in anticipation of a blow. But when he risked a glance over his shoulder, the men hadn't moved. Still not close enough to do harm. Yet.

"You'd rather the dead stayed put," Tim said, "because you put some of them there, am I right?"

O' Dowd glared at him. "What right have you to walk onto our island diggin' up things that are no business of yers?"

"I have every right, O' Dowd," Tim told him. "Because the mistakes and the evil deeds of others end up *being* my problem. If the dead got up of their own accord and came looking for you, then that'd be rosy. You could do whatever the hell you pleased. But they don't. They wait for me to cross their paths, to make the connection that allows them to set things right. *That's* why it's my business. I'm a garbage man, only these days I'm having trouble telling which side of the fence the trash is really on."

"This fella's out of his tree all together, Michael," one of the men said.

O' Dowd ignored him. He shoved the empty glass away and rose. His dark eyes bulged with rage.

Worry might have made these men hurt him, Tim realized, but fear was going to make them kill him.

"My father was right," Tim said, with a bitter grin. "Destiny plays more of a part in my life than I give it credit for."

"That so?"

"When I saw the curragh on the beach yesterday, you were quick to introduce yourself and quiz me about my intentions. I'm wondering now if you'd have been so quick off your chair if I hadn't mentioned the boat."

Again, the men shuffled. This time it sounded closer. From the corner of his eye, Tim saw Madigan raise a hand to stop them. It was not a gesture he suspected the policeman would have employed. Sweat oozed from Tim's body, his heart pounding painfully fast.

"Maybe," he said, "that was because the last time you'd seen an empty curragh on that particular part of the beach, your wife was lying dead in the water next to it."

O' Dowd hit him. It was a clumsy blow, powered by rage but weakened by alcohol. Still, Tim reeled, his jaw aflame with pain as he grabbed the bar to keep from falling. After a moment, he flexed his jaw and straightened, defiance burning in his eyes. They could kill him, but he'd be damned if they wouldn't hear the truth first, the truth about what they had set in motion, and what would happen after they took his life.

"I'm...I'm guessing Father Brennan didn't care much for the traditional values that came with his collar," Tim said. "Maybe he was a bit of a ladies man. The younger, the better. So, here's my theory—"

O' Dowd smirked. "I'm all ears." He motioned for Madigan to pour Tim a drink. Tim wanted to refuse, but kept talking instead.

"He was having an affair with your wife. You found out and lost it. You made her leave the island, and Brennan, and after she was gone you fabricated the cancer story. Then maybe you discovered somewhere along the line that she was making occasional trips back to the island to see her beloved. And it wasn't you. So you killed

Brennan, took his clothes and waited on the beach for your wife that night. Then you killed her too."

Dead silence filled the bar. Then: "Quite a story," O' Dowd said. "It's a shame you've got it arseways."

"You're denying it?"

"Yes I am."

"Are you going to tell him?" the barman asked O' Dowd. There was worry in his voice. "You know what it means if you do."

"Tell me what?"

Madigan looked at Tim. "Shut your mouth fer a second. You've caused enough trouble."

Tim did as he was told.

O' Dowd sighed. "Drink yer whiskey."

"I don't want it."

"Fine." The policeman reached over and snatched the glass from in front of Tim. With a rueful shake of his head, he grinned and downed the whiskey. When he was done, he looked from Madigan, who looked like anxiety personified, to Tim.

"You claim your world revolves around murder. Fer a time, so did ours," he said. "But I didn't kill my wife."

Tim couldn't see the lie in O' Dowd's bloodshot eyes, and that confused him. Had he got it wrong?

"Then who did?"

"Cancer."

"That's the truth?"

"Given the deep shit in which you find yerself all of a sudden, what possible motive could I have fer lyin'?" He shook his head dismissively. "I took her to a clinic on the mainland but there was nothin' they could do fer her. She died there. She always loathed this island, so I had her buried in Dublin, where she was born."

"Then who did Brennan kill?"

"How do you know he killed anyone?"

"I saw it."

Madigan tensed. "Michael…"

O' Dowd wiped a hand over his face as if it was nothing but a window from which he could clear the pain. When he was done, tears glistened in his eyes.

"What happened?" Tim asked him, after a quick glance around to ensure the men were holding their positions. All eyes were on O'

Dowd.

"My daughter, Aoife," he answered, voice trembling. "Prettiest girl on the whole island."

"Michael," Madigan said again. A warning.

"What?"

"Don't."

"Well we're not going to let him walk off the island anyway, are we? So what difference does it make?"

Tim felt his stomach plummet. All remaining doubt evaporated. They were going to kill him. A curious, distant part of him welcomed the idea. It would mean an end to the torture of serving the murdered. But that small shadowy corner of his mind was soon flooded with the panicked light of self-preservation and the awareness of what might follow death. Life was but a cocoon, he knew, but sometimes rather than becoming a creature of beauty and light, the silken butterfly emerged malformed, a withered, crooked thing, trapped in a bell jar waiting to be let out, waiting to hurt those responsible for its condition.

He had to survive this night, and the island, despite the odds being stacked against it. But what hope did he have against four men, all of them larger than him and steeled by the weathering of life spent on the island? For now, all he could do was to keep talking and, like all the bad movies he'd ever seen, pray for last-minute salvation.

"D'you have any children?" O' Dowd asked him.

"No."

"You're lucky. They're great until they start thinkin' fer themselves; then they become monsters. They get to that 'oul fork in the road, you know? Where they get to decide whether or not yer worth their time? Well, after her mother died, my Aoife decided I was an *inconvenience* to her chosen way of life, and went out of her way to show it. She grew...what's the word...*promiscuous*. Chasing horny little feckers away from the door became a full-time job for me. But she found a way around that. At first she took them behind the school shelter, then down by the park." A hardness had entered his eyes, but it was clear the memory pained him. "Then Brennan came to the island and everythin' changed. She started hangin' around him, somethin' I thought—maybe because I was desperate—would be a positive thing, that maybe he'd talk some sense into her. Of course, that's not what happened. She ended up sleepin' with him. Whether it was his idea or hers doesn't really matter. I'm sure she didn't try to stop it. As you've discovered, there are no secrets on Blackrock Island. I found out and I wanted to kill him. I would have too, if she hadn't stopped me."

Unbidden, Madigan quietly slipped a drink before the policeman.

"She was pregnant," O' Dowd said. "And that put a whole different spin on things. I decided to confront Brennan, but she forced me to put it off."

"How?"

"She threatened to kill herself if I did. Even tried once by drinkin' a bottle of Jameson's and swallowin' all my painkillers." He grinned but there was no humor in it. "All she got out of that were three days of vomitin' green sludge and the mother of all hangovers. But I got the message. I left it alone. Then one night she came to me, in tears." He paused to sip his drink and almost choked as the emotion conflicted with the alcohol. Madigan averted his gaze. Feet shuffled in the shadows.

O' Dowd coughed violently into the back of his hand, sniffed, and continued. "She asked me to help her get rid of the baby."

"Did you?"

"I sent her off to a place I knew from my days on the beat in Dundalk. They specialize in family plannin', which is really a front for illegal abortions. When we got there, she said she wanted me to go home, that she'd get someone to call me when it was time fer her to leave. I didn't want to go, but she pleaded with me until I gave in. I was probably deludin' myself into thinkin' that by followin' her wishes to the letter I'd get her back to her old self forever and we'd be a family again. I'd already lost my wife, I couldn't stand the thought of losin' her too." He drained his drink and closed his eyes. "Didn't matter though. I lost her anyway."

Despite the realization that this man might very well be *his* murderer, Tim felt a stab of pity for him. "What happened?"

"She snuck out of the clinic a few hours before they were due to...before the procedure. She rang Brennan, then hitched a ride as far as the dock. She used the money I'd given her fer the operation to bribe a fisherman into lettin' her 'borrow' his curragh — the feckin' eejit. Then she rowed home, while I sat in front of the television tryin' to keep myself from ringin' the clinic to make sure she was okay."

"And Brennan was waiting for her on the shore," Timmy said. "But how do you know what happened after she met him?"

O' Dowd opened his mouth to answer but instead of speaking, he emitted a sudden strangled gasp and tears began to spill down his cheeks. Madigan, clearly uncomfortable, replied for him.

"Aoife had many admirers," he said, his voice coarse and low, as if afraid the devil might overhear him and consider it an invitation. "She really was a strikin' young lady. One of her admirers was Tomas over there." He nodded at the man in the raincoat standing behind Tim. "He's not the quickest rock in the landslide, and he's never learned how to deal with rejection. It's gotten him into trouble more than once."

Tim turned. Tomas stared vacantly at him. Though clean-cut, his eyes were wild and dark as if all his thoughts and aspirations were trapped in the small black worlds of his pupils.

"Tomas was on the beach the day Michael here took his daughter to the mainland. For some reason only Tomas himself will understand, he decided to wait fer her to return, even if it took a month. As you now know, she returned a lot sooner than expected, but Tomas got frightened when he saw the priest. Thought Brennan might be able to read his mind and punish him fer his unclean thoughts." He smiled faintly.

Tim wondered why Tomas had not stepped up to give his account, or object to Madigan's interpretation of his motives. He concluded that the man was probably unaware that his name had even been mentioned. The distant look in his eyes suggested he was a better brawler than a thinker.

"He saw Aoife runnin' to meet Brennan," Madigan continued, as he fingered a crack in the surface of the bar. "Then he saw him kill her."

O' Dowd spoke suddenly. "Drowned her in the tide like a bloody unwanted kitten."

Or an unwanted baby, Tim thought.

Madigan gave a single sad nod. "Tomas came bustin' in here that night, blabberin' about a murder and a priest. Took us ages to figure out what he was talkin' about. After we got him calmed down, we asked him what Brennan had done with the body; he said he saw him put her in the boat and set it driftin' out.

"I closed up the bar and the five of us, me, Michael, Tomas,

Doyle, and Peader..." he said, indicating the bearded man, "...we headed down to the beach and found Brennan right where Tomas had said he was. Until then I think we were ready to dismiss the whole thing as a mistake, or Tomas drunk out of his skull and seein' things. But Brennan was there, watchin' the tide take the curragh away with poor Aoife dead inside it."

"He never saw us comin'," O' Dowd said, with the beginnings of a smile. "He was still standin' there...I think he was prayin', the mad bastard...when we reached him."

"You killed him."

"He was dead before he ever reached that cross," O' Dowd said, pride in his voice. "The fucker got what he deserved."

"How did you do it?"

"We hanged him from the old chestnut tree by the cove, then brought his body to the chapel. We made it look like a suicide, like he was hopin' fer forgiveness if he copied the sufferin' of Jesus Christ."

"Why didn't you just call the police on the mainland?"

"As I've told you before, we're a close community here. We have to be. Outsiders only mean more trouble, as you've adequately demonstrated. We take care of each other, and as archaic a principle as that might sound to you, it doesn't change the fact that that's the way it's done."

"So with no interference from the mainland authorities, you could have a hasty burial and be done with the whole thing."

The policeman scoffed. "Oh, no. Nobody would miss that particular holy man. I found out the rest of Brennan's sordid story in the weeks afterward. Apparently he'd been removed from his parishes on three separate occasions because of accusations of child molestation and lewd behavior toward teenage girls. Sometimes boys. In the last parish he had on the mainland, two girls went missin'. Neither of them was found, but with so much suspicion, the church had no choice but to send Brennan somewhere low-key and under the radar where they wouldn't have to deal with him. Can you guess where they sent the bastard?"

"Yeah, I can. So no one ever asked about him?"

"They almost seemed to have expected he'd take his own life. They probably prayed he would before he caused them any more hassle."

"So you did the world a favor, then, is that the way you see it?

Everything wrapped up in a neat little package?"

"*No*," O' Dowd snapped. "How the hell would we ever be done with somethin' like that? We killed a man; I lost my daughter! You think I needed you to come strollin' onto Blackrock to tell me they were haunting me? I'm no monster, Quinn. The moment that bastard put a hand on my daughter he condemned us all. Every shadow I see, every strange face that pops up out here, everythin' could mean the end fer us, fer everyone. We have to live with what we did, and that's more terrifyin' than anythin' *you* might conjure up fer us."

"But what about your daughter? Didn't anyone find her death unusual?"

"She'd been drinkin' and fell out of the curragh, as far as anyone was concerned," O' Dowd said. "The surf and rocks did the rest. We're an island of fishermen here, Quinn. People drown all the time."

"Brennan said 'dune var fore' when he saw you. What does it mean?"

"Gaelic. It means 'murderer,'" Madigan said.

Tim nodded. "And here you are getting ready to do it all again," he said, aiming for a nerve.

O' Dowd started to say something but was stopped by the intrusion of a sound that drew everyone's attention away from Tim.

Madigan hushed them all.

Someone knocked on the door.

CHAPTER FIFTEEN
"Only This, And Nothing More..."

"Don't open it," Tim whispered but was either not heard or ignored.

"Go on," Madigan told Tomas and clamped a hand down on Tim's arm. "It's probably only Doyle. Dense bugger was supposed to be here an hour ago."

Tim suddenly remembered the cross in the chapel, and the man he'd glimpsed hanging from it. *Doyle?* Instinct suggested it was, and if the next man through the door wasn't their friend, he'd know for sure.

"Say a word and we'll end it right here and now," Madigan said. Although he had no weapon to speak of, Tim didn't doubt for a second that he meant it.

Peadar moved back into the shadows opposite the door.

Tim looked at O' Dowd. The fear was written all over his face.

The wind soughed through the eaves, a dry lingering moan.

Tomas moved to stand before the door. Looked down, as twin conical shadows seeped beneath the oak.

"Go on," Madigan urged. "Open the bloody thing, would you?"

Tomas nodded, looked at each of them in turn, then slipped the latch and tugged the door open just enough to see who was there.

Thunder.

For a moment, nothing but darkening daylight filled the gap between door and jamb, then an ancient face, pale and wrinkled, swept into view, startling Tomas so badly he released the door and staggered back a step, an almost comical look of fright molded into his doughy features.

The shadow in the corner chuckled.

"Jesus Mary and Joseph!" Madigan said with forced joviality. "You scared the shite out of the poor lad."

"Well what's the feckin' door locked fer anyway, and at this time of the day?" Bernie Lohan said, pushing his way inside and slamming the door closed behind him. His threadbare tweed jacket was damp, his cap drenched. Once inside the room proper, he shook himself off and straightened with a wince.

Peader stepped back into the light.

Madigan sighed.

O' Dowd gave his eyes a few surreptitious wipes, and Timmy felt himself relax just a little. *More time. God bless you, Bernie.*

"Arrah!" the old man proclaimed with a smile, and pointed a gnarled finger at Tim. "Sure, there's the very fella I'm lookin' fer."

Tim composed a smile, though a plea for help was locked behind it. But even as he contemplated how best to signal Bernie, he realized it was pointless. As much as he wanted to believe Bernie could assist him, the man was simply too old, too frail. Drawing him into it would likely only get him hurt. Or worse.

"I wanted to let you know," Bernie continued, as he shrugged off his jacket, apparently oblivious to the impatience that hung like catgut among the men, "that not ten minutes after we spoke, I saw that lovely woman of yours. I tried to catch up with you but..." He gestured toward his reed-thin legs. "I'm not as spry as I used to be."

"Thank you," Tim said. "Where did you see her?" *Not that it matters a damn if I don't get out of here somehow*, he thought.

"Down on the beach, lad. Standin' there starin' out at the waves. I suppose they're an impressive sight fer someone who hasn't seen their like before. The storm's made 'em tall enough to scrape the arse off the clouds."

He hung his coat on a small brass hook affixed to the wall opposite the bar.

Tim nodded. "Thanks. I appreciate you letting me know. She had me worried sick."

Bernie waved away the thanks as he approached the bar. "So what's the idea of the locked door, Madigan? Air raid or celebration?"

O' Dowd cleared his throat. "Bernie, we shut the place up because we needed to have a chat with Mr. Quinn here. A private consultation of sorts."

Bernie spread his hands. "Well then, maybe I can be of some help?"

"I doubt it, Bernie. It's a legal matter. Very important, and we'd prefer to keep it private."

"A legal matter?" The old man looked around at the gathering, suspicion gleaming in his eyes. He jerked a thumb toward Peadar and Tomas. "I must have missed the newspaper the day they announced that these two had joined the force, or have they sold their souls to the divil in exchange for law degrees?"

"They're witnesses," O' Dowd said evenly.

"To what?"

No one responded. The look on Bernie's face suggested he thought aliens might have landed and replicated his drinking buddies. He shrugged. "Fine then. Madigan, toss me out a hot port for the road, and I'll be on my way."

"It's not a good time, Bernie. You'd better come back later on."

The resultant silence was so heavy it fought the veil of smoke in the room for dominance.

Bernie studied the somber faces around the bar for a few moments then looked directly at Tim. "You all right, lad?"

Not by a long shot, he thought, desperation biting at the inside of his throat like barbed wire. But all he could say to ensure at least Bernie walked out of here unhurt was, "Fine. Thanks."

The ferryman was clearly offended and unaccustomed to being locked out of anything, especially his local watering hole, where banishment was as unlikely as an adherence to closing times.

With a disdainful snort, Bernie headed for the door. "I may not come back tonight or any time after that if all I'm doin' is intrudin' on other people's business." He patted Tim's shoulder as he passed. "You take care of yourself, lad. Keep your eye on these 'oul drunks for me, will ya?" He continued on without waiting for a reply. Then, without so much as a scornful look over his shoulder, he cracked the front door and leaned out into the wind.

He was gone.

Tomas locked the door behind him.

O' Dowd coughed and stood up. His face had lost all color, even the blush the alcohol had afforded him. The trembling in his hands had spread. The air in the room seemed to stretch—the elasticity of tension. The shadows began to move. Tim swallowed, felt a fresh burst of adrenaline shoot through his veins. The taste of copper filled his mouth.

"I don't suppose promising I won't talk about this would satisfy you?"

O' Dowd looked genuinely apologetic as he shook his head. Madigan came around the bar. The anticipation of pain chilled his skin and threatened to force his bladder to let go.

"What about Kim?"

"Don't worry about her. We'll put her on the first ferry out of here tomorrow."

"Yeah, I'll bet. But will she be breathing?"

"That'll be up to her." O' Dowd was visibly steeling himself for what he was about to do.

Tim tensed. "She doesn't know anything about this. You don't have to hurt her."

"We won't," Madigan promised, and to Tim's relief, it sounded sincere.

Another knock on the door and he almost leapt free of his skin. O' Dowd flinched and clenched his teeth. Tomas's voice drifted over Tim's shoulder.

"His coat," he said. "The eejit forgot it."

Tim looked over in time to see Tomas tugging Bernie Lohan's

tattered jacket from the hook on the wall.

"It might be Doyle," Peader said.

Tim almost shook his head. *It isn't.*

O' Dowd swore. "Don't let him in this time." His gaze returned to Tim. "You'll find this hard to believe, and I don't blame you, but I *am* sorry."

"You're right. I don't believe it. There's always another way."

The clack of the latch being opened.

The creak of the door.

The roar of the wind.

A scream.

Tim flinched and whirled, forgetting how close O' Dowd and Madigan were. But Madigan at least had lost interest, startled by Tomas's cry.

"What—?" O' Dowd started to say but his words were lost beneath the continuing scream of utter horror from the man at the door.

Rain-flecked wind raged through the narrow opening as that scream dwindled to a gurgle. Peadar had scampered across the floor until the bar was at his back. There he sat, whispering to himself and shaking his head, his skin chalk-white.

Tomas was being lifted off his feet by a pale and slender hand that seemed to have grown from the door itself. Filthy nails dug into his throat.

"What the fuck is goin' on?" Madigan cried, but it was clear by his voice that he already knew.

My father cut him down, Tim thought, and watched in horror as blood began to flow from the incisions the priest's nails had made in Tomas's skin. His grip was tightening and now came the sound of glass being crunched underfoot.

At last the door swung open and the priest stepped into the room, still holding Tomas aloft. The young man's face was turning darker by the minute.

"Let him go!" Madigan yelled, fists clenched uselessly at his side.

"*Sinners...*" hissed the priest.

Even over the howling of the wind, they all heard the crack, as Tomas's neck conceded to the strain of the priest's vise-like grip. With a smile, Brennan tossed Tomas's limp body the full length of the bar, where it hit the far wall headfirst, smashing pictures, sending them tumbling down with the body as it dropped heavily to the floor.

"Oh Jesus," O' Dowd moaned, drawing Tim's attention. "Stop him," he pleaded.

"I can't!"

"Why? Why did you cut him down?"

Tim couldn't answer. That he hadn't freed the priest didn't matter now, and certainly wouldn't matter to O' Dowd, who was now looking at Tim as the only possible way of ridding the island of the walking dead man.

"I don't know how to stop him!"

The storm rushed through the door like a freight train but the priest stood in a perfect calm.

A clatter of feet and Madigan rounded the bar. He tripped twice before he reached the door he'd been waiting behind when Tim had arrived.

On the floor, Peadar wept.

With a sibilant sigh, the priest fell on him. Peadar screamed and thrashed as the sound of something being torn ripped across the bar.

O' Dowd ran, newfound sobriety and shock propelling him around where the vampiric-looking figure was savaging his friend. But Tim couldn't move.

God help me. Please. For once just listen. You owe me. Make this stop.

The door behind the bar flew open just as O' Dowd dove through the main entrance. The black eyes of Madigan's shotgun barrels stared at Tim for a heartbeat before gliding to his left. Tim ducked. An explosion rang out and punched a hole in the wall opposite the bar, and a little to the left of where Brennan seemed to be *feeding* on the stricken Peadar. Splinters flew. Dust rained down. Glass shattered. The wind snatched the smoke from the gun and curled it into imitation breakers.

Peader screamed his last.

The priest shuddered, the shredded tails of his black cassock moving like serpents, and rose.

Tim, stricken, watched the trembling barrels of Madigan's gun slide over the counter.

"You bastard," the barman said, his voice choked with tears. "You sick, twisted bastard."

The gun went off and the priest whirled to face the blast. For one heart-stopping moment, Tim thought it was over, that Brennan's skull had been obliterated by Madigan's bullet, as it would have been, had the priest been alive. But as the smoke and acrid stench of cordite twisted away, a nightmare version of the Cheshire Cat's disembodied grin appeared, and quickly, too quickly, the rest of the face began to return as if sewn back by frantic weavers.

The storm showed no respect for tidiness as it ripped through the room, just as Brennan showed no respect for the limitations of the human body, or more accurately, Madigan's body.

Tim waited until even the paralysis of fear could hold him no longer. As the barman was dragged atop the mahogany counter by long dead hands, Tim ran in a crouch to the door, aware he was whimpering, aware he had wet himself after all, but uncaring. The light in the doorway shrieked salvation at him. He lunged for it, the sound of breaking bones like firecrackers beneath his heels, propelling him onward.

Two feet from that glorious light, Brennan eclipsed it. For a moment he said nothing, just stared, his teeth bared in a bloodstained grin. Then he leaned forward, like an old friend preparing to divulge a secret and said, "I want to kill you, Timmy."

Tim realized then that he had been obeying their demands for so long he'd missed a crucial revelation, or buried it in the back of his mind somewhere it couldn't hurt him. Either way, it had gladly been forgotten: The dead were no better than their killers.

Sometimes, they were worse.

"Then do it," Tim said, aware that he had been saved from the lynch mob only to have the nightmare escalate in a matter of minutes. Perhaps being condemned to the Curtain would not be so bad after all. It was still freedom, of a kind. There, he'd never have to serve them again. He'd only have to stand in the Stygian dark for a short forever, peering through the rents in the fabric of reality and wait for his chance to kill. Wait for some other poor son of a bitch cursed with the power to let them out to unwittingly cross his door. But if Brennan killed him, would he be *able* to come back? Could the dead return if another one of their number was the murderer? So many unanswered questions, but at that very moment, he didn't want the answers. He didn't care. He was so sick of the whole damn thing, so sick of his miserable excuse for a life in which every glimmer of light was buried before he reached it, every joy crushed before it had a chance to blossom, every friendship destroyed, and every hope obliterated.

Too long. It had gone on too long.

A blizzard of leaves hissed in around the priest.

"Do it," he said again, and watched, shaking violently, as Brennan straightened, a disappointed look on his decayed face. "Would that I could, but I can't. He won't allow it. Mores the pity."

"What did you do to Kim?"

"Nothing," Brennan said, the disappointment more potent now. "There are rules."

"Then get out of my way."

The priest smiled. The wind howled. As thunder shattered the Heavens, the lightning revealed the cracks.

Brennan leaned close once more. "There are, however, no rules to say I can't hurt you."

CHAPTER SIXTEEN
"Children Planted By Curtain Mothers"

I'm injured, he thought with a queer sense of dislocation from the pain, and his surroundings, though he still felt the wind's cold caress, the rain's icy touch against his skin. It was the world around him, the dark gray sky, the long grass moving beneath his feet, the sea a giant rising and falling in his peripheral vision—all of these things were like melting pictures, refusing to stay on the canvases upon which they'd been painted. But in the foreground of this picture, the predominant color was red and Tim's focus jumped as his eyes found the source of the incongruity in this lush gray-green scene.

There was something wrong with his hand.

Something...

As if the thunder that rattled the Heavens had provided a hint, Tim slowed his pace to a halt and squinted, shivering, as he raised the hand he'd been cradling since staggering out of Madigan's bar.

His disorientation was so profound he had to raise both hands up before his face and examine them before he could fully comprehend what was wrong. And with the realization, came the memory of Brennan's words.

You know why they never found those girls, Timmy?

He sobbed, but began to walk before he allowed the shock to bury him where he stood. The wind threatened to send him toppling over the cliff before he reached the steps to the shore and distantly, he wondered what such a death would be like. There would be no pain, only instant oblivion. No hate, no revenge, no murder. But he couldn't be sure that was what he'd find, and the uncertainty, the not knowing what follows life no matter how virtuous, was, he decided, yet another level of the labyrinthine hell that had been unraveling before his eyes for as long as he could recall.

Because I ate them...

At the foot of the steps, vertigo threatened to send him reeling. The tide below seemed nothing more threatening than a dark comforting blanket, beckoning to him with maternal whispers. *Come...*

Slowly, carefully, he reached out with his right hand, his good hand, the hand with none of the fingers missing, and clutched the steel safety railing. Blood pattered onto his shoe and spattered the stone, and down he went, every step jarring him, tugging the pain closer to the surface, drawing it up through the panacea of shock.

Don't give up, he told himself, as he reached the middle step and leaned against the railing to catch his breath. He could barely stand up straight. It felt as if a jackhammer had been rammed into his chest and was shaking him apart from the inside out. *Not yet. Don't give up just yet.* He moved on, slower this time, the susurrant sea filling his mind with clouds, daring him to let go, coaxing him into an embrace it promised would only be cold for a second, then warm forever. He felt his eyelids trying to close, to give in to the voice of the tide and, panicked, he shook his head, breathed deep of the salty air.

Last step, and he looked to his left, to the curved stretch of sand awaiting his unsteady legs. Tangled black clumps of seaweed were strewn across the beach like discarded strands of knotted hair, wrenched free from the scalp of the sea by the combing of the waves. A jagged rock sprouted from the breakers and wore their breaking well, as it had for longer than Tim had been alive. Beyond it, tilted on its side, sat the curragh, shifting slightly in the foam. A figure stood before it.

He reached the bottom of the steps and his legs gave out. He collapsed, his forehead smacking against a sea-slimed rock. Dull pain danced across his skull, igniting a dim fire where Brennan had struck him with Agnes's bible. A mouthful of cold damp sand forced him to spit and choke.

Inky darkness began to seep into his eyes. His eyelids fluttered. Dizzy. The world swirled, the ocean became a vortex of sound and fury.

The sea hushed him, drawing him into sleep. He drifted.

She's standing by the boat...

His mind snapped from the spell into immediate and fiery pain and paralyzing cold washed over him. He struggled to get his feet beneath him, but it was as if they, like the fingers on his left hand, had been severed and cast away from his body. The absence of a response from his limbs filled him with terror, but the emotion was quickly superseded by mind-numbing agony. He was soaking wet and freezing. He turned his head and filthy foam-laden water exploded into his face, filling his mouth until he gagged. *Jesus, the tide!* It dawned on him then that even though it had felt like only a split-second of unconsciousness, it had been long enough for the water to creep in around him. Mustering every ounce of strength, he rolled over on his side, screaming as the saltwater washed over the ragged stumps of his fingers. White sparks flickered across his vision and he felt his gorge rise, the sour taste of the water only aiding his nausea. He feared another blackout and frantically tried to rise, the sand sucking greedily at his sodden shoes. The sea washed against his ankles, sending sharp chills up his legs and making his spine ache from the cold. He rose unsteadily, every muscle in his body protesting and sending requests for mercy to his addled brain.

A gull screeched. Somewhere in the distance, the thunder rumbled, its rage spent.

Tim staggered out of the tide, the force of the water propelling him forward. What remained of his fingers burned and he hissed air through his teeth. The bleeding had stopped, however, and for that much he was grateful, though he could hardly bear to look at what Brennan had done to him.

"Do you see her?"

Startled, Tim spun, and saw O' Dowd standing at the foot of the steps, his arms by his sides, eyes wide and dark. Empty. "Do you see how pretty she is?"

Tim turned to follow his gaze.

It was Kim. She was still there. The brief swell of elation was quickly vanquished as a question occurred to him. *She must have seen me. Why is she still standing there? Why isn't she moving?* Shadows of dread clawed their way across his heart, and he glanced back at the chalk-faced policeman.

"Where's Brennan?"

"My daughter," O' Dowd said, ignoring him.

His voice was filled with pride.

His jacket was covered with someone else's blood.

"She's come back to me."

His eyes were electric with the desperate madness of hope.

"That's not your daughter."

"She's come back. You brought her back to me."

"*Listen* to me. That's Kim down there." *Still,* he silently added. *She's still just standing there.* When the policeman offered nothing but an unsettling grin in response, Tim turned away from him and started down the beach, heading for the curragh and the woman who stood frozen before it, staring out to sea, as if waiting for it to reveal its mysteries.

"Kim!" The cry was like a shard of glass scraping free of his throat, but he called out again, eyes watering, salt coating his tongue. The breeze made her hair flow and thrust sea spray into her face. Yet she did not flinch, or wipe it away.

"Kim!"

He's done something to her, he thought then, the sorrow preparing to steal his breath. *Brennan lied.* He was suddenly deluged with dreadful images of what the priest might have done to cause her to stay where she stood, to stand so still, so motionless. He pictured rusted spikes thrust through flesh, wooden beams driven into the ground, ropes, blades, nails, and her precious blood feeding the tide...

No.

If she were lost, then he would be too, he decided, and damn the consequences. He would take her and walk them both into the ocean. Let the dead become someone else's responsibility. There was no sane reason why he should *have* to live with this horror anymore.

"Kim." He stopped a few feet away from her. He didn't need to scream any more. Her hair passed over her face like a shadow across the sun and though her face didn't move, her eyes moved to look at him. Tim sobbed in anguish and fell to his knees. He didn't understand, didn't want to.

There were no spikes, or beams, no blades or nails, and no blood.

It was the boat that had her held in place. The boat and the weaving mass of white threads that stretched from its belly to enter Kim's mouth. He saw them moving beneath her skin like worms, forcing their way down her throat, threading their way inside her, a million strings tied to the fingers of an invisible puppeteer. Occasionally she would twitch, as if in sudden pain, but she made not a sound. Instead it seemed as if the hush of the tide was pouring from her mouth.

"Oh God," he moaned, grabbing handfuls of his hair. "Kim..."

Her mouth opened wider. Her eyes opened wider. Tim looked away and saw the unmoving shape of O' Dowd by the steps, still watching.

"Help me!" Tim screamed at him, the pain forgotten, even as he thumped his ruined fist into the sand, imagining it was the face of whatever god had done this to him. "*Fuck!*" He raised his head, tears streaming down his face and roared at the policeman, stopping only when he saw that O' Dowd was no longer alone.

Brennan was there, descending the steps. Even from here, Tim could feel the smile radiating from the priest's face, the utter joy at what he was about to do.

O' Dowd never saw it coming. Tim cried out a warning, but knew it was useless. Before the words had crossed the short distance between them, the policeman's shadow had split in half and vanished into the sand beneath a spray of crimson. Tim groaned, swallowed bile, and quickly got to his feet. He turned to Kim.

"Let her go," he whispered, then louder, "Let her go, damn it. She hasn't hurt you." He took a step forward, and now he could see that the threads were not coming from the boat, but from something that lay in the bottom of it.

A corpse.

The remains of a dark dress clung to the bones, the skull obscured by a mass of matted black hair. From a space within the fleshless body, just below the sea-bleached ribs where the material had been torn, a ball of light, a miniature sun, revolved furiously, soundlessly, spinning out the threads bound for Kim's mouth.

When it finally dawned on him what he was looking at, it brought with it a hammer-strike blow to the window of his sanity. *Aoife...her baby...*

The ball of light was the dead girl's womb. The threads were her...

Oh Christ.

"My pretty girl," said a voice behind him, but he did not turn to face it. "A good mother, even in death."

"You said there were rules. She can't do this."

"I think it's quite obvious that she can," Brennan said.

Tim could hardly speak over his own sobbing. "But, for Christ's sake, the baby's *dead!*"

"If a child has never been given the chance to live, how can it die? For an intelligent man like you, you're really not that quick a thinker, are you?"

The threads finally stopped, the last of them trailing over Kim's lower lip. But she did not collapse, or come back to herself. The light continued to spin in the bottom of the boat. The wind had died a quiet death.

The Scholar clucked his tongue. "There are always options, as my church used to say. The unwanted can always be dealt with."

"How?"

"By killing Kim, of course. If she dies, then the baby will return to Aoife until another suitable carrier can be found. Of course, then your beloved will come back for *you*. Which leaves you in a bit of a bind, I suppose."

"Why is she doing this?"

"Come now...you've heard of the circle of life, surely? Well, in this world of opposing forces, did it never occur to you that there must also exist a circle of death? It's why the term 'newborn' isn't always entirely accurate. For every brand new shiny baby, there is also an old one, a baby that is embarking on its second attempt at real life. Some of those children grow up with a belief in reincarnation, convinced they've had former lives. And they're correct, but not in the way they think. They're no historical heroes or archetypal villains, merely children planted by their Curtain mothers."

At last, Tim turned to face him. "Why Kim?"

"That, I can't answer. If it were up to me, she'd be dead now."

It might have been better if she had died, Tim thought.

"But," Brennan continued. "I assume it's because the child is destined to have a pivotal role in the revolution. It has to be born and she," he said, pointing a blood smeared finger at Kim, "must be the one to bear it."

"Will it be normal?"

"As normal as you are."

"And Kim?"

The answer came from behind him, a woman's voice. "She'll be fine."

Aoife. Slowly, he looked over his shoulder at her—a corpse wearing Kim's body as a costume. Black rage spread across his insides. He wanted nothing more than to be able to tear these things apart with his bare hands but he knew it would never happen. If they didn't stop him, then the architect of this insanity, the Wizard behind the Curtain—a man he knew only by the enigmatic handle *Peregrine*—surely would.

"Give her back to me."

"Not just yet," Aoife said and looked past him to where Brennan stood grinning. "I need her help with one final task."

Tim watched the grin slip from the priest's face.

Aoife began to walk toward him. "Lover," she said, and there was murder in her voice.

Brennan's grin returned, but there was an edge of uncertainty to his tone. "Don't be silly, child. There's nothing you can do to me. As I've explained to our friend here, there are rules."

"Not anymore," Aoife said and as she reached for him, the slightest vibration in the air made the ground appear to shake. The priest raised his head and watched, awe and delight brightening his rotted face as the sky turned the color of dusk.

Time slowed. There came the distant sound of a fingernail tapping a bell.

With a scream of rage, Aoife sundered The Scholar's throat.

Blood flowed.

And the Curtain fell.

CHAPTER SEVENTEEN
"Grave New World"

The swollen sea teemed with them.

The beach erupted; the air cracked and split and darkened, and out they came.

From high on the cliff at the opposite side of the island, Bernie

Lohan knelt down on the grass, ignoring the pain in his arthritic knees, and prayed to God Almighty as he watched a hundred pale faces rise from the tide.

In the chapel, Agnes Noonan also prayed, fear seizing her ailing heart as long shadows stretched up from the altar, whispering.

Memories walked the narrow village paths, searching.

And Madigan's, though closed, was no longer empty.

Tim and Kim sat side by side on the sand, like lovers enjoying the sunset, but there was nothing to celebrate now. She wept, and he held her as they watched the sky twist itself into a panoply of colors and the sea proffered its dead.

"What are we going to do?" Kim asked, trembling, and he pulled her close as someone or something cold brushed against the back of his neck, causing him to flinch and grit his teeth.

"Find Peregrine," he said. "And make him stop this."

"Will they hurt us?"

"No. I don't think so."

"I feel sick."

Fearfully, he watched her hands stray to her stomach. He kissed the top of her head. "It'll be all right. I promise."

But he couldn't believe it, even as she buried her face in his neck, her breath warm against his skin. He couldn't believe the world would ever be right again. The dead didn't need him now, but in giving him what he'd wanted for so long, they had taken the world instead.

How easy it would be to walk into the tide, as he had promised he would if all was lost, as it seemed to be now. How easy it would be to take her hand and spare them both the hell that lay before them.

But then he thought of his father, what he had become, and what he had said about destiny.

He thought of his mother, still alive.

And Kim, who in seeking him out had altered her world forever more.

He owed it to them all not to give up.

He looked at the empty curragh.

It was time to go.

BOOK FOUR
Peregrine's Tale

I

1979

His name was Perry Griffin, but before he'd learned the proper way to pronounce it, he'd simply run it together into one word: Pergrin, which as the years went by mutated into *Peregrine* in the mouths of all who repeated it. Annoyed at first by what he considered a ridiculous title, it wasn't until he realized what the name meant that he stopped trying to dissuade people from using it. An awkward child, he found the image of the bird of prey that came to mind whenever someone addressed him to be somewhat bolstering, and more than a little cool. The christening of this new name, then, officially took place on his eighth birthday, when his mother presented him with his cake. Amid the twisted turrets of icing was a picture of a falcon in flight, its body skewered by dripping birthday candles, talons bared as it prepared to snatch its meal. Written in white icing across the cake was: HAPPY BIRTHDAY PEREGRINE. From then on, only the teachers at his school would insist on using his birth name. Everyone else used Peregrine, which the boy discovered meant "traveler," and though his ambitions of seeing beyond the woods in which he lived had not yet graduated beyond a mild curiosity, it would not be long before he was forced to live up to his name.

II

Peregrine didn't believe in ghosts, but only because he had never seen one. He heard the stories, of course, and sometimes lay awake attributing the chorus of night-sounds below his window to the wanderings of the dead, but always in the morning he would feel silly. The dead stayed dead, he knew. His mother had told him so and she had no reason to lie. The topic was occasionally broached in their house, but seldom discussed in-depth because for Peregrine, thinking about ghosts forced him to think of death, and that was infinitely more terrifying than anything that he might hear rustling around in the dark. So far as he knew, there was no proof that ghosts existed anywhere outside the realm of the campfire, but the reality of death could not be denied. It was a shadow the sun would never chase away, and the awesome inevitability of it terrified the boy to the core of his being.

Despite his convictions, however, he awoke one gloomy overcast morning to find a ghost sitting in the kitchen.

At least he assumed she was a ghost, for she would not look at him, but continued to stare at a point somewhere east of the window overlooking the woods. When he spoke to her, she did not answer, and after a prolonged moment of indecision, Peregrine went to his mother's side and shook her. She was cold. Still she did not move, or acknowledge his presence. She just stared, her rocking chair frozen in mid-swing by the heel of her tattered gray slipper. Frightened, the boy followed her gaze but saw nothing he deemed worthy of such intense focus.

He spoke; she ignored him.

He wept; she was silent.

A newspaper sat folded on the table, with only the word 'MURDER!' visible above a grainy photograph and lines of tiny print. On the stove, the pots and pans were cold, the customary smell of bacon and eggs absent from the air. There was only the smell of wood smoke as the embers of last night's fire hissed and spat, as if to assure the curious that there was life in its ashen bones yet.

Beyond the window, low purplish clouds rolled over the woods, rumbling. A flock of Canadian geese honked their way across the bruised pallet of the sky, plowing forth through a strengthening wind as lightning made dark veins of the trees.

Peregrine swallowed, panic clawing its way up his throat. "Mom?"

She didn't answer. He was beginning to feel as if he'd woken up in a strange house, or a nightmare. He wished for the latter, because all nightmares had to end eventually.

His mother hadn't combed her hair—a lapse in her strict daily routine that only reinforced his unease. Her eyes were wide and bloodshot, as if she hadn't slept. A part of him he had to struggle to ignore wondered if she was dead, if she had seen him to bed last night then come downstairs to sit in her favorite chair and die. She had certainly been quiet and sad enough over the past few weeks, ever since The Man left. Maybe the sadness had stopped her heart?

The mere thought of such a thing almost stopped his own.

Gently, so as not to startle her if she was simply lost in a fanciful daydream, he put his slim fingers on the arm of her chair, pausing when the pressure made it creak forward a notch. He hoped the movement wouldn't hurt her heel, braced as it was against the runner. Breath held, he drew close enough to her to notice that only the faintest scent of perfume lingered on her skin. Another ritual missed. She always squirted some on her neck just before she made him breakfast. Eggs and bacon, usually. Sometimes waffles, if he had done something to make her proud.

But there were no waffles this morning, and he couldn't remember the last time he'd made his mother proud, couldn't remember the last time he'd seen her smile. Ever since The Man left, slamming the door and leaving only a waft of whiskey, cigarettes, and sweat in the air behind him, she hadn't been herself.

Peregrine had done everything he could think of to cheer her up, but nothing worked. As the days passed and The Man didn't return, her face grew so tight and pinched he gave up trying to make her smile for fear it would split like an overripe melon.

The chair creaked again and his heart leapt. He leaned closer, listening for the reassuring sound of her breathing, then gently, gently, pressed his ear to her chest.

When he didn't hear the slightest sound, he almost screamed, but before the horror could claw its way out, a dull thud sounded and he lunged forward, forgetting his concern for his mother's foot in favor of confirming what he hoped and prayed he'd heard.

Thudump.

He smiled.

Thudump.

Allowed himself to breathe.

Thudump.

"Mom?" he whispered and drew back to look into her wan face.

She was no longer watching the wall. Her eyes had found him. He was almost overwhelmed with relief. *She's alive.*

"Mom?"

Her eyes were still glassy, but at least she'd shown some sign that she could see him. She was not a ghost, after all.

"Mom?" he said again, wishing more than anything that she would answer, even if only to tell him to shut up. "Can you hear me?"

But to his disappointment, she frowned, just a little, and her gaze returned to the wall.

I should call a doctor, Peregrine realized. *She's sick. There's something wrong with her. Why won't she talk?*

Although she hadn't spoken much at all after The Man walked out, she had at least moved and said a word here and there to him. She had continued to make him breakfast every morning, even though he could tell she didn't want to.

Secretly, he was glad The Man was gone. He remembered waking in his bed one night with the realization that it had been weeks since he'd last heard voices coming through the wall from his mother's bedroom. No voices, no booming laughter, no crying, no tortured squeaking of the bed, or moans, or animal grunting. Just quiet. Peregrine liked that just fine. He wouldn't be so tired in the mornings anymore after being kept awake by those godawful sounds; he wouldn't have to lie awake at night staring at the shadows the moon cast through the trees, wondering what peculiar things his mother and The Man were doing in her room. Wondering if The Man was hurting her. He wouldn't have to wait in bed in the mornings until he heard the sound of The Man's car starting up.

No, he didn't miss The Man at *all.* He'd rarely set eyes on him, but the glimpses he'd caught had been enough—a bearish man who wore large overcoats that only served to make him seem even bigger; hair long, dark and unruly; spade-shaped face with coal-dark eyes glaring out above a bulbous nose and worm-like lips.

But mostly it was the smell of him that bothered the boy. Whenever The Man showed up, the house filled with a sickly sweet smell so pungent Peregrine had to sleep with his face buried in the pillow. Even after the man was gone, the smell would linger for days afterward, as if there were dead flowers somewhere inside the walls.

Peregrine had learned not to ask about his mother's "guest" after his one and only inquiry had inspired her to knock out his two front teeth and chip a third with the edge of a frying pan.

His father was gone, and now The Man was gone too. He only had the faintest recollection of what his father had been like, but he missed him, if only because he had to have been better, and kinder, than the monster his mother had let into their house.

He tried to feel sorry for her, but it was difficult. He hated what the monster's absence was doing to his mother, but was overjoyed and relieved that The Man was gone. Whenever that dead flower smell choked the house, it frightened him. The Man's oily shadow, slithering across the stair steps as if coming to get him, frightened him even more. He didn't care if he never saw him again.

Then an awful thought occurred to him: What if the only way he would ever get his mother back to herself was if The Man came back? What if the doctor called round, shook his head, clucked his tongue and suggested the only remedy was to fetch The Man at once. Then her mother's visitor might never leave, and that was too awful a possibility to contemplate. He could almost smell that terrible stench already, eager to be let back inside.

A bubbling whine in his stomach reminded him he had yet to eat, and after a final, longing look at his mother, he sighed and went to fix himself some toast. He released the arm of the chair and it heaved forward with an odd clattering sound. He looked in time to see an empty whiskey bottle spinning away from his mother's feet, and watched as it came to rest pointing toward the window, like the needle of a compass following the direction of his mother's gaze.

Peregrine frowned and went to fetch the bottle. He couldn't remember ever seeing his mother drink liquor before. Perhaps The Man had left it behind.

As he slipped his hand around the bottle, there was another noise. Behind him. A scraping sound he couldn't immediately identify. He straightened, bottle in hand and turned.

A creak.

He jolted and almost dropped the bottle, then felt the tension drain from his body. A smile warmed his face. The rocking chair creaked again, settling back on its runners. His mother was awake, *proper* awake, and standing up, if a little unsteadily. It bothered him that she was still staring at the wall, though. He tried again to locate the object of her fascination but saw nothing but flaking paint and their cheap old clock, keeping time with his heart.

"Mom...you scared me," he said, reaching out a hand in case she needed to steady herself. Her lips parted with a dry rasping sound. She continued to sway, as if she was still in synch with the movement of the rocking chair. Peregrine moved closer. He wasn't sure he could do anything if she did fall over, but it was only right to try.

And then she did speak, though it took Peregrine a moment to decipher what she'd said.

Her voice was faint, little more than a whisper, so much so that at first, he thought it was the wind he'd heard fluttering through the gutters. But her mouth had moved to shape the words and there could be no mistaking they were hers.

She said: "He didn't want you."

Her eyes widened, as if she'd just realized something. Peregrine didn't think it possible for her skin to get any whiter than it was already, but it did. She was now so pale her eyes were like splotches of dark ink on a white sheet of paper.

Peregrine was confused. He'd seen drunk people before—in all the times they'd visited Uncle Marty in Indiana, he'd never once seen the old man sober—and wanted to believe his mother had simply had too much to drink, and that was why she was acting so weird, and saying things that made no sense.

But though young, he was no fool. He knew what her words *might* mean, and tried hard not to think about it.

She turned her head, just a fraction of an inch, and her eyes moved. Any joy or relief Peregrine might have felt at this was immediately obliterated by the cold fury he saw in them. Her hatred radiated out toward him, an almost palpable thing, hazing the air between them. She sucked in a deep, shuddering breath, and it emerged in a soft groan.

"Mom...what is it?"

"He didn't want you," she repeated, this time louder.

"Who?"

"'Him or me,' he said, and guess...who I chose?"

Peregrine was about to ask her to stop, tell her that she was frightening him, but an icy needle of realization slid into his brain and stole the breath from his lungs.

His mother blamed him for making The Man go away. He didn't think that fair at all, but knew it meant he'd be black and blue by bedtime. All because of that foul-smelling giant with the crawling shadow.

He made her choose between us. He was grimly satisfied that his hatred of The Man had been justified, but the fear overruled it. There was something in his mother's eyes he'd never seen before, and it made him want to run from her. But before he could move, his mother's left hand rose. He was now able to see what the scraping sound had been and it made every hair on his body stand to attention.

It was the long cast iron poker that had always hung on its hook by the fireplace. His mother's knuckles were white around its faux bronze handle. She held it as if it were a sword, the business end whitened by ash and wavering in the air between them.

"'Children are like houses' he told me, 'You can always leave 'em and get yourself a new one if the old one starts to stink'." Tears spilled down her cheeks. Peregrine wished he could believe they were for him. "He wanted me to send you away so we could be together, so I could be happy. And don't you think that's only fair? Your father left me here alone, with nothing but bills and no money, no fucking *life!* How is that fair, huh? That I have to spend my whole life cooped up in here with you while the rest of the world gets to live their dreams and ambitions. Tell me, Peregrine…how is that *fair?*"

Peregrine shook his head, wishing now that she'd stayed in her trance. He knew protesting and pleading was useless. When she lost her temper she would talk and beat him at the same time, her efforts increasing if he tried to wriggle away or apologize for whatever had incited her fury. This was no ordinary temper though. He had never seen such alien hatred in his mother's eyes and it terrified him. Helpless, he stood frozen, legs trembling, while above the house the sky bellowed and white light seared the windows.

She was steady for a moment, momentarily distracted by the burgeoning storm, then her gaze flitted back to Peregrine, and she smiled.

It was the most hideous thing he'd ever seen. He had done nothing wrong and yet in a heartbeat his mother had become a monster, just like The Man. He wanted to know where his mother had gone, the mother who'd joked with him over breakfast for years, hugged him and protected him...and loved him. He wondered if that's what The Man had been doing to his mother at night—poisoning her somehow. For there was no love in the eyes of the woman towering over him now.

"Mom..." he whispered.

"But I turned him down," she said, still smiling that terrible smile, "I let another man walk out of my life with my dreams in his pocket."

"Please..."

"But you know something, Peregrine. *You're* not going to leave with anything of mine. Nothing."

It seemed the air grew heavy then, as she took an uneven step forward, the weight of the poker conspiring with gravity to drag her to the floor. Peregrine felt a cold streak of despair freeze the flesh between his shoulder blades and he began to sob.

It was a mistake.

"Don't you cry, Peregrine," his mother said and in the next flash of lightning, her smile was gone, pulled back into an inhuman snarl that heralded her killing blow. "Don't you fucking *dare* cry!" She steadied herself and raised the weapon over her head.

"Please Mommy..."

For a split second, Peregrine thought he saw a flicker of doubt cross his mother's face, but then it was gone and he knew by the way her body tensed that she was preparing to hit him. He braced himself for unimaginable pain, perhaps the last he would ever feel.

There was a *whoosh* as the poker came down and Peregrine wailed, hands raised to ward off the blow. Thunder rolled boulders across the roof. The wind buffeted the house. Instinct forced him to dodge the arc of her strike and he staggered back a few steps, hands still in front of him as if will alone could make a metal shield of his fingers.

"Don't..."

She shrieked and drew her arm back, eyes so wide he could only see the whites and in that moment, he realized his mother was truly gone. The lightning made a witch of her, a foul, snarling thing straight out of a Grimm Fairy Tale.

"Trust me, Peregrine. It will be better for us both when you're gone."

She swung the poker at his head but this time he didn't wait for it. Despite the terror that made his limbs feel full of lead, he broke for the door, phantom pain already punching icy holes in his skull. But all he felt was the poker cut the air; all he heard was his mother's enraged cry; and then he was colliding painfully with the kitchen table, spinning, then once more running, the short path to the front door reeling away from him as it might in dreams and nightmares.

The poker whooshed again and connected with something that shattered on impact. Peregrine did not stop or look back to see what had taken the blow meant for him. He fumbled at the door handle with panicked fingers. It wouldn't open. Behind him, his mother's breath whistled through her nose and the sound drew closer.

He wrenched at the door handle once, twice, and again but it wouldn't budge. He pounded desperately at the wood. Weeping uncontrollably, snot dribbling from his nose, he shook his head, denying the cruel reality he had suddenly found himself thrust into, and punched the door hard enough to crack his knuckles. The pain brought a new wave of sobs and he almost gave up, almost sagged to the floor to await a punishment he didn't deserve.

"Wait there, Peregrine," his mother commanded, her breathing like a bellows in the small room. "I'm going to fix it."

She was behind him, he heard her thump against the kitchen table, only a few feet away.

"Wait for me. I'll make it better. John will come back. You'll see."

John. The Man. The Devil.

"You'll see," she said again, and now she was towering over him.

"Please," he whimpered and almost felt the air strain as she hefted the poker again.

"Hush now," she soothed.

She locks the door, he realized then and his chest almost exploded with hope. *Every night she locks the door*. In his panic, he had forgotten.

He lunged forward.

The poker whipped through the air.

He fumbled, grabbed, snapped back the lock and pulled.

The door opened, but not before the wicked iron thudded against his back, almost crippling him. He screamed. Fireworks erupted before his eyes and liquid flame raced up his spine. For a fleeting instant, he wondered if she'd killed him, if the floating, dizzying sensation meant *he* was now a ghost. He staggered, collided with the door, forcing it to close. The darkening light of morning recoiled from the jamb.

Peregrine choked on his own cries, then forced himself to stand. The muscles in his back sang with agony. Needles danced across the skin. It felt as if a cannonball had been shot into him, but despite the torture of standing, he managed it. Knew he had to. He was not yet dead. There was still a chance to get away.

"You're making this harder than it needs to be…"

Her words were muffled, as if his ears had been stuffed with cotton.

His hands, trembling so badly he missed the doorknob twice and ended up scrabbling at the lock, finally found purchase and he tugged with all the strength he had left.

Daylight, tainted by the storm, seeped in again and this time he lurched forward, blindly, hands outstretched to grab freedom, even as stars peppered his vision. The pain raged, tried to drag him to the ground.

Outraged screams trailed him as he blundered out into the rain. The sky boiled black and silver, the clouds churning. Thunder crackled and split the heavens.

Peregrine stumbled on.

III

Peregrine stumbled across the yard, collided with the fender of his mother's Buick, then quickly made for the woods that stood patiently on the borders of the property. Thick limbs of spruce tried to slow his passage, but he fought through them until the air around him grew denser and the light faded. When he paused and took in his surroundings, he could see nothing but trees, some dead and fallen, most standing tall and creaking in the wind.

A fresh wave of fear flooded through him. He had been in the woods a thousand times, but never when the light was seeping from the day. Never when a storm was shredding the sky over the trees, and never to escape death at the hands of his own mother. He bent a hand back to knead the throbbing at the base of his spine, recalling as he did so the time he'd asked his mother why Uncle Marty walked around with one arm permanently crooked behind his back.

Spine trouble, she'd told him.

As he trudged his way through the trees, picking his way over deadwood and avoiding critter holes, he thought he finally understood the pain Uncle Marty had had to live with. He wondered if that was the reason the old man drank so much.

The sky thrust a spear of lightning and cracked the earth somewhere up ahead. The furor made Peregrine hunker down, his arms clasped protectively around his head. He was still crying, but the tears were near their end, his eyes swollen and sore. A startled bird fluttered from the brush and took to the air, quickly vanishing into the storm.

Why is she doing this to me? Peregrine thought, miserably. Already he wanted to go home. He liked the woods when it was light, but now that the light was almost gone, the place looked almost as hostile as his own home had become. In all likelihood there might be worse things waiting for him out here. It also occurred to him that if he wandered too far and it got dark, he might get lost and die out here anyway, so he continued on until he was far enough away from the house, but not so far that he couldn't find his way back if he needed to, found a rotted stump, and sat. His back protested by tugging the muscles tight, pain thrumming along his spine. He winced.

Thunder rumbled; the rain sizzled down around him.

How could she choose him over me?

Confusion buzzed within him as he stared at the carpet of twigs, pine needles, and moss beneath his feet. Cold droplets weighed down the leaves of a walnut tree close by and he watched them dripping.

It was The Man's fault, The Man who had turned his mother against him.

"John," he said aloud, as if it were a curse word.

He imagined *John* now, stalking around the corner of the house. His mother would drop the poker and run to him, joy on her face, her arms wide to receive her guest. She would shower him with affection and bring him inside out of the storm, maybe for some hot soup and some dry clothes. A warm bed. And when he asked what had happened with Peregrine, his mother would smile and shrug and tell him: *Spine trouble.*

An involuntary moan slid from Peregrine's mouth. His shivering intensified, but there was rage there now, shaking him from the inside out. *She doesn't want me. She doesn't care.*

Amid the fury, he tried desperately to latch onto a memory of better times, but his head was pounding, the shivering making his teeth click together. All the good times seemed forced and contrived now. Every kind word, every kiss on the cheek, every promise...all lies, all an act. His mother had been stringing him along...using him until her knight came along to take her away to better things. He snorted laughter then, and the sound of it was so alarming, he flinched and huddled in on himself.

No, you've got it wrong. She's just a little sick, that's all. She needs help.

Maybe that was true, but it didn't change the fact that she was trying to kill him. If he tried to tackle the twelve-mile walk into town, she'd only have to take the car and she'd have caught up to him in minutes. The only other option was to wait it out in the darkening woods with the storm forcing the trees to dance around him.

He didn't think it possible for the rain to get any heavier, but it did, and when it pelted his scalp hard enough to sting, he stood, sodden and trembling and screamed at the trees, at the house beyond, and at the evil, wicked woman who'd pretended to be his mother all these years:

"I don't care if you kill me! You don't love me anyway! You only love *him*."

Thunder responded and it made the forest seem full of ravenous creatures, their dark bellies roiling with hunger. Lightning splashed its cobalt shadow over the trees. Peregrine, fists clenched, teeth gritted, turned to his left and walked on, away from the house and deeper into the woods. He ignored the pain in his back, though now it seemed as if the last flash of lightning had set it aflame. Nevertheless, thoughts of escape helped him maintain the pace. He was still afraid, still weeping. He felt betrayed and unsure. He wanted to go home, to open the door and find his mother sitting by the fire, mad only with worry, and looking just like she had in the old days. Before *John* came. Peregrine would tell her he'd gotten lost in the woods and fallen asleep, and she would scold him, but with love in her eyes. She would cry, her skin soft, her perfume untainted by alcohol as she drew him into her embrace. Then she would carry him upstairs to sit with him until the storm moved on. The thought almost stopped him in his tracks. The hope was so strong he wondered if, as in some of the stories he'd read, a wish could really come true if you wanted it badly enough.

Heartsick, he moved on. Real life was nothing like that. In real life, mothers pretended to love their children and beat them for no reason. Sometimes, they even tried to kill them.

"Peregrine."

He stopped dead. Every muscle grew taut.

Imagination, he told himself. *I imagined it. There's no one here but me.*

Overhead, the trees swished like ocean waves in the wind, while those with bare branches tapped gnarled knuckles together. The sky sounded as if it would come tumbling down around him.

He turned.

"Mom?"

She was standing behind him.

His most recent imaginings made him relieved to see her, even though wet and shivering, she looked more like a witch now than ever before. Her hair hung in her face, the lightning revealing only a bone-white curve of cheek. She twitched, rain sluicing down her arms, her nightdress drenched so that he could see the bare flesh beneath.

He wanted to throw his arms around her, despite how she had hurt him, despite the certainty that she didn't love him and never had. Despite her betrayal. But he couldn't see her eyes through the sodden mop of her hair, and was sure if he could, they'd be filled with lightning. *She's gone*, he knew, and felt the last vestiges of hope flee on the wind.

At last he convinced himself to turn and run, to keep going on until he reached town, and safety, but when he turned, her bony white hand clamped down like a steel claw—a falcon's claw—on his shoulder. He spun back to face her, intending to thrash and kick and bite his way free. And stopped.

She was holding the poker above her head. He'd waited too long. Now, she drew her hand back further still and muttered something the storm made difficult to hear. He wanted to believe it was *I love you*. But it sounded more like *Hush Now*.

His heart and soul ran and cleared the forest screaming, but his body stood and wept. Any minute now he would wake up, he knew he would.

The air crackled and for a moment seemed to shimmer, as if made of water. He watched it, weeping, as the storm exploded through the woods.

The poker came down.

Then all fell quiet in Peregrine's world as he died at his mother's feet.

IV

Peregrine opened his eyes and fire filled them, sudden agony chasing away the words he dreamt had been whispered in his ear. And over the pain that shrieked at him now, he thought that maybe there had been a boy in his dream, a child his own age, who had been afraid of something. His fear had been palpable. Peregrine tried to recall more but a solid bar of pain clamped down between his eyes and he whimpered, rolled onto his side and was numbly aware of cold water seeping through his shirt. The rest of his dream floated away like a kite in the wind, still tethered but too far away to reach. For now, the relentless agony held court and he brought his hands to his temples and squeezed. A gentle breeze tousled his hair as he tried to raise his head. His brain ignited; he winced and coughed dark shadows onto the mossy carpet beneath him while his bones tried to initiate a dance the chaperone of pain denied.

Then, abruptly, there was a voice, and it dragged him out of his disorientation.

"She's gone."

With great effort, Peregrine turned his head. The first thing he noticed was the sunlight, which fell in lazy honey-colored streams and seemed not at all normal. The air itself was thicker, darker than it should have been and appeared to move with a subtle fluid-like grace. Now and again something would ripple through it, like fish moving beneath the water, and it would distort the world around it. But however unusual these things were to the boy's pained eyes, when he tilted his head and looked up at the canopy of trees above him, he saw that up there, it was much worse.

The pines had been stripped of leaves, their trunks aged, and now they craned forward to regard him, their boles warped and twisted, infested with shadows which ran like oil from the bark. Branches wound downward with spindly fingers, each one resembling a hand that had been charred and broken. Every one of them seemed to be struggling to reach him. Thick slimy roots had been frozen while flailing from gaping maws in the floor of the woods, the leaves around them black.

Still dreaming, Peregrine thought. It had to be a fantasy, a nightmare from which he would soon awake. But would he feel this much pain in a dream?

Across from where he lay, a man sat on a felled tree, watching him.

"Who are you?"

"Who do you think?"

And now Peregrine knew it was a dream, because only a miracle could have brought his father back to him.

His father, who seemed to have been crudely whittled from ember and swollen dark, and exuded the smell of tobacco and earth. His father, a crooked question mark pressed against the deadfall.

His father, who had died, but only for a little while.

"Get up."

The boy rose, but only in his mind. A whirlwind of pain kept his body nailed to the floor. "I can't," he sobbed and was sure his tears were red. "It hurts." He became aware that one of his hands was soaked in blood. "It hurts," he repeated, and even his tears burned. His father clucked his tongue with the sound of a twig snapping.

"Get up. We've got work to do."

"I think I'm dying, Dad," he whimpered, as the pain exploded across his skull. "I think she killed me."

"Stop whining and get to your feet." The words were flat, the tone murderous, and now the boy could feel his father's cold hard eyes drilling through the back of his neck. "We're gonna set this right."

"I can't."

"I said, get *up*."

"Help me."

"I aim to help us both, but the getting up you have to do on your own."

It felt as if lead weights had been tied to his face, dragging it back down to a promise of painless sleep. He thought his brain might have been mashed to bits, but was afraid to raise a hand—even if he could—to probe the damage there. Angry hornets stung his skull, but every attempt to shake away their assault threatened to send him spinning into oblivion. Besides, his father was here, and he dare not disappoint him, not when he'd gone to the trouble of raising himself from the dead to come get him, not when he was all Peregrine had left. So he grit his teeth, held a breath that tasted like copper-colored vomit, and planted his hands on either side of him, palms sinking into the moss.

"That's it..."

He grunted and tried to push the carpet away into the gloom that lay beneath him. Twigs snapped and pine needles stabbed his skin, but he ignored them. The fire turned to molten lava in his head, lapping against the backs of his eyes, sending hot rivers running from his nose, and in that moment, as he rose unsteadily, the breath escaping between the gaps in his teeth in a series of tortured hisses, he knew without a doubt that he was not dead. There could never be this much pain after death, unless you ended up in Hell, and he was pretty sure he hadn't done anything wicked enough in his eleven years of life to deserve that.

The air moved sluggishly around him. *Where am I?*

As if of their own volition, Peregrine's elbows continued to straighten, levering him up ever so slowly. The agony was unbearable, his body shuddering with the strain as his heart drove fiery blood into his head. Sweat ran in rivulets down his face. His eyes stung.

"Dad..." he whispered, pleading.

"Keep going." There could be no denying the voice came from his father, but the iciness was an alien thing. It frightened him, led him to wonder what the grave might have done to the man he'd loved.

"Why won't you help me?"

"It's not my place. Now do it, damn you."

The boy closed his eyes and pushed, pushed, pushed, imagining the world had tilted and made the forest floor an immense chamber door he needed to open if he wanted to escape the hurtful dark. His whole body vibrated as if electricity had been shot through his veins and he moaned. The struggle seemed to take hours, every moment marked by his father's tangible impatience, but at last he was able to draw his knees under him, relieving some of the strain from his trembling arms.

"Good boy."

He sat up and the world spun as fresh searing agony battered his skull. He winced, wept anew and brought his hands up to find the wound. His hair was stuck to his scalp, hardened by old blood. Sobbing uncontrollably, he turned to look at his father.

"Why'd she kill me?"

"She didn't," his father told him. "But not for the want of trying."

"It was *him*, wasn't it? John."

"Yes it was. You were an inconvenience."

"Did she...?"

"Enough questions. Time to find your feet."

He did, though it took even longer to stand than it had to get on his knees, and it left him staggering, with nausea swirling through him. He was cold, and quaking, and sweating profusely. More than anything he wanted to sleep, in his own bed—the only place he could think of that might end this dreadful nightmare and see him safely back to the sunshine world: a place where a mother's love was pure and violence was something that happened to everyone else.

"Good. Now we can go."

"Go where?"

His father rose. "To find your mother."

The boy frowned, his legs like jelly, and the words came out before he thought to stop them. "You're dead."

"Yes."

"How can I see you?"

"Because you've been made to."

Peregrine didn't understand, but resisted saying so in case it made his father angry. So instead he asked, "What are we going to do when we find her?"

His father stood motionless for a moment. Then he turned and began to walk away. "We're going to set things right," he called back over his shoulder. "Teach them that people aren't houses. We're going to kill them."

The words were so wrong, so blasphemous, and so terrible that Peregrine knew he should have felt terror seizing his heart, panic playing his nerves like violin strings. But he didn't. Instead he felt a disorientating sense of *right*; that whatever happened once he started on this path would be as it was supposed to be. And while it scared him, he also realized he had no choice. He could not stay here, or risk going back to the house alone.

Father was here. Father would guide him.

On unstable legs, he took a few tentative steps. Every one shot thunder into his brain and he narrowed his eyes, willing it away. Still disturbed by the cast of this new reality, he nevertheless forced himself to quicken his pace. But as he stepped wide to avoid the tentacles of a pine tree, he stopped dead, startled to see that there were other people in the woods, watching him. A legion of people, their pale faces drawn, shadows leaking from their eyes as if their heads were pillowcases stained with oil.

A chill rippled through him. "Who are they?"

His father glanced sidelong at him, and now, in the amber daylight, as an unnaturally slow wind tugged at the trees and the crowd in the woods looked on, he saw that a thick dark fissure bisected his father's face, forcing his eyes too far apart. The eyes themselves were swollen with blood.

"Dad?"

"You brought them here, Peregrine," his father said. "You led all of us here."

He walked off, through the trees, pausing once only to check that his son was following. Peregrine trailed him at a distance, no longer sure he could trust this ruined image of the man he'd once known, and as he approached the watchers, they glared at him, as if he'd done something to draw their ire. For the rest of the journey, he averted his gaze from them, and tried to will away the pain that pulsed behind his eyes.

He had awakened into a place he didn't recognize, a place better suited to the fairytales—a haunted forest. And who knew what else might be hiding in the coiling dark? But no matter how frightening it was, it still didn't feel wrong, and as silent tears rolled down his face, he wondered what he would say when they found his mother; what *she* would say when she saw who had brought him to her.

Worse, he couldn't stop imagining how it was going to feel to watch her die.

V

Here the new world ended.

Peregrine stood at the entrance to the woods, the house standing a few feet away looking quiet and unassuming, as if a madwoman hadn't betrayed and attempted to murder her child here a few hours before.

But the boy was not looking at the house. He stood with his back to it, despite the fear that his mother might come shrieking out of it, poker raised, to finish what she'd started. The fear could wait. For now, awe had possessed him, as he watched the trees shift and bend and tremble in their dark amber world, a world he had stepped out of as simply as stepping over a crack in the pavement. It had tried to hold onto him, the thick air rushing into his lungs, the lazy amorphous light scrabbling at his back, but then he was free and gasping for breath while his father looked on. Now that world stood before him, framed by the trees, and it would only take a step to be immersed in its darkness once more. It was incredible. He had ventured into these woods hundreds of times, to play, or read, or play Robin Hood, and not once had he sensed anything amiss about it. The trees were just trees, the air sweet and clear. How could he have known that it was a fragile picture, pasted over something terrible? How could he ever have believed there was another world, another plane, waiting for him to see it?

"Peregrine."

He turned to face his father, who nodded pointedly at the house. "She's inside."

The boy looked at the house. He had been born and raised here. The cedar walls glistened from the recent rain. The lace curtains gave the windows a tired look. As he watched, a squirrel ran across the roof, walnut in mouth, and vanished behind the house. To anyone else, it would look like a quiet, peaceful place, as it had been for many years. But now it was a place of corruption, a poisoned, evil thing that had spat him out as soon as it was done with him. As soon as *she* was done with him.

"She's sleeping," his father said.

"What do I do?"

He watched an unconvincing smile quarter his father's cloven mouth as he dropped to his haunches and retrieved something long and black from where it had been hidden among the leaves. He turned and held it out to Peregrine.

The poker.

"Bring her into our world," he said.

VI

Let him run let him go let him get away…

Debilitating pain brought Peregrine to his knees, hands clutched to the sides of his head as if they might keep it from shattering. His vision jolted and he shut his eyes. The images came without warning, a stuttering film pulled through his head almost too fast to see, but figures lingered and rose like ghosts in his mind.

The boy again, and a railroad. It was clearer this time than it had been in the dream. A blond-haired boy, about Peregrine's age, running…

Not yours to keep we need him let him go…

There was a dead man chasing him.

And the whisper—

Don't touch him he's ours leave him alone…

It's my voice, Peregrine realized, his confusion deepening. *I'm telling him to leave the boy alone. But who is he?*

A moment later, there was nothing but darkness and the muttered jumble of his own thoughts. Gradually, the pain began to ebb away, until only the discomfort from his head wound remained. He opened his eyes, felt the weight of the poker in his clammy hand.

"Do it." His father stood close by, head bowed as if in prayer. "You won't be killing her, so quit thinking that. You'll be releasing her, freeing her."

As angry as he was, Peregrine didn't think he could do it. The mere thought of it appalled him. And what if he went inside and she wasn't sleeping? What if his father was wrong and she was waiting behind the door with an ax in her hand? What if The Man—*John*—was there? Then it would all be over.

Listen to yourself, said a voice he wasn't sure was his own. *You're afraid of harming her but you're worried she might kill you first. Sounds to me like you already know what has to be done.*

He gave a slight shake of his head. "Why?" he moaned aloud, and his father was suddenly right there, gruesomely bisected face shoved into Peregrine's own.

"Because she *murdered* me, you little prick, and whether you like it or not, executing murderers is your job now. Hers is only the first of many lives whose fate you'll have to decide, and you'll get to like it, because you'll have to." With a snarl, he grabbed Peregrine by the collar of his shirt and flung him toward the door. "Now get to work. We have more visits to make after this one."

Peregrine staggered to a halt and looked pleadingly at his father. At length, the sorrow left his face, replaced by a flush of anger, "You're not my father, are you? No more than she's my mother anymore."

His father smiled. "Get it done. You'll have all eternity to ask her to forgive you when she's by our side."

Will she really come back? Peregrine felt sick, and wondered what would happen if he just tossed the poker away and ran. Somehow he didn't think he'd get very far.

The breeze tossed leaves at the house and smacked them against the window. Clouds obscured the sun and shadows crawled through the woods. When Peregrine raised his face, the crowd of ghosts had formed a circle around the house. Around *him*. A gathering of tangible figures, a phantasmagoria of flesh and blood men, women, and children, all of them unified by the expressions of undiluted contempt they wore. Torn faces, broken bones and ruptured skin—a display of shattered things. They seethed and their hate kept him from running; the threat in their eyes kept him from trying.

This is the right thing to do, he told himself. *I know it is, I feel it, even if I don't want it to be.*

"Do it, boy."

Peregrine made one final, feeble effort to wake from the nightmare, but when he opened his eyes and saw the wet leaves beneath his shoes and the open door before him, he glanced down at the poker, tightened his grip on the cold handle, and entered the house.

VII

She was in her room, sleeping, just as his father had said. Her mouth was open. She sucked in great big breaths that scratched at her throat and made her snoring sound like the last choking gasps of a dying woman. Her hands were across her chest, fingers twitching as her dreams took sharp turns. A graying spray of auburn hair all but occluded the pillow.

Peregrine stood by the bed, watching her. *I can't do this. She's my mother. I love her.* This was not the woman who had tried to kill him, not the woman who had blamed him for her misery. This was his mother as he knew her, albeit without the noxious stench of whiskey that shared her room. This was how he'd found her whenever the nightmares had propelled him from his bedroom and into hers, with a plea on his lips for protection from the demons still stalking him. And yet this was the worst nightmare he'd ever had and it seemed there would be no waking from it. And here she was in her bed, but it wasn't the same, no matter how much he wanted it to be. The reality of what he was doing here came crashing down and a loud sob escaped him.

"I'm sorry," he whispered, his mother's form melting and shattering as tears filled his eyes. "I'm so sorry."

Something eclipsed the daylight, painting shadows on the walls. Fearful, Peregrine looked away from his mother, to her window, with its floral drapes and painted frame, to the dreadful aspect of his father's mutilated face pressed against the glass.

"See her," he said, his eyes so black they looked like pools of oil. "See her for what she is." Then the darkness clambered from his eyes in an explosion of tendrils, penetrating the glass without shattering it and climbing the walls, spreading outward, consuming the light at a frightening speed. The room darkened quickly, as if the curtains had been hastily drawn. Peregrine began to back away, his pulse quickening, breath rapid as he raised the poker to ward off whatever might lunge at him from the sepia-toned gloom. And he was certain something would. His skin crawled as the sensation of a million watching eyes flooded over him. His father seemed to grow and stretch until he'd filled the window, still spinning out oily black threads that had all but devoured the light in the room. Abruptly the air turned cold, licking Peregrine's skin with icy tongues. Overhead, the light bulb shattered. The pieces took impossible time in falling.

Rasping, hitching breath drew his gaze downward. To the bed.

To his mother, or what she had once been before the shadows had mauled her, leaving behind an ancient, crumbling thing with deep lightless caverns for eyes. On the pillow, soiled with inky smudges, her hair writhed, struggling to be free of her diseased skull. Dead. She had to be. And yet she moved. Some hideous trickery made her twitch and shift beneath the off-white sheets, still visible despite the increasing weight of darkness. Amber light dappled the walls, *beneath* the walls, glowing dully from under the flaking paint. He should not have been able to see her, would have preferred blindness to looking at what she had become, but her bed it seemed was the sole source of illumination in the room, possessed of a purity that seemed alien in this awful room, and incongruous given the monstrosity atop it.

"Oh how we laughed," she said, her lips moving slower than she spoke. "How we laughed about what I was going to do to you."

"Stop it," Peregrine said, but not to her, not to anyone but the unseen engineer of this horror. "I want to go home." On some level, he knew he *was* home, but fear compelled him to beg for a return to the sane safe place, the *other* place, where mothers didn't try to kill their sons and darkness was only an absence of light, not a cloak used by unspeakable things.

"I wanted him to kill you," his mother continued, in that terrible croaking whisper. "It was his idea so I told him he should be the one to do it. He has much more experience with these things. But he wouldn't." Her laughter sounded like fabric tearing. "He couldn't kill a child, he said. Anything else, but not a child. How noble of him to leave me with the dirty work. I have to admit though...I kinda liked it."

"Please stop." The poker felt like a sword in Peregrine's hand, a blade he could use to slice open this darkness and free himself.

"So here I am. And here you are, and one of us will die."

This was not his mother. This was some corrupt thing—the monster he'd always feared lived beneath his bed. He wanted to cry. He wanted to scream. He wanted to run. But he couldn't.

"And I won't be the one with *spine trouble*," said his mother and without warning she was sitting bolt upright, darkness flooding from her mouth, eyes filled with cold blue light. "It will be better soon, you little bastard," she said and lunged at him. But as with everything else in this skewed version of the world, her assault was slowed down by the viscous air.

Peregrine didn't move. His eyes were focused on her hands, sundering the air between them.

They were claws. No, not claws, talons, better suited to a bird of prey. And as she neared him he saw the skin sloughing from them in messy lumps that slopped to the floor in slow motion. Her hands, he thought with a curious calm. They were the talons from the falcon on his birthday cake.

Sickened, he did the only thing he could think of.

He clutched the poker with both hands, brought it back as if preparing to hit a home run, and swung it out in front of him. And as the iron cut through the gelatinous air, everything changed.

There was no darkness.

There was no diseased woman with falcon claws.

There was no slow motion.

Only his mother, looking at him with bloodshot, barely awake eyes. "Peregrine?"

He screamed, but it was too late to slow the impetus of his weapon.

His mother opened her mouth as if to cry out and the poker hit the side of her head with a dull crunch. With a grunt, she spun sideways in a whirl of blood and auburn hair, and hit the wall beside her bed face-first, hard enough to dent the plaster. Her head lolled, and for a moment she remained upright, her limbs jerking crazily. Then she fell backward, feet kicking beneath the covers as confused signals shot through her brain.

Peregrine wept, and started to drop the poker. A hand on his shoulder stopped him. "You must finish it," his father said.

The boy did not look at his father, could not look away from his shuddering mother. She convulsed, right hand thumping against the wall. Her pupils overwhelmed her eyes.

"End it."

"I can't."

"You want her to suffer?"

His mother whimpered and arched her back, head snapping from side to side. She seemed to be squirming her way beneath the blankets, and when finally her struggling ceased, only her eyes could be seen above the sheet. Her chest rose and feel with impossible speed.

"I want to go."

"She's still breathing," said his father.

Sobbing, Peregrine looked at the bed. His father was right. She was not yet dead.

"Make it stop," he pleaded.

"Only you can do that. And the longer you delay, the more agony she'll have to endure. She deserves every breath of pain, but if you don't wish to see it, then put her out of her misery. Bring her to us."

Do it, said the voice inside, that sneering voice he had apparently acquired on stepping foot into the horrible new world. *Do it and get it over with. Your life won't properly begin until you do.*

With a scream of utter helplessness, rage and sorrow, he took a single step closer to the bed, brought the poker over his head in a two-handed grip, and closed his eyes.

Before the killing blow was struck, he heard his mother whisper, in a voice not her own. "*There were turtles the size of Buicks in there. Snapping, snappity-snap.*"

VIII

He sat on a fallen log beside his father, watching the house burn. Soot and ash had made a dark mask of his face. The tracks of his tears were all that allowed a glimpse of the grieving boy beneath. But something had changed, had been forced to change inside him. He felt it growing in his belly, a black mass sprouting tendrils like those he'd seen spilling from his father's eyes. It promised a reprieve from the hurt, an escape from the pain, if he only let it consume him.

Something inside the house crackled and fell, and a tongue of red-yellow flame exploded from the door, sending a wave of heat rolling toward them. The breeze fanned the flames, coaxing them higher, until the house was lost within a fiery cage. His father didn't move, but Peregrine narrowed his eyes and raised a hand to shield his face. As he did so, he caught sight of something tumbling and leaping across the yard toward him. It wrapped around his right ankle and fluttered like a trapped bird.

It was the newspaper he'd seen on the kitchen table this morning.

This morning. It felt like a lifetime ago.

He picked up the paper and numbly scanned the pages, not looking for anything but feeling as though he was supposed to. Most of the paper had been lost, or burned, but on the inside page of what remained, Peregrine's eyes halted on a headline:

11-YEAR-OLD BOY RESURRECTS THE DEAD, SOLVES MURDER!

Dirty light crept across the shadowy wasteland the past few hours had made of his mind. He looked at the grainy picture of the smiling boy—

Let him run let him go let him get away—and read the story.

I've seen him.

When he was done, he looked up at the inferno, the heat now so intense his clothes were starting to scorch him, and stood.

"I want to know why I'm here, why this is happening to me," he said. For the first time his father offered a smile that even his mangled mouth couldn't spoil.

"It's happening because it's supposed to," his father replied.

Peregrine showed him the crumpled soot-stained newspaper page. With one trembling finger, he indicated the smiling child. "And I want to know who this is."

"That," his father replied, "is your brother."

COMING SOON IN PAPERBACK

NEMESIS: THE DEATH OF TIMMY QUINN

THE CONCLUDING NOVEL-LENGTH VOLUME OF THE TIMMY QUINN STORY

Now available in limited edition hardcover from Thunderstorm Books:
www.thunderstormpress.com/burke.php

And in digital via Amazon, B&N, Smashwords, Kobo, iTunes, Sony, and all other vendors

ABOUT THE AUTHOR

Called "one of the most clever and original talents in contemporary horror" (BOOKLIST), Kealan Patrick Burke is the Bram Stoker Award-Winning author of five novels (MASTER OF THE MOORS, CURRENCY OF SOULS, THE LIVING, KIN, and NEMESIS), nine novellas (including the Timmy Quinn series), over a hundred short stories, and six collections. He edited the acclaimed anthologies: TAVERNS OF THE DEAD, QUIETLY NOW, BRIMSTONE TURNPIKE, and TALES FROM THE GOREZONE.

An Irish expatriate, he currently resides in Ohio. Visit him on the web at http://www.kealanpatrickburke.com or find him on Facebook at facebook.com/kealan.burke

Made in the USA
Lexington, KY
09 June 2013